Bethlehem Road

Also by Anne Perry

Silence in Hanover Close
Cardington Crescent
Death in the Devil's Acre
Bluegate Fields
Rutland Place
Resurrection Row
Paragon Walk
Callander Square
The Cater Street Hangman

Anne Perry

Bethlehem Road

SOUVENIR PRESS

First published in the U.S.A. by
St. Martin's Press, New York

First British Edition published 1991 by
Souvenir Press Ltd., 43 Great Russell Street London WC1B 3PA

ISBN 0 285 63042 3

Printed and bound in Great Britian by
Billing and Sons Ltd, Worcester

To Ruth, for her many gifts to me

Bethlehem Road

1

HETTY STOOD AT THE edge of Westminster Bridge and stared across the dark roadway at the man lounging rather awkwardly against the beautiful three-headed lamppost on the far side. A hansom cab passed between them, clattering northwards over the great span towards the Houses of Parliament on the far side, and the newly installed electric lights like a row of golden moons along the Victoria Embankment.

The man had made no move since she had come. It was after midnight. Such a well-dressed gentleman, with his silk hat and white evening scarf and the fresh flowers in his buttonhole, would hardly be lounging around here waiting for an acquaintance! He must be a likely customer. What else would he stand here for?

Hetty sauntered over to him, swishing her gold skirts elegantly and cocking her head a little to one side.

"Evenin' ducky! Lookin' fer a little comp'ny, are yer?" she asked invitingly.

The man made no move at all. He could have been asleep on his feet, for all the notice he took of her.

"Shy, are yer?" she said helpfully—some gentlemen found themselves tongue-tied when it came to the point, especially if it was not their habit. "Don' need ter be," she went on. "Nothin' wrong in a spot o' friendship on a cold night. My name's 'Etty. Why don't yer come along o' me. 'Ave a nice tot o' gin, an' get ter know each other, eh? Don' corst much!"

Still the man neither moved nor spoke.

"'Ere! Wot's wrong wiv yer?" she peered at him, noticing for the first time that he was leaning back in rather a strained position, and that his hands were not in his pockets, as she would have expected at this time of a spring night in such chill, but were hanging by his sides. "Are yer sick?" she said with concern.

He remained motionless.

He was older than he had looked from the far side of the road, probably into his fifties; silver-gray hair caught the lamplight, and his face had a blank, rather wild stare.

"You're soused as an 'erring!" she exclaimed with a mixture of pity and disgust. She understood drunkenness well enough, but one did not expect it from the gentry, not in so public a street. "You better go 'ome, before the rozzers get yer. Go on! Yer can't spend all night 'ere!" No custom after all! Still, she had not done badly. The gentlemen on the Lambeth Walk had paid handsomely. "Silly ol' fool!" she added under her breath to the figure against the lamppost.

Then she noticed that the white scarf was round not only his neck but round the wrought iron decorative fork of the lamppost as well. Dear God—he was tied up to it—by his neck! Then the hideous truth struck her: that glassy stare was not stupor, it was . . . *death.*

She let out a shriek that cut through the night air and the deserted road with its beautiful lamps and triple pools of light and shot up into the empty void of the sky above. She shrieked again, and again, as if now she had started she must continue on and on until there were some answer to the horror in front of her.

At the far side of the bridge dim figures turned; another voice shouted and someone began to run, footsteps clattering hollowly towards her.

Hetty stepped back away from the lamppost and its burden and tripped over the curb, falling clumsily into the road. She lay stunned and angry for a moment. Then someone bent over her, and she felt her shoulders lifted.

"You all right, luv?" The voice was gruff but not ungentle, and she could smell damp wool close to her face.

Why had she been so stupid? She should have kept quiet and gone on her way, left some other fool to find the corpse! Now a little knot of people was gathering round her.

"Gawd!" someone squealed in sudden horror. "'E's dead! Dead as a mackerel, poor beggar!"

"You'd better not touch him." This was an authoritative voice, quite different in tone, educated and self-confident. "Someone send for the police. Here, you go, there's a good chap. There should be a constable along the Embankment."

There was the sound of running feet again, fading as they drew farther off.

Hetty struggled to stand up, and the man holding her hoisted her with good-natured concern. There were five of them, standing shivering and awed. She wanted to get away, most particularly before the rozzers arrived. Really, she had not used the wits she was born with, yelling out like that! She could have held her tongue and been half a mile away, and no one the wiser.

She looked round the ring of faces, all shadows and eerie highlights from the yellow lamps, breath making faint wisps of vapor in the cold. They were kindly, concerned—and there was no chance whatsoever she could escape. But she might, at least, get a free drink out of it.

"I've 'ad an 'orrible shock," she said shakily and with a certain dignity. "I feel all cold an' wobbly like."

Someone pulled out a silver flask, the light catching on its scrolled sides. It was a beautiful thing. "Have a sip of brandy?"

"Thank you, I'm sure." Hetty took it without protestation and drank every drop. She ran her fingers over it, tracing the engraving, before reluctantly handing it back.

Inspector Thomas Pitt was called from his home at five minutes past one in the morning, and by half past he found himself standing at the south end of Westminster Bridge in the shivering cold looking at the corpse of a middle-aged man dressed in an expensive black overcoat and a silk hat. He was tied by a white evening scarf round his neck to the lamp-post behind him. His throat had been deeply cut; the right jugular vein was severed and his shirt was soaked in blood. The overcoat had hidden it almost entirely; and the folded scarf, as well as holding him up and a trifle backwards so the stanchion of the lamp took some of his weight, had also covered the wound.

There was a group of half a dozen people standing on the far side of the bridge, across the road from the body. The constable on duty stood beside Pitt with his bull's-eye lantern in his hand, although the streetlamps provided sufficient light for all that they could do now.

"Miss 'Etty Milner found 'im, sir," the constable said helpfully. "She said as she thought 'e were ill, an' inquired after 'is 'ealth. Reckon more like she were toutin' fer 'is business, but don't suppose it makes no difference, poor devil. 'E's still got money in 'is pockets, an' 'is gold watch 'n chain, so it don't look as if 'e were robbed."

Pitt looked again at the body. Tentatively he felt the lapels of the coat, taking off his own gloves to ascertain the texture of the cloth. It was soft and firm, quality wool. There were fresh primroses in his buttonhole, looking ghostly in the lamplight, with the faint wisps of fog that drifted like chiffon scarves up off the dark swirling river below. The man's gloves were leather, probably pigskin; not knitted, like Pitt's. He looked at the gold-mounted carnelian cuff links. He moved the scarf aside, revealing the blood-soaked shirt, studs still in place, and then let it fall again.

"Do we know who he is?" he asked quietly.

"Yes sir." The constable's voice lost some of its businesslike clarity. "I knows 'im meself, from bein' on duty round 'ere. 'E's Sir Lockwood 'Amilton, member o' Parliament. 'E lives somewhere souf o' the river, so I reckon as 'e was goin' 'ome after a late sittin', like usual. Some o' the gennelmen walks of a fine night, if they lives close, an' a lot o' them do, wherever they're a member for." He cleared his throat of some impediment, perhaps cold, perhaps a mixture of pity and horror. "Could be some town the other end of the country. They 'as to 'ave a place in town w'en the 'ouse is in session. And o' course them as is 'igh in government 'as ter be 'ere all the time, 'cept fer 'olidays and the like."

"Yes," Pitt smiled bleakly. He already knew the customs of Parliament, but the man was trying to be helpful. It was easier to talk; it filled the silence and drew one's mind from the corpse. "Thank you. Which one is Hetty Milner?"

"'Er over there, with the light-colored 'air, sir. T'other girl's in the same line o' business, but she isn't got nothin' ter do with this. Just nosy."

Pitt crossed the road and approached the group of people. He looked at Hetty, noted the painted face, hollow in this harsh lamplight, the low neckline of her dress, the fair skin which would be coarse in a handful of years, and the cheap, gaudy skirts. They were torn from when she had stumbled off the curb, showing slender ankles and a fine leg.

"I'm Inspector Pitt," he introduced himself. "You found the body tied up to the lamppost?"

"Yeah!" Hetty did not like the police; it was an occupational hazard that her associations with them had all been to her disadvantage. She had nothing against this one in particular, but she must do what she could to rectify her earlier stupidity by saying as little as possible now.

"Did you see anyone else on the bridge?" he asked.

"No."

"Which way were you going?"

"'Ome. From the souf."

"Over towards the Palace of Westminster?"

She had a suspicion he was laughing at her. "That's right!"

"Where do you live?"

"Near the Millbank Prison." Her chin came up. "That's close on to Westminster, in case as you dunno!"

"I know. And you were walking home alone?" There was nothing sardonic in his face, but she looked at him disbelievingly.

"Wot's the matter wiv yer? You daft or suffink? Course I was alone!"

"What did you say to him?"

She was about to say who? and realized it would be pointless. She had just virtually admitted she was there plying her trade. Bleedin' rozzer had led her into saying that!

"Asked 'im if 'e was ill." She was pleased with that answer. Even a lady might ask after someone's health.

"So he looked ill?"

"Yeah—no!" She swore under her breath. "All right, so I asked 'im if 'e wanted a spot o' comp'ny." She twisted her face in an attempt at sarcasm. "'E didn't say nuffin'!"

"Did you touch him?"

"No! I in't no thief!"

"And you're sure you saw no one else? Nobody 'going home'? No tradespeople?"

"At this time o' night? Sellin' wot?"

"Hot pies, flowers, sandwiches."

"No I didn't; just a cab as passed wivout stoppin'. But I didn't kill 'im. I swear by Gawd, 'e were dead w'en I got 'ere. Why would I kill 'im? I in't crazy!"

Pitt believed her. She was an ordinary prostitute, like countless thousands of others in London in this year of grace, 1888. She might or might not be a petty thief, she would probably unwittingly spread disease and herself die young. But she would not kill a potential customer in the street.

"Give your name and address to the constable," he said to her. "And make it the truth, Hetty, or we'll have to come looking for you, which would not be good for trade."

She glared at him, then swung round and walked over to

the constable, tripping again on the curb but this time catching herself before she fell and continuing with her chin even higher.

Pitt went over to the other people and spoke to them, but none had seen anything, having come only when they heard Hetty's screams. There was nothing more he could do there, and he signaled to the mortuary carriage waiting at the far end of the bridge that it could come and remove the body. He had looked carefully at the scarf: the knot was such as anyone would tie without thinking, one end over the other, and then again. The man's weight had pulled it so tight it could not be undone. He watched them cut it with a knife and lower the corpse, then put it gently in the carriage, which drove away, a black shadow against the lights, clattering across the bridge and turning under the great statue of Boadicea in her chariot with the magnificent horses, and right along the Embankment till it disappeared. Pitt went back to the constable and the second uniformed man who had arrived.

Now came the duty that Pitt hated more than almost any other, except perhaps the final unwinding of the solution, the understanding of the passions and the pain that produced tragedy. He must go and inform the family, watch their shock and their grief and try to disentangle from their words, their gestures, the fleeting emotions on their faces any thread that might tell him something. So often it was some other pain or darkness, some other secret that had nothing to do with the crime, some ugly act or weakness that they would lie to protect.

It was not difficult to discover that Sir Lockwood Hamilton had lived at number seventeen Royal Street, about half a mile away, overlooking the garden of Lambeth Palace, the official London residence of the Archbishop of Canterbury.

It was hardly worth seeking a cab; it would be a short walk, and on a clear night very pleasant—no doubt that was what Lockwood Hamilton himself had thought when he left the House. And it would give Pitt time to think.

Ten minutes later he was standing on the step rapping with the brass knob on the fine mahogany door. He waited several moments, then rapped again. Somewhere in the attics a light came on, then one on the second floor, and finally one in the hallway. The door opened, and a sleepy butler in hastily donned jacket blinked at him, realized he was a stranger, and drew breath to be indignant.

"Inspector Thomas Pitt, of the Bow Street Station," Pitt said quickly. "May I come in?"

The butler sensed a certain gravity, perhaps a shadow of pity either in Pitt's face or voice, and his irritation dissolved.

"Is something wrong? Has there been an accident?"

"I'm sorry—it is more distressing than that," Pitt replied, following him in. "Sir Lockwood Hamilton is dead. I would omit the circumstances if I could, but it will be in the morning newspapers, and it would be better if Lady Hamilton were prepared for it, and any other members of the family."

"Oh—" The butler gulped, took a moment to gain his composure while all sorts of horrors raced through his mind, scandals and disgrace. Then he straightened himself and faced Pitt. "What happened?" he said levelly, his voice very nearly normal.

"I am afraid he was murdered. On Westminster Bridge."

"You mean . . . pushed over?" The man's face registered disbelief, as though the idea were too ludicrous to credit.

"No." Pitt drew a breath. "He was attacked with a razor, or a knife. I'm sorry. It will have been very quick, all over in a moment, and he will have felt very little. I think you had better have her maid call Lady Hamilton, and prepare some restorative; a tisane, or whatever you think best."

"Yes—yes sir, of course." The butler showed Pitt into

the withdrawing room, where the embers of the fire were still glowing, and left him to turn up the gas lamps and find a seat for himself while he set about his unhappy task.

Pitt looked round the room; it would tell him something of the people who lived here and made it their home while Parliament was sitting. It was spacious, far less cluttered with furniture than was the fashion. There was less fringing on couches and chairs, fewer hanging crystals on the light fixtures, no antimacassars or samplers, no family portraits or photographs, except one rather severe sepia tint of an elderly woman in a widow's white cap, framed in silver. It was at odds with the rest of the room, a relic of another age. If this was Lady Hamilton's choice of decor, then the woman might be Sir Lockwood's relative, perhaps his mother.

The pictures on the walls were cool, romantic, after the style of the Pre-Raphaelites; women with enigmatic faces and lovely hair, knights in armor, and twined flowers. On the decorative tables by the wall there were pewter ornaments of considerable age.

It was ten minutes before the door opened and Lady Hamilton came in. She was of above average height, with interesting, intelligent features which in her youth had probably had a certain loveliness. Now she was in her middle forties, and time had taken the first bloom from her skin and replaced it with marks of character which to Pitt were far more appealing. Her dark hair was coiled in the hastiest of knots at the nape of her neck, and she wore a dressing robe of royal blue.

She made an immense effort to remain dignified. "I understand you have come to tell me that my husband has been killed," she said quietly.

"Yes, Lady Hamilton," Pitt answered. "I am extremely sorry. I apologize for distressing you with the details, but I believe you would prefer to hear them from me, rather than from the newspapers or from other people."

She paled so markedly he was afraid for a moment she

might collapse, but she drew in her breath and let it out very slowly, managing to retain her composure.

"Perhaps you should sit down?" he suggested. He held out his hand, but she ignored it and made her way to the couch, indicating that he be seated as well. Her fists were clenched and shaking where she held them in her lap, to hide them from him, and perhaps from herself.

"Pray proceed," she instructed him.

He felt her pain and was powerless to do anything but add to it.

"It appears that Sir Lockwood was walking home after a late sitting of the House of Commons," he continued. "When he reached the south end of Westminster Bridge he was attacked by someone with either a knife or a razor. He sustained only one injury, in the neck, but it was fatal. If it can be of any comfort to you, he will have felt only the briefest instant's pain. It was extremely rapid."

"He was robbed?" She spoke only to maintain the show of composure she was fighting so hard to keep.

"No, it would appear not—unless he carried something we don't know of. He still had his money, watch and chain, and cuff links. Of course, the thief may have been interrupted before he could take anything. But that does not seem likely."

"Why—" Her voice broke; she swallowed. "Why not?"

Pitt hesitated.

"Why not?" she repeated.

She would have to know; if he did not tell her, someone else would, even if she refused to read the newspapers. By tomorrow it would be all over London. He did not know whether to look at her or away, but to avoid her eyes seemed cowardly.

"He was propped up against a lamppost and tied to it by his neck scarf. No one who was interrupted would have had time to do such a thing."

She stared at him speechlessly.

He pressed on because he had no choice. "I must ask

you, ma'am, if Sir Lockwood had received any threats that you were aware of. Had he any rivals in office, or business that might have wished him harm? This may have been done by a lunatic, but it is possible that it was someone who knew him."

"No!" The denial was instinctive, and Pitt had expected it. No one wished to think such an atrocity could be anything but random fate, an accident of mischance in time and place.

"Did he often walk home after a late sitting?"

She collected herself with difficulty. He could see from her eyes that her inner vision was on the bridge in the darkness, imagining the horrific act. "Yes—yes, if the weather was pleasant. It takes only a few minutes. It is well lit—and—"

"Yes, I know, I walked it myself. So many people might well have expected that sooner or later he would do so."

"I suppose they might, but only a madman would . . ."

"Jealousy," Pitt said, "fear, greed can strip away the normal restraints and leave naked something that is not unlike a kind of madness."

She made no reply.

"Is there anyone you would like me to inform?" he asked gently. "Any other relatives? If we could save you distress . . ."

"No—no thank you. I have already had Huggins call my brothers." Her face tightened, a strange, bleak, wounded look. "And Mr. Barclay Hamilton—my husband's son by his first marriage."

"Call. . . ?"

She blinked, then realized the meaning of his question. "Yes, we have one of those telephones. I don't care for it much myself. I think it is a little uncivil to be speaking to people when you cannot see their faces. I prefer to write if a visit is not possible. But Sir Lockwood finds—found it convenient," she corrected herself.

"Did he keep any business papers here in the house?"

"Yes, in the library. I cannot see that they would be of any use to you. There is nothing of a confidential nature. He did not bring those home."

"Are you certain?"

"Quite certain. He told me so on several occasions. He was Parliamentary Private Secretary to the Home Secretary, you know. He knew how to be discreet."

At that moment there was a noise in the hallway. The front door opened and closed, and two men's voices were plainly audible above the butler's murmured protestations. Then the withdrawing room door swung wide and one of the men stood in the entrance, his silver hair gleaming in the lamplight, his handsome face with its powerful nose and sweeping brow now strained and bleak with shock.

"Amethyst, my dear." He came in, ignoring Pitt, and placed his arm round his sister. "This is appalling! I cannot tell you how I grieve for you. We shall do everything we can to protect you, of course. We must avoid a lot of stupid speculations. It might be less disagreeable for you if you were to leave London for a little while. You are welcome to stay at my home in Aldeburgh if you wish. You will have privacy there. A change, a little sea air." He swung round. "Jasper, for heaven's sake, don't stand there! Come in. You've brought your bag with you; haven't you anything to help?"

"I don't want anything, thank you," Lady Hamilton replied, hunching her shoulders a little and turning away from him. "Lockwood is dead—nothing any of us do will alter that. And thank you, Garnet, but I won't go away yet. Later perhaps."

Garnet Royce turned finally to Pitt.

"I assume you are from the police? I am Sir Garnet Royce, Lady Hamilton's brother. Do you require her to remain in London?"

"No sir," Pitt said levelly. "But I imagine Lady Hamilton is anxious to assist us as much as possible in catching whoever is responsible for this tragedy."

Garnet regarded him with cold, clear eyes. "I cannot imagine how. She is hardly likely to know anything about whatever lunatic did this. If I can persuade her to leave London, can I assume you will not make yourself objectionable?" There was a plain warning in his voice, the voice of a man used to having not only his orders but his wishes obeyed.

Pitt met his gaze without a flicker. "It is a murder inquiry, Sir Garnet. So far I have no idea at all who is responsible, or what motive there can have been. But as Sir Lockwood was a public figure of some note, it is possible someone bore him an enmity for whatever reason, real or imagined. It would be irresponsible to come to any conclusions so soon."

Jasper came forward, a younger, less forceful version of his brother, with darker eyes and hair and with none of the magnetism. "He's quite right, Garnet." He put his hand on his sister's arm. "You'd best go back to bed, my dear. Have your maid make a tisane of this." He proffered a small packet of dried herbs. "I'll come by again in the morning."

She took the packet. "Thank you, but you need not neglect your usual patients. I shall be quite well. There will be much to do here: arrangements to make, people to inform, letters and other business to see to. I have no intention of leaving town now. I suppose later—afterwards—I may be glad to go to Aldeburgh. It is considerate of you, Garnet, but now, if there is nothing more. . . ?" She looked questioningly at Pitt.

"Inspector Pitt, ma'am."

"Inspector Pitt, if you would excuse me, I would prefer to retire."

"Of course. Will you permit me to speak again to your butler tomorrow?"

"Naturally, if you feel it necessary." She turned and was on her way out when there was another sound in the hall and another man appeared in the doorway, slender and dark, very tall, perhaps ten years younger than she. His face was pinched with shock and his eyes had the wide, white-rimmed staring look of someone under a great strain.

Amethyst Hamilton froze, swaying a little, and every vestige of color left her skin. Garnet, a step behind her, put out his arms, and she made an ineffectual brushing movement to get rid of him, but her strength failed.

The young man also stood rigid, struggling to control some deep emotion that threatened to overwhelm him. There was pain in the set of his mouth; his face had a numb, almost broken look. He tried to form some sentence appropriate to the situation and could not.

It was she who commanded herself first.

"Good evening, Barclay," she said with a supreme effort. "No doubt Huggins has told you about your father's death. It was considerate of you to come, especially at this hour. I am afraid there is nothing to be done tonight, but I thank you for your presence."

"Accept my condolences," he said stiffly. "If there is any assistance I can give, please allow me. People to inform, business affairs—"

"I shall make all the arrangements," Garnet put in. Either he was unaware of the young man's emotion, or he wished to ignore it. "Thank you. Naturally I shall keep you informed."

For a long moment no one moved or spoke. Jasper looked helpless, Garnet perplexed and impatient, Amethyst close to collapse, and Barclay Hamilton so tortured by anguish that he had no idea what to say or do.

Then at last Amethyst inclined her head with a courtesy so chill, in other circumstances it would have been blatantly rude.

"Thank you, Barclay. I am sure you must be cold. Huggins will bring some brandy, but if you will pardon me I will retire."

"Of course. I—I—" he stammered.

She waited, but Barclay found nothing further to say. In silence she passed him and with Jasper at her elbow walked out into the hall. They heard her footsteps on the stairs and dying away across the landing.

Garnet turned to Pitt. "Thank you, Inspector, for your . . . civility," he said, choosing the word carefully. "Now I assume you have inquiries to make; we will not detain you. Huggins will show you out."

Pitt remained where he was. "Yes sir, I do have inquiries to make, and the sooner they are begun the better my chances of success. Perhaps you could tell me something about your brother-in-law's business interests?"

Garnet's eyebrows rose in incredulity. "Good God! Now?"

Pitt held his ground. "If you please, sir. It would then make it unnecessary for me to trouble Lady Hamilton tomorrow morning."

Garnet looked at him with growing contempt. "You cannot possibly imagine some business associate of Sir Lockwood's would commit such an outrage! You should be combing the streets, looking for witnesses or something, not standing here warming yourself by the fire and asking damn-fool questions!"

Pitt remembered the shock and perhaps grief that must be afflicting him, even if for his sister rather than himself, and his temper dissolved. "All that has been begun, sir, but there is only a certain amount that we can do tonight. Now, can you tell me something about Sir Lockwood's career, in business and in Parliament. It will save time, and the unpleasantness of having to ask Lady Hamilton tomorrow."

The irritation smoothed out of Garnet's face, leaving only tiredness and the dark, smudged shadows of exhausting emotion.

"Yes—yes, of course," he conceded. He took a breath. "He was member of Parliament for a country constituency in Bedfordshire, but he spent nearly all his time in London; he was obliged to when Parliament was sitting, and he greatly preferred city life anyway. His business was fairly commonplace: he invested in the manufacture of railway carriages somewhere in the Midlands, I don't know where precisely, and he was a senior partner in a firm dealing in property here in London. His chief associate is a Mr. Charles Verdun, whose address I cannot give you, but no doubt it will be simple enough for you to find.

"His Parliamentary career is a matter of record. He was successful, and all successful men make enemies, even if mainly of those less able or less fortunate, but I was unaware of Sir Lockwood's having any of violent disposition or unbalanced mind." He frowned, staring past Pitt towards the closed curtains at the window, as if he would see beyond them. "Of course there is a certain instability in some quarters at the moment, among a section of the community, and there are always those ready to foment dissatisfaction and attempt to gratify their desire for power by exploiting restless people with little moral sense or knowledge of their own best interests. I suppose this could be political—the work of some anarchist, either acting alone or as part of some conspiracy." He looked at Pitt. "If it is, you must apprehend them rapidly, before we have panic in the streets, and all sorts of other elements seize their opportunity to create civil unrest. I don't suppose you know fully how very serious this could be? But I assure you, if it is anarchists, then we have grounds for grave concern, and it is our duty, those of us with sense and responsibility, to take care of those less fortunate. They rely upon us, as they have a right to. Inquire of your superiors and they will confirm to you that I am correct. For the good of everyone, this must be stopped before it goes any further."

These thoughts had already crossed Pitt's mind, but he was surprised that Garnet Royce was aware of the unrest in the vast slums and docklands of the East End, and the whispers of riot and revolution over the last few months. He had thought Parliament largely blind to such things. Certainly reform was hard and slow, but perhaps that was not what was desired by the agitators Royce was referring to. There was no power to be gained from a satisfied people.

"Yes sir, I am aware of the possibilities," he replied. "All our sources of information will be tried. Thank you for your help. Now I shall return to the police station and see if anything further has been learned, before I report the matter to Mr. Drummond."

"Is that Micah Drummond?"

"Yes sir."

Garnet nodded. "Good man. I'd be obliged if you would keep me informed, for Lady Hamilton's sake as well as my own. It is a very dreadful business."

"Yes sir. Please accept my condolences."

"Civil of you. Huggins will show you to the door."

It was dismissal, and there was no point in trying to pursue anything further here tonight. Barclay Hamilton, white-faced and drained of all vitality, sat on the couch as if drugged, and Jasper had come downstairs again and was in the hall waiting until he could decently leave. He could prescribe sleeping drafts, tisanes for the nerves, but he could not alleviate the grief or the inevitable pain that would come with the morning when the first numbness had worn off.

Pitt thanked them and walked out into the hall, where the butler, still with his jacket a trifle crooked and his nightshirt tucked into his trousers, gave a sigh of relief and let him out with barely a word.

There were no hansoms about at this hour, and Pitt walked briskly back, turning left down Stangate Road to Westminster Bridge Road, across the bridge itself and past the statue of Queen Boadicea, the huge tower of Big Ben to his left, and the gothic mass of the Houses of Parliament. On the Embankment he found a cab to take him to the Bow Street Police Station, just off the Strand. It was a little before three o'clock in the morning.

The duty constable looked up and his face took on an added gravity.

"Any reports?" Pitt asked.

"Yes sir, but nothin' a lot o' use so far. Can't find no

cabby, not yet. Street girls in't sayin' nothin', 'cept 'Etty Milner, an' she can't 'zactly take it back now. Reckon as she would if she could. Got one gent as said 'e walked over the bridge abaht ten minutes afore 'Etty yelled, and there weren't nobody 'angin' on the lamppost then, as' 'e remembers. But then o' course 'e prob'ly weren't lookin'. 'Nother gent abaht the same time said 'e saw a drunk, but took no notice. Don't know if it were poor 'Amilton or not. An' o' course Fred sellin' 'ot pies down by the steps to the river, but 'e 'adn't seen no one, 'cause 'e's the wrong end o' the bridge."

"Nothing else?"

"No sir. We're still lookin'."

"Then I'll kip down in my office for a couple of hours," Pitt replied wearily. There was no point in going home. "Then I'll go and see Mr. Drummond."

"Want a cup o' tea, sir?"

"Yes, I'm perished."

"Yes sir. It in't goin' ter get no better, sir."

"No, I know that. Bring me the tea, will you."

"Right you are, sir. Comin' up!"

At half past six Pitt was in another cab, and by quarter to seven he stood in a quiet street in Knightsbridge, where the spring sun was clear and sharp on the paving stones and the only sounds were those of kitchen maids beginning their breakfast preparations and footmen collecting newspapers to be ironed and presented to their masters at table. Fire grates had long since been cleaned out, blacked, and relit and carpets sanded and swept so that they smelled fresh.

Pitt climbed the steps and knocked on the door. He was tired and cold and hungry, but this news could not wait.

A startled manservant opened the door and regarded Pitt's lanky disheveled figure, clothes askew, knitted muffler wound twice round his neck, unruly hair too long and ill-acquainted with barbers' skill. His boots were immaculate, soft leather, highly polished, a present from his sister-in-law, but his coat was dreadful, pockets stuffed with string, a pocketknife, five shillings and sixpence, and fifteen pieces of paper.

"Yes sir?" the man said dubiously.

"Inspector Pitt from Bow Street," Pitt told him. "I must see Mr. Drummond as soon as possible. A member of Parliament has been murdered on Westminster Bridge."

"Oh." The man was startled but not incredulous. His master was a senior commander of police, and alarms and excursions were not uncommon. "Oh yes, sir. If you'll come in I'll tell Mr. Drummond you are here."

Micah Drummond appeared ten minutes later, washed, shaved and dressed for breakfast, albeit somewhat hastily. He was a tall, very lean man with a cadaverous face distinguished by a handsome nose and a mouth that betrayed in its lines a quick and delicate sense of humor. He was perhaps forty-eight or forty-nine, and his hair was receding a trifle. He regarded Pitt with sympathy, ignoring his clothes and seeing only the weariness in his eyes.

"Join me for breakfast." It was as much a command as an invitation. He led the way to a small hexagonal room with parquet flooring and a French window opening onto a garden where old roses climbed a brick wall. In the center of the room a table was set for one. Drummond swept some of the condiments aside and made room for another setting. He pointed to a chair and Pitt drew it up.

"Did Cobb have it right?" Drummond sat down and Pitt did also. 'Some member of Parliament has been murdered on Westminster Bridge?"

"Yes sir. Rather macabre. Cut the poor man's throat and then tied him up to the last lamppost on the south side."

Drummond frowned. "What do you mean, tied him up?"

"By the neck, with an evening scarf."

"How the devil can you tie somebody to a lamppost?"

"The ones on Westminster Bridge are trident-shaped," Pitt replied. "They have ornamental prongs, a bit like the tynes of a garden fork, and they're the right height from the ground to be level with the neck of a man of average build. It was probably fairly simple, for a person of good physical strength."

"Not a woman, then?" Drummond concentrated on his inner vision, his face tense.

Cobb brought in a hot chafing dish of bacon, eggs, kidneys, and potatoes and set it down without speaking. He gave each man a clean plate and then left to fetch tea and toast. Drummond helped himself and offered the server to Pitt. The steam rose deliciously, savory, rich, and piping hot. Pitt took as much as he dared consistent with any kind of good manners and then replied before he began to eat.

"Not unless she was a big woman, and unusually powerful."

"Who was he? Anyone in a sensitive position?"

"Sir Lockwood Hamilton, Parliamentary Private Secretary to the Home Secretary."

Drummond let out his breath slowly. He ate a little more before speaking. "I'm sorry. He was a decent chap. I suppose we have no idea yet whether it was political or personal, or just a chance robbery gone wrong?"

Pitt finished his mouthful of kidney and bacon. "Not yet, but robbery seems unlikely," he said. "Everything of value—watch and chain, keys, silk handkerchief, cuff links, some nice onyx shirt studs—was still on him, even the money in his pockets. If someone meant to rob him, why would they tie him up to a lamppost beforehand? And then leave before anyone even raised an alarm?"

"He wouldn't," Drummond agreed. "How was he killed?"

"Throat cut, very cleanly, so probably a razor, but we haven't got the surgeon's report yet."

"How long had he been dead when he was found? Not long, I imagine."

"A few minutes," Pitt agreed. "Body was warm—but

apart from that, if he'd been there longer, someone would have seen him sooner."

"Who did find him?"

"Prostitute called Hetty Milner."

Drummond smiled, a brief humor lighting his eyes, then dying immediately. "I suppose she tried to solicit a little business—and found her prospective client was a corpse."

Pitt bit his lip to hide the shadow of a smile. "Yes—which was a good thing. If she hadn't been so startled she wouldn't have screamed; she'd have collected herself and walked straight on, and we might not have known about him for a lot longer."

Drummond leaned forward, all the irony gone from his features, a thin line of anxiety between his brows. "What do we know, Pitt?" he asked.

Briefly Pitt summarized for him the events on the bridge, his visit to Royal Street, and finally his return to the station.

Drummond sat back and wiped his lips with his napkin. "What a mess," he said grimly. "The motive could be almost anything—business or professional rivalry, political enmity, anarchist conspiracy. Or it could be the work of a random lunatic, in which case we may never find him! What do you think of a personal motive: money, jealousy, revenge?"

"Possible," Pitt answered, remembering the widow's stricken face and her gallant struggle to maintain composure, the cool civility between her and her stepson that might cover all manner of old wounds. "Very ugly. It seems a bizarre way to do it."

"Smacks of madness, doesn't it," Drummond agreed. "But perhaps that doesn't mean anything. Please God we can settle it soon, and without having to go into family tragedies."

"I hope so," Pitt agreed. He had finished his breakfast, and in the warm room he was overwhelmingly tired.

Cobb came in with the newspapers and handed them

wordlessly to Drummond. Drummond opened the first and read from the headlines, "'Member of Parliament Murdered on Westminster Bridge,'" and from the second, "'Shocking Murder—Corpse on the Lamppost.'" He looked up at Pitt. "Go home and get some sleep, man," he ordered. "Come back this afternoon when we have had a chance to find a few witnesses. Then you can start on the business associates, and the political ones." He glanced at the papers on the table. "They aren't going to give us much time."

CHARLOTTE PITT HAD NOT yet heard about the murder on Westminster Bridge, and at the moment her mind was totally absorbed in the meeting she was attending. It was the first time she had been a part of such an assembly. Most of those gathered had little in common with each other, except an interest in the representation of women in Parliament. Most had no thought beyond the wild and previously undreamed of possibility that women might actually vote, but one or two extraordinary souls had conceived the idea of women as members of that august body. One woman had even offered herself for election. Of course, she had sunk with barely a trace, a joke in the worst taste.

Now Charlotte sat in the back row of a crowded meeting hall and watched the first speaker, a stout young woman with a strong, blunt face and red hands, as she got to her feet and the muttering gradually fell to silence.

"Sisters!" The word stuck oddly on such a mixed company. In front of Charlotte a well-dressed woman in green silk hunched her shoulders a little, withdrawing from the touch and the association of those she was forced to be so close to. "We're all 'ere for the same reason!" the young woman on the platform continued, her voice rich, and hardened with a strong northern accent. "We all believe as 'ow we should 'ave some say in the way our lives is run, wot laws is made an' oo makes 'em! All kinds o' men get a chance to choose their members o' Parliament, an' if 'e wants to get elected, that Member 'as to answer to the people. 'Alf the people, sisters, just 'alf the people—the 'alf that's men!"

She went on speaking for another ten minutes, and Charlotte only half listened. She had heard the arguments before, and in her mind they were already irrefutable. What she had come for was to see what support there was, and the kind of women who were prepared to come from conviction rather than curiosity. Gazing round at them as discreetly as she could, she saw that a large number were soberly dressed in browns and muted tones, and the cut of their coats and skirts was serviceable but not smart, designed to last through many changes of fashion. Several wore shawls pulled round their shoulders for warmth, not decoration. They were ordinary women whose husbands were clerks or tradesmen, struggling to make ends meet, perhaps striving after a little gentility, perhaps not.

Here and there were a few who were smarter; some young with a touch of elegance, others matronly, ample bosoms draped with furs and beads, hats sprouting feathers.

But it was their faces that interested Charlotte most, the fleeting expressions chasing across them as they listened to the ideas that almost all society found revolutionary, unnatural, and either ridiculous or dangerous, depending on their perception of any real change awakening from them.

In some she saw interest, even the glimmer of belief. In others there was confusion: the thought was too big to accept, required too great a break with the inbred teaching of mother and grandmother, a way of life not always comfortable but whose hardships were at least familiar. In some there was already derision and dislike, and the fear of change.

One face held Charlotte's attention particularly, round and yet delicately boned, intelligent, curious, very feminine, and with a strong, stubborn jaw. It was the expression which drew Charlotte, a mixture of wonder and doubt, as though new thoughts were entering the woman's mind and enormous questions arose out of them instantly. Her eyes were intent on the speaker, afraid lest she lose a word. She seemed oblivious of the women packed close to her; indeed, when one jostled against her and a feather from a rakish hat brushed her cheek she did no more than blink without turning to see who the offender might be.

With the third speaker, a thin, overearnest woman of indeterminate age, the hecklers began. Their voices were still moderately good-natured, but their questions were sharp.

"Yer sayin' as women knows as much abaht business as men? That don't say much fer yer man, then, do it?"

"That is if yer 'as one!" There was a roar of laughter, half raucous, half pitying: a single woman was in most eyes a sad object, a creature who had failed in her prime objective.

The woman on the platform winced so very slightly that it might even have been Charlotte's imagination. She was used to this particular taunt and had grown to expect it.

"You have one?" she flung back with certainty blazing in her face. "And children, do you?"

"Sure I 'ave! Ten of 'em!"

There were more shouts of laughter.

"Do you have a maid, and a cook, and other servants?" the woman on the platform asked.

"Course I don't! Wotcher think I am? I 'ave one girl as scrubs."

"Then you manage the household yourself?"

There was silence, and Charlotte glanced at the woman with the remarkable face and saw that already she understood what the speaker was intending. Her face was keen with appreciation.

"Course I do!"

"Accounts, budgeting, the purchase of clothes, the use of fuel, the discipline of your ten children? Seems to me you know a great deal about business—and people. I daresay you are a pretty good judge of character too. You know when you are being lied to, when someone is trying to give you short change or sell you shoddy goods, don't you?"

"Yeah . . ." the woman agreed slowly. She was not yet ready to concede, not in front of so many. "Don't mean I know 'ow ter run a country!"

"Does your husband? Could he run a country? Could he even run your house?"

"In't the same!"

"Does he have a vote?"

"Yeah, but—"

"Isn't your judgment as good as his?"

"My dear good woman!" another voice burst in, rich and piled with scorn, and heads turned towards the wearer of a plum-colored hat. "You may be very proficient at buying enough potatoes to feed your family and assessing the cost any given week; I don't doubt you are. But that is hardly on the same level as choosing a Prime Minister!"

There were giggles of stifled mirth, and someone called out, "Hear, hear," in agreement.

"Our place is in the home," the woman with the plum hat continued, gathering momentum. "Domestic duties are among our natural gifts, and as mothers, of course we know how to discipline our children—such instincts awake in us when we bear our young. It is God's order of the world. But our judgments on matters of high finance, foreign affairs, and concerns of state are utterly hopeless. Neither nature nor the Lord designed us to meddle in such things, and we rob ourselves and our daughters of our proper place, and the respect and protection due us from men, if we try to go contrary to it!"

There were more murmurs of approval, and a sprinkling of tentative applause.

The woman on the platform was exasperated at the irrelevance of the argument. There were spots of color high on her thin cheeks. "I am not suggesting you become a Minister of State!" she said sharply. "Only that you have as much right as your butler or your poulterer has to choose who shall represent you in the Parliament of your country! And that your judgment of character is probably just as competent as theirs!"

"Oh! You impertinent creature!" The woman in plum was quite outraged; her face colored darkly and her rather heavy jowls shook as she raced through her mind for words scalding enough to satisfy the occasion.

"You are quite right!" Suddenly the woman who had drawn Charlotte's attention broke the silence. Her voice was husky and pleasant; both her diction and her poise revealed she was of considerable breeding. "Women's judgment of character is quite as good as men's; on the whole, I think very often rather better. And that is all that is required to have a useful opinion as to who should represent one in Parliament!"

Everyone in the cramped hall swung round to look at her, and she blushed with slight self-consciousness, but it did not prevent her continuing.

"We are bound by the laws; I think it is only proper that we should have some say as to what they shall be. I—"

"You are quite wrong, madame!" A deeper voice cut across her, the rich contralto of a very large woman with jet beads across her bosom and a fine mourning brooch on her lapel. "The law, framed by men whom you so despise, is our finest protection! As a woman you are guarded by your husband, or should you be single, your father; he provides for your needs both spiritual and temporal; he exercises his wisdom to gain what is best for you, without the least exertion on your part; he undertakes your well-being; should you transgress or fall into debt, it is he, not you, who answers the magistrates and must satisfy your creditors. It is only just that he should also frame the laws, or elect those who do!"

"Stuff and nonsense!" Charlotte said loudly. She could contain herself no longer. "If my husband falls into debt, I shall be just as hungry as he is; if I commit a crime, the general public may look down upon him, but it is assuredly I who shall go to prison, not he! And if I kill someone, it is I who will hang!"

There was a sharp collective intake of breath and a little hiss of surprise at such unnecessary coarseness of reference.

Charlotte was not deterred: she had intended to shock, and the feeling of success was quite exhilarating.

"I agree with Miss Wutherspoon—women's judgment of character is easily as good as men's. What could be more important in your life than who you marry? And upon what basis does a man choose, if left to himself?"

"A pretty face!" someone answered sourly.

Someone else gave a reply a good deal less refined, and raised a loud laugh.

"Beauty, charm, a winning way," Charlotte answered her own question before the purpose of it was lost. "Often upon flattery, and the color of her eyes, or the way she has of laughing. A woman chooses a man who can provide for her and her children." Here she winced at her duplicity, she who had chosen Pitt entirely because he intrigued her, charmed her, frightened her with his directness, made her laugh, fired her with his anger at injustice, and because she both loved and trusted him. The fact that he was socially and financially a disaster, and like to remain so, had not weighed an ounce with her. But she knew unquestionably that most women had more sense. She sailed on regardless both of that, and of her earlier infatuation with her brother-in-law Dominic, for which she did blush, but it was lost under the high colour of her zeal. The principle was right.

"Men may go on all manner of adventures and brave the result, come what may, but most women will look to the outcome of a thing, knowing that their children must eat and be clothed, that there must be a safe home for them not only today and tomorrow, but next year and ten years from now! Women are less reckless." She thought of all the wise and brave women she had known, discounting the idiotic things she had done herself, and the risks both she and Emily had taken. "When all the shouting and the heroics are over, who is it that will tend the sick, bury the dead and start over? Women! Our opinions should count, our judgment of a man's honesty and worth to represent us should weigh in the balance too."

"You're right!" Miss Wutherspoon cried from the platform. "You're absolutely right! And if Members of Parliament had to account to women as well as men to get elected, there wouldn't be the injustices there are now!"

"What injustices?" someone demanded. "What does a good woman need that she does not have?"

"No natural woman wants to expose herself to ridicule," the woman in the plum-colored hat said loudly, her voice rising with increasing indignation, "by parading for people to accept or reject her, pleading with them to listen to her, choose her, believe in her opinions or trust her judgment in affairs she knows nothing about! Miss Taylor is a laughing-stock, and far from being a friend to women, she is our worst enemy. Not even Dr. Pankhurst would be seen in public with her! Standing for Parliament, indeed! Next thing you know we'll become harridans, like that miserable Ivory woman, who has abandoned all semblance of decency and restraint which is essential to a woman and all that is precious to society—indeed to civilization!"

There were several cries of approval and even louder hisses and expostulations of outrage. Some even demanded that the traitors to the cause should leave and go back to their nurseries, or whatever other confining place they usually inhabited.

A stout woman in bombazine raised an umbrella, unfortunately catching the ferrule of it in an elderly housemaid's skirts. There was a hiccup and a shriek of alarm. The housemaid, thinking she was being assaulted for her abuse of the lady in the plum hat, whisked her handbag round and landed it soundly on the head of the woman in bombazine, and the resulting melee had very little to do with the exercise of privilege or responsibility, and even less to do with Parliament.

Having no wish to become involved in a brawl, Charlotte withdrew. She was only a few yards outside the hall via the rear exit when she saw the woman whose face had drawn her attention. She was standing quite close, unaware of Charlotte, her attention caught by a hansom drawn up at the curb. The woman had her back to Charlotte and was arguing fiercely with a slim, elegantly dressed man whose fair hair shone almost white in the sun. He was obviously extremely annoyed.

"My dear Parthenope, this is both unseemly, and to be frank, a trifle ridiculous. You are letting me down by even being seen in such a place, and I am distressed that you should not have realized it!"

Charlotte could not see the woman's face, but her voice was thick with a confusion of emotions.

"I am tempted to make the obvious answer to excuse myself, Cuthbert, and say that no one there knew who I was. But that is irrelevant."

"Indeed it is! The risk—"

But she cut him short. "I am not talking about the risk! What if I am known to care that women should be represented in Parliament?"

"Women are represented!" He was exasperated now, and there was a flash of impatience in his face. "You are excellently represented by the present members of the House! For heaven's sake, we don't legislate simply for ourselves! Who on earth have you been listening to? Have you seen that wretched Ivory woman again? I most specifically told you that I did not wish it! Why do you insist on disobeying me? The woman is a virago, a miserable, unbalanced creature who embodies everything that is most to be deplored in a woman."

"No I have not seen her!" Parthenope's voice was low, but it now held an intensity of anger. "I told you I would not, and I have not! But I shall not stop listening to what people have to say about women one day obtaining the franchise."

"Then listen at home; read articles, if you must—although it will never happen. It is quite unnecessary and unsuitable. Women's interests are very well cared for now, and all women with any sense are fully aware of it!"

"Indeed!" Her voice grew harder, and high with sarcasm. "Then I have little sense! Only that which is required to govern a household of eight servants, see to the accounting, maintain discipline and good order and fellowship, raise and teach and nurse my children, entertain our business and parliamentary friends and provide them with fine meals in charming surroundings, and always see that no one is offended, embarrassed, excluded, or paired with someone unsuitable, and to keep the conversation charming, witty but never offensive, and never, never boring! And naturally always to look beautiful while doing all of this! I am sure that does not make me competent to decide which of two or three candidates should represent me in Parliament!"

The fair-haired man's face was tight and his blue eyes blazed. "Parthenope! You are becoming absurd!" he hissed. "I forbid you to stand out here and argue this in public any longer. We are going home, where you should have been all the time!"

"Of course." Still she did not shout, but her whole body was rigid with fury. "Perhaps once you have me there you would care to lock the door."

He put out both his hands and held her arms, but she did not yield in the slightest.

"Parthenope, I have no desire to curtail your pleasures or to be harsh with you. For heaven's sake, you know that! And you are excellent—no, brilliant—at running the house. I have always said so, and I am profoundly grateful for all you do. You are a perfect wife in every way—" He could see he was still losing; she did not want flattery, not even acknowledgment. "Damn it, madame, you are not selecting a housemaid! At that you are unequaled, but choosing a member of Parliament is utterly different!"

"Indeed?" Her eyebrows rose sharply. "Pray how? Would you not wish your Member of Parliament to be honest above question, of sound moral character, discreet about what he knows that is confidential, loyal to his cause, and competent in the skills of his job?"

"I don't want him to dust the furniture or peel the potatoes!"

"Oh Cuthbert!" She knew she had won the argument,

and lost the issue. He had not changed his mind in the slightest, nor was he likely to. His urgency was still all bent on getting her to climb into the cab and leave the areaway before someone came who might recognize one of them. Reluctantly she yielded and allowed him to hand her up. Charlotte saw her sensitive, stubborn face for a moment as she turned on the step, and the confusion in it; the new ideas could not be extinguished, nor could the old loyalties be denied. Parthenope looked at her husband with a sharp, unresolved anxiety.

Then he climbed up beside her and pulled the door shut, leaving Charlotte to come out of the shadows and walk along the footpath as if she had only this moment come out of the exit.

BY MIDAFTERNOON PITT WAS back in Bow Street. It was one of those vivid spring days when the air is sharp and the sun falls clean and pale on the pavement stones, and there was still a tingle of coldness in the wind, keen-edged and bringing a smell of dampness up from the river. A string of carriages clattered by along the Strand, harnesses polished and jingling, horses stepping high, and the crossing boys swept up behind them, cleaning away the droppings. A barrel organ churned out a popular music hall song. Somewhere out of sight a street vendor called his wares—"Hot plum duff, hot plum!"—and gradually his voice faded away as he moved towards the embankment. A newspaper boy was shouting his "extra"—"'Orrible Murder on Westminster Bridge! M.P. Dead—Throat Cut!'"

Pitt climbed the steps and went into the station. It was a different sergeant on duty, but he had obviously been fully caught up on the case.

"Arternoon, Mr. Pitt," he said cheerfully. "Mr. Drummond's in 'is office. Reckon there's a bit in—not much. Found a cab or two, for wot it's worth."

"Thank you." Pitt strode past him and into the corridor, which smelled of clean linoleum, a comparatively new invention. He went up the stairs two at a time and knocked on the door to Drummond's office. His memory went back to a few months ago, when Dudley Athelstan had occupied it. Pitt had found Athelstan pompous and, with the insecurity of the socially ambitious, never sure which master to serve. Athelstan had resented Pitt's impertinence, his untidiness—but above all his impudence in marrying Charlotte Ellison, so much his social superior.

Drummond was a totally different man, having sufficient family background and private means not to care about either. He called his permission to enter.

"Good afternoon, sir." Pitt looked round the room, full of mementos of past cases, many of which he had worked on himself; tragedies and resolutions, darkness and light.

"Come in, Pitt." Drummond waved him towards the fire. He fished among papers on his desk, all handwritten in copperplate of varying degrees of legibility. "Got a few reports, nothing very helpful so far; a cabby crossing the bridge who noticed nothing at a quarter past midnight, except perhaps a prostitute at the north side, and a group of gentlemen coming up from the House of Commons. Hamilton could have been one of them; we'll have to ask around tonight when the House rises. No good looking now. We'll find out which members live on the south side of the river and might have gone home that way. Got a man on it now."

Pitt stood by the fire, the warmth delicious up the backs of his legs. Athelstan always used to monopolize it.

"I suppose we have to face the remote possibility it was one of his colleagues?" he said with regret.

Drummond looked up sharply, instant disagreement on his face. Then reason overtook distaste. "Not yet, but it may have to be considered," he conceded. "First we'll look at personal or business enemies and—God help us—the possibility it was some lunatic."

"Or anarchists," Pitt added glumly, rubbing his hands down the back of his coat where the fire warmed it.

Drummond regarded him, a bleak and not unsympathetic humor in his eyes. "Or anarchists," he agreed. "Unpleasant as it is, we had better pray it is personal. Which is the line you must pursue today."

"What have we so far?" Pitt asked.

"Two cabbies, the one at a quarter past midnight who noticed nothing, one at approximately twenty past, seen by

Hetty Milner, who also says he saw nothing; but since Hetty saw him immediately before she spoke to Hamilton, that doesn't mean much. Poor devil must have been there then, possibly before. But it shouldn't be hard to establish what time he left the House, so we have a space of twenty minutes or so. Might help with determining where suspects were, but I doubt it: if it was family they may well not have committed the crime personally." He sighed. "We'll probably be looking at movement of money, bank withdrawals, sales of jewelry or pictures, acquaintances of unusual nature." He rubbed his hands over his face wearily, only too aware of the closing of ranks that scandal inspired among the upper classes. "Look into his business affairs, will you Pitt? Then you'd better see what political matter he was involved with. There's always Irish Home Rule, slum clearance, poor law reform—heaven knows what else someone might feel violent about."

"Yes sir." It was what he would have done anyway. "I suppose we've got someone checking on all the known agitators?"

"Yes, all that is being done. At least we've got only a narrow space of time to cover. Might get something from the other people who came running when Hetty Milner screamed. So far they've given us nothing useful, but memory does sometimes dredge up a face or a sound afterwards, something seen out of the corner of the eye." Drummond pushed forward a sheet of paper with a name and address on it. "That's Hamilton's business partner. You could start with him. And Pitt . . ."

Pitt waited.

"For heaven's sake be tactful!"

Pitt smiled. "I assume that is why you chose me for the case—sir."

Drummond's mouth quivered. "Get out," he said quietly.

Pitt took a hansom along the Strand, Fleet Street and Ludgate Hill past St. Paul's and up to Cheapside, along Cheapside and down Threadneedle Street past the Bank of

England to Bishopsgate Street Within and the offices of Hamilton and Verdun. He presented his card, an extravagance he had indulged in a while ago and indeed found useful.

"'Inspector Thomas Pitt, Bow Street,'" the clerk read with patent surprise. Policemen did not carry calling cards, any more than did the ratcatcher or the drain man. Standards had declined appallingly lately! What was the world coming to?

"I would like to speak with Mr. Charles Verdun, if I may," Pitt continued. "About the death of Sir Lockwood Hamilton."

"Oh!" The clerk was considerably sobered—and a little elated, in spite of himself. There was a certain grisly glamor in being connected with a famous murder. He would tell Miss Laetitia Morris all about it this evening, over a glass of stout at the Grinning Rat. That should make her sit up and take notice! She would not find him boring after *this*. Harry Parsons would not seem half so interesting with his common bit of embezzlement. He looked at Pitt.

"Well if you wait 'ere, I'll see what Mr. Verdun says. 'E don't see people just for the askin', you know. Perhaps I could tell you somethin'? I saw Sir Lockwood reg'lar. I 'ope you're well on your way to catchin' the criminal what done this. Per'aps I saw 'im—without knowin', like?"

Pitt read him like one of the clerk's own copperplate ledgers. "I shall know better what to ask you after I've seen Mr. Verdun."

"Course. Well I'll go and see wot 'e says." And dutifully the clerk retired, to come back in a few moments and usher Pitt into a large untidy room with a good fire, which was smoking a little, and several armchairs in green leather, comfortable and polished to a shine by use. Behind an antique and battered desk piled with papers sat a man of anything between fifty and seventy, with a long face, tufted gray eyebrows, and a benign and whimsical expression. He composed his features into an expression of suitable gravity and waved his hand towards a chair, inviting Pitt to sit down. Then he wandered over himself, took a look at the fire, and swung his arms round as if to dispel the smoke.

"Damn thing!" He glared at it. "Can't think what's the matter with it! Maybe I'd better open a window?"

Pitt prevented himself from coughing with difficulty and nodded his head. "Yes sir. A good idea."

Verdun strolled back behind the desk and yanked on the lower half of the sash window. It shot up with a thump, letting in a gust of cool air.

"Ah," he said with satisfaction. "Now, what can I do for you? Police fellow, eh? About poor Lockwood's death. Shocking thing to happen. I suppose you've no idea who did it? No, you wouldn't have—too soon, eh?"

"Yes sir. I understand Sir Lockwood was in business partnership with you?"

"Yes, in a manner of speaking." Verdun reached for a humidor and took out a cigar. He lit it with a spill from the fire and blew out a smoke so pungent it made Pitt gasp.

Verdun mistook his expression entirely.

"Turkish," he said with satisfaction. "Have one?"

Camel dung, Pitt thought. "Very kind of you, but no thank you, sir," he replied. "In what manner of speaking, sir?"

"Ah." Verdun shook his head. "Wasn't in here much. Keener on his politics—had to be. Parliamentary Private Secretary, and all that. One has a duty."

"But he had a financial interest in the company?" Pitt persisted.

"Oh yes, yes. You could say that."

Pitt was puzzled. "Was he not an equal partner?" His name had been first on the plate outside the door.

"Certainly!" Verdun agreed. "But he didn't come here more than once a week at most, often less." He said it without the slightest resentment.

"So you do most of the work?" Pitt asked. He wanted

to be tactful, but with this man it was difficult. Obliqueness seemed to be misunderstood altogether.

Verdun's eyebrows shot up. "Work? Well, yes, I suppose so. Never thought of looking at it like that. Fellow's got to do something, you know! Don't like hanging around clubs with a lot of old fools talking about cads, the weather, who said what, and how everybody dresses—and who's having an affair with whose mistress. I always find it too easy to see the other chap's point of view to get heated about it."

Pitt hid a smile with difficulty. "So you deal in property?" he prompted.

"Yes, that's right," Verdun agreed. He puffed at his cigar. Pitt was profoundly glad the window was open; it really smelled appalling. "What's this got to do with poor old Lockwood being killed on Westminster Bridge?" Verdun went on, puckering up his face. "Don't think it was over some property deal, do you? Hardly seems likely. Why should anybody do that?"

Pitt could think of several reasons. He would not be the first slum landlord to charge exorbitant rents and cram fifteen or twenty people into one damp and rat-infested room. Nor would he be the first to use his properties as brothels, sweatshops, and thieves' kitchens. There was the possibility Hamilton had been doing this and had been killed for revenge or from outrage—or that Verdun had done it, and when Hamilton found out and threatened to expose him, Verdun killed him to keep him silent.

Or it might simply have been someone acting out of fury at having been evicted from a home, undersold, or beaten to a lucrative deal. However, Pitt did not speak any of these thoughts aloud.

"I imagine there's a good deal of money involved," he said instead, as innocently as he could.

"Not a lot," Verdun replied candidly. "Do it to keep busy, you know. Wife dead twenty years ago. Never felt like marrying again. Couldn't ever care for anyone as I did for her. . . ." For a moment his eyes were gentle, faraway, seeing some past happiness that still charmed him. Then he recalled himself. "Children all grown up. Got to do something!"

"But it brings a good income?" Pitt looked at the quality of Verdun's clothing. It was shabby, worn into comfort, but his boots were excellent, and the cut of his jacket Savile Row, his shirts probably Gieves and Son. He did not look fashionable; he looked as if he was sufficiently sure of himself and his place in society that he did not need to. His was old money, quiet money.

"Not terribly," Verdun interrupted Pitt's thoughts. "No need. Hamilton made his income from something to do with railway carriages, in Birmingham or somewhere like that."

"And you, sir?"

"Me?" Again the wispy, tufted eyebrows shot up, and the round gray eyes beneath were bright with irony and suppressed humor. "Don't need it; got enough. Family, you know."

Pitt had already known it; in fact he would not have been surprised had there been an honorary title Verdun declined to use.

There was a rattling outside, a steady arrhythmical clatter.

"You can hear it!" Verdun said quickly. "Horrible contraption! A typewriter, if you please! Got it for my junior clerk—boy can't write so anyone but an apothecary can read it. Hideous thing. Sounds like twenty horses sliding round a cobbled yard."

"Would you mind giving the police a list of your property deals in the last twelve months, Mr. Verdun?" Pitt requested, biting his lip. He was predisposed to like this man, but his mild, slightly vague manner might hide far uglier passions. Pitt had liked people before and discovered them to be capable of killing. "And anything proposed for the future," he added. "It will be treated with as much confidence as possible."

"My dear fellow, you'll find it excessively tedious. But if you like. Can't imagine you'll catch Lockwood's killer in the list of semidetached houses in Primrose Hill, Kentish Town, or Highgate, but I suppose you know what you're doing."

The neighborhoods he mentioned were all respectable suburban areas. "What about the East End?" Pitt asked. "No properties there?"

Verdun was quicker than Pitt had thought. "Slum landlords? Suppose you were bound to think of that. No. But you can look through the books if you feel it's your duty."

Pitt knew it would be pointless, but a clever auditor might find some discrepancy that would point to other books, other deals—even embezzlement? He profoundly hoped not. He would like Verdun to be exactly what he seemed.

"Thank you, sir. Are you acquainted with Lady Hamilton?"

"Amethyst? Yes, slightly. Fine woman. Very quiet. Imagine there's some sadness there; no family, you know. Not that Lockwood ever mentioned it—very fond of her. Didn't say much, but it was there. Knew that. Do, if you've ever cared for a woman yourself."

Pitt thought briefly of Charlotte at home, the warmth and the heart of his own life. "Indeed." He seized the opportunity the subject of family offered him. "But there is a son by Sir Lockwood's first marriage?"

"Oh, Barclay, yes. Nice fellow. Didn't see much of him. Never married—no idea why."

"Was he close to his mother?"

"Beatrice? No idea. Didn't get on with Amethyst, if that's what you mean."

"Do you know why?"

"No idea. Might have resented his father marrying again, I suppose. Bit silly, I always think. Should have been pleased for him he was happy, and Amethyst certainly made him an excellent wife. Supported him in his career, entertained his friends with skill and tact, and kept an excellent house. In fact I would say he was happier with her than with Beatrice."

"Maybe Mr. Barclay knew that, and resented it on his mother's behalf," Pitt suggested.

Verdun's face dropped. "Good heavens, man, you're not going to suggest he waited twenty years, then suddenly one night crept up behind his father on Westminster Bridge and cut his throat for it, are you?"

"No, of course not." It was preposterous. "Is Mr. Barclay Hamilton reasonably well provided for financially?"

"Happen to know that: inherited from his maternal grandfather. Not a lot, but comfortable. Nice house in Chelsea—very nice. Near the Albert Bridge."

"I suppose you have no idea if there's any rival or enemy who might have wished Sir Lockwood harm? Any threats you know of?"

Verdun smiled. "I'm sorry. If I did I should have mentioned it, distasteful as it is. After all, you can't have chaps running around killing people, can you!"

"No sir." Pitt stood up. "Thank you for your help. If I may look at those records of yours? The last year or so should be sufficient."

"Of course. I'll have Telford make a copy for you on that awful contraption, if you like. Might as well do something useful on it. Sounds like a hundred urchins in hobnail boots!"

It was quarter past six when Pitt was finally ushered into the Home Secretary's office in Whitehall. It was very large and very formal, and the officials in their frock coats and wing collars made it plain that it was a considerable favor granted in extraordinary circumstances that Pitt was even allowed across the threshold, let alone into a Cabinet Minister's private office. Pitt attempted to straighten his tie, making it worse, and ran his fingers through his hair, which was no improvement either.

"Yes, Inspector?" the Home Secretary said courteously. "I can give you ten minutes. Lockwood Hamilton was my Parliamentary Private Secretary, and very good at it, efficient and discreet. I am deeply sorrowed by his death."

"Was he ambitious, sir?"

"Naturally. I should not promote a man who was indifferent to his career."

"How long had he held the position?"

"About six months."

"And before that?"

"A backbencher, on various committees. Why?" He frowned. "Surely you don't think this was political?"

"I don't know, sir. Has Sir Lockwood been involved in any issues or legislation that might arouse strong feelings?"

"He hasn't proposed anything. For Heaven's sake, he's a Parliamentary Private Secretary, not a minister!"

Pitt realized he had made a tactical error. "Before you appointed him to this position, sir," he went on, "you must have known a considerable amount about him: his past career, his stand on important issues, his private life, reputation, business and financial affairs . . ."

"Of course," the Home Secretary agreed somewhat tartly. Then he realized Pitt's purpose. "I don't think I can tell you anything of use. I don't appoint men I consider likely to be murdered for their private lives, and he wasn't important enough to be a political target."

"Probably not, sir," Pitt was forced to agree. "However, I would be neglecting my duty if I didn't look at all the possibilities. Someone unbalanced enough to think of murder as a solution to their problems may not be as rational as you or I."

The Home Secretary gave him a sharp glance, suspecting sarcasm, and he did not like the impertinence of Pitt's equating a Cabinet Minister with a policeman in an estimate of rationality, but he met Pitt's bland blue stare and decided the matter was not worth pursuing.

"We may be dealing with the irrational," he said coldly.

"I hope so most profoundly. Any society may be subject to the occasional lunatic. A family or business crime would be unpleasant, but it would be a nine-day scandal, forgotten afterwards. Immeasurably worse would be some conspiracy of anarchists or revolutionaries who were not after poor Hamilton in particular but bent on generally destabilizing the government and causing alarm and public outcry." His hands tightened imperceptibly. "We must clear up this matter as soon as possible. I assume you have all available men on it?"

Pitt could see his reasoning—and yet there was a coldness in him that Pitt found himself disliking as he stood there in the elegant and well-ordered office, which smelled faintly of beeswax and leather. The Home Secretary would prefer a private tragedy with all its pain and ruined lives to an impersonal plot hatched by hotheads dreaming of power and change in some back room, and he felt no compunction about saying so.

"Well?" the Home Secretary demanded irritably. "Speak up, man!"

"Yes sir, we have. You must have considered other men for the position of your Parliamentary Private Secretary, as well as Sir Lockwood?"

"Naturally."

"Perhaps your secretary would give me their names." It was not a question.

"If you think it necessary." He was reluctant, but he took the point. "Hardly a position a sane man kills to achieve."

"What sort of position would a sane man kill to achieve, sir?" Pitt asked, his voice as devoid of expression as he could manage.

The Home Secretary shot him a look of chill dislike. "I think you must look outside Her Majesty's government for your suspect, Inspector!" he said acidly.

Pitt was unruffled: it was faintly satisfying that their dislike was mutual. "Can you tell me Sir Lockwood's views on the most contentious current issues, sir? For example, Home Rule for Ireland?"

The Home Secretary pushed out his lower lip thoughtfully, his irritation submerged. "I suppose it could be something to do with that, not directed at poor Hamilton so much as at the government in general. Always an issue that raises heated emotions. He was for it, and fairly outspoken. Though if people were going to murder each other because they disagreed over the Irish question, the streets of London would look like the aftermath of Waterloo."

"What about other issues, sir? Penal reform, the poor laws, factory conditions, slum clearance, women's suffrage?"

"What?"

"Women's suffrage," Pitt repeated.

"Good God, man, we've got some strident and misguided women who don't know where their best interests lie, but they'd hardly cut a man's throat just to make a plea for the franchise to be extended!"

"Probably not. But what were Sir Lockwood's opinions?"

The Home Secretary was about to dismiss the subject but seemed grudgingly to realize that it was as valid as any other possibility so far raised. "He wasn't a reformer," he replied. "Except in the most moderate terms. He was a very sane man! I wouldn't have had him as my P.P.S. if I didn't trust his judgments."

"And his reputation in his personal life?"

"Impeccable." The briefest of smiles flickered across the home secretary's face. "And that is not a diplomatic answer. He was extremely fond of his wife, a very fine woman, and he was not a man to seek . . . diversions. He had little art of flattery or trivial conversation, and I never observed him to admire another woman."

Having met Amethyst Hamilton, Pitt did not find it hard to believe. Charles Verdun had said the same.

"The more I hear of him, the less does he sound like a

man to have inspired a personal hatred violent enough to incite murder." Pitt had a faint satisfaction in seeing the Home Secretary's appreciation of the turn of his argument, little as he liked it.

"Then you had better pursue whatever evidence you have and look into all the agitators and political groups we know of," he said grimly. "Keep me informed."

"Yes sir. Thank you."

"Good day to you." He was dismissed.

The House of Commons was still sitting; it was too early to attempt to retrace Hamilton's steps the night before. Pitt was cold and hungry and knew little more than when he had left his home that afternoon after a snatched few hours of sleep. He would go back to Bow Street and have a sandwich and a mug of tea and see if there was any news from the constables out pursuing witnesses.

But when he reached the station the duty sergeant told him that Sir Garnet Royce, M.P., had called to see him.

"Bring him to my office," Pitt replied. He doubted it would be a helpful visit, but he owed the man the courtesy of seeing him. He pushed some papers off the second chair to make room for Royce to sit down if he wished and went behind his desk, glancing to see if there were any messages or new reports. There was nothing except the pile of house transactions from Verdun, with a note from one of the officers specializing in fraud, saying that as far as he could see they were exactly what they appeared to be; there was nothing to be deduced from them except that the firm conducted fairly efficient dealings in domestic property in several agreeable suburbs.

There was a knock on the door, and a constable showed in Garnet Royce. He was smartly dressed in a velvet-collared coat and carried a silk hat, which he put on the table. He was an imposing figure in this very ordinary gaslit office.

"Good evening, sir," Pitt said curiously.

"Evening, Inspector." He declined the chair. He was still

holding a silver-headed cane, and he turned it restlessly in his strong hands as he spoke. "I see the newspapers have made headlines of poor Lockwood. Suppose it was to be expected. Distressing for the family. Makes it hard to manage affairs with any dignity; lot of idle people hanging around like ghouls, people one barely knows trying to scrape an acquaintance. Disgusting! Brings out the best and the worst in people. You'll understand my distress for my sister."

"Of course, sir." Pitt meant it.

Royce leaned forward a little. "If it was some random madman, as seems much the likeliest thing, what are your chances of apprehending him, Inspector? Answer me honestly, man to man."

Pitt looked at his face: the power in the sweep of nose and cheek, the wide mouth and sloping brow. It was not a sensitive face, but there was strength and intelligence in it.

"With luck, sir, quite fair; without a witness of any sort, and if the man doesn't attack anyone else, not great. But then if he is a madman, he will continue to behave in a way to draw attention to himself, and we will find him."

"Yes. Yes of course." Sir Garnet's hands closed on the cane. "I suppose you have no ideas as yet?"

"No sir. We're working through the obvious possibilities: business rivalry, political enemies."

"Lockwood was hardly important enough to earn political enemies." Royce frowned. "Of course, there were a few people who lost promotions because he gained them, but that's what one expects, for heaven's sake. It's true of anyone in public life."

"Was there anyone who might have taken it especially hard?"

Royce thought for a moment, searching his memory. "Hanbury was pretty upset over the chairmanship of a parliamentary committee several years ago and seems to have held something of a grudge. And they quarreled over Home Rule—Hanbury was very much against it, and Lockwood was in favor. Rather felt he'd let the side down. But one doesn't commit murder over such things."

Pitt regarded the other man's face in the lamplight. There was no shadow of double-mindedness or deception in it, no irony, no humor. He meant exactly what he said, and Pitt was obliged to agree with him. If the motive for murder was political, it lay in something far deeper than any issue they had touched on yet; it was a rivalry or a betrayal more personal, far more bitter than the question of Irish Home Rule or social reform.

Royce took his leave, and Pitt went upstairs to see Micah Drummond.

"Nothing of much use." Drummond pushed a pile of papers across his desk towards Pitt. He looked tired, and there were dark patches under his eyes where the skin was thin and delicate. This was only the first day, but already he had felt the pressure, the anger of the people as horror turned to fear, and the alarm of those in power who knew the real danger.

"We've narrowed down the time," he said. "He must have been killed between ten to midnight, when the House rose, and twenty past, when Hetty Milner found him. We ought to be able to cut it down further when we talk to the members when the House rises tonight."

"Did we find any street vendors who'd seen him?" Pitt asked. "Or any who'd been around that area and hadn't seen him, which would narrow things down?"

Drummond sighed and shuffled through the papers. "Flower seller said she didn't see him. She knows him, so I presume she's fairly reliable. Chap who sells hot pies on Westminster steps, Freddie something, but he saw nothing useful: half a dozen men, any one of whom could have been Hamilton, but he can't swear to it. Distinguished-looking fellow in good dark coat and silk hat with a white scarf, average height, gray at the temples—the streets round the bridge are crawling with them when the House rises!"

"Of course, it may not be Hamilton they were after," Pitt said quietly.

Drummond looked up, his eyes hollow and anxious. "Yes, I had thought of that. God help us, if he was after someone else where do we even begin? It could be almost anyone!"

Pitt sat down on the hard-backed chair in front of the desk. "If it is a random attack against the government, and Hamilton just happened to be the one," he said, "then it must be anarchists or revolutionaries of some sort. Don't we have some knowledge of most of these groups?"

"Yes." Drummond fished out a sheaf of papers from a drawer in the desk. "And I've got men looking into it, trying to trace the activities of known members of all of them. Some want to do away with the monarchy and set up a republic, others want total chaos—they're fairly easy to spot: usually just hotheaded talk in pubs and on street corners. Some are foreign-inspired, and we're chasing those as well." He sighed. "What have you found, Pitt? Is there anything personal?"

"Not so far, sir. He seems to have been an unremarkable man, successful in business, but I can't find anything to inspire hatred, much less murder. His partner Verdun is a civilized, moderate man who deals in suburban properties, more for something to do than for profit."

Drummond's face showed imminent criticism.

"I've got the accounts," Pitt said quickly. "There's nothing shown except ordinary property transactions in respectable residential areas. If they're dealing in slum properties as well, they have a perfect set of alternative books."

"Likely?" Drummond asked.

"Not in my opinion."

"Well, have someone look up Verdun and see if he is what he says. See if he gambles, or keeps women."

Pitt smiled grimly. "I will, but I'll lay any odds you like that he doesn't."

Drummond's eyebrows rose. "How about your job? Would you lay that? And mine, if we don't clear this up."

"I don't think we'll do it through Charles Verdun, sir."

"What about political motive? What did the Home Secretary say?"

Pitt summed up what he'd learned from Hamilton's superior, watching Drummond's face gradually fall.

"A random victim?" he mused unhappily. "Mistaken for someone else, someone more important? God, I hope not; that would mean the murderer might try again!"

"Back to anarchists," Pitt said, rising. "I'd better go and see what I can find out as the members leave the House of Commons—who spoke to Hamilton last, what time, and if they saw anyone approach him."

Drummond pulled out a gold watch from his waistcoat. "You might have a long wait."

Pitt stood in the cold at the north end of Westminster Bridge for over an hour and a half before he saw the first figures coming out of the House of Commons and turning towards the river. By then he had eaten two hot pies and a plum duff, watched innumerable courting couples walk arm in arm along the embankment and two drunks singing "Champagne Charlie" out of time with each other, and his fingers were numb.

"Excuse me, sir?" He stepped forward.

Two members stopped, scowling at being accosted by a stranger. They noted his bulging pockets and woolen muffler and made to walk on.

"Bow Street Police, sir," Pitt said sharply. "Inquiring into the murder of Sir Lockwood Hamilton."

"They were shaken, reminded forcibly of something they had preferred not to consider. "Fearful business," one said. "Fearful!" the other echoed him.

"Did you see him yesterday evening, sir?"

"Ah, yes, yes I did. Didn't you, Arbuthnot?" The taller

turned to his companion. "Don't know what time it was. As we were leaving."

"I believe the House rose at about twenty minutes past eleven o'clock," Pitt offered.

"Ah yes," the stockier and fairer man agreed. "Probably so. Saw Hamilton as I was leaving. Poor devil. Shocking!"

"Was he alone, sir?"

"More or less; just finished speaking to someone." The man's eyes looked blank, benign. "Sorry, don't know who. One of the other members. Said good night, or something of the sort, and walked off towards the bridge. Lives on the south side, you know."

"Did you see whether anyone followed him?" Pitt asked.

The man's face looked suddenly pinched as the reality hit him. It ceased to be an exercise in memory. A vivid picture forced itself on his inner mind; he realized he had witnessed what was about to become a murder. His years of composure and self-confidence fled, and he saw the vulnerability of the lone man on the bridge, stalked by death, as if it were his own. "Poor devil!" he said again, his throat tight, his voice constricted. "I rather think someone did, but I haven't the slightest idea who. It was just the impression of a figure, a shadow as Hamilton started off across the bridge past the first light. I'm afraid rather a lot of us walk home on a decent night, if we live close by. Some took carriages or cabs, of course. Late sitting, rather a bore. I wanted to get home and go to bed. I'm sorry."

"Any impression of the shadow, sir? Size, manner of walking?"

"I'm sorry—I'm not even sure I saw it. Just a sort of movement across the light. . . . How frightful!"

"And you, sir?" Pitt turned to the other man. "Did you see Sir Lockwood with anyone?"

"No—no, I wish I could help, but it was all rather more an impression than anything. Don't see a chap's face under the light and you don't really know—just an idea—pretty dark between the lamps, you know. I'm sorry."

"Yes, of course. Thank you for your help, sir," Pitt inclined his head in a salute and passed on to the next group of men, already beginning to leave either in carriages or on foot.

He stopped half a dozen others, but learned nothing which enabled him to do more than narrow the time more exactly. Lockwood Hamilton had set off across Westminster Bridge at between ten and twelve minutes past midnight. At twenty-one minutes past, Hetty Milner had screamed. In those nine or eleven minutes someone had cut Hamilton's throat, tied him to the lamppost, and disappeared.

Pitt arrived home just before midnight. He let himself in with his key, and took his boots off in the hall to avoid making a noise as he crept along to the kitchen. There he found a dish of cold meat on the table, with fresh homemade bread, butter, and pickles set out, and a note from Charlotte. The kettle was to the side of the hob and only needed moving over, the water in it hot already. The teapot was on the stove, and beside it the tea caddie, enameled and painted with a picture of flowers, and a spoon.

He was halfway through his meal when the door opened and Charlotte came in, blinking in the light, her hair round her shoulders in a polished cascade like mahogany in the firelight. She wore an old dressing robe of blue embroidered wool, and when she kissed him he caught the scent of soap and warm sheets.

"Is it a big case?" she asked.

He looked at her curiously: there was none of her usual sharp inquisitiveness, her scarcely masked desire to meddle—at which she had at times proved remarkably successful.

"Yes—murder of a Member!" He answered, finishing the last slice of his bread and pickle. He did not feel like telling her the grim details, for tonight he wished to put it from his mind.

She looked surprised, but far less interested than he had expected. "You must be very tired, and cold. Have you made any progress?" She was not even looking at him, pouring herself a cup of tea. She sat down at the kitchen table opposite. Was she being superbly devious? If so, it was not like her: she knew she was very bad at it.

"Charlotte?"

"Yes?" Her eyes were dark gray in the lamplight, and apparently quite innocent.

"No, I haven't made any progress."

"Oh." She looked distressed, but not interested.

"Is something wrong?" he asked with sudden anxiety.

"Have you forgotten Emily's wedding?" Her eyes widened, and suddenly he recognized all her emotions, the excitement, the concern that everything should be well, the loneliness at the thought of Emily's going away, the whisper of envy for the glamor and the romance of it, and the genuine happiness for her sister. They had shared much together and were closer than many sisters, their different personalities complementing each other rather than being cause for misunderstanding.

Pitt put out his hand and took hers, holding it gently. The very gesture was an admission, and she knew it before he spoke.

"Yes I had forgotten—not the wedding, but that it was Friday already. I'm sorry."

Disappointment passed over her face like the shadow of a cloud. She mastered it almost immediately. "You are coming, aren't you, Thomas?"

He had not been sure until that moment that she really wanted him to. Emily had originally married far above even their parents' very comfortable aspiring middle-class social position, becoming Lady Ashworth, with status and very considerable wealth. Recently widowed, she now proposed marrying Jack Radley, a gentleman of undoubted good breeding but who had no money at all. Charlotte had done the unspeakable and married a policeman, socially on much the same level as the ratcatcher or the bailiff!

The Ellisons had always treated Pitt with courtesy. In spite of her sharply reduced circumstances and the loss of all her previous social circle, they knew Charlotte was happy. Emily gave her cast-off gowns, and now and again new ones, and she bought them both handsome presents as often as tact allowed and shared with Charlotte the exhilaration and the tragedy, the danger and triumph of Pitt's cases.

But still Charlotte might have been secretly relieved if he were unable to attend the wedding, fearing condescension on the one hand, his social gaffes. On the other, the differences between her former world and his were subtle but immeasurable. He was unreasonably glad that she wanted him there; he had not realized how deep his suppressed hurt had been, because he had refused to look at it.

"Yes—at least for a while. I may not be able to stay long."

"But you can come!"

"Yes."

Her face relaxed and she smiled at him, putting her hand over his. "Good! It will matter so much to Emily, as well as to me. And Great-aunt Vespasia will be there. You should see my new dress—don't worry, I haven't been extravagant—but it really is special!

He relaxed at last, letting go all the knots inside him as the darkness slid away. It was so ordinary, so incredibly trivial: the shade of a fabric, the arrangement of a bustle, how many flowers on a hat. It was ridiculous, immensely unimportant—and sane!

PITT LEFT AT ABOUT half past seven the next morning, and Charlotte swept into action as soon as he was out of the door. Gracie, her resident maid, took care of everything in the kitchen, including getting breakfast for Jemima, now aged six and very self-possessed, and Daniel, a little younger and desperately eager to keep up. There was a tremendous air of excitement in the house, and both children were far too aware of the importance of the day to sit still.

Charlotte had their new clothes laid out on their beds: cream frills and laces for Jemima, with a pink satin sash, and a brown velvet suit with a lace collar for Daniel. It had taken over an hour's persuasion and finally a downright bribe—that next time they rode on the omnibus he would be able to pay his own bright penny fare to the conductor—to convince him that he was going to wear this!

Charlotte's dress had been specially made for her, something she had taken for granted before her marriage. Now she usually made her gowns herself, or adapted them from ones given her by Emily or on rare occasions by Great-aunt Vespasia.

But this was magnificent, the softest crushed plum-colored silk, low cut at the front to show her throat and fine shoulders and just a touch of bosom, fitted at the waist, and with a bustle so exquisitely feminine she felt irresistible merely at the sight of it. It swished deliciously when she walked, and the shade was most flattering to her honey-warm skin and auburn hair, which she had polished with a silk scarf until it shone.

It took her an hour and several unsuccessful attempts to dress, curl, and pin it exactly as she wished, and to assure that her face was improved in every way possible, short of anything which could actually be called "paint." Paint was still a cardinal sin in society and only indulged in by women of the most dubious morality.

When another thirty minutes had been taken up in minor adjustments to the children's clothing and Jemima's hair ribbons, she finally put on her own gown, to the breathless squeals and sighs of the children and the intense admiration of Gracie, who could hardly contain herself for delight. She was on the edge of the most total romance; she had seen Emily many times and thought her a real lady, and she would hang on every word when her mistress returned and told her all about the wedding. It was better than all the pictures in *The Illustrated London News,* or even the most sentimental songs and ballads she heard cried in the street. Not even the penny dreadfuls she read by candlelight in the cupboard under the stairs could match this—after all, those were people she had never met, or cared about.

Emily sent a carriage for them on the chime of ten o'clock, and by twenty minutes past, Charlotte, Jemima, and Daniel alighted at St. Mary's Church, Eaton Square.

Immediately behind her Charlotte's mother, Caroline Ellison, stepped out of her carriage and signaled her coachman to continue and find a suitable place to wait. She was a handsome woman now in her middle fifties and wearing her widowhood with vigor and a new and rather daring sense of freedom. She was dressed in golden brown, which suited her admirably, and a hat nearly as splendid as Charlotte's. Holding her hand was Emily's son Edward, now Lord Ashworth in his father's stead, wearing a dark blue velvet suit, his fair hair combed neatly. He looked nervous and very sober and held onto his grandmother's hand with small, tight fingers.

Behind them, helped discreetly by a footman, came Caroline's mother-in-law, well into her eighties, making the most of every twinge and infirmity, her bright black eyes taking in everything, and her ears with their pendulous jet earrings highly selectively deaf.

"Good morning, Mama," Charlotte kissed Caroline carefully, so as not to disarrange either of their hats. "Good morning, Grandmama."

"Think you're the bride?" the old lady said sharply, looking her up and down. "Never seen such a bustle in all my life! And you've too much color—but you always had!"

"At least I can wear yellow," Charlotte replied, looking at her grandmother's sallow skin and dark gold gown and smiling charmingly.

"Yes you can," the old lady agreed with a glare. "And it's a pity you didn't—instead of that! What do you call it? No color I ever saw before. Well, if you spill raspberry fool on it no one will ever know!"

"How comforting," Charlotte said sarcastically. "You always did know the right thing to say to make a person feel comfortable."

The old woman bent her head. "What? What did you say? I don't hear as well as I used to!" She picked up her ear trumpet and placed it ostentatiously near her hand so it would be ready for instant use to draw attention to her infirmity.

"And you were always deaf when you chose to be," Charlotte replied.

"What? Why can't you stop mumbling, child!"

"I said I would call it rose." Charlotte looked straight at her.

"No you didn't!" the old lady snapped. "You've got above yourself since you married that tom-fool policeman. Where is he, anyway? Didn't care to bring him into society, eh? Very wise—probably blow his nose on the table napkins and not know which fork to use!"

Charlotte remembered again how intensely she disliked her grandmother. Widowhood and loneliness had made the old woman spiteful; she commanded attention either by complaining or by attempting to hurt those around her.

Charlotte ceased looking for an adequately cutting reply. "He's working on a case, Grandmama," she said instead. "It is a murder, and Thomas is in charge of the investigation. But he will be here for the ceremony if he can."

The old lady sniffed fiercely. "Murders! Don't know what the world's coming to—riots in the streets last year. 'Bloody Sunday' indeed! Even housemaids don't know how to behave themselves these days; lazy, uppity, and full of impertinence. You live in sad times, Charlotte; people don't know their place anymore. And you haven't helped—marrying a policeman, indeed! Can't imagine what you were thinking of! Or your mother either! Know what I'd have said if my son had wanted to marry the parlormaid!"

"So do I!" said Charlotte, finally letting go of her temper. "You'd have said, 'Lie with her by all means, as long as you're discreet about it, but marry someone of your own social class, or above—especially if she has money!'"

The old lady picked up her cane as if she would have rapped Charlotte across the legs with it; then, realizing her granddaughter would barely feel it through the weight of her skirts, she tried to think of a verbal equivalent—and failed.

"What did you say?" she snapped in defeat. "You mumble dreadfully, girl! Have you artificial teeth or something?"

It was so ludicrous Charlotte burst into laughter and put her arm round the old lady, astonishing her into silence.

They had just got inside the church and were being ushered to their seats when Lady Vespasia Cumming-Gould arrived. She was Charlotte's height, but slender now to the point of gauntness, and stood ramrod stiff, dressed in ecru-colored lace over coffee satin, with a hat of such rakish elegance that even Caroline gasped. She was over eighty; she had stood at the top of the stairs as a girl and peeped through the banisters as the guests arrived in her father's house to dance the night away after the news of the victory of Waterloo. She had been the most startling beauty of her day, and her face, although imprinted with time and tragedy, still held the grace and proportion of loveliness that nothing would mar.

She had been the favorite aunt of Emily's late husband, and both Emily and Charlotte loved her deeply. It was an affection which she returned, even defying convention enough to include Pitt, not caring in the slightest what other people thought of her for receiving a policeman in her withdrawing room as if he had been a social entity, and not one of the less desirable tradesmen. She had always had both the rank and the beauty to disregard opinion, and as she got older she used it shamelessly. She was a keen reformer of laws and customs of which she did not approve, and she was not averse to meddling in detection whenever Charlotte and Emily provided her with the opportunity.

Church was not the place for greetings; she merely inclined her head minutely in Charlotte's direction and took her seat at the end of the pew, waiting while the other guests arrived.

The groom, Jack Radley, was already at the altar, and Charlotte was beginning to feel anxious when at last Pitt slipped into the pew beside her, looking surprisingly smart and holding a black silk hat in his hands.

"Where did you get that?" Charlotte whispered under her breath, in a moment of alarm as to the expense of such a thing he would never use again.

"Micah Drummond," he answered, and she saw the appreciation in his eyes as he saw her gown. He turned and smiled at Great-aunt Vespasia, and she bent her head graciously and slowly dropped one eyelid.

There was a buzz of excitement, then a hush, and the organ changed tone and became magnificent, romantic and a little pompous. In spite of herself Charlotte turned to gaze backwards to see Emily framed by sunlight in the arch of the church doorway, walking slowly forwards on the arm of Dominic Corde, the widower of their elder sister Sarah. A host of memories came flooding back for Charlotte: Sarah's wedding; the turmoil of her own emotions in those early years when she had imagined herself so terribly, hopelessly in love with her brother-in-law Dominic; Charlotte herself walking up the aisle on her father's arm to stand by Pitt at the altar. She had been certain then that she was doing the right thing, despite all the mounting fears, the knowledge she would lose many friends and the security of position and money.

She was still sure it was right. There had been hardships, of course, things she would have considered drudgery eight years ago. Now her world was immeasurably wider, and she knew that even on a policeman's pay, with a little allowance of her own from her family, she was by far one of the world's most fortunate souls. She was seldom cold and never hungry, nor did she lack for any necessity. She had known a multitude of experiences, but never tedium, never the fear that she was wasting her life in useless pursuits, never the endless hours of embroidery no one cared about, the painting of indifferent watercolors, the deadly calls, the dreadful tea parties full of gossip.

Emily looked marvelous. She was wearing her favorite water green silk, set against ivory and embroidered with pearls. Her hair was perfectly dressed, like a pale aureole in the sunlight, and her fair skin was flushed with excitement and happiness.

Jack Radley had no money and probably never would have, nor a title; Emily would cease to be Lady Ashworth, and it had cost her a moment's regret. But Jack had charm, wit, and a remarkable ability for companionship. And since George's death he had proved he had both courage and generosity of spirit. Emily not only loved him, she liked him enormously.

Charlotte slipped her hand into Pitt's and felt his fingers tighten over hers. She watched the ceremony with happiness for Emily and no shadow of anxiety for the future.

Pitt was obliged to leave almost as soon as the formal

part of the ceremony was over. He remained only long enough to congratulate Jack, kiss Emily, and greet Caroline and Grandmama, and Great-aunt Vespasia in the vestry.

"Good morning, Thomas," Vespasia said gravely. "I am delighted you were able to come."

Pitt clutched Micah Drummond's hat and smiled back at her.

"I am sorry for having been so late," he said sincerely, "and for having to leave in such haste."

"No doubt a pressing case." She raised her fine silver eyebrows.

"Very," he agreed, knowing she was curious. "An unpleasant murder."

"London is full of them," she replied. "Is it of personal motive?"

"I doubt it."

"Then a thankless task for you, and requiring little of your peculiar skills. No social issue, I presume?"

"None so far. It looks to be merely political, or perhaps the work of a random madman."

"An ordinary violence, then."

He knew she was vaguely disappointed that there was no opportunity for her to meddle, even vicariously through Charlotte or Emily; he knew also that she did not wish to admit it.

"Very pedestrian," he agreed soberly. "If that is what it proves to be."

"Thomas—"

"Excuse me, ma'am." And with a little bow he smiled once more at Emily, turned, and walked briskly away, through the church gateway and down Lower Belgrave Street towards Buckingham Palace Road.

A small reception was to be given in one of the town houses in Eaton Square by a good friend of Emily's, and after a few more moments they all walked across the street in the sun, first Emily on Jack's arm followed by Caroline and Edward, then Charlotte and her children. Dominic offered his arm to Great-aunt Vespasia, and she accepted it graciously, although her mind was still on the retreating figure of Pitt. Grandmama was escorted, grumbling all the way, by a close friend of the groom.

It was the beginning of a new stage of life for Emily.

Then Charlotte suddenly thought of the women in the public meeting, some so outrageously complacent, so sure of their comfort, their unassailable positions, others risking derision and notoriety to fight for a cause that was surely hopeless. How many had once been brides like this, full of hope and uncertainty, dreaming of happiness, companionship, safety of the heart?

And how many had ended a few short years later like the woman Ivory they had spoken of with such disdain—fighting for redress, a byword for unhappiness?

She had barely mentioned that meeting to Pitt, there had been so much else to think of, but it was there at the back of her mind.

This was different, though. Emily was in love, the radiance of her face mirrored that—but she had never been naïve, never lost sight of the practical in all the romance.

Charlotte smiled as she recalled their girlhood, the long hours spent talking of the futures they planned, the gallant and handsome men they would find. It was Emily who never completely let go of reality, even at twelve with her hair in pigtails and a white starched pinafore over her dress. Emily always kept one toe on the ground. It was Charlotte whose dreams took flight and soared from the world!

Champagne was poured, toasts were made, there were speeches and laughter, and Charlotte joined in, happy for Emily, delighted by the glamor and the romance, the lights and glasses, the flowers with their heady perfume, the rustle of taffeta and silk.

She put a few tiny pastries on a plate and took them over to her grandmother sitting on a chair in the corner.

The old lady took them, surveyed them carefully, and

picked out the largest. "Where did you say they were going?" she asked. "You told me, and I forgot."

"Paris, and then a tour of Italy," Charlotte replied. She tried to keep the envy from her voice. She herself had had only a long weekend at Margate, and then Pitt had had to go back on duty, and she had spent the next month moving into the first tiny house, with rooms smaller than the maids quarters in her family home. She had had to learn to manage for a month on money she would previously have spent on one gown, and how to cook, where she once would have instructed the kitchen staff. It did not matter, really, but she would have loved just once to sail off in a ship, to visit foreign places, dine splendidly, not so much for the food but for the romance of it! She would like to see Venice, to drift on a canal by moonlight and hear the gondoliers singing across the water; to see Florence, that city of great artists, and walk among the ruins of Rome dreaming of the grandeur and glory of great ages past.

"Very nice," Grandmama agreed, nodding her head. "Every young girl should do it some time in her life, the earlier the better. A civilizing influence, as long as it is not taken too seriously. One should learn about foreigners, but never imitate them."

"Yes Grandmama," Charlotte said absently.

"Of course you wouldn't know that!" the old lady went on. "I don't suppose you'll ever see Calais, never mind Venice or Rome!"

It was true, and this time Charlotte had no heart to answer.

"Told you that before," the old woman added vindictively. "But you never listen. Never did, even as a child. But you've made your bed, and you must lie in it."

Charlotte stood up and went to Emily. The formal part of the celebration was over, and she and Jack were preparing to leave. She looked so happy Charlotte felt tears in her eyes as the emotions churned inside her, joy for Emily at this moment and relief for the shadows that were past, the grief and the mourning, the terror as suspicion had hemmed her in, hope for the years ahead, envy for the adventures and the shared laughter, the new sights and the glamour.

She put her arms round Emily and hugged her.

"Write to me. Tell me of all the beautiful things you see, the buildings and the paintings, the canals in Venice. Tell me about the people, and if they're funny or charming or odd. Tell me about the fashions and the food, the weather—everything!"

"Of course! I'll write a letter every day and post them when I can," Emily promised, tightening her own arms round Charlotte. "Don't get into any adventures while I'm gone, or if you do, be careful!" She held her sister a little tighter. "I love you, Charlotte. And thank you for being there, all the time, ever since we were little." Then she was on her way, clinging to Jack's arm and smiling at everyone, her eyes full of tears, her gorgeous dress sweeping and rustling.

Several days passed by, with Pitt pursuing every avenue in the investigation of the murder of Sir Lockwood Hamilton. The details of his business were checked more thoroughly, but the accounts of the firm's property purchases and sales yielded nothing more than they had at first glance. Not one of them was out of the ordinary with regard either to unfair acquisition through pressure of any kind, or to any advantage being taken of others' misfortune, nor had any holding been sold at unreasonable profit. It appeared that it was exactly as Charles Verdun had said, a business in which Hamilton took some share of the profit but little in the conduct, and in which Verdun himself employed his time because he enjoyed it.

The business in Birmingham from which Hamilton drew most of his income was merely a matter of inherited shares, and unremarkable in any way Pitt could discover.

Barclay Hamilton owned a very pleasant house in Chelsea and was reputed to be quiet, a little melancholy, but perfectly respectable. No one had ill to speak of him, and his financial affairs were in excellent order. He was a highly eligible young man at whom many young ladies of fine family had set their caps, without success. But nothing was said, even in a whisper, to his discredit.

Nor had the cold breath of scandal ever touched Amethyst Hamilton. She did not overspend on gowns or jewelry, she ran her house with skill but without extravagance, she entertained generously in her husband's interest. She had many friendships, but none of a closeness that caused even the most critical to make comment that was worth Pitt's time to consider.

A more thorough investigation of Hamilton's political career, the account of which Pitt spent many hours reading and rereading, produced no injustices so glaring as to have provoked anything like murder. He had been the object of envy perhaps, of resentment that favors had been unequally given, but all this was a part of a hundred other political lives as well. He appeared to have taken no remarkable stand on any issue that could single him out as the object of violent feeling. He was a competent man, both liked and respected, but not marked for that greatness which inspires passion.

In the meantime Micah Drummond had as many of his force as he could spare in pursuit of every known band of anarchists or pseudo-revolutionaries who might have used such a means to further their cause. He spoke to senior officers in many other police districts of London, and even to the Foreign Office to see if they were acquainted with any other nation or power who might have had an interest in the death of a member of Parliament. Eventually he gave what he had to Pitt and told him to try his own sources in the underworld and its fringes, to see if he could pick up any whispers.

Pitt read the reports and discarded three quarters of them. The constables had done their job thoroughly, and their own informant had exhausted everything likely to produce any information of use. Of the last quarter he chose the few he could follow through fences, petty thieves, or small-time forgers who owed him a favor, or who were seeking some advantage.

He changed out of his own clothes, removed the beautiful boots Emily had given him, and got into some shapeless trousers and a jacket so old and rimed with dirt he could pass without comment in the poorest of tenements or rookeries, the grimmest of East End docks or public houses. Then he went out, took a cab for two miles eastward and got out just short of the Whitechapel Road.

In the next three hours he spoke to half a dozen petty criminals, always moving eastward towards Mile End, and then south to the river and Wapping. He had a thick sandwich and glass of rough cider in a public house overlooking the water and then set off again deeper into the slums and narrow, fetid streets within sound and smell of the Thames, looking towards Limehouse Reach. At last, in the late afternoon, he had enough information to trade for what he wanted.

He found the right man up crooked stairs, damp with the rot of ages, a thousand yards from the pier stakes where once they had tied pirates and let the tide rise to drown them. He stopped at a doorway and knocked on the warped panels.

After several minutes it was opened a crack and there was a rumbling growl with a high-pitched menace at the back of it—a dog who would attack at the slightest misstep. Pitt looked down and saw the beast's head, a white blur in the shadows, a piglike cross between a bull terrier and a setter.

The door swung a little wider to show yellow oil light behind and a squat man with a thick neck and pale bristly hair cut in the "terrier crop" of one recently in prison. His face was ruddy and his eyebrows so pale they seemed colorless, almost translucent. It was not until he pulled the door fully open that Pitt saw he had a wooden leg below a fat thigh cut off above the knee. He knew he had the right man.

Pitt eyed the dog which stood between them. "Deacon Stafford?" he asked.

"Yeah—'oo're yer? Wotcher want? I dunno yer." He surveyed Pitt up and down, then looked at his hands. "Yer a crusher out o' twig!"

So his disguise was far less effective than he had thought. He must remember his fingernails next time.

"Thin Jimmy said you might be helpful," Pitt said quietly. "I have certain information you would find useful."

"Thin Jimmy . . . Well, come in. I in't standin' 'ere; I got a bad leg."

Pitt had heard Deacon's story. His father had "got the boat" to Australia back when deportation was still a common punishment for petty robbery, and his mother had been sent with her three children to the workhouse. Young William Stafford had been set to work "picking oakum"—unraveling old rope—at the age of three. At six he had run away, and after begging and stealing till he was on the point of starvation, he had been picked up by a kidsman, a man who trained and ran a bunch of child thieves and pickpockets, taking the largest portion of their profits, fencing them, and in return giving them food and protection. William had picked pockets successfully "cly faking," then progressed to a higher form of the art, specializing in stealing from women—"fine-wiring." After a spell in the Coldbath Fields jail, the damp had got into his bones and his fingers lost their nimbleness. He took to "flying the blue pigeon"—stealing roofing lead, most particularly from churches, which earned him his nickname. A bad fall on a freezing night had resulted in a splintered thigh, which became gangrenous, costing him his leg. Now he sat in this narrow room piled with furniture by the embers of a smoky fire and traded information and power.

Deacon offered Pitt a seat in the huge overstuffed chair opposite his own, a yard from the fire, and the dog waddled in and lay between them, watching Pitt with its pink piggy eyes.

"So wotcher got?" Deacon asked curiously. "Thin Jimmy knows me, 'e's a downy little swine, but 'e don' give me no flam—so don' you neither, or yer'll get a right dewskitch afore yer leaves Lime'ouse."

Pitt had no doubt that indeed he would be thrashed soundly if he gave Deacon any "flam." Word for word, he passed on the information he had gleaned so carefully all day. Deacon looked satisfied; the light of a deep inner jubilation spread over his broad face, and his lips parted in a gummy smile.

"Right. So wotcher want from me, then? This in't fer nuffin'!"

"Westminster Bridge murder," Pitt replied candidly. "Anarchists? Irish Fenians? Revolutionaries? What do you hear?"

Deacon was surprised. "Nuffink! Least, o' course I 'eard a bit! Ten years ago I'd 'a said 'Arry Parkin. Great one fer the anarchists, 'e were, but 'e were crapped in 'eighty-three. Three week in the saltbox, then the long drop fer 'im. 'E were never good fer nuffink but bug 'unting anyway, poor bastard."

"They don't hang people for robbing drunks," Pitt pointed out.

"Killed some shofulman," Deacon explained. "Paid 'im in fakement, an Parkin cracked 'is 'aed open. Stupid bastard!"

"Not much help," Pitt said dryly. "Try a little harder."

"I'll ask Mary Murphy," Deacon offered. "She's an 'ore. Sails on 'er bottom—no pimp. She'll 'ave 'eard if it's the Fenians, but I reckon it in't."

"Anarchists?" Pitt pressed.

Deacon shook his head. "Nah! That in't the way their minds goes. Stick a shiv in some geezer on Westminster Bridge! Wot good'd that do 'em? They'd go fer a bomb, summink showy. Loves bombs, they do. All talk, they are—never do nuffink so quiet."

"Then what is the word down here?"

"Croaked by someone as 'ated 'im, personal like." Deacon opened his little eyes wide. "In't no flam—I makes me livin' by blowin', I'd be a muck snipe in a munf if I done that! In't quick enough to thieve no more. I'd 'ave ter try a scaldrum dodge, an that in't no way ter live!"

No, begging by fake or self-inflicted wounds would hardly fit Deacon's sense of his own dignity.

"No," Pitt agreed, standing slowly, keeping his eye on the dog. "Nor is sitting in lavender in some deadlurk the rest of your days." It was a cant term for hiding from the police in an empty house.

Deacon understood the threat perfectly, nor did he appear to resent it: it was an expected part of trade.

"That murder in't nuffink ter do wiv us in the East End," he said with total candor. "Don' do us no good. An' we knows abaht anarchists and the like, because it pays us ter. I'll keep an ear for yer, seein' as yer gave me wot I wanted. But me best word to you is that it in't nuffink revolutionary, yer'd best look to 'is own sort."

"Or a random lunatic," Pitt said grimly.

"Oh." Deacon sighed deeply. "Well, there's some o' vem an' all, but not from 'ere. We takes care o' vem our own way. Look to 'is own sort, mister, vat's wot I says. 'Is own sort."

It was five days after Emily's wedding and departure on the boat train for Paris that Pitt was awakened from his first early night since the murder by a loud and urgent knocking on his front door. He emerged slowly from the soft, sweet darkness of sleep into a realization that the thumping was no part of a dream but persisted into reality, demanding his attention.

"What is it?" Charlotte asked drowsily at his side. Funny how she could sleep through this noise, and yet if one of the children but whispered she was wide awake and up on her feet getting into her robe before he had struggled to consciousness.

"Door," he said blearily, reaching in the dark to find his

jacket and trousers. It could only be for him, and he would be required to go somewhere out into the sharp night. He fumbled for his socks and found only one.

Charlotte sat up and felt around for a match to light the gas.

"Don't," he said softly. "It's around here somewhere."

She did not ask who it was at the door; she knew from experience it could only be a constable with some urgent news. She did not like it, but she accepted the fact that it was a part of his life. What she dreaded was the knock that might come when he was not here, and that the news would be that which she could not bear.

Pitt found his other sock, put it on, and stood up. He leaned over and kissed her, then tiptoed to the bedroom door and downstairs to find his boots and answer the summons.

He unlocked the front door and swung it open. There was a constable on the step, the streetlamp beyond lighting one side of his face.

"There's been another one!" His words came out in a rush, relief that Pitt was there easing his lonely horror. "Mr. Drummond says as you're to come right away. I got a cab, sir, if you're ready."

Pitt noticed the hansom standing a few doors along, horse restless, cabby sitting on his box with the reins in his hands, a blanket round his knees. The horse's breath formed a thin cloud of vapor in the air.

"Another what?" Pitt was confused for a moment.

"Another Member of Parliament, sir, with 'is throat cut an' tied up to the lamppost on Westminster Bridge—just like the last one."

For a moment Pitt was stunned. He had not expected it; he had been convinced by Deacon that it was a personal crime, motivated by fear or greed or some long-sought revenge. Now it seemed the only answer was the worst of all: a random lunatic was at work.

"Who is it?" he said aloud.

"Vyvyan Etheridge. Never 'eard of 'im meself," the

constable answered anxiously. "But then, I don't know much abaht politicians, 'cept them as everyone knows."

"We'd better go." Pitt reached for his coat, gloves still in his pockets, and then closed the door and followed the constable along the damp pavement, the dew condensing on the walls, which gleamed in the gaslight. They climbed into the cab, and immediately it set off back towards the bridge.

Pitt wriggled round tucking in his shirttails under his coat. He should have put more clothes on; he was going to be cold.

"What else do you know?" he asked in the rattling darkness, bumping against the sides of the cab as they swung sharply round a corner. "What time is it?"

"It must be about quarter to midnight, sir," the constable replied, hitching himself back into his seat more comfortably, only to be thrown out of it again as they swung the other way. "Poor soul was found just after eleven o'clock. 'Ouse sat late again. 'E was prob'ly killed on the way 'ome, like the other one. 'E lives off the Lambeth Palace Road, south side o' the river again."

"Anything else?"

"Not as I knows, sir."

Pitt did not ask who had found the body; he preferred to make his own judgment when he got there. They careered through the spring night in silence, bumping against each other as the cab jolted and jarred round corners, righted itself again, and charged on.

They drew up at the far end of Westminster Bridge and Pitt scrambled out into the glare of the lamplight. A group of people stood frightened, at once fascinated and repelled. None of them was permitted to go, neither did anyone want to. Some horror kept them close to each other, as though they were unwilling to leave those who had shared the knowledge here in the pool of light, islanded amidst the shadows.

Micah Drummond's lean figure was easily distinguished, and Pitt went to him. On the ground, laid in some semblance of decency, was the body of a man of late middle age, dressed in sober clothes of excellent quality, a silk hat beside him on the pavement. A white silk scarf had been cut with a knife, and lay a little to one side of his neck. It was soaked with blood, which also drenched his shirtfront, and there was a single fearful wound in his neck from one side right across to the other.

Pitt knelt and looked more closely. The face looked calm, as if he had not seen death coming. It was a narrow patrician face, not unpleasing, with a long nose, a good brow, the mouth perhaps a little lacking in humor but without cruelty. The man's hair was silver, but still thick. There were fresh flowers pale in the buttonhole.

Pitt looked away and up at Drummond.

"Vyvyan Etheridge, M.P.," Drummond said quietly. He looked haggard, his eyes hollow, his mouth pinched. Pitt felt a quick stab of pity for him. Tomorrow all London, from the scrubwoman to the Prime Minister, would be calling for a solution to these outrages, stunned that members of the establishment, whether loved or hated, men considered safe above all others, could be killed silently and unseen within a few hundred yards of the Houses of Parliament.

Pitt stood up. "Robbed?" he asked, although he knew the answer.

"No," Drummond replied, barely shaking his head. "Gold watch, very expensive, ten gold sovereigns and about ten shillings in silver and coppers, a silver brandy flask, still full. Looks in this light like an extremely fine one, solid, not plate, and scrolled and engraved with his name. Gold cuff links, and he carried a cane with a silver top—all here. Oh, and French leather gloves."

"No paper?"

"What?"

"No paper?" Pitt repeated, although he had little hope of it. He had to ask. "I wondered if perhaps whoever did it left some note, a threat, a demand. Some sort of identification."

"No. Only Etheridge's own papers: a couple of letters, calling cards, that sort of thing."

"Who found him?"

"Young fellow over there." Drummond gestured very slightly with his head. "I think he was a little drunk then, but he's certainly sober enough now, poor devil. Name's Harry Rawlins."

"Thank you, sir." Pitt stepped off the curb and crossed the road to the group of people standing under the lamp opposite. It all had a dreamlike quality, as if he were reliving the first time. The night sky was the same vast cavern overhead, the smell of the air sharp and clean here on the river, the water gleaming black and satin bright beyond the balustrade, reflecting the lights all along the Embankment, the triple globes of the lamps, the outline of the Palace of Westminster black gothic against the stars. Only the little knot of people was different; there was no Hetty Milner, with her fair skin and gaudy skirts. Instead there was an off-duty cabby, a taproom steward on his way home, a clerk and his lady friend, frightened and embarrassed, a railway porter from Waterloo Station just across the bridge, and a young man with blond hair falling over his brow, face now pallid as marble, his eyes staring with horror. He was well dressed, obviously a young gentleman out for a night on the town. Every vestige of indulgence had fallen from him like a dropped garment, and he was appallingly sober.

"Mr. Rawlins." Pitt had no need to ask which he was: his experience was written in his face. "I am Inspector Pitt. Would you tell me exactly what happened, sir?"

Rawlins gulped. For a moment adequate speech eluded him. It was not some tramp he had found, but a man of his own class, tied up ludicrously, lounging against the lamp, silk hat askew, white scarf too tight under his chin, head lolling in a mockery of drunkenness.

Pitt waited patiently.

Rawlins coughed and cleared his throat. "I was coming

home from a late party with a few friends, don't you know, and—"

"Where?" Pitt interrupted.

"Oh—Whitehall Club, just over there." He pointed vaguely towards the other end of the bridge beyond Boadicea. "Off Cannon Street."

"Where do you live, sir?"

"Charles Street, south of the river, off the Westminster Bridge Road. Thought I'd walk home. Do me good. Didn't want the pater to see me a—a little tiddly. Thought the fresh air, and all that."

"So you were walking home over the bridge?"

"Yes, that's right." For a moment he teetered a little on his feet. "God! I've never seen anything so awful! Poor devil was leaning backwards against the lamppost, sort of lolling, as if he were three sheets to the wind. I took no notice until I got level with him, and then I realized who he was. Met him a couple of times, you know; friend of the pater's, in a mild sort of way. Then I thought, Vyvyan Etheridge'd never be caught like that! So I went over, thinking he must be ill, and—" He swallowed. There was a fine sweat on his face now, in spite of the cold. "—and I saw—saw he was dead. Of course, I remembered poor Hamilton then, so I walked back towards the Parliament side, pretty smartly—I think maybe I ran—and I shouted out something. Anyway, the constable came and I told him what . . . er, what I'd seen."

"Was there anyone else on the bridge, or coming from the bridge as you approached it?"

"Er . . ." He blinked. "I don't rightly recall. I'm fearfully sorry. I was definitely a bit—high—until I saw Etheridge and realized what'd happened."

"If you could search your memory, sir?" Pitt pressed, looking at the fair, earnest, rather placid face.

Rawlins was very pale. He was neither so drunk nor so shaken that he did not realize the implication of Pitt's insistence.

"I think there was someone on the opposite of the bridge. I mean across the road, coming towards me; a big stout person. I have the impression of a longish coat, dark—that's really what I remember, a sort of darkness moving. That's about it. I'm sorry."

Pitt hesitated a moment longer, half hoping Rawlins would think of something more. Then he accepted that the young man's mind had been in such a muddled state that that was really all there was.

"And the time, sir?" he asked.

"What?"

"The time? Big Ben is just behind you, sir."

"Oh. Yes. Well, I definitely heard it strike eleven, so about five past. Not later."

"And you are sure you saw no one else? No cabs passing, for instance?"

There was a flicker of light in his eyes. "Oh yes—yes I did see a cab. Came off the bridge and went along the Victoria Embankment. Remember now that you mention it. Sorry Constable."

Pitt did not bother to correct Rawlins as to his rank. The man had intended no insult; he was shocked past everyday niceties.

"Thank you. If you think of anything else, I'm at the Bow Street Station. Now you had better go home and have a hot cup of tea and go to bed."

"Yes—yes I'll do that. Good night, er—good night!" He went off rapidly and rather unsteadily, lurching from one pool of light to the next on up Westminster Bridge Road and disappearing behind the buildings.

Pitt crossed the street back to Drummond. Drummond met his eyes, searching for some sign of hope and finding little.

"There's nothing else," he said bleakly. "Looks political after all. We'll get the men out tomorrow morning after conspiracies, but we're already doing all we can. There isn't a single piece of evidence of any sort to connect anyone with this. Dear heaven, Pitt, I hope it isn't some lunatic."

"So do I," Pitt said grimly. "We'll be reduced to doubling police on duty and hoping to catch him in the act." He said it in desperation, but he knew there was little else they could do if indeed that were the case. "There are still other possibilities."

"Someone mistook the first victim?" Drummond said thoughtfully. "They intended Etheridge, but got Hamilton by mistake? It's dark enough in the stretches between the lamps, and if he'd had his back to the light and his face in shadow when he was attacked, their features are enough alike, and with the same light hair—a frightened or enraged person—" He did not finish; the vision was clear enough.

"Or the second crime is an imitation of the first." Pitt doubted it even as he spoke. "Sometimes it happens, especially when a crime gains a lot of publicity, as Hamilton's murder did. Or it could be that only one of the murders matters, and we are intended to believe it is anarchists or a madman, when one cold-blooded crime was committed to mask another."

"Who was the intended victim, Hamilton or Etheridge?" Drummond looked tired. He had slept little in the last week and now this cold horror with all its implications stretched darkly in front of him.

"I'd better go and tell the widow." Pitt was shivering. The night air seemed to eat right through his clothes into his bones. "Have you the address?"

"Three Paris Road, off the Lambeth Palace Road."

"I'll walk."

"There's a hansom," said Drummond.

"No, I'd rather walk." He needed time to think, to prepare himself. He set off briskly, swinging his arms to get warm and trying to form in his mind how he would tell this new family of its bereavement.

It took him over five minutes of knocking at the door

and waiting before a footman turned on the light in the hall and gingerly opened the door.

"Inspector Thomas Pitt, Bow Street Station," Pitt said quietly. "I'm sorry, but I have bad news for Mr. Etheridge's family. May I come in?"

"Yes—yes sir," the footman stepped back and pulled the door wider. The hall was large and lined with oak. A single gaslight showed the dim outlines of portraits and the soft blues of a Venetian scene. A magnificent staircase curved up towards the shadows of the gallery landing and the one light glowing there.

"Has there been an accident, sir?" the footman asked anxiously, his face puckered with doubt. "Was Mr. Etheridge taken ill?"

"No, I am afraid he is dead. He was murdered—in the same way as Sir Lockwood Hamilton."

"Oh my Gawd!" The footman's face blanched, leaving the freckles across his nose standing out sharply. For a moment Pitt was afraid he was going to faint. He put out his hand, and the gesture seemed to recall the man. He was probably no more than twenty at most.

"Is there a butler?" Pitt asked him. The youth should not have to bear the burden of such news alone.

"Yes sir."

"Perhaps you should waken him, and a lady's maid, before we tell Mrs. Etheridge."

"Mrs. Etheridge? There in't no Mrs. Etheridge, sir. 'E's—'e were a widower. Long time now, before I come 'ere. There's just Miss Helen—that's 'is daughter; Mrs. Carfax, she is—and Mr. Carfax."

"Then call the butler, and a maid, and Mr. and Mrs. Carfax. I am sorry, but I shall need to speak to them."

Pitt was shown into the morning room, austere in dark green, with early spring flowers in a misty blue Lalique bowl and paintings on the wall, at least one of which Pitt believed to be an original Guardi. The late Vyvyan Etheridge had had not only fine taste, but a great deal of money with which to indulge it.

It was nearly a quarter of an hour before James and Helen Carfax came in, pale-faced and dressed in nightclothes and robes. Etheridge's daughter was in her late twenties and had his long, aristocratic face and good brow, but her mouth was softer, and there was a delicacy in her cheekbones and the line of her throat which, while it did not give her beauty, certainly spoke of an imagination and perhaps a sensitivity not apparent in her father. Her hair was thick but of no particular depth of shade, and disturbed from sleep and caught by tragedy, she was bereft of color or animation.

James Carfax was far taller than she, lean and slenderly built. He had a magnificent head of dark hair and wide eyes. He would have been handsome had there been strength in his face instead of mere smoothness. There was in his mouth a mercurial quality; it was a mouth that would be as quick to smile as to sulk. He stood with his arm round his wife's shoulder and stared defensively at Pitt.

"I am extremely sorry, Mrs. Carfax," Pitt said immediately. "If it is of any comfort to you, your father died within seconds of being attacked, and from the look of peace upon his face, I think he probably knew no fear, and barely a moment's pain."

"Thank you," she said with difficulty.

"Perhaps if you were to sit down," Pitt suggested, "and have your maid bring you some restorative?"

"It is not necessary," James Carfax snapped. "Now that you have told us the news, my wife will retire to her room."

"If you prefer that I return tomorrow morning," Pitt said looking not at James but at Helen, "then of course I shall. However, the sooner you give us all the information possible, the better chance we have of apprehending whoever is responsible."

"Rubbish!" James said instantly. "There is nothing we can tell you that would help! Obviously whoever murdered

Sir Lockwood Hamilton is still at large and murdered my father-in-law as well. You should be out in the streets hunting for him—or them. It's either a madman, or some anarchist plot. Either way, you won't find any guidance to it in this house!"

Pitt was used to shock and knew the first wave of grief often showed itself as anger. Many people fought against pain by driving it out with some other intense emotion. The desire to blame someone seemed to come most readily.

"Nevertheless, I must ask," Pitt insisted. "It is possible the attack may have been personally inspired, made by someone who had some political animosity—"

"Against both Sir Lockwood and my father-in-law?" James's dark eyebrows shot upward in sarcastic disbelief.

"I need to investigate, sir." Pitt held his gaze steadily. "I must not decide in advance what the solution is going to be. Sometimes one man may commit murder in imitation of another, hoping the first will be blamed for both crimes."

James lost his fragile temper. "More likely it's anarchists, and you're simply incompetent to catch them!"

Pitt overlooked the jibe. He turned to Helen, who had taken his advice and seated herself uncomfortably on the edge of the wide, forest green sofa. She was hunched forward, arms folded across herself as if she were cold, although the room still retained the warmth of the smoldering fire.

"Are there any other members of the family we should inform?" he asked her.

She shook her head. "No, I am the only child. My brother died several years ago, when he was twelve. My mother died shortly after. I have an uncle in the Indian Army, but I shall write to him myself, in a day or two."

So she would inherit. Pitt would make sure, of course, but it would be extraordinary if Etheridge had left his fortune outside the family. "So your father had been a widower for some time," he said.

"Yes."

"Had he ever considered marrying again?" It was a reasonably tactful way of inquiring whether Etheridge had any romantic alliances. He hoped she understood what he meant.

A wan smile lit her face for an instant, and vanished. "Not so far as I know. That is not to say there were not several ladies who considered it."

"I imagine so," Pitt agreed. "He was of fine family, had a successful career, an impeccable reputation, was charming and personable, and was of very substantial means, and still young enough to have another family."

James's head came up sharply and his mouth fell slack with some emotion of alarm or loss that Pitt could see for an instant, before it was masked, but he could not be sure of its nature.

Helen's eyes flashed upward to her husband's face; she grew even more pale, then the color rushed up in her cheeks. She turned to Pitt and spoke so quietly he had to lean forward to catch her words.

"I don't think he . . . ever had any desire to marry again. I'm sure I should have known of it."

"Would any of these ladies have had reason for entertaining hopes?"

"No."

Pitt looked at James, but James avoided his eyes.

"Perhaps you would give me the name of his solicitors in the morning?" Pitt asked. "And any business partners or associates he may have had?"

"Yes, if you think it necessary." She was very pale. Her hands were clenched and her body still hunched forward on the edge of the seat.

"His affairs were in excellent order," James put in, suddenly looking at Pitt and frowning. "Surely they have no bearing on this? I think you intrude on our privacy without justification. Mr. Etheridge's wealth was inherited through lands in Lincolnshire and the West Riding, and shares in several companies in the City. I suppose there may be some malcontents or would-be revolutionaries who resent that, but only the same ones who would resent anyone with property." His eyes were bright, his jaw a little forward. He was half challenging Pitt, as if he suspected Pitt might have some secret sympathy with those James considered to be his own class.

"We are looking into that, of course." Pitt smiled briefly back at him and held his gaze. It was James who looked away. "I will also inquire into his political career as well," he continued. "Perhaps you can give me an outline from which to begin?"

Helen cleared her throat. "He has been a Liberal Member of Parliament for twenty-one years, from the general election in December 1868. His constituency is in Lincolnshire. He served as a junior minister in the Treasury in 1880 when Mr. Gladstone was Prime Minister and Chancellor of the Exchequer, and in the India Office when Lord Randolph Churchill was Secretary for India, I think that was 1885. And he was Parliamentary Private Secretary to Sir William Harcourt when he was Home Secretary, but only for about a year—I think it was 1883. At present he has—he had," she said, hesitating for only a moment, "no particular office, so far as I know, but a great deal of influence."

"Thank you. Do you happen to know if he held strong views on the Irish question? Home Rule, for example."

She shivered and glanced again at James, but he was apparently unaware of it, his mind absorbed with something else.

"He was against Home Rule," he answered very quietly. Then her eyes widened and there was a flash, a quickening of something within. Anger and hope? Or merely intelligence? "Do you think it could have been Fenians? An Irish conspiracy?"

"Possibly." Pitt doubted it; he remembered Hamilton had been strongly in favor of Home Rule. But then perhaps Hamilton had been killed by mistake. At night with the distortion of the lamplight . . . the two men were of a height, roughly of an age, and not dissimilar in coloring and features. "Yes—possibly."

"Then you had better begin inquiring," James said. He seemed a little more relaxed. "We will retire. My wife has had a profound shock. I am sure you can learn anything else you need from my father-in-law's political colleagues." He turned to leave. His concern for Helen did not extend to offering her his arm.

The merest flicker of hurt crossed Helen's face before it was mastered and concealed again. Pitt debated for an instant whether to offer his hand. He wished to, as he would have to Charlotte, but he remembered his position: he was a policeman, not a guest or an equal. She would regard it as an impertinence, and more powerful in his mind, it would highlight the fact that her husband had not done so. James was standing by the door, holding it open.

"Have you been at home all evening, sir?" Pitt said with an edge to his voice he had not intended, but his anger at the man was too strong.

James looked surprised. Then a wave of color spread up his cheeks, dim in the light of the two lamps that had been turned up but unmistakable to someone staring at him as Pitt was.

He hesitated. Was he debating whether to lie?

"Never mind." Pitt smiled sourly. "I can ask the footman. I need not detain you. Thank you, Mrs. Carfax. I am deeply sorry to have had to bring you such news."

"We don't need your apologies—just get off about your business!" James said waspishly. Then realizing at last how he betrayed himself by unnecessary rudeness, he turned and walked out of the door, leaving it wide and unattended for Helen to follow.

She stood still, her eyes on Pitt's face, struggling with herself whether to speak or not.

Pitt waited. He was afraid she would retreat if he prompted her.

"I was at home," she said, then instantly seemed to regret it. "I mean, I went to sleep early. I—I am not sure about my husband, but—but my father did receive a . . . a letter that troubled him. I think he may have been threatened in some way."

"Do you know who sent this letter, Mrs. Carfax?"

"No. It was political, I think. Maybe regarding the Irish?"

"Thank you. Tomorrow perhaps you would be kind enough to see if you can remember any more. We will inquire at his office, and among his colleagues. Do you know if he kept the letter?

She looked almost at the point of collapse. "No. I have no idea."

"Please don't destroy anything, Mrs. Carfax. It would be better if you were to lock your father's study."

"Of course. Now if you will excuse me, I must be alone."

Pitt stood to attention. It was an odd gesture, but he felt a profound sympathy for her, not only because she had lost her father in violent and peculiarly public circumstances, but because of some other pain he sensed in her, a loneliness that had something to do with her husband. He thought perhaps she loved him far more than he did her, and she knew it, and yet there was also something beyond that, another wound he could only guess at.

The footman showed him out, and he went down the steps into the quiet lamplit street with a deep feeling that there were other tragedies to be revealed.

5

THE FOLLOWING DAY CONSTABLES set about finding any witnesses who might have seen anything from which a fact could be deduced: a more exact time, whether the attacker had come from the north side of the bridge or the south, which way he had gone afterwards, whether by cab or on foot. There was little they could do until the evening, because those who frequented the streets close to midnight were in their own homes, shops, or lodgings through the day, which could be almost anywhere, and even the members of Parliament were at home or in offices and ministries.

By midweek they had found four of the cabbies who had crossed the bridge between half past ten and eleven o'clock. None of them had seen anything that was of any help, nothing out of the ordinary, no loitering figures except the usual prostitutes, and they, like Hetty Milner, were merely pursuing their trade. One had seen a man selling hot plum duff, but he was a regular, and when the police met the man in the early evening he could tell them nothing further.

Other members of Parliament had spoken with Etheridge shortly before they all left the House and went their several ways. None had seen him approached by anyone or could remember his actually walking towards the bridge. They had been busy in conversation themselves, the night was dark, it was late, and they were tired and thinking of home.

All that the day's labor, walking, questioning, and deduction produced by midnight was the confirmation of a very ordinary evening. No unusual person had been noticed, nothing had disturbed Etheridge or caused him to behave other than after any late night sitting of the House. There had been no quarrels, no sudden messages, no haste or anxiety, no friends or acquaintances with him except other members.

Etheridge had been found dead by Harry Rawlins within ten minutes of his last words to his colleagues outside the entrance of the House of Commons.

Pitt turned his attention to the personal life of Etheridge, beginning with his financial affairs. It took him only a couple of hours to confirm that he had been an extremely wealthy man, and there was no heir apart from his only child, Helen Carfax. The estate was in no way entailed, and the house in Paris Road and the extremely fine properties in Lincolnshire and the West Riding were freehold and without mortgage.

Pitt left the solicitors' offices with no satisfaction. Even in the spring sunshine he felt cold. The lawyer, a small, punctilious man with spectacles on the bridge of his narrow nose, had said nothing of James Carfax, but his silences were eloquent. He pursed his mouth and gazed at Pitt with steady sadness in his pale blue eyes, but his discretion had been immaculate; he told Pitt only what was in due course going to become public knowledge when the will was probated, not that Pitt had expected anything else. Families of Etheridge's standing did not employ lawyers who betrayed their clients' trust.

Pitt took a quick lunch of bread, cold mutton, and cider at the Goat and Compasses and then hired a hansom through Westminster and across the bridge back to Paris Road. It was an acceptable hour to call, and even if Helen Carfax were not well enough to receive him herself, it would not matter; his primary purpose was to search Etheridge's papers to see if he could find the letter she had spoken of, or any other correspondence which would indicate an enemy, a woman who felt ill-used, a business or professional rival, anything at all.

When he alighted from the cab he found the house as he had expected, all the curtains drawn and a dark wreath on the door. The parlormaid who answered his knock wore black crepe in her hair instead of the crisp white cap she would normally have had, and no white apron. It was on the tip of her tongue to tell him to go to the tradesmen's entrance, but some mixture of uncertainty, fear, and the aftermath of shock made her choose the simpler measure and ask him in.

"I don't know whether Mrs. Carfax will see you," she said warningly.

"How about Mr. Carfax?" Pitt asked as he followed her into the morning room.

"He's gone out to attend some business. I expect he'll be back after luncheon."

"Would you ask Mrs. Carfax if I may have permission to look through Mr. Etheridge's study to see if I can find the letter she mentioned to me last night?"

"Yes sir, I'll ask," she said doubtfully, and left him to wait alone. He looked round the room more closely than he had the previous night. Guests who might call unexpectedly would be received here, and residents of the house might spend a quiet morning attending to correspondence. The mistress would come here to order the affairs of the day, give the cook and the housekeeper their instructions, and discuss some domestic or cellar matter with the butler.

There was a Queen Anne writing desk in one corner, and a table with a number of framed photographs on it. He studied them carefully; the largest was obviously Etheridge himself as a young man, with a gentle-faced woman beside him. They looked stiff as they faced the photographer, but even in the formal pose there was a confidence that shone through, a composure that had more to do with happiness than discipline. To judge from the fashions it had been taken about twenty years ago. There was also a picture of a boy of about thirteen, thin, with the large, intense eyes of an invalid. The picture was mounted in black.

The elderly woman who reminded Pitt of a benign, rather lugubrious horse was presumably Etheridge's mother. The family resemblance was there; she had the good brow and tender mouth, recalling her granddaughter as she might have been in another age.

To the left side of the table was a large picture of Helen herself with James Carfax. She looked startlingly innocent, her face very young, eyes full of hope and the kind of radiance that belongs to those in love. James also smiled, but only with his mouth and his beautiful teeth; his eyes held satisfaction, almost relief. He seemed more aware of the camera than she.

The date was in the corner, 1883. Possibly it was shortly after their marriage.

Pitt went to the bookcase. A man's choice of books said much of his character, if the books were actually read; if, on the other hand, they were meant to impress, they revealed something of the people whose opinion mattered to him. If they were merely to decorate the wall they revealed nothing, except the certain shallowness of a person who used books for such a purpose. These were well-used volumes of history, philosophy, and a few classic works of literature.

It was Helen herself who appeared nearly ten minutes later, ashen-faced and dressed entirely in black, which made her look younger, but also wearier, as if she were recovering from a long and confining illness. But her composure was admirable.

"Good morning, Inspector Pitt," she said levelly. "I believe you wish to search for the letter I mentioned last night? I doubt you will find it—I don't imagine my father will have preserved it. But of course you may look."

"Thank you, Mrs. Carfax." He wanted to apologize for disturbing her, but he could think of nothing that would not sound trivial in the circumstances and so found himself following her silently across the gaslit hallway. An upstairs maid with a pile of laundry and a tweeny of about fourteen with a mop in her hand were both leaning over the landing rail watching. If the housekeeper caught them, they would be disciplined sharply and told precisely what happened to girls who could not attend to their work but interested themselves in the affairs of their betters.

The library was another spacious room, with two oak-paneled walls, one with large windows, the curtains drawn as suited a house in mourning; the other two walls were lined with glass-fronted bookcases. The fire was unlit, but the ashes had been cleared and the grate freshly blacked.

"There is my father's desk," Helen said, indicating a large oak desk inlaid with tooled leather in dark maroon and containing nine drawers, four on either side and one central one. She held out her thin hand, offering him a little carefully wrought key.

"Thank you, ma'am." He took it, and feeling even more intrusive than usual, he opened the first drawer and began to look through the papers.

"I presume these are all Mr. Etheridge's?" he asked. "Mr. Carfax never uses this room?"

"No, my husband has offices in the City. He never brings work home. He has many friends, but little personal correspondence."

Pitt was sorting through unanswered constituency letters, small matters of land boundaries, bad roads, quarrels with neighbors, all trivial compared with violent death. None of them were written with ill will; simple irritation, more than rage or despair, seemed the ruling emotion.

"Has Mr. Carfax been obliged to go into the City this morning?" he asked suddenly, hoping to surprise something from her.

"Yes. I mean—" She stared at him. "I—I am not sure. He told me, and I—forgot."

"Is Mr. Carfax interested in politics?"

"No. He is in publishing. It is a family interest. He does not go in every day, only when there is a board meeting, or . . ." She trailed off, changing her mind about discussing the subject.

Pitt came to the second drawer, which was full of various tradesmen's bills. He looked at them closely, interested to see that apparently they were all addressed to Etheridge, none to James Carfax. Everything was accounted for here that he might have expected would be required for the running of the establishment: the purchase of food, soap, candles, polishes, linen, coal, coke and wood; the replacement of crockery and kitchenware, servants' uniforms, footmen's livery; the maintenance of the carriages and supplies for the horses, even the repair of harness. Whatever James Carfax contributed, it must be very little indeed.

The only thing absent was any account of expenditure for feminine clothing, shoes, dress fabrics or dressmakers' bills, millinery or perfumes. It would seem Helen had either an allowance or money of her own; or perhaps these were the things which James provided.

He continued with the next drawer, and the next. He discovered nothing but old domestic accounts and some papers to do with the properties in the country. None of it bore the faintest resemblance to a threat.

"I did not imagine he would keep it," Helen said again, when Pitt completed his search. "But it was . . . it must have meant something." She looked away towards the curtained windows. "I had to mention it."

"Of course." He had seen the compulsion that had driven her to speak, although he was less sure of is nature than his polite agreement led her to suppose. Some nameless anarchist, out there in the streets, come at night from the tangle of the slums, was frightening enough, but so infinitely better than that a passion to murder had been born here in the house, living here, bound here, forever a part of them and their lives, its shadow intruding across every hush in conversation, every silence in the night.

"Thank you, Mrs. Carfax," he said, turning from the desk. "Is it possible this letter could be in some other room? The morning room perhaps, or the withdrawing room? Or might your father have taken it upstairs to prevent someone finding it by chance and being distressed?" He did not for a moment think it likely, but he would like to spend a little longer in the house and perhaps speak to the staff. Helen's lady's maid could probably tell him all he wanted to know, but of course she would not. Discretion was her chief qualification, more even than her skill at dressing hair and at fine needlework, and in the art of trimming and pressing a gown. Those who betrayed confidences never found work again. Society was very small.

It seemed Helen did not want to abandon the possibility either, no matter how slim.

"Yes—yes, he may have put it upstairs. I will show you his dressing room; that would be a private place to keep such a thing. There would be no chance of my finding it and being distressed." And she led him out into the hall and up the lovely curved staircase and along the landing to the master bedroom and the dressing room beside it. Here the curtains were not fully drawn, and Pitt had time to notice the view across the mews to the loveliness of the gardens of Lambeth Palace.

He turned to find Helen standing beside a dresser, the top drawer of which had a brass-bound keyhole. Silently she unlocked it for him and pulled out the drawer. It contained Etheridge's personal jewelry, two watches, several pair of cuff links set with semiprecious stones and three plain gold pair, engraved with a crest, as well as two finger rings, one a woman's with a fine emerald.

"My mother's," Helen said softly at Pitt's shoulder. "He kept it himself. He said I should have it after he was . . . dead. . . ." For a moment her composure broke and she swung round to hide her face till she should regain it.

There was nothing Pitt could do; even to show that he had noticed would be inappropriate. They were strangers, of opposite sexes, and socially the gulf between them was unbridgeable. To share whatever pity he felt, whatever understanding, would be inexcusable.

Instead he searched the drawers as quickly as possible, seeing quite easily that there was nothing of a threatening nature: an old love letter from Etheridge's wife, two bank notes, for ten pounds and twenty pounds, respectively, and some photographs of his family. Pitt slid the drawer shut and looked up to find that Helen had turned to face him again, the moment mastered.

"No?" She spoke as though she had known the conclusion.

"No," he agreed. "But then, as you say, ma'am, it is the sort of thing one destroys."

"Yes. . . ." She seemed to want to say something more, but could not find the form of it.

Pitt waited. He could not help her, although he was as aware of her anxiety as of the sunlight which filled the room. Finally he could bear it no longer."

"It may be in his office in the House of Commons," he said quietly. "I have yet to go there."

"Ah, yes, of course."

"But if you think of anything else to tell me, Mrs. Carfax, please send a message to Bow Street, and I shall call on you at your first convenience."

"Thank you—thank you, Inspector," she replied, seeming a little relieved. She led him back onto the landing. As he was passing the top of the stairs he noticed two faded patches on the wallpaper, only slight, but it seemed a picture had been removed, and two others changed in position to return the balance.

"Your father sold one of his paintings recently," he said. "Would you know to whom?"

She was startled, but she did not refuse to answer. "It was my painting, Mr. Pitt. It can have nothing to do with his death."

"I see. Thank you." So she had recently acquired an amount of money. He would have to investigate it discreetly and discover how much.

The front door opened and James Carfax came in on a gust of spring wind and sunlight. The footman came forward and took his hat, coat, and umbrella, and James strode across the hall, stopping as the movement at the top of the stairs caught his eye, his face darkening with irritation and then, as he recognized Pitt, anger.

"What in hell are you doing here?" he demanded. "For God's sake, man, my wife's just lost her father! Get out on the streets and look for whatever lunatic's responsible. Don't waste your time here harassing us!"

"James—" Helen started down the stairs, her hand white, on the bannister. Pitt waited well behind because he could hardly see her black skirts on the gaslit stair and feared lest he might tread on them. "James, he came back to see if he could find a threatening letter I told him Father had received."

"We'll look for it!" James was not to be so easily soothed. "If we find it we'll inform you. Now good day to you, sir—the footman will show you out."

Pitt ignored him and turned to Helen. "With your permission, ma'am, I would like to speak to the footmen and coachmen."

"Whatever for?" Clearly James still considered his presence a trespass.

"Since Mr. Etheridge was attacked in the street, sir, it is possible he was followed and watched some time beforehand," Pitt replied levelly. "On recollection one of them may bring something helpful to mind."

Anger stained James' cheeks with color; he should have seen that point himself. In many ways he was younger than the thirty or so years Pitt judged him to be. His sophistication was a thin skin over his emotions, over the rawness of someone unproved in his own eyes. Perhaps his father-in-law's complete control of the household had oppressed him more than he could admit to himself.

Helen put her hand on her husband's arm, her fingers resting very lightly, as if she were half afraid he might brush her off and she wanted to be able to pretend not to have noticed.

"James, we have to help all we can. I know they may never catch this madman, or anarchist, whoever it is, but—"

"That hardly needs to be said, Helen!" He looked at Pitt; they were much of a height. "Question the outside staff, if you must—and then leave us alone. Let my wife mourn in private, and with some decency." He did not put his hand over hers, as Pitt would have done in his place. Instead he moved away from her hand, and then put his arm round her shoulders, holding her by his side for a moment. Pitt saw Helen's face relax and a soft pleasure relax her features. To Pitt it was a colder gesture than the touching of hands would have been, a masked thing, kept apart by layers of cloth. But one does not know what happens in the relationships of others. Sometimes what seems close hides voids of loneliness whose pain outsiders can never conceive: others who sound to be remote, pursuing their own paths without regard, actually understand each other and silences exist because there is no need for speech, as quarrels are the strange coverings of enfolding warmth and intense loyalties. Perhaps James and Helen Carfax's love was not as one-sided as he had imagined, not so full of pain for her, nor so cramping and unwelcome to him.

He excused himself and went through the green baize door to the servants quarters, explaining to the butler who he was, and that he had Mr. Carfax's permission to speak to them. He was met with cool suspicion.

"Mrs. Carfax told me her father had received a threatening letter," he added. "She naturally wished me to pursue it, to discover anything I can."

The watchfulness relaxed. The thought of James Carfax giving or withholding permission in the household was obviously so unfamiliar to them it had not registered. The mention of Helen, however, was different.

"If we knew anything we'd have told you," the butler said grimly. "But if you want to ask anyone, then of course I'll see that they're brought, and that they answer you as best they can."

"Thank you." Pitt had thought of several questions, not that he expected helpful answers to any of them, but it gave him an opportunity to make a better judgment of the household. The cook offered him a cup of tea, for which he was grateful, and during the conversation he saw the extent of the establishment. Etheridge had kept ten maids altogether, including an upstairs maid, a downstairs maid, the tweeny, a lady's maid for Helen, laundresses, a parlourmaid, a kitchenmaid, and scullery maids. And of course there was a housekeeper. There were two footmen, both six feet tall and nicely matched, a butler, a valet, a bootboy, and outside, two grooms and a coachman.

He watched them all relax and become easier as he told them one or two mildly humorous stories of his experience and shared tea and some of the cook's best Dundee cake, which she kept for the servants hall. He observed the lady's maid more closely than the rest of them. She accepted some good-natured teasing because her position in the servants ranking was higher, despite her being only twenty-five or twenty-six, but as soon as he turned the subject towards Helen and James there was a very slight alteration in the angle of her chin, a tightening of the muscles in her shoulders, a carefulness in her eyes. She knew the pain of a woman who loves more than she is loved, and she was not going to betray it to the rest of the servants, still less to this intrusive policeman.

It was all Pitt had wanted, and when he had eaten the last crumb of his cake, he thanked them, complimented them, and went outside to find the coachman, who was busy cleaning harness in the mews.

Pitt asked the coachman if he'd noticed anyone taking an unusual interest in Etheridge's journeys, but he did not expect to learn anything. What he wanted to know was where James Carfax went, and how often.

When he left in the late afternoon he was in time to catch a hansom back across the river to St. James's and the famous gentlemen's club of Boodle's, where the coachman had said

James Carfax was a member. The man had been discreet, naming only the places where such a young man might be presumed to go: his club, very occasionally his place of business, the theaters, balls and dinners of the usual social round, and in the summer the races, regattas, and garden parties which all Society attended, if they had the rank to be invited and the money to accept.

It was growing dark when Pitt found the doorman at Boodle's and with a mixture of flattery and pressure, elicited from him that Mr. James Carfax was indeed a regular visitor to the premises, that he had many friends among the members and they often sat far into the night playing cards, and yes, he supposed they drank a fair bit, as gentlemen will. No, he did not always leave in his own carriage, at times he dismissed it and left in the vehicle of one or another of his friends. Did he return home? Well it was not for him to say where a young gentleman went when he left.

Was Mr. Carfax overall a winner at cards, or a loser? He had no idea, but certainly he paid his debts, or he would not remain a member, now would he?

Pitt agreed that he would not and had to be content with that, although the thoughts that disturbed him were growing in his mind, and nothing he had learned dispelled them.

There was one more thing he could do before going home. He took another cab, from St. James's down the Buckingham Palace Road and south to the Chelsea Embankment to Barclay Hamilton's house close to the Albert Bridge. There was no use asking any professional or social acquaintance of James Carfax the sort of thing he wished to know. But Barclay Hamilton had recently lost his own father to the same grotesque death as Helen Carfax's father had met with. He could reasonably be pressed with questions more direct and might be free to answer them without fear of the social condemnation others might feel, the sense of having betrayed those who implicitly trusted him.

He was received with some surprise, but civilly enough. Now that he had the opportunity to see Barclay Hamilton on his own, and not in the circumstances of the immediate impact of bereavement, Pitt found him a man of quiet charm. The brusqueness of his manner at their first meeting had completely vanished, and he invited Pitt into his sitting room with as much curiosity as it was courteous to show.

It was not a large room, but graciously furnished, obviously for the comfort of its owner rather than to impress others. The chairs were old, the red and blue Turkey rug was worn in the center but at the outer edges still retained its stained glass vividness. The pictures, mostly watercolors, were not expensive, perhaps even amateur, but each had a mood and a delicacy that suggested they had been chosen for their charm rather than for monetary value. The books in the glass-fronted cases were arranged in order of subject, not to please the eye.

"I don't let my housekeeper touch anything in here, except to dust it," Hamilton said, following Pitt's gaze with a faint smile. "She complains, but obeys. She is greatly put out that I will not allow her to decorate the back of every chair with an antimacassar and put family photographs all over the table. I will permit one of my mother—that is enough. I don't care to feel stared at by an entire gallery."

Pitt smiled back. It was a man's room, and it reminded him of his own bachelor days, although his lodgings had consisted of only one room and had been far from the elegance of Chelsea. It was only the masculinity of it that held the echo, the mark of a single owner, a single taste, a man free to come and go as he pleased, to drop things where he liked without regard for another's convenience.

It had been a good time in his life, a necessary time for growing from boy to man, but he looked back on it with a tolerance that held no yearning, no desire to recapture it. No house could be home to him without Charlotte in it, her favorite pictures, which he loathed, hanging on the wall, her sewing spread out, her books left lying on the tables, her slippers somewhere for him to trip over, her voice from the kitchen, the lights on, the warmth, her touch, familiar now but still exciting, still needed with an urgency, and above all, her sharing, the talk of her day, what had been right or wrong in it, what had been funny or infuriating, and her endless concern and curiosity about his work and what mattered to him in it.

Hamilton was looking at him now, his eyes wide and puzzled. There was humor in his face, but a shadow about the bridge of the nose, a delicacy, as if he had seen his dreams die and had to rebuild with care over a loss that still pained.

"What can I tell you, Inspector Pitt, that you do not already know?"

"You have read of the death of Vyvyan Etheridge?"

"Of course. I should not think there is a soul in the city who has not."

"Are you acquainted, either personally or by repute, with his son-in-law, Mr. James Carfax?"

"A little. Not closely. Why? Surely you cannot think he has any connection with anarchists?" Again the fleeting smile, the knowledge of absurdity which amused rather than angered him.

"You don't think it likely?"

"I don't."

"Why not?" Pitt tried to put skepticism into his voice, as if it were the line of investigation he was pursuing.

"Frankly, he hadn't the passion or the dedication to be anything so total."

"So total?" Pitt was curious. It was not the reason he had expected: not moral impossibility but emotional shallowness. The perception said more of Hamilton than perhaps it did of James Carfax. "You do not think he would find it repugnant, unethical? Disloyal to his own class?"

Hamilton colored faintly, but his candid eyes never left Pitt's. "I would be surprised if he considered the question in that light. In fact, I doubt he has ever thought of politics one way or the other, except to assume that the system will remain as it is and ensure him the sort of life he wishes."

"Which is?"

Hamilton lifted his shoulders very slightly. "As far as I know, lunching with friends, a little gambling, visiting the races and the fashionable parties, the theaters, dinners, balls—and discreet nights with a trollop now and then—perhaps a visit to the dogfight or a fistfight if he can find one."

"You have no high opinion of him," Pitt said levelly, still holding his eyes.

Hamilton pulled a slight face. "I suppose he is no worse than many. But I cannot believe he is a passionate anarchist in heavy disguise. Believe me, Inspector, no disguise could be so superb!"

"Does he win at gambling?"

"Not overall, according to the gossip I've heard."

"And yet he pays up. Does he have considerable private means?"

"I doubt it. His family is not wealthy, although his mother inherited some honorary title. He married well, as you know. Helen Etheridge has tremendous expectations—I suppose now they are a reality. I imagine she pays whatever debts he runs up. He isn't a heavy loser, so far as I know."

"Are you a member of Boodle's?"

"I? No—not my sort of interest. But I have several acquaintances who are. Society is very small, Inspector. And my father lived within a mile of Paris Road."

"But you have not lived in your father's house for many years now."

All the ease and humor died out of Hamilton's face, as if someone had opened a door and let in a blast of winter. "No." His voice was tight, caught in his throat. "My father married again after my mother's death. I was an adult; it was perfectly natural and suitable that I should find my own premises. But that can have nothing to do with James Carfax. I referred to it only to show you that in Society one cannot help knowing something about other people if they move in similar circles."

Pitt regretted having inadvertently caused him pain. He liked the man, and it had been no part of his search to touch an old wound that could hardly have any bearing either on Lockwood Hamilton's death or Etheridge's.

"Of course," he agreed, leaving the apology tacit in his voice; the less the wound was touched the sooner the thin skin would heal over it again. "Did you mention other women as a supposition from his general conduct, or have you some specific knowledge?"

Hamilton breathed out, relaxing again. "No, Inspector. I regret my speculations were based solely on his reputation. It is possible I did him an injustice. I don't like the man; please consider anything I say with that in view."

"You knew Carfax's wife before her marriage?"

"Oh yes."

"Did you like Helen Etheridge, Mr. Hamilton?" Pitt asked it so candidly that it was robbed of implication.

"Yes," Hamilton said equally frankly. "But not romantically, you understand. I always felt her very young. There was something childlike in her; she was like a little girl who keeps her dreams." He smiled ruefully. "As if she had only just put her hair up and donned her first long skirts!"

Pitt pictured Mrs. Carfax, her vulnerability and her obvious adoration for her husband, and silently agreed.

"Unfortunately we all have to grow up," Hamilton added with a small smile. "Perhaps women less so, on the whole." Then he bit his lips as if he wished to take the words back. "Some women, anyway. I fear I cannot help you very much, Inspector. I don't care for James Carfax very much, but I would swear he has no connection with anarchists, or any other political conspiracy, nor is he a madman. He is exactly what he appears, a rather selfish young man who is bored, drinks a little more than is wise, and likes to show off but has not the financial means to keep up with his friends without using his wife's money, which galls him, but not enough to prevent him from doing it."

"And if his wife ceased to provide the money?" Pitt asked.

"She won't. At least," he corrected himself, "I don't believe she will, unless he becomes too rash in his behavior and hurts her too much. But I don't think he's fool enough for that."

"No, I don't suppose so. Thank you, Mr. Hamilton. I appreciate your candor; it has probably saved me hours of delicate questions." Pitt stood up. It was late and growing cold outside, and he wanted to go home. Tomorrow would come soon enough, and he had achieved little.

Barclay Hamilton stood up also. He was taller than Pitt had remembered, and leaner. He looked embarrassed.

"I apologize, Inspector Pitt. I have spoken more frankly than I had a right to. It is the end of the day, and I am tired. I was less than discreet, and possibly uncharitable towards Carfax. I should not have spoken my thoughts."

Pitt smiled broadly. "You did warn me that you did not like him."

Hamilton relaxed, a sudden lightness in his face evoking the young man he must have been eighteen years ago, when Amethyst Royce had married his father. "I hope we meet again, Inspector, in happier circumstances." And instead of calling the manservant he held out his hand and shook Pitt's as if they had been friends, not gentleman and detective.

Pitt left the house and walked slowly along the Embankment until he should find a cab and at last go home. The night air was raw, and there was a mist rising from the water. Somewhere far down the river by the Pool of London, ships' foghorns were blaring out, muffled by distance and damp.

Could James Carfax have murdered his father-in-law to speed his wife's inheritance? Or, uglier and more painful than that, could Helen, in her anguish to keep her husband, have murdered her own father for his money, money she needed to give James the material things he counted so dear? To keep his attention, so she might pretend it was love? She could hardly have done it herself, but she might have paid someone else to do it. That might account as well for Sir Lockwood Hamilton's murder: a paid assassin might have mistaken him for Etheridge, something a person who knew him well would not do on a lamplit bridge like Westminster.

Tomorrow he must find out which picture she had sold, and for how much. It wouldn't be as easy to discover what had happened to the money it had brought, but that too should be possible.

Pitt went home tired after a long day, Helen's face lingering in his mind, with its painful tenderness and the fear in her eyes.

The following morning Pitt got up early and set out in the rain to report to Micah Drummond, and Charlotte received her first letter from Emily, postmarked Paris. She sat looking at it for several minutes without opening it. Half of her was eager to know that Emily was happy and well, the other half was stung by an envy for the excitement of laughter and adventure and the beginning of love.

After propping it up against the teapot and staring at it while she ate two slices of toast and marmalade, a preserve which she made extremely well—it was her best culinary achievement—she finally succumbed.

It was dated Paris, April 1888, and read:

Dearest Charlotte,

I hardly know how to begin to tell you everything that has happened. Crossing on the boat was miserable! The wind was cold and the sea rough! But once we reached dry land it all changed completely. The coach drive from Calais to Paris made me think of every adventure I've ever read, about musketeers and Louis XVI—it was the XVI, wasn't it? It was such a marvelous idea of Jack's, and full of all the things I imagined: farms with cheeses for sale, wonderful trees, little old villages with farmers' wives arguing, all delightful and romantic. And I thought of the fleeing aristocrats in the Revolution—they must have passed this way to reach the packet boats to England!

Jack had everything arranged in Paris. Our hotel is small and quaint, overlooking a cobbled square where the leaves on the trees are just unfolding, and a little man stands outside and plays an accordion in the evenings under the open windows. We sit outside at a table with a checked cloth and drink wine in the sun. It is a little cool, I admit, but how could I mind? Jack bought me a shawl of silk, and I feel very French and very elegant with it round my shoulders.

We have walked for miles and my feet are sore, but the weather has been lovely, bright with a fresh wind, and I have loved every minute of it. Paris is so beautiful! Everywhere I go I feel someone famous or interesting has walked these same streets, a great artist with unique and passionate vision, or a wild-eyed revolutionary, or a romantic like Sydney Carton who redeemed everything with the ultimate love.

And of course we have been to the theater. I did not understand most of it, but I caught the atmosphere, and that was all that mattered—and Charlotte, the music! I could have sung and danced all the way home, except that I would have been arrested for disturbing the peace! And it is all such fun because Jack is enjoying it every bit as much as I. He is such a good companion, as well as tender and considerate in all other ways that I had hoped. And I have noticed other women gazing at him with shining eyes, and not a little envy!

Paris gowns are marvelous, but I fear they would be out of fashion in no time. I can imagine spending half one's life at the dressmaker's, forever having them "made over" to keep up with madame next door!

We leave for the south tomorrow morning, and I can hardly dare hope it will be as perfect as this. Can Venice really be as marvelous as I dream it will? I wish I knew more Venetian history. I shall have to find a book and read something. My head is filled with romance and, I daresay, quite unreal notions.

I do hope you are well, and the children, and Thomas is not having to work too many hours. Does he have an interesting case? I shall look forward to hearing all your news when I return, but please take care of yourself and don't get involved in anything dangerous! Be inquisitive, by all means, but only in the mind. I am not with you just at the moment, but be assured my thoughts and my love are, and I shall see you again soon.

All my love,
Emily

Charlotte put the sheets of paper down with a smile on her face and tears in her eyes. She would not for even a second's darker thought have wished Emily anything but total happiness. It was easy to feel a welling up of gladness inside her at the thought of Emily singing and dancing along the streets of Paris, especially after the tragedy and the awful misery of George's death.

But there was also a gnawing fear of having been left out. She was sitting in a kitchen by herself, in a small house, in a very ordinary suburb of London, where in all probability she would be for the rest of her life. Pitt would always work hard, for less money a month than Emily was now spending in a day.

But it was not money, money did not provide happiness—and idleness certainly did not! The cause of the ache in her throat was the thought of walking in laughter and companionship in beautiful places with time to spend, and of being in love. That was it—it was the magic of being in love, the tenderness that was not habit but was intense and thrilling, full of discovery, taking nothing for granted, making everything infinitely precious. It was being the center of someone else's world, and they of yours.

Which was all very silly. She would not have changed Pitt for Jack Radley, or anyone else. Nor would she have changed her life for Emily's . . . except perhaps just at the moment. . . .

She heard Gracie's feet clacking along the corridor, outrage audible in every step as she came from the front door having had words with the fishmonger. Gracie had no time for tradesmen who got above themselves.

"I know," Charlotte said as soon as Gracie appeared and before she could begin her expostulations. "He's impertinent!"

Gracie saw she would find no sympathy and instantly changed tack. She was all of sixteen now, and thoroughly experienced.

"What's Mr. Pitt working on now, ma'am?"

"A political case."

"Oh. What a pity! Well never mind—maybe it'll be better next time!" And Gracie set about riddling the grate and restarting the fire.

Pitt discovered from Micah Drummond that he himself had already been to the House of Commons and spoken to several of Etheridge's colleagues.

"Nothing that I can see helps us," he said, shaking his head. He said nothing of pressure from the Commissioner of Police, or from the Home Office, but Pitt did not need to be told. They would still be subtle—it was early days yet—but the air of fear would be there, the anxiety to meet public demand, to answer the questions, quiet anxiety, and to appear to have everything in control. Some individuals would fear charges of incompetence, loss of status, even of office, and they would seek someone to blame.

"Political enemies?" Pitt asked.

"Rivals." Drummond shrugged. "But he wasn't ambitious enough to have enemies, or controversial enough to have stirred anyone to passion. And he had enough private income not to be greedy or to be tempted into graft."

"The Irish question?"

"Against Home Rule, but so were three hundred forty-two others three years ago, more in 'eighty-six. And anyway, Hamilton was for it. And on other issues Etheridge seems to have been moderate, humane without being radical. For penal reform, poor law reform, the Factories Acts—but change should be gradual, nothing that would destabilize society or industry. Very unremarkable all the way along."

Pitt sighed. "The more I look at it, the more it seems as if it might be personal after all, and poor Hamilton was simply a mistake."

"Who?" Drummond looked up with a frown. "His son-in-law, for the money? Seems a bit hysterical. He'd get it anyway in due course. No plans for disinheritance, were there? Wife not likely to leave him, surely? It would be social suicide!"

"No." Helen Carfax's worried, vulnerable face came sharply to his mind. "No, on the contrary, she's obviously very much in love with him. And probably gives him all the money he asks for; it seems to be the most attractive thing about her, to him."

"Oh." Drummond leaned back wearily. "Well you'd better go on looking at that. Unless of course Hamilton was the intended victim, and Etheridge was added to conceal the motive? But I agree, that is a bit farfetched—more of a risk than it would be worth. And there doesn't seem to be anyone in Hamilton's family or among his acquaintances with any motive that we can find. What about this picture you say Helen Carfax sold? What was it worth?"

"I don't know yet. I was going to look into that today. Could be anything from a few pounds to a small fortune."

"I'll have Burrage do that. You go back to the Carfaxes' house. I don't know what else you can do, but keep trying.

See if there're any women James Carfax is involved with, not just using. See if his debts are serious, or pressing. Perhaps he couldn't afford to wait?"

"Yes sir. I'll be back at lunchtime to see if Burrage has anything on the painting."

Drummond opened his mouth to protest, then changed his mind and said nothing, merely watching Pitt go out the door.

But when Pitt came back long after luncheon at half past two, the news that greeted him had nothing to do with the painting. There was a hand-delivered note from Helen Carfax saying that she had remembered the exact nature of the threat her father had received, and if Pitt wished to call at the house in Paris Road, she would tell him what it had been.

He was surprised. He had believed it to be an invention, born of her desire to persuade both him and herself that the violence and the hatred that surrounded the murder had its origin far from her home or family, that it was something outside, beyond in the darkness of the streets where she never went; east in the slum and docklands, the taverns and alleys of discontent. He had not expected her to mention it again, except as a vague possibility, undefined.

Still, she had sent for him, so he left Bow Street and took a cab south across the river to Paris Road.

She greeted him quietly, her eyes one minute downcast, the next seeking his face. Her hands, clenching and unclenching at her sides, seemed stiff, and she fumbled with the door handle as she led him into the morning room. But then she was speaking of people whom she considered might have cut her father's throat and tied him to a lamppost like an effigy, a lampoon of authority and order.

"I daresay you know of it, Mr. Pitt, being a policeman," she began, looking not at him but at a patch of sunlight on the carpet in front of her. "But three years ago there was a woman named Helen Taylor who tried to become a candidate for Parliament! A woman!" Her voice was growing a little sharp, as though underneath her stillness there was a rising hysteria. "Naturally it caused a certain amount of feeling. She was a very odd person—to call her eccentric would be charitable. She wore trousers! Dr. Pankhurst—you may have heard of him—chose to walk with her in public. It was most unbecoming, and quite naturally Mrs. Pankhurst objected, and I believe he ceased to do so. Mrs. Pankhurst is one of those who desires women to be given the franchise."

"Yes, Mrs. Carfax, I had heard there was such a movement. John Stuart Mill wrote a very powerful tract on the Admission of Women to Electoral Franchise in 1867. And a Mary Wollstonecraft wrote about political and civil equality for women in 1792."

"Yes, yes I suppose so. It is something in which I have no interest. But some of the women who espouse the cause do so very violently. Miss Taylor's behavior is surely an example of their—their disregard of the normal rules of society."

Pitt kept his expression one of continued interest. "Indeed it would seem to have been unwise, at the least," he offered.

"Unwise?" Her eyes flew wide open and for a moment her hands were perfectly still.

"It failed to produce any of the results she desired," he answered.

"Surely it was bound to? No sane person could imagine she might succeed?"

"Who is it you believe threatened your father, Mrs. Carfax?"

"A woman—one of the women who want suffrage. He was opposed to it, you know."

"No, I didn't know. But surely he is with the majority in Parliament, and in the country. Quite a considerable majority."

"Of course, Mr. Pitt." The nervous tension in her was so great she was shaking. The color drained out of her skin and her voice was a whisper. "Mr. Pitt, I do not say they are sane. A person who would do . . . what was done to my father, and to Sir Lockwood Hamilton, cannot be explained by any normal means."

"No, Mrs. Carfax. I am sorry to have pressed you." He was apologizing for being there to witness her distress, not for asking her to explain, but it did not matter if she did not understand that. All that mattered was that she should know of his sympathy for her.

"I appreciate your—your tact, Mr. Pitt. Now I must not take more of your time. Thank you for coming so quickly."

Pitt left in deep thought. Was it really conceivable that some woman, passionate for electoral justice, should cut the throat of two members of Parliament, simply because they were among the vast majority who felt her cause was untimely, or even ridiculous? It did not seem sane. But then as Helen Carfax had pointed out, such an act was not that of a person whose mind worked as others did, whatever the reason for it.

He still found his own thoughts returning to James Carfax, whose motive was far easier to understand, and to believe. He wanted to know more about him, see something besides the rather spoiled and shallow young man seen by Barclay Hamilton, or the shocked and rattled husband he had seen himself.

Accordingly at a little after four o'clock he presented his card to the parlormaid at Lady Mary Carfax's Kensington residence and requested half an hour of her time, if she would be so gracious. It was in the matter of the recent violent death of Vyvyan Etheridge, M.P.

She sent back a message that he should wait in the morning room, and when it was convenient she would see him.

She chose to make it three quarters of an hour, in order that he should not give himself airs or imagine she had nothing better to do. Then she yielded to her curiosity and sent the maid to fetch him to the withdrawing room, where she sat in a bright pink overstuffed chair. It and three similar chairs and a chaise longue almost filled the room. There were one or two agreeable paintings on the walls and many photographs and portraits of family groups. At least a dozen of them showed the development of James Carfax from an infant to the thoughtful, rather self-conscious young man pictured with his arm round his mother's shoulders.

Lady Mary Carfax was not a tall woman, but she sat with imperious rigidity, and of course she did not rise when he came in. She had a coronet of gray hair, naturally curling. She must have been a beauty in her youth; her skin was still fine and her nose straight and delicate, but there was a coldness in her blue-gray eyes and a slack line now to her jaw and throat. Her mouth might have been charming in her early years; now there was a tightness in it that betrayed an inner chill, a ruthlessness that for Pitt dominated her face.

She did not care to crane her neck backwards, so reluctantly she gave him permission to sit.

"Thank you, Lady Mary," he said, and sat down opposite her.

"Well, what can I do for you? I know a certain amount about politics, but I doubt I can tell you anything of anarchists or other revolutionaries and malcontents."

"Your daughter-in-law, Mrs. James Carfax, believes that her father was threatened by a woman who was passionate about obtaining the right to vote for Parliament."

Lady Mary's slightly downward sloping eyebrows shot upward. "Good gracious! I knew of course that they were the most brazen creatures, bereft of the sensitivities of feeling, the refinements that are natural to a woman. But I must admit that until now it had not entered my mind that they might take such complete leave of all sanity. Of course I did advise Mr. Etheridge against having any sympathy with them, right from the beginning. It is not natural for women to desire to dominate public affairs. We do not have the brusqueness of nature; it is not our place."

Pitt was surprised. "You mean that at some time there

was a question of his being in favor of the franchise for women?"

Her face was full of distaste. "I am not sure that he would have gone as far as that! He did consider there was some argument that women of maturity and a certain degree of property—not just any woman—should be able to vote for local councils and, in certain cases, should have the right to custody of their children when separated from their husbands."

"Women of property? What about other women, poorer women?"

"Are you trying to be amusing, Mr.—what was your name?"

"Pitt, ma'am. No, I just wondered what Mr. Etheridge's ideas were."

"They were misplaced, Mr. Pitt. Women have no education, no understanding of political or governmental affairs, no knowledge of the law and seldom any of finance, other than of a merely domestic nature. Can you imagine the sort of people they would elect to Parliament if they had the vote? We might find ourselves governed by a romantic novelist, or an actor! Who else in the world would take us seriously? If we became weak and foolish at home it would be the beginning of the end of the Empire, and then the whole Christian world would suffer! Can anyone wish that? Of course not!"

"And would women having the vote do that, Lady Mary?"

"There is a certain order in society, Mr. Pitt. We break it at our peril."

"But Mr. Etheridge did not agree?"

Her face tightened at the memory, but there was only irritation and impatience at the foolishness that had required her guiding hand.

"Not at first, but he came to see that he had allowed to get out of hand his natural sympathies for a certain woman who had behaved quite irresponsibly and brought upon herself a domestic misfortune. She appealed to him, in his parliamentary capacity, and for a short while his judgment was affected by her extreme and rather hysterical views. However, he did realize, of course, that the whole suggestion was absurd, and after all, it was not as if it were the desire of a large number of people! No one but a few hotheaded women of a most undesirable type has ever entertained such an idea."

"Was that Mr. Etheridge's conclusion?"

"Naturally!" The slightest smile flickered over her lips. "He was not a foolish man, only susceptible to a sentimental pity for people who do not warrant it. And Florence Ivory certainly did not. Her influence was short-lived; he very soon perceived that she was a most undesirable person, in all ways."

"Florence Ivory?"

"A very strident and unwomanly creature. If you are looking for a political assassin, Mr. Pitt, I should look to her, and her associates. I believe she lives in the same area across the river, somewhere near the Westminster Bridge. At least, that is what Mr. Etheridge told me."

"I see. Thank you, Lady Mary."

"My duty," she said with a lift of her chin. "Unpleasant, but necessary. Good afternoon, Mr. Pitt!"

6

IT TOOK PITT ALL the morning of the next day to catch up on the news which had reached Bow Street regarding the case, namely that Helen Carfax's painting had been very fine and fetched five hundred pounds—enough to employ a maid every day of her life from childhood to old age and still have some to spare. What had she done with so much money? Surely it had gone to James, in some form or other: a present? an allowance? in payment of his debts at Boodle's?

There was more in from cabdrivers, but nothing that added to what they already knew. No one had any word on anarchists or Fenians, or any other violent group.

The newspapers were still featuring the story in headlines, with speculations on civil riot and dissolution below.

The Home Secretary was becoming anxious and had informed them of his profound wish that they bring the case to a speedy conclusion, before public unrest became any more serious.

The briefest of inquiries ascertained that Florence Ivory lived in Walnut Tree Walk, off the Waterloo Road, a short distance to the east of Paris Road and Royal Street, and the Westminster Bridge. She was acknowledged by the local police station with frowns and slight shrugs. There was no record of any offense against the law. Their attitude seemed to be a mixture of amusement and exasperation. The sergeant answering Pitt's questions pulled his features into a grimace, but it was good-natured.

Pitt called in the early afternoon. It was a pleasant house, modest for the area, but well cared for, sills recently painted and chintz curtains in the open windows and a jar of daffodils catching the sun.

A maid of all work opened the door, the apron round her broad waist obviously for service, not ornamentation, and a mop leaned against the wall where she had rested it to attend to the caller.

"Yes sir?" she asked, looking surprised.

"Is Mrs. Ivory at home? I am Inspector Pitt, from the Bow Street Police Station, and I believe Mrs. Ivory may be able to help us."

"I can't see 'ow she could do that! But if you want I'll go an' ask 'er." She turned and left him on the step while she retreated somewhere into the back of the house, leaving her mop behind.

It was only a moment before Florence Ivory appeared, whisking the mop out of the hallway and into the door of a room to the right, then facing Pitt with a startlingly direct gaze. She was of average height and slender to the point of gauntness. She had no bosom to speak of, and her shoulders were square and a trifle bony; nevertheless she was not unfeminine, and there was a considerable elegance to her, of a quite individual nature. Her face was far from traditionally beautiful: her eyes were large and wide set, her brows too heavy for fashion, her nose long, straight, and much too large; there were deeply marked lines round her mouth. In spite of the fact, Pitt judged her to be thirty-five at the very most. When she spoke her voice was husky, sweet, and completely unique.

"Good afternoon, Mr. Pitt. Mrs. Pacey informs me you are from the Bow Street Police Station and believe that I can help you in some way. I cannot imagine how, but if you care to come in I shall try."

"Thank you, Mrs. Ivory." He followed her through the hallway into a wide room at the back of the house, dark-paneled, and yet creating an illusion of light. A polished table held a porcelain dish, cracked but still retaining much of its delicate beauty, and on it was a bowl of spring blossom. The far wall was almost entirely taken up with windows and a French door opening onto a small garden. The curtains were pale cotton, sprigged with some sort of flower design, and the seat beneath the windows was covered with cushions in the same material. It was a room in which he felt immediately comfortable.

Beyond the windows he could just see the figure of a woman bending in the garden, working the earth. She was not far away, for the garden was small, but through the panes, unless he stared, he could make out no more than a white blouse and the sun on a cloud of auburn hair.

"Well?" Florence Ivory said briskly. "I would imagine your time is precious, and mine certainly is. What is it you imagine I know that could possibly interest the Bow Street police?"

He had been turning over in his mind how he could approach the subject with her, both yesterday evening and this morning, and now that he had met her all his preparations seemed inadequate. Her penetrating stare was fixed on him with impatience ready to become dislike; deviousness would be torn apart and would alienate her by insulting her intelligence, an act which he judged she would take very ill.

"I am investigating a murder, ma'am."

"I know no one who has been murdered."

"Mr. Vyvyan Etheridge?"

"Oh." She had been caught out, not in a lie, in an inaccuracy. And the foolishness of it caused a flush of irritation to rise to her cheeks. "Yes, indeed. Somehow the word 'murder' brought to my mind something more—more personal. I think of that as an assassination. I am afraid I do not know anything about anarchists. We live a very quiet life here, very domestic."

He had no idea from her face whether the word was meant in praise or bitterness. Had she imagined herself in Parliament too? Or was Lady Mary Carfax simply repeating a mixture of gossip and her own prejudices?

"But you were acquainted with Mr. Etheridge?"

"Not socially." There was laughter in her voice now. It was a beautiful instrument, rich and passionate, flexible to a hundred shades of thought and meaning.

"No, Mrs. Ivory," he agreed. "But I believe you had some occasion to appeal to him professionally?"

Her face hardened, the light vanished from it, and something crossed it which was so intense it was frightening, a hatred that threatened to rob her of breath and twist her very body with its violence.

Pitt instinctively started forward, then caught himself and waited. This woman might have taken an open razor and crept up behind a man and cut his throat from ear to ear. She did not look to have the strength, but certainly she had all the force of emotion.

The silence hung between them so thickly every other tiny sound was magnified—the clatter of the maid somewhere in the kitchen, a child's feet running on the pavement beyond the curtained windows, a bird singing.

"I did," she agreed finally. Her voice seemed pressed from between her teeth, and her eyes did not move from his. "And if he dealt with others as he did with me, then I am not surprised someone killed him. But it was not I."

"What did he do, Mrs. Ivory, that you found so irredeemable?"

"He elicited trust—and then betrayed it, Mr. Pitt. Do you excuse betrayal? As perhaps you have not experienced it very often? No doubt you have ways to fight, recourse when you are used, wronged—oh don't look like that!" Her face was suddenly full of scorn mixed with a furious humor, a kind of derision he had never seen before. "I do not mean that he seduced my girlish heart—although, God knows, that has happened to enough women. I had no personal relationship with Mr. Etheridge, I assure you!"

For an instant there was an element of the absurd in it; then he remembered how unlikely a thing love can be, let alone that hunger that attracts people in the mask of love. She was a woman of character, high individuality; it was not impossible, her wry interest in everything could have drawn Etheridge. His dismissal died before it reached his lips.

"I understand his connection with you was as a member of Parliament, and I assumed your feeling of injustice was in that regard," he said instead.

Her hard laughter came again. "How painfully tactful you are, Mr. Pitt. Whose feelings are you trying to spare? Not mine! Nothing you could say of Mr. Etheridge could be as harsh as what I might say of him myself. Or is it your duty to speak well of your superiors?"

A dozen answers flashed through Pitt's mind, most of them sarcastic or critical, and he restrained himself. He would not allow her to dictate how he did his job, or what his manner should be.

"It is my duty, Mrs. Ivory, to discover who murdered Mr. Etheridge. My opinion of him is immaterial," he said coolly. "A lot of the people who are murdered are not those I would necessarily like, had I known them. Fortunately the freedom to walk about without fear of being murdered does not depend on one's friendship with policemen, or the lack of it."

For an instant she was furious, then her face relaxed into a sudden smile. "I suppose that is as well, or I should live in terror. You have a sharp tongue, Mr. Pitt. You are quite right, I did appeal to Mr. Etheridge to help me, as a constituent of his, which I was at the time. I lived in Lincolnshire."

"And I assume he did not help you?"

Again the hatred twisted her face and made it ugly; her mouth, which had been mobile, soft, and intelligent a moment before became a flat, bitter line.

"He promised to, and then like all men, he rallied to his own kind in the end. He betrayed me and left me with nothing!" She was shaking, her thin body beneath the cotton of her gown was tense with passion, shoulders rigid. "Nothing!"

The French doors opened and the other woman came in, obviously having heard the anguish ringing in Florence's voice. She was several years younger, barely twenty. She was of a completely different build, taller and softer in outline, with a delicate bosom and rounded arms. Rosetti could have used her perfect Pre-Raphaelite face in one of his Arthurian romances; she had all the earthy naivete and the unconscious strength of his subjects.

She went to Florence Ivory and put an arm round her defensively, facing Pitt with anger.

Florence put one had on the girl's. "It is all right, Africa. Mr. Pitt is from the police. He is inquiring into the murder of Vyvyan Etheridge. I was telling him what kind of a person Mr. Etheridge was. Naturally that involved my own experiences with him." Her eyes met Pitt's again. "Mr. Pitt, my friend and companion, Miss Africa Dowell, whose house this is, and who has been generous enough to take me in and give me a home when I would otherwise have nothing."

"How do you do, Miss Dowell," Pitt said gravely.

"How do you do," she answered guardedly. "What do you want from us? We despised Mr. Etheridge, but we did not kill him, nor do we know who did."

"I did not suppose you knew who did," Pitt agreed. "At least, not that you were aware. But you may well know something that helps when it is put together with what I know or may yet learn."

"We don't know any anarchists." There was something in the lift of her chin, her frank-eyed defiance, that made Pitt think it was at least in part a lie.

"You believe it was anarchists? Why, Miss Dowell?"

She swallowed, confused. It was not the reply she had expected.

Florence stepped in. "Well, if there were a personal motive, a matter of inheritance, or passion, you would hardly imagine that we should know anything of help to you. And as far as I know we are also acquainted with no lunatics."

Only part of Pitt was irritated by them, standing close

together, defensively; they had been hurt and they were protecting themselves against being hurt again.

"But possibly some people disliked Mr. Etheridge for political reasons?" he continued.

"Dislike is far too mild a term, Mr. Pitt," Florence said, the bitterness returning. "I hated him." Her hand tightened on Africa's arm. "I daresay there were others he treated similarly, but I do not know of them, nor would I tell you if I did."

"People who might have been sufficiently angered to behave violently, Mrs. Ivory?"

"I've told you, I have no idea. But sometimes all the pleading and protestations in the world do no good, when the people who have power are comfortable themselves, when they have warmth, food, safety, social rank, families around them, and the position to see that everything remains that way. They cannot and do not want to believe that other people are suffering any pain or injustice, that things should be changed—most especially if the changes involve questioning an order which they find so satisfactory."

He saw the passion in her face, the vehemence with which she spoke, and he knew this was no instant response to his words, it was a conviction boiling under the surface, awaiting the right moment to burst out with all the strength of years of suffering, however occasioned.

He must keep his emotions quiet. This was no time to give his own answers, to speak of the injustices that made his own anger burn or the complacency he would have scalded with his contempt. Nor was it time to philosophize. He was here to learn if this woman could have abandoned pleading and argument and the consent to law that kept the community from barbarism, if she had put her own sense of right and equity before all others and cut the throats of two men.

"All you seem to be saying, Mrs. Ivory, is that the satisfied do not often seek change; it is the dissatisfied who press for improvement, or merely for their turn to have the power and the rewards."

Again her face tightened with anger, which was now directed at him.

"For a moment, Mr. Pitt, I thought you had imagination, pity even. Now I see you are as complacent, insensitive, and frightened for your own miserable little niche in society as the rest of your kind!

His voice dropped. "Who are my kind, Mrs. Ivory?"

"The people with power, Mr. Pitt!" She almost spat the words. "Men—almost all men! Women are born into life and must take our father's name, his rank in life. He decides where and how we will live. In the house, his word is law—he decides whether we shall be educated or not, what we will do, if we shall marry, when, and to whom. Then our husbands decide what we shall say, do, even think! They decide what faith we shall profess, what friends we may or may not meet, what shall happen to our children. And we have to defer to them, whatever we actually think, to pretend they are cleverer than we are, subtler, wiser, have more imagination—even if they are so stupid it is painful!" She was breathing hard, her whole body shaking.

"Men make the laws and administer them; the police are men; judges are men—everywhere I turn my life is dictated by men! Nowhere can I appeal to a woman, who might understand what I really feel!

"Do you know, Mr. Pitt, it is only four years ago that I ceased to be in law a chattel to my husband? A thing, an object belonging to him like his other household goods, a chair or a table, or a bale of linen. Then the law—man's law—at last recognized that I am actually a person, a human being, independent of anyone else, with my own heart and my own brain. When I am hurt it is not my husband who bleeds, it is I!"

Pitt had not known it. The women in his own family were so mightily independent it had never occurred to him to consider their legal standing. He did know that married women had been entitled to retain and administer their own property only six years ago; in fact when he had first met Charlotte in 1881, he would in law have been the owner of her money, such as it was, even her clothes, upon their marriage. He had not thought of it until someone had made a vicious remark as to his change in fortune.

"And you find protestations and pleadings are no use?" he said fatuously, hating having to be so false to the understanding, even the empathy he felt. He had grown up the son of servants on a country estate; he knew about obedience and ownership.

Her disgust stung. "You are either a fool, Mr. Pitt, or else you are deliberately patronizing me in a fashion both contemptible and completely pointless. If you are trying to make me say that I consider there are occasions when violence is the only means left to someone suffering intolerable wrongs, then consider me to have said it." She glared at him, defying him to make the next, inevitable charge.

"I am not a fool, Mrs. Ivory," he said instead, meeting her blazing eyes. "Nor do I imagine you are. Whatever you pleaded for to Mr. Etheridge, it was not that he should change the whole order of society and give to women an equality they have never enjoyed in all our two thousand years. You may be marvelously ambitious, but you will have started with something more specific, and I think more personal. What was it?"

The rage died away again suddenly, like a force that has been so violent it has consumed all its fuel, and only the pain was left. She sat down on a cushioned wood settle and stared not at him but at the garden through the open window.

"I imagine if I do not tell you, then you will only go and dig it up elsewhere, perhaps less accurately. I was married fifteen years ago, to William Ivory. My property was not great, but it would have been more than enough for me to live on in some comfort. Of course, on my wedding day it became his. I have never seen it since."

Her hands were completely calm in her lap; she held a

lace handkerchief, which she had pulled from her pocket, but she did not twist it. Only the whiteness of her knuckles betrayed the straining muscles.

"But that is not my complaint—although I find it monstrous. It was an institutionalized way for men to steal women's money and do whatever they pleased with it, on the grounds that we were too feeble-witted and too ignorant of financial affairs to manage it ourselves. We must watch our husbands squander it, and never speak a word, even if we had a hundred times more sense! And if we did not know how to manage affairs, whose fault is that? Who forbade our education in anything but the most trivial matters?"

Pitt waited for her to return to her grievance. All this time Africa Dowell stood at the far end of the settle, a figure of startling immobility, as if she had indeed been one of the romantic paintings she resembled, and like them all manner of passion and dreams were in her face; she might well just this instant have seen the mirror of Shalott crack from side to side, sealing her doom. Whatever Florence Ivory was recounting, it was well known to her, and she felt the same unhealed wound.

"We had two children," Florence continued. "A boy, and then a girl. William Ivory became more and more dictatorial. Our laughter offended him. He thought me light-minded if I enjoyed my children's company, told them stories or played games, and yet if I wished to talk of politics, or of changes in the laws which might help the poor and the oppressed, he said I meddled in things that were too weighty for me and were not my concern, and I had no idea what I was talking about. My place was in the parlor, the kitchen, or the bedroom; nowhere else.

"Finally I could bear it no longer, and I left. I knew from the outset that I could not have my son, but my daughter, Pansy, who was then six years old"—even speaking the name seemed to wrench her—"I took with me. It was very hard for us. We had little money, and few means of earning any. At first I was given shelter by a friend here in London who had some understanding of my plight, and some pity for me. But her own circumstances became severely reduced, and I was obliged by honor not to burden her with our care any longer.

"It was then, about three years ago, that Africa Dowell took us in." She looked round and saw Pitt's face, perhaps detecting in him confusion and a certain impatience. It was indeed a sad story, but she had in no way touched upon Vyvyan Etheridge, nor had she any reason to blame him for any part of it.

"I supported electoral reform," Florence said wryly. "I even went so far as to endorse Miss Helen Taylor's attempt to stand for Parliament. I freely expressed my feelings on the subject of women's rights—that we should be able to vote and to hold office, to make decisions, both as to our money and our children, even to have access to that knowledge which would enable us to choose what number of children we had, rather than spend all our adult years bearing one child after another until exhausted in body and heart, and destitute in pocket."

Her voice grew harsher, and the humiliation and bitterness lay like an open wound, still lacerated, still pouring blood.

"My husband heard of it and pressed the courts that I was an unfit person to have custody of my daughter. I pleaded my cause to Vyvyan Etheridge. He said he saw well that my political views were no part of my fitness as a mother, and I should not be deprived of my child because of them.

"I did not know at that time that my husband had friends of such influence as he might bring to bear on Mr. Etheridge. He used them, he spoke man to man, and Mr. Etheridge sent word to me that he regretted he had misunderstood my case, and on closer investigation he agreed with my husband that I was an unstable woman, of an hysterical and ill-informed nature, and my daughter would be better with her father. That same day they came and took her from me, and I have not seen her since." She hesitated a moment, mastering herself with difficulty, forcing the memory out of her mind, and when she continued her voice was flat, almost dead. "Am I sorry Vyvyan Etheridge is dead? I am not! I am sorry only that it was quick and that he probably did not even know who had killed him, or why. He was a coward and a betrayer. He knew I was neither a hysterical person nor light-minded. I loved my daughter more than any other person on earth, and she loved me and trusted me. I could have cared for her above all other interests or causes, and I would have taught her to have courage, dignity, and honor. I would have taught her she was loved, and how to love others. And what will her father teach her? That she is fit for nothing but to listen and to obey, never to feel all her passion, to think or to dream, never to stand up for what she believes is right or good. . . ." Her voice faltered with the extremity of her loss and the waste of a child's life, the daughter she had borne and loved, tearing at her heart. It was several long minutes before she could speak again.

"Etheridge knew that, but he bowed to pressure from other men, from the people who might make it uncomfortable for him if he supported me. It was easier not to fight, and so he allowed them to take my child and give her to her autocratic and loveless father. I am not even permitted to see her." Her face was a mask of such anguish Pitt felt it was intrusive even to look at her. The tears ran down her cheeks, and she wept without a grimace; it had a kind of terrible beauty, simply from the power of her passion.

At last Africa knelt down and gently took her hand. She did not hold Florence Ivory in her arms; perhaps the time for that had already been and gone. Instead she looked across the flowered muslin of Florence's skirt at Pitt.

"Such men deserve to die," she said very quietly and gravely. "But Florence did not kill him, nor did I. If that is what you came hoping to discover, then your journey has been wasted."

Pitt knew he should press them now as to where they

had been at the times Hamilton and Etheridge had been killed, but he could not bring himself to ask it. He assumed they would swear that they had been here at home in their beds. Where else would a decent woman be at close to midnight? And there was no proving it.

"I hope to find out who did murder both Mr. Etheridge and Sir Lockwood Hamilton, Miss Dowell, but I do not hope it is you. In fact I hope you can show me that it was not."

"The door is behind you, Mr. Pitt," Africa replied. "Please have the courtesy to leave us."

Pitt arrived home at dusk, and as soon as he was in the door he tried to put the case from his mind. Daniel had had his supper and was ready for bed, it was merely a matter of hugging him good night before Charlotte took him upstairs. But Jemima, being two years older, had privileges and obligations commensurate with her seniority. They were alone in the parlor by the fire. She bent and picked up all the pieces of her jigsaw puzzle, muttering to herself as she did so. Pitt knew immediately that the mess had been left largely by Daniel, and that she was feeling weightily virtuous clearing it up. He watched her small figure, careful to hide his smile, and when she turned round with immeasurable satisfaction at the end, he was perfectly grave. He did not comment: discipline was Charlotte's preserve while the children were still so young. He preferred to treat his daughter as a very small friend whom he loved with an intensity and a sweetness that still caught him unaware at times, tightening his throat and quickening his heart.

"I've finished," she said solemnly.

"Yes, I see," he replied.

She came over to him and climbed onto his knee as matter-of-factly as she would into a chair, turned herself round, and sat down. Her soft little face was very serious. Her eyes were gray and her brows a finer, child's echo of Charlotte's.

He seldom noticed that her hair had the curl and texture of his, only that it was the rich color of her mother's.

"Tell me a story, Papa," she requested, although from the way in which she had settled herself and the certainty in her voice, perhaps it was a command.

"What about?"

"Anything."

He was tired and his imagination exhausted by struggling with the murders of Etheridge and Hamilton. "Shall I read to you?" he suggested hopefully.

She looked at him with reproach. "Papa, I can read to myself! Tell me about great ladies—princesses!"

"I don't know anything about princesses."

"Oh." Disappointment filled her eyes.

"Well," he amended hastily, "only about one."

She brightened. Obviously one would do.

"Once upon a time there was a princess . . ." And he told her what he could remember of the great Queen Elizabeth, daughter of Henry VIII, who despite much danger and many tribulations finally became monarch of all England. He got so involved in it he did not notice Charlotte standing in the doorway.

Finally, having recalled all he could, he looked at Jemima's rapt face.

"What next?" she prompted.

"That's all I know," he admitted.

Her eyes widened in wonder. "Was she real, Papa?"

"Oh yes, as real as you are."

She was very impressed. "Oh!"

Charlotte came in. "And it's really bedtime," she said.

Jemima put her arms round Pitt's neck and kissed him. "Thank you, Papa. Good night."

"Good night, sweetheart."

Charlotte met his eyes for a moment, smiling. Then she picked up Jemima and carried her out of the room, and as Pitt watched them go, he suddenly thought again of Florence Ivory and the child she had loved, and had taken from her.

Would any judge consider Charlotte a "suitable" person? She had married beneath her, regularly meddled in the detection of crimes, had gone careering round music halls and mortuaries, had disguised herself as a missing courtesan, and had driven after a murderess in a carriage chase that had ended up in a fight on a bawdy house floor. And certainly she had campaigned in her own way for reform!

He could not think clearly of what he might feel if any law could visit him and take away his children if his social circumstances were deemed inadequate. The pain of it drenched even his imagination.

And the thought that inevitably followed it was that he could well believe Florence Ivory might have hated Etheridge enough to cut his throat, and Africa Dowell with her, had she known and loved the child too, and seen the grief. It was a conclusion he could not escape, deeply as he wanted to.

He said nothing of it to Charlotte that night, but in the morning when the post came, he noticed the letter in Emily's hand with its Venetian postmark and knew it would be full of news, excitement, and romance. Emily might have debated whether to talk of all the glamor she was enjoying or to temper it, in view of the fact that Charlotte would never see such things, but knowing Emily, he believed she would not patronize Charlotte with such an evasion. And he guessed the mixture of happiness and envy, and the sense of being left out, that Charlotte would feel.

She would say nothing, he knew that. She had not shown him the first letter, nor would she show him this one, because she wanted him to think she cared only that Emily was happy, not about all the things Emily had, and indeed in her heart that was what mattered to her.

He chose this moment to tell her of his involvement in the Westminster murders, both to take her mind from Emily's new and glittering world and to ease a certain loneliness he felt in not so far having shared with her his feelings, his frustration, confusion, and deep awareness of pain.

He sat at the breakfast table eating toast and Charlotte's sharp, pungent marmalade.

"Yesterday I spoke to a woman who may have cut the throats of two men on Westminster Bridge," he said with his mouth full.

Charlotte stopped with her cup halfway to her mouth. "You didn't tell me you were working on that case!" she exclaimed.

He smiled. "There hasn't been much opportunity, what with Emily's wedding. Then I suppose I became involved in the routine, rather sad questions. It doesn't concern anyone you know."

She pulled a little half apologetic face, realizing his unsaid need to speak of something that had puzzled or grieved him. He read her expression, the understanding between them wry and sweet.

"A woman?" she said with raised brows. "Could it really have been a woman? Or do you mean she paid someone else?"

"This woman, I think, could have done it herself. She has the passion, and believes she has cause—"

"Has she?" Charlotte interrupted quickly.

"Perhaps." He took another bit of the toast and it crumbled in his hand. He picked up the pieces and finished them before taking another slice. Charlotte waited impatiently. "I think you would feel she had," he said, and he outlined for her all that had happened so far, enlarging his opinions of Florence Ivory and Africa Dowell, finding depth and subtlety in them as he searched for the precise words he wanted.

She listened almost without interruption, only mentioning briefly that Florence Ivory's name had been spoken in the public meeting, but since she had learned nothing of her, except that she was an object of pity or contempt, she did not elaborate, and when he finished there was no time to discuss it. He was already late, but he felt lighter-footed and easier of heart, though nothing had changed, no new insight had flashed on his inner mind.

But as he walked along the damp street towards the thoroughfare where he could get a hansom to Westminster, he did wish he could take her just once to someplace exciting and different, give her one glamorous memory to rival Emily's. But stretch his imagination as he might, he could see no way of affording it.

When he was gone Charlotte sat for several minutes thinking of Florence Ivory, her loss and her anger, before she pushed the matter aside and opened the letter. It was headed Venice and read:

> My dearest Charlotte,
>
> What a journey! So long—and noisy. There was a Madame Charles from Paris who talked all the way and had a laugh like a terrified horse. I never want to hear her voice again! I was so tired and dirty when I got here I was ready to cry. It was dark, and I simply fell into a carriage and was taken to our hotel, where all I wanted was to wash off some of the soot and grime before climbing into bed to sleep for a week.
>
> Then in the morning, what magic! I opened my eyes to see light rippling across an exquisite ceiling and to hear, beauty of beauties, the sound of a man's voice singing, lyrical as an angel, drifting across the morning air outside, almost echoing!
>
> I jumped up, mindless of my nightgown or my hair in a tangle, not caring in the slightest how I looked or what Jack would think of me, and ran to the great window, at least two feet deep, and leaned out.
>
> Water! Charlotte, there was water everywhere!

Green and like a mirror, lapping right up to the walls. I could have leaned out and dropped no more than ten feet into it! It was the light reflected from its wind-dappled surface that I had seen on the ceiling.

The man who sang was standing up as graceful as a reed in the stern of a boat that drifted along, moved by a long pole or oar, I'm not certain which. His body swayed as he moved, and he was singing from pure joy at the loveliness of the day. Jack tells me he does it for money from tourists, but I refuse to believe him. I should have sung for joy, had I been afloat on that canal in the sparkling morning.

Opposite us there is a palace of marble—honestly! I have been for a ride in one of the boats, which are called gondolas, and have been right across the lagoon to the Church of Santa Maria della Salute. Charlotte, you never even in your dreams saw anything so utterly beautiful! It seems to float on the very surface of the sea like a vision. Everything is pale marble, blue air and water, and gold sunlight. The quality of the light is different here, there is a clarity to it—it is a different color, somehow.

I love the sound of the Italian language, there is a music in it to my ear. I prefer it to the French, although I understand scarcely a word of either.

But the smell! Oh dear—that is something quite different, and very trying. But I swear I shall not let it destroy one moment of my pleasure. I think I am noticing it less as I become accustomed to it.

It has also taken me a little time to become used to the food, and I am terribly tired of the same clothes all the time, but I can pack and carry only so much. And the laundry service is far from what I might wish!

I have bought several paintings already, one for you, one for Thomas, and one for Mama, and two for myself, because I want to remember this for ever and ever.

I do miss you, in spite of everything I am seeing and even though Jack is so sweet and full of conversation. Since I do not know where I am going to be, or when, or how long letters will take to reach me, I cannot send you an address so that you may write to me. I shall just have to look forward to seeing you when I get home again, and then you must tell me everything. I am longing to hear what you have done, and thought, and felt—and learned?

Give my love to Thomas and the children. I have written separately to Mama and Edward, of course. And don't get into any adventures without me,

Your loving sister,
Emily

Charlotte folded the letter and slipped it back into its envelope. She would put it in her work basket; that was one place Pitt would not find it. She would tell him that Emily was having a wonderful time, of course, but it would only hurt him to read of all the things Emily and Jack were able to see, and he and Charlotte were not. She could not pretend to him she was not envious, that she did not want to see Venice, the beauty and history and romance of it: he would not believe her if she did.

Better just to tell him Emily was enjoying herself. He would suppose she did not show him the letter because it contained some secret between sisters, perhaps even some details of personal life. After all, Emily was on her honeymoon.

She got up from the kitchen table and put the letter in her apron pocket and began organizing the day. It was spring; she would do some fierce cleaning and renew everything possible. She already had an idea for new curtains on the landing.

Pitt went to the House of Commons in the Palace of Westminster and sought permission to go to Etheridge's office and examine what papers were there, in search of letters and documents that might have to do with William or Florence Ivory. He would also inquire whether there was an office in Etheridge's constituency which might have notes or correspondence on the matter.

A junior official in a stiff winged collar and gold-rimmed pince-nez looked at him dubiously.

"I don't recall the name. What was it concerning? Mr. Etheridge had many constituents appeal for his time or intervention in matters of all natures."

"The custody of a child."

"There is an ordinary law which deals with such matters." The clerk looked over the top of his pince-nez. "I imagine Mr. Etheridge will have replied to Mr. or Mrs. Ivory informing them of the fact, and that will be all the record we have, if indeed we have that. Space is limited; we cannot store trivial correspondence forever."

"The custody of a child is not trivial!" Pitt said with barely controlled rage. "If you cannot find the correspondence, then I'll send in men and they can go through every piece of paper there is until either we find it or we know that it is not here. Then we will look in Lincolnshire."

The man flushed faintly pink, but it was irritation, not embarrassment.

"Really Inspector, I think you forget yourself! You have no mandate to search all Mr. Etheridge's papers."

"Then find me the ones referring to William and Florence Ivory," Pitt snapped. "I imagine you have concluded for yourself that it may have to do with murder."

The man's lips tightened and he swung round and marched away along the corridor, with Pitt at his heels. They came to the office Etheridge had shared with another member of Parliament, and the official muttered a few words under his breath to a more junior clerk. Standing at a cabinet full of files, the clerk looked with some alarm at Pitt.

"Ivory?" he looked confused. "I don't recall anything. What date was it?"

Pitt realized he did not know; he had not asked. It was a stupid omission, but too late to rectify now.

"I don't know," he replied with as much coolness as he could muster. "Start at the present and work backwards."

The clerk looked at him as if he had been something alive on the dinner plate, then swiveled round to a set of files and began searching, moving his fingers through the piles of papers.

The official sighed and excused himself, and his heels tapped away along the corridor into the distance; Pitt stood still in the office and waited.

It did not take as long as he had expected. Within five minutes the clerk pulled out a thin file and produced one letter. He held it up with a pinched look of distaste.

"Here you are, sir, a copy of one letter from Mr. Etheridge to a Mrs. Florence Ivory, dated the fourth of January, 1886." He held it out for Pitt to take. "Although I cannot imagine how it will be of interest to the police."

Pitt read it.

Dear Mrs. Ivory,

I regret your very natural distress in the matter of your daughter, but it has been decided, and I fear I cannot enter into any further correspondence with you upon the subject.

I am sure you will come in time to appreciate that all actions that have been taken were in the best interests of the child, which you as her mother must in the end also desire,

Yours faithfully,
Vyvyan Etheridge, M.P.

"That cannot be all!" Pitt said peremptorily. "This is obviously the end of a considerable correspondence! Where is the rest of it?"

"That is all I have," the clerk said with a sniff. "I expect it is a constituency matter. I daresay it is in Lincolnshire."

"Then give me the address in Lincolnshire," Pitt demanded. "I shall go and search there."

The man wearily wrote several lines of instruction on a piece of paper and passed it over. Pitt thanked him and left.

Back at Bow Street he went straight up to Micah Drummond's office and rapped impatiently on the door.

"Come in!" Drummond looked up from a pile of papers, and seemed relieved to see Pitt. "Any news? The further we look at the various anarchist groups we know, the less we find anything."

"Yes sir." Pitt sat down without being invited; he was too preoccupied with his thoughts for it to have crossed his mind. "There is a past constituent of Etheridge's it appears he promised to help in a matter of child custody, and then he sided with the father. She lost the child and is distraught with the pain of it. She has admitted she considers there are times when violence is the only recourse for certain wrongs. The evidence is that Etheridge betrayed her. However, she denies having murdered him."

"But you think she did?" Drummond's pleasure at the thought of a solution was already dimmed by his own perception of the motive, and by something in Pitt's anger, a darkness that Drummond knew was not directed at the woman.

"I don't know. But it is too probable not to investigate. Most of the letters may be at the constituency office, which is in his country home in Lincolnshire. I will have to go there and search. I shall need a warrant, in case some clerk or secretary refuses me permission, and a rail ticket."

"Do you want to go tonight?"

"Yes."

Drummond considered Pitt for a moment. Then he reached for a bell and rang it, and as soon as a constable appeared he gave his orders.

"Go to Inspector Pitt's home and inform Mrs. Pitt that he will be away tonight; have her pack him a valise, including sandwiches, and return here as quickly as you can. Keep the cab at the door. On your way out tell Parkins to make out a search warrant for the Lincolnshire home of Mr. Vyvyan Etheridge, for papers or letters that might contain threats to his life or his welfare, and anything to or from. . . ?"

"Florence or William Ivory," Pitt supplied.

"Right. Jump to it, man!"

The constable disappeared. Drummond looked back at Pitt. "Do you think it conceivable this poor woman did it alone?"

"Not likely." Pitt remembered her slender frame and the passion in her face, and the protective arm of the younger, bigger woman. "She was taken in by a Miss Africa Dowell, who knew the child as well, and seems to sympathize with the Ivory woman intensely."

"Not unnatural." Drummond's face was grave and sad. He had children of his own, who were grown now, and his wife was dead. He missed family life. "What about Hamilton? A mistake?"

"Almost certainly, if it was she. I don't know how many times she actually met Etheridge, if at all."

"You said this Africa Dowell—you did say Africa?"

Pitt gave the ghost of a smile. "Yes, that's what Mrs. Ivory called her: Africa Dowell."

"Well if this Africa Dowell took her in, that suggests Mrs. Ivory has little means, so she could not have paid anyone else to kill Etheridge. It seems a very . . . a very efficiently violent method for a woman. What is she like, what background? Was she a farm girl or something that she might be so skilled in cutting throats?"

"I don't know," Pitt admitted. It was another thing he

had forgotten to inquire. "But she is a woman of great passion and certainly intelligence, and I think courage. I imagine she would be equal to it, if she set her mind to it. But I gathered from the home, which was very attractive and in a good area, that Miss Dowell has money. They could have paid someone."

Drummond pulled a small face. "Well, either way it could account for Hamilton's having been the first victim through a mistake of identity. You'd better go to Lincolnshire and see what you can find out. Bring everything back with you." He looked up, his eyes meeting Pitt's, and for several seconds it seemed he was about to add something. Then at last he changed his mind and shrugged slightly. "Report to me when you get back," was all he said.

"Yes, sir." Pitt left and went downstairs to await the constable's return with his things. He knew what Drummond had wanted to say: the case must be solved, and soon. As they had feared, the public outcry was shrill, in some of the newspapers almost to the point of hysteria. The very fact that the victims had been the representatives of the people, that the crimes had struck at the foundation of everything that was freedom, stability, and order, made the violence in the heart of the city a threat to everyone. The murders seemed to reflect the soul of revolution itself, dark and savage, an unreasoning thing that might run amok and destroy anyone—everyone. Some even spoke of the guillotine of the Reign of Terror in Paris, and gutters running with blood.

And yet neither Drummond nor Pitt wanted to think that one woman had been driven to take insane revenge for the loss of her child.

Pitt arrived at the Broad Street Station of the Great Northern Railway just in time to catch his train to Lincolnshire. He slammed the carriage door as the engine started to belch forth steam and the fireman stoked the furnace, and with a roar and a clash of iron they moved out of the vast, grimy dome into the sunlight and began the long journey past the factories and houses and through the suburbs of the largest, wealthiest, and most populous city in the world. Within its bounds lived more Scots than in Edinburgh, more Irish than in Dublin, and more Roman Catholics than in Rome.

Pitt felt a sense of awe at the city's sheer teeming enormity as he sat in his carriage watching the rows and rows of houses rush past him, grimed with the flying steam and smuts of innumberable trains just like his. Nearly four million people lived here, from those ashen-faced waifs who perished of cold and hunger, to the richest, most talented and beautiful people in all a civilized nation. It was the heart of an empire which spanned the world—the fount of art, theater, opera and music hall, laughter, law, and abuse and monumental greed.

He ate his sandwiches of cold meat and pickle and was glad to get out and stretch his cramped legs at last when he arrived at Grantham in midafternoon. It took him another hour and a half to travel by a branch line and then a hired pony and trap to the country home of the late Vyvyan Etheridge. The door was opened by a caretaking manservant, whom Pitt had some difficulty in persuading of his errand, and that it was legitimate.

It was after four o'clock when he finally stood in the waning light in Etheridge's study, another sumptuous and elegant room lined with books, and began to search through the papers. He was reading by lamplight and hunched up with cold an hour later when he finally found what he had come for.

The first letter was very simple and dated nearly two years ago.

Dear Mr. Etheridge,

I appeal to you as my member of Parliament to assist me in my present distress. My story is a simple one. I married at nineteen at my parents' arrangement, to a man several years older than myself and of a nature most grim and autocratic. I endeavored to please him and to find some happiness, or at least to learn it, for twelve years. During that time I bore him three children, one of whom died. The other two, a boy and a girl, I cared for and loved with all my heart.

However, in time my husband's manner and his unyielding domination of my life, even in the smallest things, made me so wretched I determined to live apart from him. When I broached the subject he was not at all unwilling, indeed I think he had grown quite tired of me and found the prospect of his release from my company without disgrace to himself an agreeable solution.

He insisted that my son remain with him, in his sole custody, and that I should have no influence upon him nor say in his future life. My daughter he permitted to come with me.

I asked no financial provision, and he made none either for me or for our daughter, Pamela, known to us as Pansy, then aged six. I found lodgings and some small labor with a woman of reasonable means, and all was well, until this last month my husband has suddenly demanded the custody of our daughter again, and the thought of losing my child is more than I can bear. She is well and happy with me and wants for none of the necessities of life, nor does she lack regarding her education and moral welfare.

Please defend me in this matter, as I have no other to turn to.

I remain most sincerely yours,
Florence Ivory

There followed a copy of Etheridge's response.

My dear Mrs. Ivory,

I am most touched by your plight, and will look into the matter immediately. It seems to me that your original agreement with your husband was a most reasonable one, and since you asked of him no support, he has acted less than honorably and can have no claim upon you, still less to remove so young a child from her mother.

I shall write to you again when I have further information.

Until then I remain yours sincerely,

Vyvyan Etheridge

The next letter was also Etheridge's own copy of one he had written to Florence Ivory, dated two weeks later.

My dear Mrs. Ivory,

I have inquired further into your situation, and I see no cause for you to distress yourself, or fear for yourself or your daughter's happiness. I have spoken with your husband and assured him that he has no grounds for his demand. A child of Pansy's tender years is far better in the care of her natural mother than that of some housekeeper or hired nurse, and as you have stated, she does not lack for any of the appurtenances of health, education, and a sound moral upbringing.

I doubt that you will be troubled further in the matter, but if you are, please do not hesitate to inform me, and I will see that legal counsel is obtained and a decision handed down that will ensure you are not threatened or caused anxiety again.

I remain yours sincerely,

Vyvyan Etheridge.

This was followed by a letter in a quite different hand.

Dear Mr. Etheridge,

Further to our discussion on the 4th day of last month, I think perhaps you are not aware of the conduct and character of my wife, Mrs. Florence Ivory, who somewhat misrepresented herself to you when seeking your intervention to prevent my receiving custody of my daughter, Pamela Ivory.

My wife is a woman of violent emotions and sudden and immature fancies. She has unfortunately little sense of what is fit, and is most self-indulgent of her whims. It pains me to say so, but I cannot consider her a suitable person to undertake the upbringing of a child, most especially a girl, whom she would imbue with her own wild and unbecoming ideas.

I do not wish to have to inform you, but circumstances compel me. My wife has taken up several socially contentious and radical causes, including that of desiring the parliamentary franchise for women. She has taken her support for this extraordinary cause so far as publicly to visit and be seen with Miss Helen Taylor, a most fanatic and revolutionary person who parades herself wearing trousers!

She has also sought the company and expressed considerable admiration for a Mrs. Annie Bezant, who has also left the home of her husband, the Reverend Bezant, and employs herself stirring up industrial ill-will among match girls and the like employed in the factory of Bryant and Mays. She is fomenting unrest and advocating strikes!

I am sure you can see from this that my wife is no fit person to have the custody of my daughter, and I therefore request that you offer her no further assistance in the matter. It can only lead to distress for my daughter, and if her mother should prevail, to her ruin.

Your obedient servant,
William Ivory

And Etheridge's copy of his reply:

Dear Mr. Ivory,

Thank you for your letter regarding your wife, Florence Ivory, and the custody of your daughter. I have met with Mrs. Ivory and found her a strong-willed woman of forcible and perhaps ill-found opinions regarding certain social issues, but her behavior was perfectly seemly, and she is obviously devoted to her daughter, who is well cared for, in good health, and progressing with her education in a most satisfactory manner.

While I agree with you that Miss Taylor's behavior is quite extreme and cannot possibly profit her cause, I do not believe that your wife's support of her constitutes sufficient ill judgment to make her unfit to care for her child, and as you know, the law now allows a woman, if widowed, to be sole guardian of her children. Therefore I feel in this instance that so young a girl as Pansy is best cared for by her mother, and I hope that this will continue to be the case.

Yours sincerely
Vyvyan Etheridge

Here, as was clear from the handwriting of the letter which followed, a fourth voice joined the correspondence.

Dear Vyvyan,

I hear from William Ivory, a good friend of mine, that you have befriended his unfortunate wife in the matter of the custody of their daughter Pamela. I must tell you that I feel you are ill-advised in the matter. She is a headstrong woman who has publicly espoused some highly contentious and undesirable causes, including the parliamentary franchise for women, and worse than that, industrial militancy among some of the most unskilled labor in the city.

She has openly expressed her sympathy with the match girls at Bryant and Mays and encouraged them to withdraw their labor!

If we support such people, who knows where the general dissension and upheaval may end? You must be aware that there is unrest in the country already, and a strong element that desires the overthrow of the social order, to be replaced with God knows what! Anarchy, by the way they speak.

I must strongly recommend that you give no further aid of any sort to Florence Ivory, indeed that you assist poor William to obtain custody of his unfortunate child forthwith, before she can be further injured by the eccentric and undisciplined behavior of her mother.

I remain yours in friendship,
Garnet Royce, M.P.

Garnet Royce! So the civilized and arbitrary Garnet Royce, so solicitous of his sister's affairs, so concerned to be helpful, was the one who had sided with convention, and robbed Florence Ivory of her child. Why? Ignorance—conservatism—returning some old favor—or simply a belief that Florence did not know how to care for her own child's welfare?

He turned back to the copy of Etheridge's next letter.

Dear Mrs. Ivory,

I regret to inform you that I am looking further into the matter of your husband's plea for the custody of your daughter. I find that the circumstances are not as I first surmised, or as you led me to believe.

Therefore I am obliged to withdraw my support from your cause, and to put my weight behind your husband's effort to give his guardianship and care to both his children, and to raise them in an orderly and God-fearing home.

Yours faithfully,
Vyvyan Etheridge

Mr. Etheridge,

I could hardly believe it when I opened your letter! I called upon you immediately, but your servant would not admit me. I felt sure that after your promises to me, and your visit to my home, that you could not possibly so betray my trust.

If you do not help me I shall lose my child! My husband has sworn that if he obtains custody I shall not ever be permitted to see her, much less talk and play with her, teach her what I love and believe, or even assure her that it is not my will that we part, and that I shall love her with all my strength as long as I live!

Please! Please help me.

Florence Ivory

> You do not reply! Please, Mr. Etheridge, at least hear me. I am not unfit to care for my child! What offense have I committed?
>
> Florence Ivory

And from the last one, written in a scrawl ragged with emotion:

> My child is gone. I cannot put my pain into words, but one day you will know everything that I feel, and then you will wish with all the power of your soul that you had not so betrayed me!
>
> Florence Ivory

Pitt folded the note and put it together with the rest of the correspondence in a large envelope. He stood up, banging his knee against the desk without feeling it. His mind was in the darkness on Westminster Bridge, and with two women in a room in Walnut Tree Walk, a room full of chintz and sunlight, and pain that spilled out till it soaked the air.

7

IT WAS THE DAY after Pitt went to Lincolnshire that Charlotte received a hand-delivered letter a little before noon. She knew immediately she saw the footman with the envelope in his hand that it was from Great-aunt Vespasia; her first dreadful thought was that some illness had befallen the old lady, but then she saw that the footman was in ordinary livery, and his face bore no mark of grief.

Charlotte bade him wait in the kitchen. Hurrying into the parlor, she tore open the paper and read Vespasia's thin, rather eccentric hand:

> My dear Charlotte,
>
> An old friend of mine, whom I am perfectly sure you would like, is greatly afraid that her favorite niece is suspected of murder. She has come to me for help, and I come to you. With your experience and skill we may be able to discern the truth—at least I intend to try!
>
> If you are able to accompany my footman to visit me and begin a plan of campaign this afternoon, please do so. If you are not, then write and let me know the soonest that you will have a moment to spare. Already it grows late, and time is short.
>
> Yours affectionately,
> Vespasia Cumming-Gould

P.S. There is no need to dress glamorously for the occasion. Nobby is the least formal of people and her anxiety far outweighs her sense of occasion.

There was only one possible reply. Charlotte knew very well what it is like to have someone very dear to you suspected of murder, and to feel all the fear of arrest, imprisonment, trial, even hanging racing nightmarishly through your mind. She had known it with Emily so very recently. Aunt Vespasia had stood by them then. Of course she would go.

"Gracie!" she called as she walked back from the parlor towards the kitchen. "Gracie, I have been called away, to help someone in trouble. Please give the children their lunch, and their tea if necessary. This is an emergency; I shall return when the matter is in hand."

"Oh yes, ma'am!" Gracie turned her attention from the footman and the cup of tea she was passing him. "Is it illness, ma'am, or"—she tried to keep the light of excitement out of her eyes, and failed—"is it . . ." She could not find the right word for the mixture of peril and adventure dancing on the edge of her imagination. She knew of Charlotte's battles with crime in the past, but she did not dare speak of them openly now.

Charlotte smiled wryly. "No Gracie, it is not illness," she conceded.

"Oh, ma'am!" Gracie breathed out a sigh of exquisite anticipation. Dark and wonderful adventures raced through her mind. "Do be careful, ma'am!"

Forty minutes later Charlotte alighted from the carriage, assisted by the footman, and climbed the stairs to the front door of Great-aunt Vespasia's town house. It opened before she raised her hand to the knocker, indicating that she was expected, indeed awaited, but she was surprised to see that it was the butler himself who stood in the entrance, grave and elegant.

"Good morning, Mrs. Pitt. Lady Cumming-Gould is in the withdrawing room, if you care to go through. Luncheon will be served presently in the breakfast room."

"Thank you." Charlotte handed him her cape and followed him across the parquet floor of the hallway. He opened the door for her, and she passed into the withdrawing room.

Great-aunt Vespasia was sitting in her favorite chair by the fire. Opposite her was a woman almost gawkily lean, with a face of marvelous, dynamic ugliness, so full of intelligence it had its own kind of beauty. Her eyes were very dark, her brows fiercely winged, her nose too powerful, mouth humorous, perhaps in youth even tender. She was nearly sixty, and her complexion had been ruined by all kinds of weather, from the extremes of ocean wind to the heat of a tropical sun. She gazed at Charlotte with quite undisguised curiosity.

"Come in, Charlotte," Vespasia said quickly. "Thank you, Jeavons. Call us when luncheon is ready." She turned to the other woman. "This is Charlotte Pitt. If anyone can give us really practical help it is she. Charlotte, Miss Zenobia Gunne."

"How do you do, Miss Gunne," Charlotte said courteously, although a single glance at the woman made her feel sure such formality was soon going to be dismissed.

"Sit down," Vespasia directed, waving her lace-cuffed hand. "We have a great deal to do. Nobby will tell you what we know so far."

Charlotte obeyed, catching the urgency in Vespasia's voice and realizing the other woman must be profoundly worried to have come for help to a person she had never met before, nor even heard of socially.

"I am most grateful for your attention," Zenobia Gunne said to Charlotte. "The situation is this: My niece owns a house south of the river, inherited from her parents, my younger brother, and his wife upon their death some twelve years go. Africa—my brother called her after that continent because I spent a great many years exploring it, and he was fond of me—Africa is a girl of intelligence and independent opinions, and a very lively compassion, especially for those whom she feels to have suffered injustice."

Zenobia was watching Charlotte's face as she spoke, trying already to ascertain what impression she might be forming.

"Some two or three years ago Africa met a woman a few years older than herself, perhaps twelve or fourteen, who had left her husband, taking with her her young daughter. She had managed quite adequately on her own resources for some time, but when some change in circumstance made this no longer possible, Africa offered both the woman and the child a home. She grew very fond of both of them, and they of her.

"Now, the part of the story that concerns us is that the woman's vicious husband sought to obtain custody of the child. She appealed to her member of Parliament, who promised to assist her, which for some time he did. Suddenly he changed his mind and instead gave his aid to the husband, who then won his custody order for the child and forthwith removed her. The mother has not seen her since."

"And the husband has been murdered?" Charlotte asked, fearing already that there was going to be nothing she or anyone could do to help.

"No." Zenobia's remarkable eyes held hers unflinchingly, but for the first time Charlotte realized that there was both resolution and pain in them, clearly justifying all Vespasia's fears. "No, it is the member of Parliament who has been murdered, Mrs. Pitt."

Charlotte felt a chill, as if that night on the Bridge with its chill and fog from the river had entered the room. This was Thomas's case that he had told her of with such confusion and pity. She knew all London was appalled by the crimes, not merely by their nature but by the identity of the victims and the apparent ease with which able men, men both cherished and respected, the makers of law, had been killed within sight of the Mother of Parliaments.

"Yes," Zenobia said very quietly indeed, her eyes on

Charlotte's face. "The Westminster Bridge murders. I fear the police may believe it was Africa and her lodger who committed these terrible acts. The poor woman certainly had motive enough, and neither she nor Africa can prove themselves innocent."

Pitt's description of them was sharp in Charlotte's memory, his sense of Florence Ivory's anger and grief, and the passion he was sure could bring her to kill. The question beat in Charlotte's head so, nothing else could form itself or find shape. Had they? *Had they?*

"Charlotte, we must do all we can to help," Vespasia said briskly, before the silence could become painful. "Where do you suggest we begin?"

Charlotte's mind was whirling. How well did Great-aunt Vespasia know this woman with the extraordinary face? Were they lifelong friends, or merely social acquaintances? They were a generation apart. If they had been friends years ago, what had happened to them since? How much had they changed and grown separate, been marked by experience, learned to value different things, to love different people? What sort of a woman explored Africa? Why? With whom? Did she perhaps count family loyalty above the lives of those who were not of her class or kin? It was ridiculous to be discussing this in front of her, where Charlotte could not be frank.

"At the beginning," Zenobia said gravely into the silence, answering Vespasia's question. "No, I do not know that Africa is innocent. I believe it, but I cannot know it, and I realize that if we attempt to help her, there is a possibility that we may do exactly the opposite. I am prepared to take that risk."

Charlotte collected her thoughts and attempted to set them forth logically. "Then if we cannot prove them innocent," she said, "we shall have to see if we can discover who is guilty—and prove that." There was no purpose in being falsely modest or decorous with this woman. "I have read something of the matter in the newspapers," she admitted.

At this point she would not say that her husband was the detective in charge of the case—Zenobia might find it impossible to believe she could be impartial, and it would place an intolerable burden of double loyalty upon Vespasia.

She knew it was not the thing for ladies of quality to read anything in the newspapers except the society pages, and perhaps a little of the theater or reviews of suitable books or paintings, but there was no point in pretending she was of delicate sensibilities—even could she have carried it off—if they were going to discover the authors of any crimes at all, let alone such as these.

"What do we know of the facts?" she began. "Two members of Parliament have been murdered at night, upon Westminster Bridge, by having their throats cut, and then their bodies were tied up by their evening scarves to the lamppost at the south end of the bridge. The first was Sir Lockwood Hamilton, the second a Mr. Vyvyan Etheridge." She looked at Zenobia. "Why should this woman—what is her name?"

"Florence Ivory."

"Why should Florence Ivory kill both men? Were they both connected in some way with the loss of her child?"

"No, only Mr. Etheridge. I have no idea why the police believe she should have killed Sir Lockwood as well."

Charlotte was puzzled. "Are you sure she has reason to be afraid, Miss Gunne? Is it not possible the police are merely questioning everyone who had cause to hold a grudge against either victim, in the hope they might discover something, and entertain no real suspicions towards Mrs. Ivory or your niece?"

A fleeting smile crossed Zenobia's face, a mixture of irony, amusement, and regret. "It is a hope to cling to, Mrs. Pitt, but Africa said the policeman who came to see them was an unusual man; he did not bluster or threaten them in the least and seemed to find no satisfaction whatever in having discovered the power of their motive. Florence told him her story and made no attempt to hide either the depth of her grief at the loss of her child or her hatred of Etheridge. Africa said she watched the man's face, and she believes he would have preferred to discover an alternative solution to his case; indeed, she was convinced the story weighed him down. But she was also equally certain that he will investigate it and return. And since they have no witness that they were at home alone in the house, which is not far from Westminster Bridge, and as they have abundant motive, and as indeed Africa has sufficient money to have employed someone else to perform the actual task, they fear they may well be arrested."

Charlotte could not help but believe it also, except for the unlikelihood of their having killed Lockwood Hamilton as well. And it seemed improbable, but not impossible, that there was another such murderer loose in London.

"Then if it was not Africa and Mrs. Ivory," she answered. "It must have been someone else. We had better set about finding out who!"

Zenobia fought against a rising panic. She mastered it, but Charlotte could see clearly in her eyes her knowledge of the enormity of the task, the near hopelessness of it.

Vespasia sat up a little straighter in her chair, her chin high, but it was courage speaking rather than belief, and they all knew it.

"I am sure Charlotte will have an idea. Let us discuss it over luncheon. Shall we go through to the breakfast room? I thought it would be pleasant there; the daffodils are in bloom and there is always an agreeable view." And she rose, brushing away Charlotte's assistance, and led the way through as if it had been the most casual of occasions, the renewing of an old friendship and the making of a new one, and there was nothing more serious to consider than what to wear this evening and upon whom they might call tomorrow.

The breakfast room was parquet-floored like the hall and had French windows opening onto the paved terrace. There were china cabinets full of Minton porcelain in blue and white round the walls, and a full service of white Rockingham scrolled and tipped in gold. A gateleg table was set for three, and the parlormaid waited to serve the soup.

When they began the second course, which was chicken and vegetables, and the servants had temporarily left, Vespasia looked up and met Charlotte's gaze, and Charlotte knew it was time to begin. She forgot the succulence of the meat and the sweetness of the spring sprouts.

"If it is anarchists or revolutionaries," she said carefully, weighing her logic as she went and trying not to think of Florence Ivory and her child, or of Zenobia Gunne, calm, attentive, but under her composure desperately aware of tragedy, "or a madman, then there is very little chance that we shall discover who it is. Therefore, we had best direct our efforts where we have some possibility of success—which is to say we must assume Sir Lockwood and Mr. Etheridge were killed by someone who knew them and had a personal reason for wishing them dead. As far as I can think, there are very few emotions strong enough to drive an otherwise sane person to such extremes: hatred, which covers revenge for past wrongs; greed; and fear, fear of some physical danger, or more likely the fear of losing something precious, such as one's good reputation, love, honor or position, or simply peace from day to day."

"We know very little about either of the victims," Zenobia said with a frown, and again a touch of understanding that the task might be far greater than she had hoped when she appealed to Vespasia.

It was not the difficulty that disturbed Charlotte, but the fear that in the end they would discover it was indeed Florence Ivory who had brought about the murders, if not directly, then by the even greater misdeed of employing someone else to commit the act.

"That is what we must set ourselves to do," she said aloud, pushing the vegetables round her plate—suddenly the delicacy of their taste no longer mattered. "We are in a far better position than the police to meet the appropriate people at a time and in a manner we can observe them unguarded.

And because we are in many ways of a similar station in life, we can understand what is in their minds, what lies behind their words."

Vespasia folded her hands in her lap and paid attention like a schoolgirl in class. "With whom shall we begin?" she asked.

"What do we know of Mr. Etheridge?" Charlotte inquired. "Has he a widow, family, a mistress?" She saw with some satisfaction that Zenobia's face registered no horror, nor any indication that her sense of decency had been offended. "And if those avenues prove fruitless, then had he rivals in business, or professionally?"

"The *Times* said that he was a widower and leaves one daughter, married to a James Carfax," Vespasia offered. "Sir Lockwood left a widow, and a son by his first marriage."

"Excellent. That is where we shall start. It will always be easier for us both to meet with women and to make judgments and observations of them that may be useful. So we have Mr. Etheridge's daughter—"

"Helen Carfax," Vespasia supplied.

Charlotte nodded. "And Lady Amethyst Hamilton. Is the son married?"

"Nothing was said of a wife."

Zenobia leaned forward. "I have a very slight acquaintance with a Lady Mary Carfax; it was some time ago now, but I believe, if I remember accurately, that her son was named James."

"Then renew the acquaintance," Vespasia said instantly.

Zenobia's mobile mouth turned down. "We disliked each other," she said reluctantly. "She disapproved of me for going to Africa, among other things. She felt—and said—that I disgraced both my birth and my sex by behaving totally unsuitably on almost every occasion. And I thought her pompous, narrow-minded, and completely without imagination."

"No doubt you were both correct," Vespasia said tartly. "But since she is unlikely to have improved with time, and you wish information of her, not she of you, then it is you who will have to accommodate yourself to her social prejudices and remember your niece profoundly enough to force yourself to be agreeable to her."

Zenobia had faced the insects and heat of the Congo, the discomforts of trekking across deserts and sailing in canoes, fought against exhaustion, disease, outraged family, stubborn officials, and mutinous natives. She had endured heartache, ostracism, and loneliness. She was more than equal now to the self-discipline required of her to be civil to Lady Mary Carfax, since it was so evidently necessary.

"Of course," she agreed simply. "What else?"

"One of us will visit Lady Hamilton," Charlotte went on. "Aunt Vespasia, perhaps that had better be you. None of us knows her, so we shall have to invent an excuse. You can say you knew Sir Lockwood through your work for social reform, and you have come to express your condolences."

"I did not know him," Vespasia replied, waving one long hand in the air. "Which I agree is immaterial. However, since it is a lie, you can tell it just as well as I. I shall go and see Somerset Carlisle and learn everything I can from him as to the political lives of both men. It is always possible that the crime is political, and it would be wise of us to cover that area of investigation as well."

"Who is Somerset Carlisle?" Zenobia asked curiously. "I am sure I have heard the name."

"He is a member of Parliament," Vespasia answered. "A man of anger, and humor." She smiled as she said it, and Charlotte guessed precisely what wild adventure of the past she was remembering. Vespasia's blue gaze was faraway and almost innocent. "And with a passion to reform. If I tell him our situation, he will help us all he can."

Zenobia tried to look hopeful and nearly succeeded. "When shall we commence?"

"When we have finished luncheon," Vespasia answered her, and a flicker of satisfaction crossed her face as she saw incredulity, then a sudden real hope light Zenobia's eyes, and at last her body lost some of its rigid tension.

When the meal was finished there was very much to be done. The clothes each had worn for the consultation and the laying of plans were not at all suitable for the errands they proposed. Zenobia's very casual attire, with little matching anything else, would be an immediate insult to anyone of Lady Mary Carfax's social susceptibilities, therefore she left to go home and change into the very latest fashion she possessed, which was last year's and very plain, but a great improvement on her present garb nevertheless. It was not that she lacked means, simply that she considered clothes only for their practicality, not their appearance beyond the requirements of decency.

She asked Charlotte if there was anything in particular she should say to Lady Mary, but Charlotte, fearing the meeting was going to be hazardous enough anyway, advised that simply to reopen the acquaintance would be sufficient for now.

Vespasia changed from her light gown, suitable for the house, into something warmer in sky blue wool and with a matching jacket, so she might walk outside without chill. She added something of glamor because she loved beauty and could not abandon it whatever the circumstances. Had she contemplated anything so extraordinary as rowing up the Congo, she would have done so with her hair arranged and in a gown that was both fashionable and individual. Also, she was fond of Somerset Carlisle and retained enough vanity to wish to appear well before him. He might be thirty-five years her junior, but he was still a man.

And for Charlotte Vespasia looked out an anthracite gray gown with a delicious bustle, which was both sober enough in which to express condolences, and sufficiently fashionable to proclaim the wearer a lady. It needed no attention now, because Vespasia had indulged in detecting before, and she had known what some of the requirements would be before she had dispatched the footman to collect Charlotte. Vespasia's lady's maid had been busy most of the morning.

Therefore Charlotte rode with Vespasia in her carriage, setting her down at the residence of Somerset Carlisle before proceeding on to Royal Street.

Her courage was high to begin with, but when she saw Vespasia, her back ramrod straight and wearing her hat at a superbly rakish angle, disappear through the doorway, suddenly she was overcome by the recklessness and the sheer folly of the entire scheme. She had been flattered because Great-aunt Vespasia had turned to her, and she had led both her aunt and Zenobia Gunne to believe she was capable of far more than in truth she was. She was going to end up making a fool of herself, and worse than that, she was going to insult a woman recently bereaved in the most appalling circumstances, and even *more* painful, she was misleading and offering false hope to two elderly women who had trusted her, when they would so much better have placed their faith in the police, or a good lawyer, which they could certainly afford.

The carriage bowled down Whitehall at an excellent pace; there were few afternoon callers with the necessity to pass this way and traffic was very light. They would be under the shadow of Big Ben any minute. She would scarcely have time to compose herself before they reached the Westminster Bridge and crossed it to Royal Street less than a mile on the other side. What on earth was she going to say? It had seemed an adventure over luncheon; now it was merely ridiculous, and very ill-mannered!

Should she tell the coachman to drive twice round the block while she scrambled to devise some believable account she might give of herself? Such as what? "Good afternoon, Lady Hamilton, you don't know me, but my husband is a policeman—actually he is working on your husband's murder—and I have delusions that I can detect. I am going to discover who did it, and why—and I mean to begin by scraping an acquaintance with you! Tell me everything about yourself!"

Should she try to be subtle? Or was some degree of frankness the only way?

The carriage stopped and a moment later the door opened and she was obliged to take the footman's hand and climb out. There was no more time!

Her legs felt weak, as if her knees had no bones in them. She stood on the pavement, knowing the footman and the coachman were both looking at her.

"Please wait," she said breathlessly, and picked up her skirts and walked up to the front door. She did not even have a calling card to present! There was nothing in the world she could do about it now.

The door opened and a parlormaid in black appeared, too well trained to show her surprise.

"Yes ma'am?"

There was nothing to do but plunge ahead.

"Good afternoon. My name is Charlotte Ellison," she said—they might know or remember the name Pitt. "I hope I do not intrude, but I had such an admiration for Sir Lockwood that I wished to call in person to express my condolences to Lady Hamilton, rather than merely to write, which seems so slight a thing to do." She glanced at the silver tray the parlormaid held out, waiting for a card, and felt the color rise in her cheeks. "I am so sorry, I have been abroad and unpacked in such a hurry." She forced a smile. "Would you be kind enough to tell Lady Hamilton that Miss Charlotte Ellison wishes a few moments of her time to express the thoughts of many people who admired Sir Lockwood for his courtesy and compassion, and the wisdom with which he counseled us during our struggle to bring to pass certain reforms in the poor laws and regarding the education of pauper children." That would do; she knew something of that from her desperate struggle with Great-aunt Vespasia and Somerset Carlisle for such a bill when there had been the murders in Resurrection Row. She smiled her most charmingly at the maid, and stood her ground.

"Of course, ma'am." The maid put the empty tray down on the hall table and turned away, closing the door. "If you would care to wait in the morning room, I will see if Lady Hamilton is free to receive you."

In the morning room Charlotte looked round hastily to make some judgment of the woman whose house this was. It was elegant, individual, not overcrowded. Nor did she see the struggle of two personalities, two tastes, any sign that a second wife had taken over from a first. There was nothing discordant, no jarring memories. The only thing she guessed to come from the past was a painting of a cottage garden, faded, a little oversweet, out of character with the cooler watercolors on the other walls, but not displeasing, a sentimental gesture rather than an intrusion.

The door opened and a woman in black came in. She was tall and slender, perhaps in her mid or late forties, with dark hair winged with gray. Her face had known sadness long before this latest blow, but in it there was no anger, no rage at life, and certainly no self-pity.

"I am Amethyst Hamilton," she said politely. "My maid tells me you are Charlotte Ellison, and that you have come to express your condolences for my husband's death. I confess he did not mention your name, but it is very considerate of you to have come in person. Naturally at the moment I am not making or receiving calls, other than those of sympathy, so I shall be taking tea alone. If you care to join me, you are welcome." The briefest of smiles crossed her face and vanished. "Very few people find themselves comfortable in the houses of those in mourning. I should find your company welcome. But of course I understand if you have other calls to make."

Charlotte was assailed with guilt. She knew the terrible isolation of mourning: she had seen Emily's loneliness after George's death the previous year, which, like this woman's, was compounded by the horror of murder, the burdens of a police investigation, and the scandal, and ultimately the terrible fear and suspicion of people one likes and loves intruding into the mind, smearing every memory, touching everything with doubt. And here she was telling lies, using the mask of sympathy to try and learn the secrets of this poor woman's family, learn facts and emotions normally guarded in the presence of the police, all because Charlotte thought her own judgment keener, better able to penetrate the vulnerabilities of her own class and sex.

"Thank you," she replied, her voice cracking, and she swallowed hard. Quite possibly Florence Ivory had killed this woman's husband, mistaking him in the lamplight for another man. "I should like to."

"Then please come through to the withdrawing room. It is warmer. And tell me, Miss Ellison, how you came to know my husband?"

There was no answer except to mix as much of a lie as necessary with all the truth she could remember.

"I worked some time ago on an attempt to have the workhouse laws altered. Of course, I was just a very small part of the attempt; I merely collected a little information. There were others far more important, people with influence and wisdom. Sir Lockwood was most kind to us then, and I felt he was a man of both compassion and integrity."

"Yes," Amethyst Hamilton agreed with a smile, leading the way into the withdrawing room and offering Charlotte a chair by the fire. "You could not have described him better," she said, sitting down herself. "There were many who disagreed with him over one subject or another, but none I ever knew who felt he had been either self-seeking or dishonest." She pulled the bell rope at her elbow, and when the maid appeared she ordered tea to be brought, and after a glance at Charlotte, sandwiches and cakes as well. When the maid had gone she continued speaking.

"It is strange how many people do not wish to speak of the dead. They send cards or flowers, but if they call they talk of the weather or my health, or of their own. Of anything but Lockwood. And I feel as if they are wishing him out of existence. It is most unreasonable of me; I daresay they do it out of consideration for my feelings."

"And perhaps out of embarrassment," Charlotte added, before remembering that this was a formal visit; she did not know this woman at all, and her frank opinions were not called for. She felt the heat rise in her face. "I am sorry."

Amethyst bit her lip. "You are perfectly right, Miss Ellison. We so seldom know how to deal honestly with other people's emotions when we do not share them. It is most unpatriotic of me to say so, but I fear it is something of a national failing."

"Indeed." Charlotte had never been anywhere else, so she had no idea whether it was so or not, but she had just rashly claimed to have returned from a visit abroad, so she could only nod and agree.

"I had a sister," she rushed on, "who died in most tragic circumstances, and I found it exactly the same. Please, if you wish to, tell me of Sir Lockwood, anything you care to recall. I should be neither embarrassed nor uninterested. It is part of the respect we feel for those we admire that we should continue to speak of them when they are no longer with us, and to praise them to others."

"You are very kind, Miss Ellison."

"Not at all." Charlotte felt again a guilt which she expected would hurt her indefinitely, but she could not stop now. "Tell me how you met? I expect it was romantic?"

"Not in the slightest!" Amethyst nearly laughed, and her face became soft at the memory, the echo of the girl she'd been was in the lines of her mouth and the momentary smoothness of her brow. "I bumped into him at a political meeting where I had gone with my elder brother. I remember I was wearing a cream hat with a feather on it, and a necklace of amber beads of which I was so fond I kept fingering it. Unfortunately it broke and scattered all over the floor. I was very upset, and bent to pick the beads up, and only made it worse. The rest cascaded all over the place. One gentleman stepped on one and lost his balance, falling against a large lady with a dog in her arms. She shrieked, the dog jumped and ran away under her neighbor's skirts. All of which put the speaker off, who quite lost his place. Lockwood glared at me and told me to compose myself, because I am afraid I was beginning to giggle. But he did help me find the beads."

Tea was brought and she poured it, having dismissed the maid, and for the next thirty minutes Charlotte listened while she recounted her courtship, and one or two later events in her marriage. None of them showed Lockwood Hamilton as anything but a gentle, rather serious person who, beneath his outer, comfortable, rather pompous public face, was a vulnerable man, deeply in love with his second wife. How he had come to have his throat cut in the darkness on Westminster Bridge grew more inexplicable with every sentence.

It was well after four when the parlormaid knocked and announced that Mr. Barclay Hamilton had called.

Amethyst's skin drained of color and all the life left her eyes. In the midst of the recollections of happiness some pain had plunged right through her and brought back all her present loneliness and tragedy in its wake.

"Ask him to come in," she said, forcing her voice a little. She turned to Charlotte. "My husband's son by his first wife. I hope you do not mind? It will only be a matter of courtesy, and I do not wish you to feel as if you must leave."

"But if it is a family matter," Charlotte felt compelled by duty to offer, "might my presence not cause embarrassment? Surely—"

"No, not at all. We are not close. Indeed your presence may very well make it easier—for both of us."

It was so clearly a plea, for all the formality of her words, that Charlotte felt excused to stay, and wished she had not been.

The parlormaid returned and showed in a man perhaps ten years younger than Amethyst, very lean, with a sensitive face now almost white with tension. He looked only momentarily at Charlotte, but she knew he was disconcerted to see her there, and it robbed him of what he had intended to say.

"Good afternoon," he said uncertainly.

"Good afternoon, Barclay," Amethyst replied coolly. She turned deliberately to Charlotte. "Mr. Barclay Hamilton, Miss Charlotte Ellison, who was kind enough to call in person to express her condolences."

Barclay's face softened in recognition of a generosity.

"How do you do, Miss Ellison." Then before she could reply, he turned back to Amethyst and the moment was gone. "I apologize for calling at an inconvenient time. I brought a few papers regarding the estate." He held them forward in his hand, not so much offering them to her as indicating the reason for his presence.

"Very good of you," Amethyst replied. "But unnecessary. I was not anxious. You could have sent them and avoided the journey."

He looked as if he had been slapped; then his mouth hardened. "They are not of a nature I'd trust to the penny post. Perhaps I did not make myself clear: they are land deeds and rental agreements."

If Amethyst heard the edge in his voice she either refused to acknowledge it or did not care. "I am sure you are better equipped than I to deal with such things. You are, after all, the executor." She did not offer him tea or make the slightest accommodation for him.

"And it is part of my duty to see that you are aware of the circumstances, and understand the properties you now own." He was staring at her, and at last she met his eyes. The blood rushed up in her cheeks, then fled again, leaving her paler than before.

"Thank you for doing your duty." She was polite now, but remote to the point that it became rudeness. "Of course, I would have expected no less of you."

His tone was equally cold and punctilious. "Perhaps you will now do your own and look at them."

Her body stiffened and her head came up. "I think you forget to whom you speak, Mr. Hamilton!"

There were white lines round his mouth forced by the pressure of his feeling, and the effort of self-control. When he spoke his voice shook. "I never forget who you are, madame. Never from the day we met have I forgotten most exactly who and what you are, as God is my judge."

"If you have accomplished all you came to do," she said very quietly, very levelly, "then I think it would be better if you were to leave. I wish you good afternoon."

He inclined his head, first to Amethyst, then to Charlotte. "Good afternoon, ma'am; Miss Ellison." And he turned sharply and marched out, pulling the door behind him with a bang.

For an instant Charlotte considered pretending nothing had happened, but even as the idea crossed her mind she knew it was ridiculous. Before the interruption she and Amethyst had been talking together as friends; there had been a thread of understanding that would make such a charade impossible. It would be a deliberate rebuff, like walking away.

The seconds ticked by, and Amethyst did not move. Charlotte waited until the silence was oppressive, then she leaned across, poured the dregs of Amethyst's tea into the slop basin and filled her cup again from the pot. She stood and went to her.

"You had better have this," she said gently. "It is obviously a distressing relationship. It would be pointless of me to offer my help—there is probably nothing anyone can do—but please accept my sympathy. I too have relatives I find exceedingly trying." She was thinking of Grandmama, which was hardly the same, but when she had been young and living at home, it was difficult enough.

Amethyst regained control of herself and accepted the tea, sipping it in silence for some moments.

"Thank you," she said at last. "You are most considerate. I apologize for subjecting you to such an embarrassing confrontation. I had no idea it would be so—so awkward."

But further than that she said nothing, offering no explanation.

Charlotte did not expect one. It seemed that Barclay Hamilton had so violently resented her marrying his father that even after all these years he had not forgiven her. Perhaps it was a form of jealousy, perhaps a devotion to his mother which would not permit him to let anyone take her place. Poor Amethyst; the ghost of the first Lady Hamilton must have stalked her all her married life. At that moment Charlotte conceived a fierce dislike of Barclay Hamilton, in spite of all she saw in his face that she might otherwise have found peculiarly pleasing.

She was about to help herself to another cake when the parlormaid returned and announced Sir Garnet Royce. He followed her so closely it was impossible for Amethyst to deny that she would see him, and from the calm certainty in his eyes he apparently took it for granted that he was welcome. His brows rose when he saw Charlotte, but it did not disconcert him.

"Good afternoon, Amethyst; good afternoon!"

"Miss Charlotte Ellison," Amethyst supplied. "She has been good enough to come in person to express her sympathy."

"Most kind." Garnet nodded briefly. "Most kind." He had acquitted courtesy, and he ignored her now as he would have a butler or a governess. "Now Amethyst, I have completed the arrangements for a memorial service. I made a list of people it would be suitable to invite, and those who would be offended if they were not included. You can read it, of course, but I am sure you will agree." He did not make any move to pull it out of his pocket. "And I have chosen an order of prayer, and several hymns. I asked Canon Burridge if he would conduct. I am sure he is the most appropriate."

"Is there anything left for me to do?" There was a slight edge to her voice, but not enough to be exceptional in the circumstances. Charlotte would have resented anyone else's taking charge so completely, but perhaps she had become too independent since her marriage and her slide down the social scale. Garnet Royce was doing what he believed best for his sister—his face reflected decisive, practical goodwill—and Amethyst raised no objection, although for an instant a frown flickered across her brow, and she drew breath as if to say something contrary but changed her mind.

"Thank you," she said instead.

Garnet went to the table where Barclay Hamilton had left the papers he had delivered. "What are these?" He picked them up and turned them over. "Property deeds?"

"Barclay brought them," Amethyst explained, and again the shadow of anger and pain crossed her face.

"I'll look at them for you." Garnet made as if to put them in his pocket.

"I should be obliged if you would leave them where they are!" Amethyst snapped. "I am perfectly able to look at them myself!"

Garnet smiled briefly. "My dear, you don't know anything about them."

"Then I shall learn. It would seem an appropriate time," she retorted.

"Nonsense!" he said, good-natured but totally dismissive. "You don't want to be bothered with the details and administration of the estate, and with learning new terms. Law is very difficult and complex for a woman, my dear. Allow your man of affairs to ascertain that everything is in order, as I am sure it is—Lockwood was meticulous about such things—and I will explain to you what it means, what you have, and advise you what steps to take, if any. I doubt there will be much to alter. You should have a holiday, get away from this tragedy, calm your mind and your spirits. It will be good for you in all ways. Believe me, my dear, I still remember my own bereavement clearly enough." His face became shadowed with a memory he did not share except by implication, and Amethyst offered no sympathy. The loss must have been old, or crowded out by her own so current wound.

"Spend a few weeks in Aldeburgh." He looked at her, his distress replaced by solicitude again. "Walk by the sea, take the fresh air, visit with pleasant people and talk of country ways. Get away from London until all this business is over."

She turned away from him and looked out of the small space in the window that was clear beneath the blinds.

"I don't think I wish to."

"Be advised, my dear," he said quite gently, putting the papers in his pocket. "After what has happened you need a complete change. I'm sure Jasper would say the same."

"I'm sure he would!" she said instantly. "He always agrees with you! That does not make him right. I do not wish to leave at the moment, and I will not be pushed!"

He shook his head.

"You are very stubborn, Amethyst. One might almost say willful; not an attractive quality in a woman. You make it very difficult to do what is best for you."

He reminded Charlotte of her father with his blind care, his determination to protect, and at the same time his complete unawareness of the root of one's feelings, of what one might be thinking or dreaming that had nothing to do with the ordinariness of the conversation.

"I appreciate your concern, Garnet," Amethyst said, obviously struggling to keep her patience. "I am not ready to leave yet. When I am I shall ask you, and if your invitation is still open, then I shall be grateful to accept. Until then I am remaining here in Royal Street. And please put those deeds back. It is time I learned what they are and how to administer the properties myself. I am a widow and had better learn how to conduct myself like one."

"You conduct yourself excellently, my dear. Jasper and I will take care of your affairs and counsel you, and of course all legal and financial matters will be dealt with by people of those professions. And in time you may wish to marry again, and we shall keep suitable people in mind."

"I do not wish to marry again!"

"Of course you don't, now. It would hardly be seemly, even if it were desired. But in a year or two . . ."

She swung round to face him. "Garnet, for goodness' sake listen to me for once! I intend to become familiar with my own affairs!"

He was exasperated by her obduracy, her blind refusal to be sensible, but he maintained his even tone and composed expression in spite of all provocation. "You are being most unwise, but I daresay when you have had a little more time you will realize that. Naturally you are still suffering the first shock of your bereavement. I do know how you feel, my dear. Of course, Naomi died from scarlet fever"—his brow furrowed—"but the extraordinary sense of disbelief and loss is the same, whatever the cause."

For a moment Amethyst's eyes opened wide in surprise, then some memory returned, confusing her further, and incredulity and pity filled her face. But he seemed to read none of it. He was absorbed with his own thoughts and plans.

"I shall call again in a day or two." He turned to Charlotte, recalling her presence. "Very courteous of you to have come, Mrs.—er, Miss Ellison. Good day."

"Good day, Sir Garnet," she replied, standing up also. "I am sure it is time I was leaving."

"Did you come in a hansom?"

"No, my carriage is outside," she said without a flicker, exactly as if she were in the habit of having such an equipage at her disposal. She turned to Amethyst. "Thank you for giving me so much of your time, Lady Hamilton. I came to offer my condolences, and I find I have enjoyed your company more than most people's. Thank you."

For the first time since Barclay Hamilton had been announced, Amethyst smiled warmly.

"Please call again—that is, if you do not mind."

"I should be delighted to," Charlotte accepted, without knowing if it would be possible, and without the faintest hope it would further the cause of Florence Ivory and Africa Dowell. In fact her visit had done nothing except confirm that Lockwood Hamilton was exactly what he seemed, and must surely have been killed in mistake for someone else, presumably Vyvyan Etheridge.

She bade them good-bye and climbed into Aunt Vespasia's carriage feeling that she had accomplished nothing, except possibly the elimination of a certain avenue of thought. She would find it very hard to believe Amethyst Hamilton had had anything to do with her husband's death. She might ask Aunt Vespasia to inquire further about Barclay Hamilton; perhaps they might learn something of his mother. But it was a very slender thought. Sharper and blacker was the figure of Florence Ivory. The sooner she formed some personal impression of her, Charlotte felt, the better.

"Walnut Tree Walk, please," she instructed the coachman, before realizing she should not have said please; after all she was instructing a servant, not requesting a friend. She had forgotten how to behave.

Zenobia Gunne sat in her own carriage with many of the same misgivings as Charlotte had had in Vespasia's. She was not in the least afraid of Mary Carfax, but she did not like her, and she knew the feeling was returned with some fervor. It would take an extraordinary reason to bring Zenobia to call upon her unannounced, and Mary would believe nothing less. The last time they had met, at a ball in 1850, Mary had been an imperious and fragile beauty, betrothed satisfactorily but unromantically to Gerald Carfax. Zenobia was single. They had both fallen in love, in their wildly different ways, with Captain Peter Holland. To Mary he had been comely and dashing, and she had suddenly seen romance leaving her forever as she tied herself to Gerald; to Zenobia he had been a man too poor to afford a wife, but the most immense fun, full of laughter and imagination, his mouth always ready to smile, sensitive to the beautiful, and to the absurd, a brave, tender and funny man she had loved with all her heart. He had been killed in the Crimea, and she had never loved anyone since with the same depth, or without at some moment seeing Peter's face in his and feeling all the old dreams return. And with every other man at all the best, the tenderest times, it was Peter's eyes she saw, Peter's laughter she heard.

It was after that that she had first gone to Africa, scandalizing her family, as well as Mary Carfax. But what did it matter, with Peter dead? Better to be alone than live a pretense with someone else.

Now as the carriage sped through the spring streets towards Kensington she racked her brains for a credible tale. It would be hard enough even for a long-standing friend and confidante to learn anything useful that might throw light on the murder of Vyvyan Etheridge; she would learn nothing at all if she did not even get through the door! Did Mary remember that ball? Did she know that Peter had loved Zenobia, and that she would have persuaded him that she did not care about money or Society, had he not died on the battlefield of Balaklava? Or did Mary still imagine it might have been she he would have chosen, had he the freedom to choose anyone?

Desperation was the element! She must use as much of the truth as possible. She must find a reason she could lie about convincingly; emotions were far harder to simulate. She was at her wits end . . . and she needed to know—that was it! She needed to know the whereabouts of a mutual friend, someone from those far-off days, and her extremity had driven her to seek Mary Carfax. Mary would believe that. But who should she say she was searching for? It must not be someone in such current circulation that Zenobia should have found her for herself. Ah! Beatrice Allenby was just the person. She had married a Belgian cheesemaker and gone to live in Bruges! No one could be expected to know that as a matter of course. And Mary Carfax would enjoy relating that: it was a minor scandal, girls of good family might marry German barons or Italian counts, but not Belgians, and certainly not cheesemakers of any sort!

By the time she alighted in Kensington she was composed in her mind and had her story rehearsed in detail. A small boy with a hoop and a stick ran down the pavement past her, and his governess hurried along, calling after him. Zenobia smiled and ascended the steps. She presented her card to the parlormaid, outstared the rather pert girl, and watched with satisfaction as she departed to take the news to her mistress.

She returned a few moments later and showed Zenobia into the withdrawing room. As she had expected, Mary Carfax's curiosity was too sharp for her to wait.

"How pleasant to see you again, Miss Gunne, after so very long," she lied with a chill smile. "Please do take a seat." Her concern was polite, but there was also a solicitude in it, a reminder that Mary was a fraction younger, which fact she had treasured even in their youth and now found too sweet to let pass. "Would you care for some refreshment? A tisane?"

Zenobia swallowed the reply that came to her lips and forced the opening she had planned. "Thank you; most kind." She sat on the edge of her chair, as manners dictated, not farther back, as would have been comfortable, and bared her teeth very slightly. "You look well."

"I daresay it is the climate," Lady Mary answered pointedly. "So good for the complexion."

Zenobia, burned by the African sun, longed to make some withering reply but remembered her niece and forbore. "I am sure it must be," she agreed with difficulty. "All the rain—"

"We have had quite a pleasant winter," Lady Mary contradicted. "But I daresay you have not been here to experience it?"

Zenobia satisfied her.

"No, no I returned only very recently."

Lady Mary's rather straight eyebrows shot up. "And you came to call upon me?"

Zenobia did not twitch a muscle. "I wished to call upon Beatrice Allenby, but I cannot find a trace of her. No one seems to know where she is presently staying. And remembering how fond you were of her, I thought perhaps you might know?"

Lady Mary struggled, and the opportunity to relate a scandal won. "Indeed I do—although I hardly know if I should tell you!" she said with satisfaction.

Zenobia affected surprise and concern. "Oh dear! Some misfortune?"

"That is not the word I would have used for it."

"Good heavens! You don't mean a crime?"

"Of course I don't! Really, your mind is—" Lady Mary caught herself just in time before she was openly rude. That would have been vulgar, and she disliked Zenobia Gunne far too much to be vulgar in front of her. "You have become more used to the unconventional behavior of foreigners. Certainly I do not speak of a crime—rather, a social disaster. She married beneath her and went to live in Belgium."

"Good gracious!" Zenobia let her amazement register fully. "What an extraordinary thing! Well, there are some very fine cities in Belgium. I daresay she will be happy enough."

"A cheesemaker!" Lady Mary added.

"A what?"

"A cheesemaker!" She let the word fall with all its redolence of trade. "A person who manufactures cheese!"

Zenobia remembered a dozen such exchanges years ago—and Peter Holland's face so full of laughter. She knew exactly what he would have thought, what he would have said in a snatched moment alone. She raised her eyebrows. "Are you perfectly sure?"

"Of course I'm sure!" Lady Mary snapped. "It is not the sort of thing about which one makes mistakes!"

"Dear me. Her mother must be distraught!" A very clear picture came into Zenobia's mind of Beatrice Allenby's mother, who would have been delighted with any husband, so long as Beatrice did not remain at home.

"Naturally," Lady Mary agreed. "Wouldn't anyone? Although she had no one to blame but herself! She did not watch the girl as she should. One has to be vigilant."

It was the opening Zenobia had been waiting for.

"Of course, your son married very nicely, didn't he? But then I hear he was a fine-looking young man." She had not heard anything of the sort, but no mother minded having her son referred to as handsome; in her eyes no doubt he was. There were many photographs round the room, but she was too shortsighted to see them clearly. They could have been of anyone. "And with such charm," she added for good measure. "So rare. Good-looking young men are apt to be ill-mannered, as if the pleasure of looking at them were sufficient."

"Yes, indeed," Lady Mary said with satisfaction. "He could have chosen almost anyone!"

That was a wild exaggeration, but Zenobia let it pass. She recalled how sedate and pompous Gerald Carfax had been, and pictured Mary's long boredom over the years, the brief dream of love fading at last, buried, because to remember it made the present unbearable.

"Then he married with his heart?" she remarked. "How very commendable. No doubt he is very happy."

Lady Mary drew breath to declare that certainly he was, then she remembered Etheridge's murder and realized that would be a highly unfortunate thing to say. "Ah, well . . ."

Zenobia waited with the question written large in her face.

"His father-in-law died tragically a very short time ago. He is still in mourning."

"Oh dear—oh!" Zenobia affected sudden intelligence. "Oh, of course! Vyvyan Etheridge, murdered on Westminster Bridge. How perfectly wretched. Please accept my condolences."

Lady Mary's face tightened. "Thank you. For one who has just returned from the outreaches of the Empire you are very well informed. No doubt you have missed Society. I must say, one would have considered oneself safe from such outrages in London, but apparently not! Still, no doubt it will all be solved and forgotten soon. It can have nothing whatsoever to do with us."

"Naturally," Zenobia said with difficulty. She remembered acutely why she had disliked Mary Carfax so much. "It is hardly like marrying a cheesemaker."

Lady Mary was oblivious to sarcasm; it was outside her comprehension. "A great deal depends upon upbringing," she said serenely. "James would never have done such a selfish and completely irresponsible thing. I would not have permitted him to entertain such an idea when he was young, and of course now he is adult he still respects my wishes."

And your purse strings, Zenobia thought, but she said nothing.

"Not that he is without spirit!" Lady Mary looked at Zenobia with a flash of dry disapproval that contained the trace of a smile. "He has many fashionable friends and pursuits, and he certainly does not permit his wife to intrude into his . . . his pleasures. A woman should keep her place; it is her greatest strength, and her true power. As you would have known, Zenobia, if you had kept it yourself, instead of careering off quite unnecessarily to heathen countries! There is no call for an Englishwoman to go traipsing around on her own, wearing unbecoming clothes and getting in everyone's way. Adventuring is for men, as are many other pursuits."

"Otherwise one ends up marrying a cheesemaker instead of an heiress!" Zenobia snapped. "I imagine James's wife will inherit a fortune now?"

"I have no idea. I do not inquire into my son's financial affairs." Lady Mary's voice was tinged with ice, but there was a curl of satisfaction round her mouth just the same.

"Your daughter-in-law's affairs," Zenobia corrected. "Parliament passed an act, you know; a woman's property is her own now, not her husband's."

Lady Mary sniffed, and her smile did not fade. "A woman who loved and trusted her husband would still give it into her husband's charge," she replied. "As long as he was alive. As you would know, if you had enjoyed a happy marriage yourself. It is not natural for women to concern themselves in such things. If we once start doing it, Zenobia, then men will cease to look after us as they should! For goodness' sake, woman, have you no intelligence?"

Zenobia laughed outright. She loathed Mary Carfax and everything to do with her, but for the first time since they had parted thirty-eight years go, she felt a glimmer of understanding toward her, and with it a kind of warmth.

"I fail to see what is funny!" Lady Mary said tartly.

"I'm sure." Zenobia nodded through her mirth. "You always did."

Lady Mary reached for the bell. "You must have other calls to make—please do not let me take all of your time."

There was nothing Zenobia could possibly do but take her leave. She rose. The visit had been a total disaster, not a thing could be salvaged, but she would go with dignity.

"Thank you for passing on the news about Beatrice Allenby. I knew you would be the person who would know what had happened—and who would repeat it. It has been a charming afternoon. Good day to you." And as the maid opened the door in answer to the bell, she swept past her, across the hall, and out of the front door as soon as it was opened. Outside in the street she swore fluently in a dialect she had learned from a canoeist in the Congo. She had achieved nothing to help Florence Ivory, or Africa Dowell.

Vespasia had by far the easiest task, but she was also the only person suited to perform it with excellence. She knew the political world as neither Charlotte nor Zenobia could possibly do; she had the rank and the reputation to approach almost anyone, and from her many battles for social reform she had gained the experience to know very well when she was being lied to or fobbed off with an edited version of the truth suitable for ladies and amateurs.

She was fortunate to find Somerset Carlisle at home, but had he been out she would have waited. The matter was far too urgent to put off. She had naturally not said so to Zenobia, but the more she heard of the details, the more she feared that at the very least the police could make an excellent case against Florence Ivory, and at most she was actually guilty. Had Zenobia not been the character she was—eccentric, courageous, lonely, and of deep and enduring affections—Vespasia would have avoided any involvement with the affair at all. But since she had agreed to help, the least cruel thing she could think of was that they should try to discover the truth as soon as they could. There was the remote possibility that they would find some other solution; if not, they would at least end Zenobia's fearful suspense, the swings between the upsurge of hope and the plunges of cold despair as one piece of information surfaced after another. And as hard as any revelation was the gray silence of waiting, not knowing what could happen next, imagining, trying to argue in the mind what the police would be thinking.

Vespasia had experienced it all after George's death and she knew what Zenobia would feel with an immediacy no outsider could.

Therefore she did not have the slightest qualm in sending for Charlotte and dispatching her on any errand that might prove useful. She would have sent Emily as well had she not been gallivanting round Italy. And she was perfectly happy to take up Somerset Carlisle's time and employ *his* talents, should they prove to be of help.

He received her in his study. It was a smaller room than the withdrawing room, but immensely comfortable, full of old leather and old finely polished wood reflecting the firelight. The big desk was strewn with papers and open books, and there were three pens in the stand and half a stick of sealing wax and a scatter of unused postage stamps.

Somerset Carlisle was a man in his late forties, lean, with the look of one who has burnt up all his excesses of energy in relentless activity, a face where emotion and irony lay so close to the surface that only years of schooling kept them within the bounds of taste, not because he feared or believed the doctrine of others, but because he knew the impracticality of shocking people. However, as Vespasia knew very well from the past, his imagination was vivid and limitless, and he was equal to any act, no matter how bizarre, if he believed it right.

He was startled to see her, and immediately curious. A lady of her quality would never have called unannounced unless her reason were pressing; knowing Vespasia, it had probably to do with crime or injustice, about which she felt intensely.

He rose as soon as she came in, inadvertantly spilling a pile of letters, which he ignored.

"Lady Cumming-Gould! It is always a pleasure to see you. But no doubt you have come for something more than friendship. Please sit down." He rapidly pushed a great long-legged marmalade cat out of the other chair and brushed off the seat with his hand, plumping up the cushion for her. "Shall I send for tea?"

"Later perhaps," she replied. "For the moment I need your assistance."

"Of course. With what?"

The marmalade cat stalked over to the desk, jumped up onto it, and tried to climb behind a pile of books, not in alarm but from curiosity.

"Hamish!" Carlisle said absently. "Get down, you fool!" He turned back to Vespasia, and the cat ignored him. "Something has happened?"

"Indeed it has," she agreed, remembering with a sharply sweet sense of comfort how much she liked this man. "Two members of Parliament have had their throats cut on Westminster Bridge."

Carlisle's winged and rather crooked eyebrows rose. "And that brings you here?"

"No, not of itself, of course not. I am concerned because it seems the niece of a very good friend of mine may be suspected by the police."

"A woman?" he said incredulously. "Hardly a woman's

sort of crime—neither the method nor the place. Thomas Pitt doesn't think so, surely?"

"I really have no idea," she admitted. "But I think not, or Charlotte would have mentioned it, always assuming she knew. She has been somewhat preoccupied with Emily's wedding recently."

"Emily's wedding?" He was surprised, and pleased. "I didn't know she had married again."

"Yes—to a young man of immeasurable charm and no money whatsoever. But that is not as disastrous as it sounds; I think, as much as one can ever be sure, that he cares for her deeply and has the quality of loyalty in even very trying times, a sense of adventure, and a very agreeable sense of humor, so it may well prove a happy situation. At least it has begun well, which is not always the case."

"But you are concerned about your friend's niece? Why on earth should she take to murdering M.P.s?" His face was full of visions of the absurd, but she knew that beneath it he understood fear very well, and his light tone did not mean he did not appreciate the gravity of the situation.

"Because the second victim promised to help her retain custody of her child, and then reneged on his word and assisted her husband, with the result that she lost the child and will in all probability not see her again."

He was leaning forward towards her, tense now, concentrating. "Why? Why should a mother lose custody of her child?" he asked.

"She is deemed an unsuitable person to raise a girl because she has opinions. For example, she believes that women should have a right to vote for their representatives in Parliament and in local government, and she has associated herself with Mrs. Bezant and the fight for a decent wage and improved conditions for the match girls at Bryant and Mays. No doubt you are better aware than I of the numbers who die of necrosis of the jaw from the phosphorus and are bald before they reach the age of twenty from carrying boxes on their heads."

His face looked suddenly bruised, as if he had seen too much pain. "I am. Tell me, Vespasia," he said, letting the formality drop without realizing it, "do you believe this woman could have killed the M.P.s?"

"I do," she confessed. "But I have not met her yet. I may think otherwise when I have, though I doubt it: Nobby—Zenobia Gunne—thinks so too. But I have promised to help. Therefore I have come to ask you if there's anything at all you can tell me about either Lockwood Hamilton or Vyvyan Etheridge which may conceivably be of any use in discovering who murdered them, whether it is Florence Ivory and Africa Dowell or someone else."

"Two women?"

"Florence Ivory is the mother who lost her child; Africa Dowell is Nobby's niece, with whom Mrs. Ivory shares a house."

He stood up and went to the door, requested tea and sandwiches, and returned to sit down opposite Vespasia again, having to remove Hamish from his chair first.

"Naturally, when I first heard of the murders it crossed my mind to wonder whether it was anarchists, a lunatic, or someone with a personal motive, although I admit, I thought the third far less likely after Etheridge was killed as well."

"Didn't they have anything in common?"

"If they did I don't know what it was, beyond the things that are equally common to a couple of hundred other people!"

"Then we may have to assume that one was killed in mistake for the other," she concluded. "Is that imaginable?"

He thought for a moment. "Yes. They both lived on the south side of the river not far from Westminster Bridge, a pleasant walk home on a spring night. They were both of medium build, with the conspicuous feature being silver hair, and both were pale, with rather longish faces. I have never mistaken one for the other, but it would be possible for someone who had only a slight acquaintance, and in the dark. That would mean that Etheridge was the intended victim, and Hamilton a mistake; one would hardly make the mistake second."

"Tell me all you know about Etheridge." Vespasia sat back and folded her hands in her lap, her eyes on his face.

For several seconds he sat in silence, ordering his thoughts, during which time the tea and sandwiches arrived.

"His career has been solid but unspectacular," he began at last. "He has property in two or three counties, as well as in London, and is very well provided for indeed, but it is old money, not new. He did not make much of it himself."

"Politics?" she interrupted.

His mouth turned down at the corners. "That is what is difficult to understand. He didn't do anything controversial, tended to go with the party line on everything I know of. He is for reform, but only at the speed his peers approve. He's hardly a radical or an innovator, nor, on the other hand, a die-hard."

"You are saying he went whichever way the prevailing wind blew," Vespasia said with some contempt.

"I don't know that I would put it as cruelly as that. But he was very much in the mainstream. If he had any convictions, they were the same as most of his colleagues. He was against Irish Home Rule, but only on a vote; he never spoke about it in the House, so he was hardly a target for the Fenians."

"What about office?" she said hopefully. "He must have trodden on somebody's toes on the way up."

"My dear Vespasia, he didn't go far enough up to do anyone out of anything of importance—certainly nothing he'd get his throat cut for!"

"Well did he ravish someone's daughter, or seduce someone's wife? For heaven's sake, Somerset, somebody killed him!"

"Yes I know." He looked down at his hands, then up again into her eyes. "Don't you think it may be either a lunatic simply run amok, or else your friend's niece, as you fear?"

"I think it is probable, but not certain. And as long as

there is any doubt one way or the other, I shall continue to pursue it. Perhaps the man had a lover, of either sex? Or he may have gambled; maybe someone owed him more than they could afford to pay, or perhaps it was Etheridge himself who was owing. He may have gained some knowledge, quite by chance, and he was murdered to silence him."

Carlisle frowned. "Knowledge of what?"

"I don't know! For heaven's sake, man, you have been in the world long enough! Scandal, corruption, treason—there are more than enough possibilities."

"You know it always amazes me how a woman of your immaculate breeding and impeccable life could have such an encyclopedic knowledge of the sins and perversions of mankind. You look as if you've never seen a kitchen, much less a bawdy house."

"That is how I intend to look," she replied. "A woman's appearance is her fortune, and what she seems to be will be the measure of what other people assume she is. If you had a trifle more practical sense you would know that. At times I think you are an idealist."

"At times I probably am," he agreed. "But I will scrape around and see what I can learn about Etheridge for you, although I doubt it will be of much help."

So did Vespasia, but she would not give up hope.

"Thank you. Knowledge will be useful, whatever it is. Even if it merely allows us to eliminate certain possibilities."

He smiled at her, and there was some tenderness as well as respect in his eyes. She felt faintly embarrassed, which was absurd; Vespasia was above embarrassment. But she was startled to find how much his affection pleased her. She took another sandwich—they were salmon and mayonnaise—and gave one as well to the cat, and then she changed the subject.

Charlotte alighted at Walnut Tree Walk and went straight up to the door. There was no point on this call in being anything but perfectly frank. She had not asked but she presumed Zenobia Gunne had told her niece that she would do all she could to help; why else would her niece have confided in her?

The door was opened by a maid, not in uniform but in a plain blue dress with a white apron and no cap.

"Yes ma'am?"

"Good afternoon. I apologize for calling so late," Charlotte said with great aplomb. "But it is most important that I speak with Miss Africa Dowell. My name is Charlotte Ellison, and I have come from her aunt, Miss Gunne, on a matter of some urgency."

The maid stepped back and invited her in, and as soon as Charlotte came into the hallway she liked the house. It was full of bamboo and polished wood, with plenty of light. Spring bulbs and flowers bloomed in green earthenware pots, and she could see chintz curtains in the dining room through the open door.

It was only a moment before the maid returned and showed her into a large sitting room, which seemed to be the one room in the house designed for receiving guests. The far wall was entirely taken up by windows and French doors, the seats were covered in flowered cushions, and on the bamboo-legged occasional table were bowls of flowers. However, Charlotte was aware of a hollowness in it, something she would not have expected from what she already knew of these women's lives. It took her only a moment to realize what had given her the feeling: there were no photographs anywhere, even though there was plenty of space on the mantelshelf, the windowsill, the table and the top of the cabinet. Most especially, there were no pictures of the child, such as Charlotte herself had of both Jemima and Daniel. There were no mementos at all.

And though it was a woman's room, there was no needlework in progress, no wool, no sewing basket, no embroidery. A sidelong glance at the bookshelf disclosed the heaviest of material, philosophy and political history, no humor, no romance, and certainly nothing a child would read.

It was as if they had expunged all trace of painful memory and of the desire to create the heart of a home. It was pitiful; she could understand it with a part of her mind, and yet it was also chilling.

The woman who stood in the center of the room was angular, even bony, and at the same time she had a kind of perverse grace. Her plain muslin dress was oddly becoming. Frills would have been absurd with that striking face, the very wide-set eyes, the dominant nose, and the mouth etched by lines of pain. She looked to be about thirty-five, and Charlotte knew she must be Florence Ivory. Her heart sank lower. A woman with a face like this could assuredly have both loved and hated enough to do anything!

Beyond her, sitting on the window seat, a younger woman with a face straight from Rosetti stared back at Charlotte watchfully, prepared to defend what she loved, both the woman and the ideal. It was a dreamer's face, the face of one who would follow her vision, and die for it.

"How do you do," Charlotte said after a moment's hesitation. "I have spent some part of the morning in the company of Lady Vespasia Cumming-Gould, and your aunt, Miss Gunne. They invited me to take luncheon with them because they are deeply concerned about your welfare, and the possibility that you may be wrongly accused of a crime."

"Indeed?" Florence Ivory looked bitterly amused. "And how does that involve you, Miss Ellison? You cannot possibly call upon every woman in London who faces some injustice!"

Charlotte felt a prickle of irritation. "I should not wish to, Mrs. Ivory, and certainly not upon all those who thought they had!" she answered equally tartly. "I call upon you because Miss Gunne has taken it upon herself to try to prevent this particular injustice which she fears, and has asked my Great-aunt Vespasia's help, who has in turn asked me."

"I fail to see what you can do." Florence spoke from bitterness, but also from despair.

"Of course you fail to," Charlotte snapped. "If you

could see it you could probably do it yourself! You are not unintelligent." Her mind flashed back to that public meeting and the intensity of determination. "And I have few resources that are not open to you or anyone else. I simply have some experience, some common sense and some courage." She had not spoken so abruptly, or so arrogantly, to anyone as far back as she could remember! But there was an abrasiveness and an anger in this woman which she at once understood, knowing her story, and found unnecessary and self-defeating.

Africa Dowell stood up and went to Florence Ivory. She was taller than Charlotte had realized, and although slender, she looked as if she might be of athletic build under the rosy cotton of her gown.

"You cannot be a detective, Miss Ellison, if Lady Cumming-Gould is your great-aunt. What is it you are proposing to do that might be of help to us?"

Florence gave her a withering look. "Really, Africa. The police are all men, and while some of them may have reasonable manners and even some imagination, it is futile to suppose they will come to any conclusion except the most obvious and convenient one! They are hardly going to suspect Miss Ellison's family or associates, are they? Our best prayer is that some lunatic is caught before they can organize the evidence against me!"

Africa had more patience than Charlotte would have had.

"Aunt Nobby is really very good." Her chin lifted a little higher. "When she was in her early thirties she began exploring. She went to Egypt, then south to the Congo. She traveled up the great river in a canoe; she was the only white person in her party. She's had the courage to do things you would like to do, so don't dismiss her." She refrained from adding any criticism of Florence Ivory's prejudice.

Florence was moved more by Africa's loyalty than by the facts. Her face softened, and she put her hand on the younger woman's arm. "I would indeed like to do such things," she admitted. "She must be a remarkable person. But I don't see how she can help us in this."

Africa turned to Charlotte. "Miss Ellison?"

Charlotte could not find any comforting panacea. She detected by chance and instinct, by being caught up in events, by caring and observing. And most certainly she would be ill-advised to tell either of these two women that her husband was with the police.

"We will explore the other possibilities," she answered rather lamely. "Discover whether either man had any personal, business, or political enemies—"

"Won't the police do that?" Africa asked.

Charlotte saw Florence's face, the anger in it, the conviction of injustice to come. She sympathized: Florence Ivory had suffered loss already, perhaps the worst she could conceive. But her condescension, her blanket condemnation of all persons in authority, not just those who had betrayed her, lost her the warmth that Charlotte would have felt for her otherwise.

"What makes you certain the police suspect you so strongly, Mrs. Ivory?" she asked rather brusquely.

Florence's face held both pain and contempt. "The look on the policeman's face," she answered.

Charlotte was incredulous. "I beg your pardon?"

"It was in his eyes," Florence repeated. "A mixture of pity and judgment. For heaven's sake, Miss Ellison! I have motive enough, and I wrote to Etheridge and said so—no doubt the police will find my letters before long. I have the means: anyone can purchase a razor, and the kitchen is full of knives of excellent sharpness! And I was alone in the house the night he was killed; Africa went to visit a neighbor who was sick and sat up with her half the night. But the woman was delirious, so I don't suppose she knows whether Africa remained there or not! You may be very good at solving petty thefts and discovering the authors of unpleasant letters, Miss Ellison, but proving me innocent is beyond your abilities. But I am grateful for your well-meaning efforts. And it was kind of Lady Cumming-Gould to be concerned for us. Please thank her for me."

Charlotte was so angry it took all her strength of will to force herself to remember how dreadfully the woman had already been hurt. Only by recalling Jemima's face to her inner vision, by remembering the feel of her slender little body in her arms, the smell of her hair, did she quell the fury. In its place came a pity so wrenching it left her almost breathless.

"You may not be the only person he betrayed, Mrs. Ivory; and if you did not kill him, then we shall continue to search for whoever did. And I will do it because I wish to. Thank you for your time. Good day. Good day, Miss Dowell." And she turned and walked back towards the hall, out of the front door, and into the late spring sunlight feeling exhausted and frightened. She did not even know whether she believed Florence Ivory to have killed Etheridge or not. Certainly the cause was there, and the passion!

8

WALLACE LOUGHLEY, M.P., STOOD almost under the immense tower of Big Ben. It had been a long sitting, and he was tired. The debate had been really rather pointless, and in the end, nothing had been achieved. It was a lovely evening; he could think of a dozen better places to spend it than cooped up in the House of Commons listening to arguments he had heard a dozen times before. There was a jolly good Gilbert and Sullivan opera on at the Savoy Theatre, and several charming ladies he knew would be there.

The offshore breeze carried the smoke and the fog away, and he could see a dazzle of stars overhead. He had been meaning to say to Sheridan—blast! He had been a few yards away only moments ago. He could not have gone far, bound to walk on an evening like this. Only lived off the Waterloo Road.

Loughley set out smartly towards the bridge, past the statue of Boadicea with her horses and chariot outlined black against the sky, the lights along the Embankment a row of yellow moons down the course of the river. He loved this city, especially the heart of it. Here was the seat of power hallowed back to Simon de Montfort and the first Parliament in the thirteenth century, to even its concept in the Magna Charta, and Henry II's charter before that. Now it was the center of an Empire none of them could have conceived. Heavens, they had not even known the world was round, let alone a quarter of its face would be British!

Ah, there was Sheridan, leaning up against the last lamppost, almost as if he were waiting for him.

"Sheridan!" Loughley called out, raising his elegant cane to wave. "Sheridan! Meant to ask you if you'd come to dine with me next week, at my club. Wanted to talk about the . . . Whatever's the matter with you, man? Are you ill? You look . . ." The rest died away in blasphemy wrung from his heart so intensely that perhaps it was no blasphemy at all.

Cuthbert Sheridan was draped half backwards against the lamppost, his head a little on one side, his hat on the crown of his head, and one lock of pale hair over his brow, looking colorless in the strange quality of the artificial light. The white scarf round his neck was so tight his chin was tipped up, and already the dark blood was soaking the silk and running under to stain his shirtfront. His face was ghastly, eyes staring, mouth a little open.

Loughley felt the sky and the river whirl about him, and his stomach lurched; he lost his balance, stumbling and grasping for the balustrade. It had happened again, and he was alone on Westminster Bridge with the appalling corpse, so horrified he could not even shout.

He turned and stumbled away back towards the north end and the Palace of Westminster, feet slipping on the damp pavement, the lights dancing in his blurred vision.

"You or'right, sir?" a voice said suspiciously.

Loughley looked up and saw light gleaming on silver buttons and the blessed uniform of a constable. He grasped the man's arm.

"Dear God! It's happened again! Over there . . . Cuthbert Sheridan."

"Wot's 'appened sir?" The voice was heavy with skepticism.

"Another murder. Cuthbert Sheridan—with his throat cut, poor devil! For God's sake, do something!"

At any other time P.C. Blackett would have regarded the shaking, semicoherent man in front of him as a hallucinating drunk, but there was something hideously familiar about this.

"You come wiv me an' show me, sir." He was not going to let the man out of his sight. It crossed his mind that perhaps he even had the Westminster Cutthroat in his grasp now, although he doubted it. This man looked too genuinely shocked. But he was unquestionably a witness.

Reluctantly Loughley returned, feeling nauseated by horror. It was exactly as had been burned indelibly in his mind. Now it had the quality of a nightmare.

"Ah," P.C. Blackett said heavily. He looked back at Big Ben, noted the time, then pulled out his whistle and blew it long, shrilly, and with piercing intensity.

When Pitt arrived Micah Drummond was already there, dressed in a smoking jacket, as if he had just left his own fireside, and looking cold and sad. There was a hollowness in his eyes, even in the lamplight, and the bridge of his nose was even more pinched.

"Ah, Pitt." He turned and left the small group of men huddled together by the mortuary coach. "Another one, exactly the same. I thought perhaps with Etheridge we'd seen the last of it. Well, it looks as if it wasn't your woman after all. We're back to a lunatic."

For a moment Pitt felt a surge of relief mixed with the mounting horror. He did not want Florence Ivory to be guilty. Then her face came to his memory as clearly as if he had seen her the instant before. There was passion in it, intensity violent enough to carry out her will, whatever it was, and also a keen and subtle intelligence, quite enough to foresee precisely this conversation.

"Probably," he agreed.

"Probably!"

"There are many possibilities." Pitt stood still, staring at the lamppost. The body had been removed and had been laid out on the ground in an attempt at decency. He looked down at it, his mind taking in the details of clothing, the hands, the wound exactly like the two others', the pallid, terrible face with its strong nose and deep-set eyes, the hair that might have been gray or blond, silvery in the lamplight. "It could be a madman," he went on. "Or anarchists, though I doubt that; or there may be some political plot afoot that we have had no whisper of as yet. Or it could be that this has nothing to do with the other two, just someone copying. It happens. Or it could be three murders, only one of which the murderer cares about, the other two meant to lead us astray."

Drummond closed his eyes, as if his eyelids could keep out the fearfulness of the thought. He put his long hands up to cover his face for a moment before taking them away with a sigh.

"Dear God, I hope not! Could anyone be so . . ." But he could not find the word, and he let it go.

"Who is he?" Pitt asked.

"Cuthbert Sheridan."

"Member of Parliament?"

"Yes. Oh yes, he's another member of Parliament. About thirty-eight or forty, married, with three children. Lives on the south side of the river, Baron's Court, off the Waterloo Road. Up-and-coming young backbencher, member for a constituency in Warwickshire. A bit conservative, against Home Rule, against penal reform; for better working conditions in mines and factories, better poor laws and child labor laws. Very definitely against any vote for women." He looked up at Pitt and held his eyes steadily. "So is almost everyone else."

"You know a lot about him," said Pitt, surprised. "I thought he was found only half an hour ago."

"But it was one of his colleagues, following him to ask him to dine, who found him. So he knew him straightaway and told us. Poor fellow's pretty cut up. A Wallace Loughley, over there sitting on the ground by the mortuary coach. Somebody gave him a tot of brandy, but it would be a charity to see him as soon as you can and let the poor beggar go home."

"What did the surgeon say?"

"Same as the others; at least, it seems so at first glance. A single wound, almost certainly delivered from behind. Victim doesn't seem to have suspected anyone or offered any resistance."

"Odd." Pitt tried to imagine it. "If he was walking across the bridge, going home after a late sitting, he would presumably be moving at quite a good pace. Someone must have been going very briskly to overtake him. Wouldn't you think a man alone on the bridge, especially after two other murders, would at least turn round if he heard rapid footsteps approaching him from behind? I certainly would!"

"I would too," Drummond agreed with a deepening frown. "And I'd shout and probably run. Unless of course it was someone coming towards him, from the south side. But in any case, I certainly wouldn't stand still and wait for someone to come close enough to strike me from either direction." He let his breath out shakily. The air was so silent they could hear the water swirling round the piers of the bridge, and far away along the Embankment the rattle of a hansom cab. "Unless, of course," Drummond finished, "it was someone I knew, and trusted." He bit his lip. "Certainly not some unknown madman."

"What about Wallace Loughley?" Pitt raised his eyebrows. "What do we know about him?"

"Nothing yet. But it won't be hard to find out. For a start I'd better see if he is who he says he is. I suppose it would be easy enough to claim. I certainly don't know all six hundred seventy members of Parliament by sight! I'd better not let him go home until someone has identified him, poor devil."

"I'll see him." Pitt pushed his hands hard down in his pockets. He left Drummond and walked over to the mortuary carriage and the group of half a dozen men gathered round it. One was obviously the driver; he still had half his attention on the horse, although the reins were hooked to the stay. A man in early middle age, haggard, hands shaking, hair streaked across his brow, was presumably Loughley. He had been sitting on the curbside, and he stood up as Pitt approached, waiting, but he did not speak. He was very clearly suffering from shock, but there was no hysteria in him, no arrogance, no panic that Pitt could see. If he had followed Sheridan and murdered him, he had a mastery of himself to the finest detail, a brain as cold as the water of the Thames beneath them.

"Good evening, Mr. Loughley," Pitt said quietly. "What time did you last see Mr. Sheridan alive?"

Loughley swallowed, finding his voice with difficulty. "It must have been a little after half past ten, I think. I left the House at twenty minutes past, and spoke to one or two people. I—I'm not sure for how long, but I said only a few words to each of them. I saw Sheridan and said good night to him; then after he had gone Colonel Devon said something to me about business. Then I remembered I wanted to speak to Sheridan; he'd only been gone a few minutes, so I went after him, and—and you know what I found."

"Is Colonel Devon a Member of Parliament?"

"Yes—dear God! You don't think—! You can check with him. He'll remember what was said; it was about tonight's debate."

"Did you see anyone else on the bridge, either ahead of you or behind, Mr. Loughley?"

"No. No I didn't. That's the extraordinary thing: I don't remember seeing anyone else! And yet it must have been only—" He took a deep, shaky breath. "Only minutes after . . ."

There was a slight commotion at the north end of the bridge, a loud cry from some of the people being held back by the police. A woman started to scream and was led away. There were brisk footsteps, and a dark figure emerged and came towards them, overcoat flapping. As he passed under the light Pitt recognized Garnet Royce.

"Good evening, sir," Pitt said clearly.

Royce came up to him, glanced at Loughley, and greeted him by name, then looked back at Pitt and at Drummond, who had rejoined him.

"This is getting very serious, man!" he said grimly. "Have you any idea how close people are to losing control? We seem to be on the very brink of anarchy. Perfectly sane and steady people are panicking, talking about conspiracies to overthrow the throne, uprisings of workers, strikes, even revolution! I know that's absurd." He shook his head very slightly, dismissing their hysteria rather than the ideas. "It is probably an isolated lunatic—but we've got to apprehend him! This must stop! For God's sake, gentlemen, let us bend every resource we have and put an end to this horror! It is our responsibility. The weaker and less fortunate rely on us to defend them from the depradations of the lunatic underworld, and from political anarchists who would destroy the very fabric of the Empire. In God's name, it is our duty!" He was deeply earnest; there was a fire of sincerity in his eyes neither Pitt nor Drummond could doubt. "If there is anything I can do, anything whatsoever, tell me! I have friends, colleagues, influence. What do you need?" He looked urgently from one to the other of them and back again. "Name it!"

"If I knew what would help, Sir Garnet, I would assuredly ask," Drummond replied wearily. "But we have no idea of the motive."

"Surely we cannot hope to understand the reasons of a madman?" Royce argued. "You're not suggesting this is personal, are you? That there is some enemy common to all three men?" His face reflected his incredulity, and there was even a harsh gleam of humor in the brilliant eyes.

"Perhaps not common to all three," Pitt said, watching the expression of surprise, then understanding and horror that crossed Royce's features. "Perhaps the enemy only of one."

"Then not a madman, but a fiend," Royce said very quietly, his voice shaking. "How could anyone but a lunatic do such a thing to two strangers, in cold blood, to hide one intended death?"

"We don't know," Drummond replied quietly. "It is merely a possibility. But we are looking into every anarchist or revolutionary group we know of, and we do know of most of them. Every police informer we have has been asked."

"A reward!" Royce said suddenly. "I am sure I could get together with other businessmen and raise a sufficient reward, so that it would be well worth the while of anyone who knew anything to come forward. I'll do it tomorrow, as soon as this atrocity reaches the newspapers." He pushed the heel of his hand over his brow, brushing back the sweep of hair. "I dread to think what the panic will be, and you cannot blame people. My poor sister feels bound by a sense of honor or duty to remain here until the matter is closed. I beg you, gentlemen, to do everything you can. I would take it as a favor if you would keep me informed, so that I may know if there is anything I can do. I once worked for the Home Office; I am aware of police procedures, of what you can do and what is impossible. Believe me, I have the greatest sympathy. I do not expect miracles of you."

Drummond stared beyond him to the far end of the bridge, where a crowd was gathering, frightened, increasingly hostile, huddling together and staring at the little knot of police and the silent mortuary coach awaiting its terrible charge.

"Thank you, sir. Yes, a reward might help. Men have betrayed every cause they have known for money at one time or another, from Judas on down. I appreciate it."

"It will be in your hands by tomorrow evening," Royce promised. "Now I will leave you to your duty. Poor Sheridan, God help him! Oh"—he turned just as he was about to leave—"would you like me to inform his wife?"

Pitt would have liked it dearly, but it was his task, not Royce's.

"Thank you, sir, but it is necessary that I should. There are questions to ask."

Royce nodded. "Understood." He replaced his hat, and walked briskly to the south side of the bridge and up the hill on the east side of the street, towards Bethlehem Road.

Drummond stood silently for a moment or two, staring into the darkness where Royce had departed.

"He seems to have an exceptional grasp of the situation," he said thoughtfully. "And to be deeply concerned. . . ." He left the sentence hanging in the air.

The same thread of an idea was stirring in Pitt's mind, but it had no form, and he could find none for it.

"What do you know about him?" Drummond asked, facing Pitt again curiously.

"Member of Parliament for over twenty years," Pitt answered, remembering everything he had heard, directly or indirectly. "Efficient, even gifted. As he said, he has held high office under the Home Secretary in the past. His reputation seems to be spotless, both personally and professionally. His wife died some time ago; he has remained a widower. He was Hamilton's brother-in-law—but of course you know that."

Drummond inclined his head. "I suppose you looked into their relationship?" he asked wryly.

Pitt smiled. "Yes. It was civil, but not close. And there was no financial involvement that we could find, except that he seems to be taking care of his sister's affairs now she is widowed. But he is the elder brother, and that seems natural."

"Professional rivalry with Hamilton?"

"No. They served in different areas. Allies, if anything."

"Personal?" Drummond persisted.

"No. Nor political—not that you would cut a man's throat because he espouses a different cause from your own. From everything I learned of Royce he is a strongly traditional family man with a deep conviction in the responsibility of the strong to care for the weak and the able to govern the masses—in their own interest."

Drummond sighed. "Sounds like practically every other Member in the House—in fact, like most well-to-do middle-aged gentlemen in England!"

Pitt let out his breath in a little grunt, then took his leave, heading in the same direction Royce had gone, only at the end of the bridge he turned towards Baron's Place and the home of the late Cuthbert Sheridan, M.P.

It was the same as before, standing on the steps in the dark, banging again and again to waken sleeping servants, and then the wait while they relit the gas and pulled jackets on hastily to find out who could be calling at such an hour.

There was the same look of horror, the halting request that he wait, the effort at composure, then the long silence while the awful news was broken, and once again Pitt found himself standing in a cold morning room in the gaslight facing a shocked and ashen woman who was trying hard not to weep or to faint.

Parthenope Sheridan was perhaps thirty-five or thirty-six, a small woman with a very straight back. Her face was a little too pointed to be pretty, but she had fine eyes and hair, and slightly crooked teeth which gave her an individuality which at another time might well have been charming. Now she stood hollow-eyed, staring at Pitt.

"Cuthbert?" she repeated the name as if she needed to say it again to grasp its meaning. "Cuthbert has been murdered—on Westminster Bridge? Like the others? But why? He has no connection with—with . . . what? What is it about, Inspector Pitt? I don't understand." She reached for the chair behind her and sat down in it unsteadily, covering her face with her hands.

Pitt wished passionately that they were of the same social class, just for a few moments, so he could put his arms round her and let her weep on his shoulder, instead of sitting stiffly hunched up, unable to share her emotion, isolated because there was no one in the house but servants, children, and a policeman.

But there was nothing he could do. No pity in the world crossed the chasm between them. Familiarity would add to her burden, not decrease it. So instead he broke across the silence with formal words and the necessities of duty.

"Nor do we, ma'am, but we are working on every possibility. And it seems that it may be political, or it may have been someone with a personal enmity towards any one of the three men, or it may simply be someone who is mad, and we shall find no reason that we can understand."

She made a supreme effort to speak clearly, without tears in her voice, without sniffling. "Political? You mean anarchists? People are talking about plots against the Queen, or Parliament. But why Cuthbert? He was only a very junior minister at the Treasury."

"Had he always been at the Treasury, ma'am?"

"Oh no; members of Parliament move from one office to another, you know. He had been in the Home Office as well, and the Foreign Office for a very short while."

"Had he any convictions about Irish Home Rule?"

"No—that is, I think he voted for it, but I'm not sure. He didn't discuss that sort of thing with me."

"And reform, ma'am; was he inclined towards social and industrial reform, or against it?"

"As long as it was well conducted and not too hasty, he was for industrial reform." A curious look passed across her face; it seemed made up of both anger and pain.

He asked the question he least wished to. "And reform of the franchise; was he in favor of extending it to women?"

"No." The word came from between her teeth. "No, he was not."

"Was his opinion well known to others?"

She hesitated; her eyebrows went up. "I—yes, I imagine so. He expressed it quite forcefully at times."

He could not fail to see both the surprise and the distress

in her face. "Were you of the same opinion, Mrs. Sheridan?" he asked.

Her face was so white the shadows under her eyes looked almost gray, even in this yellow gaslight.

"No." Her voice was quiet, almost a whisper. "I believe very strongly that women should have the right to vote for members of Parliament, if they choose, and to stand for local councils themselves. I am a member of my local group fighting for women's suffrage."

"Are you acquainted with a Mrs. Florence Ivory, or a Miss Africa Dowell?"

There was no change in her expression, no added fear or start of apprehension. "Yes, I know them both, though not well. There are not many of us, Mr. Pitt; it is hard for us not to know of one another, especially of those few who are prepared to take risk, to fight for what they believe, rather than merely pleading for it to a government which is composed entirely of men and quite obviously not disposed to listen to us. Those who hold power have never in all history been inclined to relinquish it willingly. Usually it has been taken from them by force, or it has slipped from their hands because they were too weak or corrupt to retain it."

"Which does Mrs. Ivory believe will come to pass here?"

The first pale flush of color marked her cheeks, and her face hardened.

"That is a question you had better ask her, Mr. Pitt—after you have discovered who murdered my husband!" Then her anger dissolved in an agony of distress and she turned away from him and crumpled against the back of the chair, weeping silently, her whole body shaking with the violence of her emotion.

Pitt could not apologize. It would have been ridiculous, and without purpose; grief had nothing to do with him; to comment would have served only to show his lack of comprehension. Instead he simply left, going out into the hallway, passing the white-faced butler, and opening the front door for himself. He went down the steps into the spring darkness; a slow mist was curling up from the river now, smelling of the incoming tide. She would weep now, and probably again when the cold light of morning brought back reality and memory, and loneliness.

When Pitt reached home he went straight to the kitchen and made himself a pot of tea. He sat at the table drinking it, warming his hands on the mug, for well over an hour. He felt tired and helpless. There had been three murders, and he had no more real evidence than he'd had the night of the first one. Was it really Florence Ivory, driven beyond sanity by the loss of her child?

But why Cuthbert Sheridan? Simple hatred, because he too was against giving women more power and influence in government, perhaps in law, medicine, and who knew what else? It was only twelve years since medical schools had been opened to women, six years since married women might own and administer their own property, four since they had ceased in law to be chattel belonging to their husbands.

But surely only a madwoman would murder those who were unwilling to change? That would be almost everyone except a mere handful! It made no sense—but should he be looking for sense in these deaths?

At last he went to bed, warmer, sleepy, but no more certain in his mind.

In the morning he left early, saying little to Charlotte except a few bleak works about finding Sheridan, the horror, the rising sense of hysteria in the crowd.

"Surely it could not have been Florence Ivory?" she said when he finished. "Not this too?"

He wanted to say of course not; this changes everything. But it did not. Such a burning sense of injustice does not know the bounds of sense, not even of self-preservation. Reason was no yardstick with which to measure.

"Thomas?"

"Yes." He stood up and reached for his coat. "I am sorry, but it could still be her."

Micah Drummond was in his office already, and Pitt went straight up. The daily newspapers were in a pile on his desk, and the top one had black banner headlines: THIRD MURDER ON WESTMINSTER BRIDGE, and under it, ANOTHER M.P. BUTCHERED HALF A MILE FROM HOUSE OF COMMONS.

"The rest are much the same, or worse," Drummond said bleakly. "Royce is right; people are beginning to panic. The Home Secretary has sent for me—heaven only knows what I can tell him. What have we got? Anything?"

"Sheridan's widow knew Mrs. Ivory and Africa Dowell," Pitt replied miserably. "She is a member of her local women's suffrage organization, and her husband was fiercely against it."

Drummond sat without moving for some time. "Ah," he said at last, no conviction in his voice, no certainty. "Do you think that has anything to do with it? A women's suffrage conspiracy?"

Put in those words it sounded absurd, yet Pitt could not forget the passion in Florence Ivory, the loss that time had hardened but not touched with even the smallest healing. She was a woman who would not be stopped by fear or convention, risks to herself, or other people's doubts or beliefs. Pitt was quite sure that she was capable of it, both emotionally and physically, with Africa Dowell's help.

And would Africa have helped? He thought so. She was a young woman full of idealism and burning emotions forcefully directed towards the bitter wrongs she felt had been done to Florence and her child. She had a dreamer's or a revolutionary's dedication to her vision of justice.

"Pitt?" Drummond's voice cut across his thoughts.

"No, not really," he replied, weighing his words. "Unless two people can be called a conspiracy. But it might be a series of circumstances. . . ."

"What circumstances?" Drummond, too, was beginning to see the outline of a pattern, but there were too many unknowns. He had not met the people and so could not judge, and always at the back of his mind were the newspaper headlines, the grave and frightened faces of men in high office who now felt accountable and in turn passed on the responsibility and the blame to him. He was not frightened; he was not a man to run from challenge or duty, nor to blame others for his own helplessness. But neither did he evade the seriousness of the situation. "For heaven's sake, Pitt, I want to know what you think!"

Pitt was honest. "I fear it may be Florence Ivory, with Africa Dowell's help. I think she has the passion and the commitment to have done it. She certainly had the motive, and it is more than possible she mistook Hamilton for Etheridge. But why she then went on to kill Sheridan I don't know. That seems more cold-blooded than I judge her to be. It seems gratuitous. Of course, it could be someone else, perhaps an enemy of Sheridan's taking advantage of a hideous opportunity."

"And you have some sympathy for Mrs. Ivory," Drummond added, watching Pitt closely.

"Yes," Pitt admitted. It was true, he had liked Florence Ivory and felt keenly for her pain, perhaps too keenly, thinking of his own children. But then he had liked other murderers. It was the petty sinners, the hypocrites, the self-righteous, those who fed on humiliation and pain that he could not bear. "But I think it is also possible that we have come nowhere near the answer yet, that it is something we haven't guessed at."

"Political conspiracy?"

"Perhaps." But Pitt doubted it; it would have to be a monstrous one, touched with madness.

Drummond stood up and went to the fire, rubbing

his hands as if he were cold, although the room was comfortable.

"We've got to solve it, Pitt," he said without condescension, turning to face him; for a moment the difference in office between them ceased to exist. "I have all the men I can spare raking through the files of every political malcontent we've ever heard of, every neorevolutionary, every radical socialist or activist for Irish Home Rule, or Welsh Home Rule, or any other reform that has ever had passionate supporters. You concentrate on the personal motives: greed, hatred, revenge, lust, blackmail; anything you can think of that makes one man kill another—or one woman, if you think that possible. There are enough women in the case with the money to employ someone to do what they could not or dared not do themselves."

"I'll have a closer look at James Carfax," Pitt said slowly. "And I'd better look in more detail at Etheridge's personal life. Although an outraged husband or lover doesn't seem likely—not for all three!"

"Frankly nothing seems likely, except a remarkably cunning lunatic with a hatred of M.P.s who live on the south side of the river," Drummond said with a twisted smile. "And we've doubled the police patrol of the area. All M.P.s know enough to guard themselves—I'd be very surprised if any of them choose to walk home across the bridge now." He adjusted his necktie a little and pulled his jacket straighter on his shoulders, and his face lost even the shred of bleak humor it had shown. "I'd better go and see the Home Secretary." He went to the door, then turned. "When we've dealt with this case, Pitt, you're overdue for promotion. I'll see that you get it; you have my word. I'd do it now, but I need you on the street until this is finished. You more than deserve it, and it will mean a considerable raise in salary." And with that he went out of the door and closed it, leaving Pitt standing by the fire, surprised and confused.

Drummond was right, promotion was long overdue; he had forfeited it previously by his attitude towards his superiors, by insubordination not by his acts but by his manner. It would be good to have his skills recognized, to have more command, more authority. And more money would mean so much to Charlotte, less scrimping on clothes, a few luxuries for the table, a trip to the country or the sea, maybe in time even a holiday abroad. One day she might even see Paris.

But of course it would mean working behind a desk instead of on the street. He would detail other men to go out and question people, weigh the value of answers, watch faces; someone else would have the dreadful task of telling the bereaved, of examining the dead, of making the arrests. He would merely direct, make decisions, give advice, direct the investigations.

He would not like it—at times he would hate it, hate being removed from the reality of the passion and the horror and the pity of street work. His men would hear the facts and return to him; he would no longer be aware of the flesh and the spirit, the people.

But then he thought of Charlotte with Emily's unopened letter in her pinafore pocket, waiting until he had gone because she did not want him to see her face when she read about Venice and Rome, about the glamor and romance of wherever Emily was now.

He would accept the promotion—of course he would. He must.

But first they must catch the Westminster Cutthroat, as the newspapers were calling him.

Could it possibly be James Carfax? Pitt could not see in that handsome, charming, rather shallow face the ruthlessness necessary to kill three people, one after the other, merely to gain his wife's inheritance, no matter how much he wanted it.

What about Helen? Did she love her husband enough, want to keep him enough to commit such crimes, first for him, then to protect herself? Or him?

* * *

He spent all day pursuing finances. First he found the record of the sale of Helen Carfax's painting, then he traced further back to see if she had sold other things and found that she had—small sketches, trinkets, a carving or two—before she'd sold the painting whose absence he had noticed. There was no way of proving what she had used the money for without searching her own personal accounts, and possibly not then. It could have been for gowns and perfumes, to make herself more attractive to a wandering husband, or for jewelry, or perhaps for medical expenses, or presents for James or even for someone else. Or maybe she gambled—some women did.

He reached home a little after six, tired and dispirited. It was not only the difficulty of the case, it was the thought of promotion, of guiding other men rather than doing the work himself. But he must never let Charlotte know his feelings or it would rob her of any pleasure in the rewards it would bring. He must disguise his feeling of loss.

She was in the kitchen finishing the children's tea and preparing his. The whole room was warm, softly glowing from the gas lamps on the wall as the light faded in the sky outside. The wooden table was scrubbed clean and there was a smell of soap and hot bread and some kind of fragrant steam he could not place.

He went to her without speaking and took her in his arms, holding her closely, kissing her, ignoring her wet hands and the flour on her apron. And after her first surprise she responded warmly, even passionately.

He got it over with straightaway, before he had time to think or regret.

"I'm to be promoted! Drummond said as soon as this case is finished. It will mean far more money, and influence, and position!"

She held him even harder, burying her face against his shoulder. "Thomas, that's wonderful! You deserve it—

you've deserved it for ages! Will you still be out working on cases?"

"No."

"Then you'll be safer too!"

He had done it, told her without a shadow, without her suspecting anything but joy and pride. He felt a moment of terrible isolation. She did not even know what it cost him; she had no idea how intensely he would rather be on the street, with people, feeling the dirt and the pain and the reality of it. It was the only way to understand.

But that was foolish. Why else was he telling her like this, but precisely because he did not want her to sense his misgivings! He must not spoil it now. He pushed her away a little and smiled at her.

She searched his face, and the brilliance in her eyes turned to questioning.

"What is it? What is wrong?"

"Just this case," he answered. "The further I look into it the less I seem to have hold of."

"Tell me more about it. Tell me about this latest victim," she invited him. "I'll get your dinner. Gracie's upstairs with the children. You can explain it to me while we eat." And taking his agreement for granted she took the lid off the pan and stirred it once or twice, filling the kitchen with a delicious odor. Then she lifted plates out of the warming oven and served mutton stew with thick leeks and slices of potato and sweet white turnips and a touch of dried rosemary that gave it sharpness and flavor.

He told her all that he had omitted on his previous, rather scattered accounts, which had been more emotional than logical, together with the little of value he had learned since and the skeletal knowledge he had of Cuthbert Sheridan.

When he had finished she sat for several minutes in silence, looking down at her empty plate. When at last she did look up there was a deep color in her cheeks and the half shame-faced look of embarrassment and defiance he had seen so many times before.

"How?" he said quietly. "How are you involved? It's nothing to do with us, any of us. And Emily's in Italy—isn't she?"

"Oh yes!" She seemed amost relieved. "Yes, she's in Florence. At least, the letter I got this morning was from there. She may be somewhere else by now, of course."

"Well then?"

"Great-aunt Vespasia . . . sent for me."

He raised his eyebrows. "To discover the Westminster Cutthroat?" he said with heavy disbelief.

"Well, yes, in a way. . . ."

"Explain yourself, Charlotte."

"You see, Africa Dowell is the niece of Great-aunt Vespasia's closest friend, Miss Zenobia Gunne. And they think the police suspect her—quite rightly, as it turns out. Of course I didn't tell them it was you!"

He searched her face for several moments and she held his gaze without flinching. She could keep a secret, sometimes, and she could be evasive, with difficulty, but she was no good at all at lying to him, and they both knew it.

"And what have you discovered?" he asked at length.

She bit her lip. "Nothing. I'm sorry."

"Nothing at all?"

"Well I made friends with Amethyst Hamilton—"

"How on earth did you do that? Does Aunt Vespasia know her?"

"No—I just lied." She looked down at the table, embarrassed, then up again, meeting his eyes. "She and her stepson loathe each other so much they cannot even be civil, but I can't see anything in that which could lead to murder. She's been married for many years, and nothing new has happened . . ." she trailed off.

"And," he prompted.

"She inherits quite a lot of money, but that's hardly a reason, especially not—" Again she stopped.

"Not what?"

"I was going to say, not to kill Etheridge and Sheridan as well, but I suppose that doesn't necessarily follow, does it?"

"Not necessarily," he agreed. "It could be that the last two murders were close to hide the one that matters, or they could have been committed by a copycat. I don't know."

She put out her hand and gently covered his. "You will," she said with conviction, but he was not sure whether it was her mind or her heart which spoke. "*We* will," she added, as if as an afterthought.

CHARLOTTE SET OUT THE following morning on the omnibus to see Great-aunt Vespasia. It was a sparkling spring day, the air mild and the sun warm. It would be lovely to be in the country, or even in one of the fashionable squares with all the new leaves bursting and the sound of birdsong. Perhaps she and Pitt would be able to go to the country for a weekend this summer. Or longer—a whole week?

In the meantime she thought of the small things she could buy with the extra money Pitt would have. A new hat would be an excellent start, one with a very large brim, and pink ribbon on it, and flowers—big cabbage roses with golden centers, they were so becoming! One should wear it at a certain angle, up at the left and a little down over the right brow.

And she could get two or three muslin dresses for Jemima, instead of having to make do with only one best one for Sundays. Should she get pale blue, or a very soft shade of green? Of course, people said that blue and green should never be worn together, but personally she liked the combination, like summer leaves against the sky.

She employed the entire journey in such pleasant thoughts, so much so that she was almost carried past her stop, which would have been very annoying, since there was a considerable distance to walk anyway. People like Great-aunt Vespasia did not live on the routes of the public omnibus.

She climbed off with indecent haste and all but fell over as she reached the pavement. She ignored the critical comments of two large ladies in black, setting off at a very brisk pace towards Great-aunt Vespasia's town house.

She was admitted at once and shown into the morning room, where Vespasia was sitting with a pen in her hand and several sheets of writing paper in front of her. She put them aside as soon as Charlotte came in.

"Have you discovered something?" she asked hopefully, dispensing with the formalities of greeting.

"It is as bad as we fear," Charlotte sat down immediately. "I did not tell you before that it is Thomas who is handling the case! I was afraid Zenobia might not believe I could be open-minded, and I thought that if you knew it might place you in something of an embarrassing position. But it is Thomas who went to Mrs. Ivory, and he does indeed think it may be she. They've got everyone possible out looking for anarchists, revolutionaries, Fenians, and anyone else who might be political, but no one has found anything at all. The only ray of light, if you can call anything so tragic a light, is that Mrs. Ivory would have no sane reason for killing Cuthbert Sheridan."

"Not a light I care for," Vespasia said grimly.

"And Thomas will be promoted as soon as the case is solved."

"Indeed?" Vespasia's silver eyebrows rose minutely, but there was satisfaction in her eyes. "Not before time. You must tell me when it is official, and I shall send him a letter of congratulation. Meanwhile, what can we do to help Zenobia?"

Charlotte noted that she had said Zenobia, not Florence Ivory. She caught her eye and knew the choice was deliberate.

"I think it is time for a little cold reason," Charlotte said as gently as it was possible to say such a thing. "Thomas says they have done everything they can to discover a conspiracy of any political or revolutionary nature, and they can find nothing whatsoever. Indeed, it seems hard to imagine any political end that would be served by such acts, unaccompanied by any demand for change or reform. Except, of course, anarchy—which seems to me to be something of a lunatic idea anyway. Who can possibly benefit from that?"

Vespasia looked at her with impatience. "My dear girl, if you imagine that all political aims owe either their conception or their execution to unadulterated sanity, then you are more naive than I had supposed!"

Charlotte felt the color climb in her cheeks. Perhaps she was naive. She certainly had not mixed in the circles of government that Vespasia had, nor heard the private dreams of those who wielded power, or aspired to. She had indeed imagined them to have a degree of common sense, which on consideration might well be an unfounded conclusion.

"Sometimes those who cannot create enjoy the power to destroy," Vespasia went on. "It is all they have. After all, what else is much of violence? Think back on the crimes you yourself have helped to solve. Look at most domination of one person over another: the fishwife or the washerwoman could have told such people that it would not produce the admiration or the love or the peace they desired, but one hears what one wishes to."

"But anarchists are noisy, Aunt Vespasia. They don't want anarchy alone! And Thomas says the police are aware of a great many of them, and none seems to have been involved with the Westminster Bridge murders. After all, there is no political power in anonymous acts, is there! One has to own up to them at some point in order to reap the reward."

"One would presume so," Vespasia agreed, part of her reluctant to let go of the idea of some unknown assailant lashing out wildly for a cause. It was less ugly to her than the possibility of a friend, even a relative of the intended victim prepared to murder three people in order to mask the one murder that might implicate them. "Is it possible there is some connection between the three that we have not thought of?" she pressed.

"They are all M.P.s," Charlotte said bleakly. "Thomas has not been able to discover anything further. They have no business connections, they are not related, they are not in line for any one position, for that matter they are not even of the same party! Two are Liberal, one Tory. And they have no political or social opinions in common, not even regarding Irish Home Rule, Penal Reform, Industrial or Poor Law Reform—nothing, except that they are all against extending the electoral franchise to women."

"So are most people." Vespasia's face was pale, but sixty years' training showed in her hands, resting elegantly in her lap over the wisp of her lace handkerchief. "Anyone planning to kill members of Parliament for that reason is going to decimate both houses."

"If it is personal, then we had better begin to consider very seriously who might have motive," Charlotte said gently. "And pursue them in ways that would be impossible for Thomas. I have already made the acquaintance of Lady Hamilton, and although I find it hard to believe it was she, there may be some connection." She sighed with unhappy memories. "And of course sometimes the truth is hard to believe. People you have liked, still do like, can have agonies you never conceived, fears that haunted them until they escaped all reason and turned to violence, or old wounds so terrible they cannot leave them behind. Revenge obsesses them beyond everything else—love, safety, even sanity."

Vespasia did not reply; perhaps she was thinking of the same people, or at least one of them, for whom she too had cared.

"And there is young Barclay Hamilton," Charlotte said. "Although there seems to be a profound emotion troubling him regarding his father's second marriage, I don't know what should lead him to murder."

"Nor I," Vespasia conceded quietly, a weariness in her that she overcame with difficulty. "What of Etheridge? There is a great deal of money."

"James Carfax," Charlotte replied. "Either he himself, or his wife, in order to keep him from going to other women, or even leaving her altogether."

"How tragic," Vespasia sighed. "Poor creature. What a terrible price to pay for something that is in the end merely an illusion, and one that will not remain for long. She will have destroyed herself to no purpose."

"Or if indeed he has had other relationships," Charlotte said, thinking aloud, "some other love, or infatuation, perhaps . . ." she trailed off.

"Quite possibly he had had affairs with other women," Vespasia agreed dourly. "But even in the unlikely event they had husbands who were offended by it, to cut the throats of three members of Parliament and hang them on Westminster Bridge seems oblique, and excessive to a degree!"

Charlotte was suitably crushed. It was absurd. Had it been Etheridge alone it might have made sense. "It doesn't seem to be a crime of passion," she said aloud. "Indeed it does not appear to make any kind of sense!"

"Then there is only one conclusion," Vespasia said grimly. "There is either a passion or a reason of which we are not aware. Certainly if it is a passion, it was not momentary, but rather extremely sustained, and therefore I would suppose it is one of great depth."

"Someone has been done a wrong so terrible it corrodes their souls like a white-hot acid," Charlotte offered.

Vespasia stared at her. It was on the tip of her tongue to tell Charlotte not to be melodramatic; then she glimpsed for an instant the horror of what such a thing might be, and remained silent.

Charlotte pursued her own line. "Or there is a motive we have not seen, perhaps because we do not know the facts, or the people, or because it is too ugly to us, and we have refused to see it. All we know of what those three men had in common was a fierce disapproval of the movement to extend the franchise to women."

"Hamilton's disapproval was not fierce," Vespasia corrected automatically, but there was no lightness in her voice; it need not be said between them that Hamilton's death may have been a mistake, due to the assumption, in the dim light on the bridge, that he was Etheridge. "It could be others trying to blacken the reputation of the women fighting for suffrage," Vespasia went on, "knowing they would be blamed."

"Oblique, and excessive to a degree," Charlotte repeated Vespasia's own words, then instantly regretted the impertinence. "I'm sorry!"

Vespasia's face softened for a moment in recognition of the emotion. "You are quite right," she conceded. "If somewhat cruel in your manner of observation." She stood up and went to the window, gazing out at the sunlight in the garden, slanting pale and brilliant on the tree trunks and the first red shoots of the rose leaves. "We had best pursue what we can. Since we fear Florence Ivory may indeed be guilty, it would be profitable for you to form a further opinion of her character. You might call upon her again, if you will."

Charlotte looked at Vespasia's slender back, stiff under her embroidered lace dress, her shoulders so thin Charlotte was reminded quite painfully of how old she was, how fragile; she remembered that with age one does not cease to love or to be hurt, nor feel any less vulnerable inside. Without waiting to allow self-consciousness to prevent her, she went over and put her arms round Vespasia, regardless of whether it was a liberty or not, and held her tight as she would have a sister or a child.

"I love you, Aunt Vespasia, and there is nothing I would like in the world more than one day to become a little like you."

It was several moments before Vespasia spoke, and when she did her voice was hesitant and a little throaty. "Thank you, my dear." She sniffed very delicately. "I am sure you have made an excellent beginning—both the good and the bad. Now if you would be so good as to let go of me, I must find my handkerchief." She did, and blew her nose in a less ladylike manner than usual, with her back to Charlotte. "Now!" she said briskly, stuffing the totally inadequate piece of cambric and lace up her sleeve. "I shall use the telephone to speak to Nobby and have her call upon Lady Mary Carfax again; I shall renew some political acquaintances who may be able to tell me something of use; you will call upon Florence Ivory; and then tomorrow we shall meet here at two o'clock and go together to express our condolences to the widow of Cuthbert Sheridan. It may even be that it was he who was the intended victim." She tried hard to keep hope out of her voice—it had a certain indecency—and failed.

"Yes, Aunt Vespasia," Charlotte said obediently. "Tomorrow at two o'clock."

Charlotte set out for her visit to Florence Ivory with little pleasure. Indeed, the fear was strong inside her that she would either learn nothing at all or that her present anxieties would be strengthened and she would feel a greater conviction that Florence was both capable of such murders and likely to have committed them, with the help perhaps of Zenobia's niece Africa Dowell. She herself hoped she might find that they were not at home.

She was to be disappointed. They were at home and willing to receive her; in fact, they made her welcome.

"Come in, Miss Ellison," Africa said hastily. Her face was pale, but there were spots of color high on her cheeks, and smudges of shadow under her eyes, from fear and too little sleep. "I am so glad you have called again. We were quite concerned lest this latest horror should have turned you from our cause. The whole matter is a nightmare." She led Charlotte towards the charming sitting room, with its flowered curtains and its plants. Sunlight streamed through the windows, and three blue hyacinths filled the room with a perfume so heady, at another time it would have distracted the attention.

Now however Charlotte had eyes and thoughts only for Florence Ivory, who sat in a rattan chair with cushions of green and white, a raffia basket in her hands, which she was mending. She looked up at Charlotte with a face more guarded than her companion's.

"Good afternoon, Miss Ellison. It is very civil of you to

call. May I presume from your presence that you are still engaged in our cause? Or have you come to tell me that you now consider it past help?"

Charlotte was a little stung; there was in Florence's turn of phrase a whole array of assumptions which she found offensive.

"I shall not give up, Mrs. Ivory, until the matter is either won or lost, or until I find some evidence of your guilt which makes pursuing it further morally impossible," she replied crisply.

Florence's remarkable face, with its widely spaced eyes full of haunting intelligence, seemed for a moment on the edge of laughter; then reality asserted itself and she gestured to the chair opposite and invited Charlotte to be seated.

"What else can I tell you? I knew Cuthbert Sheridan only by reputation, but I have met his wife on a number of occasions. In fact I may have been instrumental in her joining the movement for women's suffrage."

Charlotte observed the pain in the woman's face; saw the irony in the eyes, the bitterness in the mouth, the small, bony hands clenched on the raffia basket. "May I presume that Mr. Sheridan did not approve?" she asked.

"You may," Florence agreed dryly. She regarded Charlotte closely, and her expression gradually became one of barely disguised contempt. Only her need for help and a residue of good manners concealed it at all. "It is a subject which produces great emotion, Miss Ellison, of which you seem to be largely unaware. I have no idea what your life has been. I can only assume you are one of those comfortable women who are satisfactorily provided for in all material ways and are happy to pay for your keep with a docile temperament and skill in keeping a home—or organizing others who do it for you—and that you consider yourself fortunate to be in such a position."

"You are quite right—you do have no idea what my life has been!" Charlotte said extremely sharply. "And your assumptions are impertinent!" As soon as the words were out of her mouth she remembered how this woman had suffered, had lost her children, and she realized with a flood of shame that perhaps she was precisely as comfortable as Florence had accused her of being. She had little money, certainly, but what part of life's ease or joy was that? She had enough. She had never been hungry, and she was not so often cold. She had her children, and Pitt treated her not as a possession, which in law she had indeed been until only recently, but as a friend. As she sat in the green and white chair with the sun coming in through the garden windows and the air full of the scent of the hyacinths, she realized with a powerful gratitude that she had freedom an uncounted number of women would have given all their silks and servants to possess.

Florence was staring at her, and for the first time since they had met, there was confusion in her face.

"I apologize," Charlotte said with great difficulty. She found this woman highly irritating, profound as her pity for her was. "My rudeness was unnecessary, and in some ways you are perfectly correct. I cannot truly understand your anger, because I have not been a victim of the wrongs of which you speak. Please tell me."

Florence's eyebrows rose. "For goodness' sake, tell you what? The social history of women?"

"If that is the issue," Charlotte replied. "Is that why these men were killed?"

"I've no idea! But if I had done it, it would be!"

"Why? For a vote on who sits in Parliament?"

Florence's tolerance snapped, and she stood up sharply, the raffia basket and needle falling to the carpet. She faced Charlotte with stinging condescension.

"Do you think you are intelligent? Capable of learning? Do you have emotions, even passions? Do you know anything about people, about children? Do you even know what you want for yourself?"

"Yes of course I do," Charlotte said instantly.

"Are you sure you are not just an overgrown child?"

Now Charlotte was equally angry. She rose as well, the

color burning in her cheeks. "Yes I am perfectly sure!" she hissed back through her teeth. "I am very perceptive about people, I have learned a great deal about many things, and I am quite capable of making wise and sensible judgments. I make mistakes sometimes, but so does everyone. Being adult doesn't make you immune to error, it just makes those errors more important, and gives you more power to cover them up!"

Florence's face did not soften in the least. "I agree. I am every bit as sure as you that I am no child, and I resent profoundly being treated as one, and having my decisions made for me by either my father or my husband, as if I had no will or desire of my own, or as if what they wanted was always the same as what I wanted for myself, or could be relied upon to be in my best interest." She swung round and went behind the chair, leaning forward over the back of it, the muslin of her dress straining across her thin body. "Do you suppose for one second that the law would be as it is if those who made it were answerable to us as well, instead of only to men? Do you?"

Charlotte opened her mouth to reply, but Florence cut her off.

"Do you give your mother a gift at Christmas, or on her birthday?"

"What?"

Florence repeated the question with a harsh, derisory impatience in her voice.

"Yes. What has that to do with suffrage, for heaven's sake?"

"Do you know that in law you cannot give anyone a gift, anyone at all, from the day you become betrothed—not married, *betrothed*—without your fiancé's permission?"

"No, I—"

"And that until four years ago even your clothes and effects belonged to your husband? And if you inherited money, jewelry from your mother, anything, it belonged to him also? If you worked at anything and earned money, that also was his, and he could require it be paid directly to him, so you could not even touch it. Did you think you could make a will, so you could leave your belongings to your daughter, or your sister, or a friend, or reward a servant? So you can—so long as your husband approves! And if at any time he disapproves or changes his mind, or others change it for him, then you cannot! Even after you are dead! Did you know that? Or did you imagine that your dresses, your shoes, your handkerchiefs, your hairpins were your own? They are not! Nothing is yours. Certainly not your body!" Her mouth curled in memory of an old pain, one so deep no balm had ever reached it. "You cannot refuse your husband, regardless of his treatment of you, or how many others he may have lain with, in love or in lust. You cannot even leave his roof unless he gives you his permission! If you do, he can have the law bring you back and prosecute anyone who gives you shelter—even if it is your own mother!

"And if he does allow you to leave, your property remains his, as does anything you might earn, and he has no obligation to give you, or your children, should he permit you to take them, a single penny to keep you from starvation or freezing.

"No—don't interrupt me!" Florence Ivory shouted when Charlotte opened her mouth to speak. "Damn your complacency! Did you imagine you had any say in what should happen to your children? Even your baby still at the breast? Well you don't! They are his, and he may do with them as he pleases—educate them or not, teach them anything he cares to, or nothing, discipline them and care for their health or welfare as he likes. When he makes a will he has the right to dispose of what property used to be yours before you married him however he pleases. He can leave your jewelry to his mistress, if he likes. Did you know that, Miss Ellison? Do you think Parliament would make laws like that if it were answerable to women voters as well as men? Do you?"

Again Charlotte opened her mouth to say something,

but she was overwhelmed by the flood of injustices, and over and above that the scalding outrage that burned through Florence's thin body. Charlotte sank onto the arm of her chair. Florence was not merely cataloguing the inequities of the law, she was crying out from her own pain. It was nakedly apparent, even if Charlotte had not known from Pitt how she had lost first her home and her son, then her beloved daughter. She had never considered divorce or separation because it had not occurred in her family or any of her friends. Of course she had known for years that it was commonly believed that men had natural appetites which must be satisfied, and decent women did not; therefore it was to be expected that a man might commit adultery, and a wife's only course was to conduct herself so she was never forced into a position where she was seen to know of it. It was not grounds for divorce for a wife, and anyway, a divorced woman ceased to exist in society, and a working woman would be on the streets dependent on whatever skills she had to earn her keep—and her skills would be minimal, and domestic. No one took a divorced woman into service.

"That, Miss Ellison, is a fraction of the reason why I want women to have a right to vote!" Florence was staring at her, pale now, exhausted by her own emotions and all the relieved pain, the struggles that had been lost one by one. There was hatred in her powerful enough to drown out all lesser qualms of doubt or pity, or thoughts of self-preservation. Whether she had killed three men on Westminster Bridge, Charlotte did not know, but sitting on the arm of the chintz-covered chair in this sunlit room with the odor of hyacinths, she felt again the sickening conviction that Florence Ivory was capable of it.

The three women were motionless. Florence gripped the back of her chair, her knuckles white, the cloth of her dress strained at the shoulders till the stitching thread showed at the seams. Outside in the garden a bird hopped from a low lilac branch onto the windowsill.

Africa Dowell moved from the corner by the door

where she had been listening. She made a move as if to touch Florence, then something in the rigid figure warned her away, and she turned to Charlotte, knowledge and fear in her eyes, and defiance.

"Florence is speaking for a great many people, more than you might imagine. Mrs. Sheridan had recently joined a group fighting for women's suffrage, and there are others up and down the country. Famous people have urged it. John Stuart Mill wrote a paper years ago—" She stopped, painfully aware that nothing she said would erase from their minds the skin-crawling knowledge of a passion that could have driven Florence Ivory to kill, and may have.

Charlotte looked at the carpet, framing her words carefully.

"You say many women feel the same," she began.

"Yes, many," Africa agreed faintly, her voice without conviction.

Charlotte met her eyes. "Why not all women? Why should any woman be against it, or even indifferent?"

Florence's answer was harsh and instant. "Because it is easier! We are brought up from the cradle to be ignorant, charming, obedient, and to depend completely on someone else to provide for us! We tell men we are fragile of body and of mind and must be protected from anything indecent or contentious, we must be looked after, we cannot be blamed for anything because we are not responsible! And they do look after us. They do as much for us as a mother does for a child that cannot walk: she carries it! And until she puts it down, it never will walk! Well I don't want to be carried all my life!" She struck her hand so violently against her chest Charlotte felt sure it must have bruised the flesh. "I want to decide which way I will go, not be carried whether I choose to or not where someone else wishes. But many women have been told for so long they cannot walk that now they believe it, and they haven't the courage to try. Others are too lazy; it is easier to be carried."

It was only a partial truth. Charlotte knew so many

more reasons: there was love, gratitude, guilt, the need to be loved with tenderness and without contention or rivalry, the deep pleasure of earning the respect and nurturing the best in a man, and perhaps the strongest reason of all—the need to give love, to cherish the young and the weak, to support a man, who seemed in the world's eyes to be the stronger, and yet whom one learned so quickly was easily as vulnerable as oneself, often more so. The world expected so much of him, and allowed him no weakness, no tears, no failure. A host of memories came to her of Pitt, of George, of Dominic, even of her father, seen now with the wisdom of hindsight, and of other men whom the astringent wash of an investigation had stripped layer by layer of all pretense. Their hidden selves had been as frail, as full of terrors and weaknesses, self-doubt and petty vanities and deceptions as any woman's. Only their outer garb was different, and their outer power.

But there was no purpose in telling this to Florence Ivory. Her wounds were too deep, and her cause was just. Charlotte imagined her emotions, thought for an instant how she would have felt had her own children been lost to her and knew reason would be misplaced.

But only reason could help now. She changed the subject entirely, looking at Florence with a calm she did not feel. "Where were you when Mr. Sheridan was murdered?" she asked.

Florence was startled. Then she smiled without humor, her remarkable face as quick to change as reflections in a pool of water.

"I was here, alone," she said quietly. "Africa had gone to spend a little time with a friend who is confined with her first child and feeling unwell. But why in heaven's name should I kill Mr. Sheridan? He has done me no harm—no more at least than any other man who denies us the right to be people, not merely appendages to men. Do you know you can't even make a contract in law? And if you are robbed it is your husband who is offended against, not you, even if it is your purse that is taken?" She laughed harshly. "Nor can you be sued! Or be responsible for your own debts. Unfortunately, if you commit a murder, that is your fault—your husband will not be hanged in your place! But I did not kill Mr. Sheridan, or Mr. Etheridge, or Sir Lockwood Hamilton, for that matter. Though I doubt you will prove it, Miss Ellison. Your good intentions are a waste of time."

"Possibly." Charlotte stood up, staring rather coldly. "But it is mine to waste, if I so choose."

"I doubt it," Florence answered without moving. "If you pursue the matter I daresay you will find that it is your father's, or your husband's if you have one." She turned her back and bent to pick up the raffia basket from where it had fallen, as though Charlotte had already left.

Africa showed her to the door, white-faced, searching for words and discarding each before it touched her lips. Every line of her body, every stiff, awkward movement betrayed her fear. She loved Florence, she pitied her desperately, she burned for her injuries and injustices, and she was mortally afraid that the torment of the loss of her child had driven her to creep out at night with a razor in her hand, and kill—and kill—and kill.

The same thought was in Charlotte's mind, the same chill voice inside her, and she could not pretend. She looked at the girl with her ashen Pre-Raphaelite face, strong and young and so frightened, full of resolve to fight a losing battle, and she grasped her cold hands and held them tightly for a moment. There was nothing useful or honest to say.

Then she turned away and walked briskly down the street towards the place where the public omnibus might be caught for the long ride back.

Zenobia Gunne faced the prospect of calling upon Lady Mary Carfax a second time with the same resolve of fortitude she had summoned to sail up the Congo River in an open canoe, only this was a task which promised less reward. There would be no brazen sunsets, no mangrove roots rising out of the dawn-lit water, no screaming birds the color of jewels flung haphazard against the sky. Only Mary Carfax's thirty-year-long remembrance of contempt and a hundred old grudges.

With deep misgivings, a churning in the pit of her stomach, and a sense of her own inadequacy, she had her carriage brought round and obeyed Vespasia's instructions. She had nothing in common with Mary Carfax but old memories.

She was also afraid that Florence Ivory might well be guilty, and that Africa's overactive sense of pity might have driven her, if not actually to help Florence, then at least to shield her now the deed was done.

And then a grimmer, uglier thought forced itself upon her. Was it done? Or would it continue? Sheridan had been killed after any injustice by Etheridge was more than avenged. Did Africa know it was Florence, or did her sympathy permit her to be blind?

Zenobia should have befriended her, visited her more often, not allowed her to become so close to so compelling a woman in such distress, one so passionate about her injustices, so likely to lose her emotional balance and her sanity. Africa was her youngest brother's child; she should have taken her duties more seriously after her parents' death. She had followed her own interests across the world, selfishly.

But it was too late now to offer time and friendship; the only thing that could help would be to prove Florence innocent, and as Charlotte Pitt had said—what a curious woman Charlotte was, so divided between two worlds, and yet apparently at home in both—as she had pointed out, that could only be accomplished by proving that someone else was guilty.

She leaned forward and rapped on the front wall of the carriage. "Please hurry!" she shouted urgently. "You are going too slowly! What are you waiting for?"

She presented her card to Lady Mary's maid and watched the ramrod back of the girl as she took it away to show her mistress. Zenobia did not intend to lie as to her purpose in coming; it was not in her nature to tell petty lies, she had no art for it, and she could not think of a lie grand enough to serve the purpose.

The girl returned and showed her into the withdrawing room, where a large fire burned in spite of the clement weather. Mary Carfax sat upright in a gold-ornamented French chair. She concealed her surprise because her curiosity overrode it, and since that was an ill-bred emotion she did not own, she did her best to conceal that also.

"How agreeable to see you again—so soon," she said in a voice that veered from one tone to another as she tried to decide which attitude to adopt. "I feared that—" but she changed her mind again, that was too inferior. "I supposed it would be a dull afternoon," she said instead. "How are you? Please do sit down and be comfortable. The weather is most pleasant, don't you think?"

Zenobia had barely noticed it, but the conversation must be conducted with civility, whatever it cost.

"Delightful," she agreed, taking the seat farthest from the fire. "There are numerous blossoms out, and the air is quite mild. I passed several people walking in the park, and there was a German band playing in the rotunda."

"One looks forward to the summer." Lady Mary was bursting with inquisitiveness as to why Zenobia, who patently disliked her, should have called at all, let alone twice in the space of a fortnight. "Shall you be attending Ascot, or Henley? I find the races tire me, but one should be seen, don't you agree?"

Zenobia swallowed her retort and forced an amiable expression to her face. "I am sure your friends will be disappointed if you do not go, but I fear I may not find it suitable. There is a member of my family touched at present by a tragedy, and if matters get worse, I shall not feel in the slightest like enjoying such social events."

Lady Mary shifted minutely in her seat and her fingers closed over the ornate curlicues on the ends of the chair arms. "Indeed? I am sorry." She hesitated, then plunged ahead. "Can I offer any assistance?"

Zenobia swallowed hard. She thought of Peter Holland that last night before he sailed for the Crimea. How he would have laughed at this! He would have seen the danger—and the absurdity. "You might tell me something about those women who are striving to obtain the franchise." She saw the immediate tightening of disapproval in Lady Mary's face, the drawing together of the brows and the sharpening of the pale blue eyes. "What manner of people are they? Indeed, who are they?"

"What they are is very easy," Lady Mary replied. "They are women who have failed to make a suitable marriage, or who have an unnaturally masculine turn of mind and desire to dominate rather than be the domestic, gracious, and sensitive creatures they were intended to be, both by God and nature. They are women who have neither made themselves attractive nor acquired such arts and accomplishments as are becoming to a woman and useful in her natural functions of bearing and raising children and ordering a house which is a refuge of quiet and decency for her husband, away from the evils of the world. Why any woman should choose otherwise I cannot imagine—except, of course, as a revenge upon those of us who are normal, whom they cannot or will not emulate. I regret to say there is a growing number of such creatures, and they endanger the very fabric of society." Her eyebrows rose. "I trust you will have nothing to do with them, even if your natural instincts and your spinster circumstances tempt you!" For a moment malice was plain in her eyes, and old memories sharp. Mary Carfax's pretense at pity was a sham; she had forgotten and forgiven nothing.

"Heaven knows," she continued in her rather thin voice, "there is enough unrest and distress in the country already. People are actually criticizing the Queen, and I believe there is talk of revolution and anarchy. Government is threatened on all sides." She sighed heavily. "One only has to consider these ghastly outrages on Westminster Bridge to realize that the whole of society is in peril."

"Do you think so?" Zenobia affected a mixture of doubt

and respect, but there was a fleeting smile inside her, an old fragment of warmth, like a snatch of song returning.

"I am certain of it!" Lady Mary bridled. "What other interpretation would you put upon affairs?"

Now it was time for innocence. "Possibly the tragedies you speak of arise from a personal motive: envy, greed, fear—perhaps revenge for some injury or slight?"

"Revenge on three such men, all of them members of Parliament?" Lady Mary was interested in spite of herself. She breathed in slowly, glanced at the photographs of Gerald Carfax and of James on top of the piano, then let out a sigh. "One of them was the father-in-law of my son, you know."

"Yes—how very tragic for you," Zenobia murmured superficially. "And, of course, for your son." She was not sure how to proceed. What she needed was to know more about James and his wife, and asking Lady Mary would produce only her own opinion, which was inevitably biased beyond any use. But she could think of no other avenue to pursue. "I imagine he is very much affected?"

"Ah, yes—of course. Of course he is." Lady Mary bristled a trifle.

Zenobia had watched people of many sorts, gentry and working people, artisans, gamblers, seamen, adventurers and tribesmen. She had learned much that all had in common. She recognized embarrassment under Lady Mary's stiff hesitation and the very slightest tinge of color staining her scrubbed and pallid cheeks—Mary would never descend to paint of any sort! So James Carfax was not grieving for his father-in-law.

Zenobia tried a more sympathetic tack, sensing an opening. "Mourning is very hard for young people, and of course Mrs. Carfax is no doubt most distressed."

"Most," Lady Mary agreed instantly this time. "She has taken it very hard—which is only natural, I suppose. But it puts a great strain upon James."

Zenobia said nothing, her silence inviting further enlightenment.

"She is very dependent upon him," Lady Mary added. "Very demanding, just at the moment."

Again Zenobia understood the hesitation, and the wealth of memory behind it. She recalled Lady Mary as she had been thirty years ago: proud, domineering, convinced she knew what was best for all and determined—in their interest—to accomplish it for them. No doubt James Carfax had been prime among them, and Lady Mary would not approve the vying demands of a wife.

Any further thought along this line was prevented by the entrance of the parlormaid, who returned to say that Mr. James and Mrs. Carfax had called, and indeed they were right behind her. Zenobia regarded them with profound interest as they came in and were introduced. James Carfax was above average height, elegantly slender, with the kind of easy smile she had never cared for. But was that a judgment of him, or of herself? Not a strong man, she thought, not a man she would have taken with her up the great rivers of Africa—he would panic when she most needed him.

Helen Carfax was a different matter. There was strength in her face, not beauty, but a balance of bone and a width to her mouth which was pleasing, and which would grow more so with time. But she was a woman under extreme stress. Zenobia had seen the signs before: she did nothing so obvious as wringing her hands, tearing her handkerchief, pulling at her gloves, or twisting a ring; it was in the eyes, a rim of white between the pupil and the lower lid, and a stiffness in her walk as if her muscles ached. It was more than grief or the pain of a loss already sustained; it was the fear of a loss yet to come. And her husband appeared to be unaware of it.

"How do you do, Miss Gunne." He bowed very slightly. He was charming, direct, his eyes were handsome and he met hers with a candid smile. "I do hope we do not interrupt you? I call upon Mama quite regularly, and I have nothing of urgency to say. In time of mourning there are so few calls one can make, and I thought it would be so pleasant to be out for a little while. Please do not curtail your visit on our account."

"How do you do, Mr. Carfax," Zenobia answered, regarding him without disguising her interest. His clothes were beautifully cut, his shirts of silk, the signet ring on his hand in perfect taste. Even his boots were handmade and, she guessed, of imported leather. Someone was making him a handsome allowance, and it was not Lady Mary, unless she had changed out of all character! She would give a little at a time, Zenobia knew, carefully, watching how each penny was spent: it was her form of power. "You are very gracious," Zenobia said aloud. It was habit, not any liking for him that prompted her words.

He gestured towards Helen. "May I present my wife."

"How do you do, Miss Gunne," Helen said dutifully. "I am delighted to make your acquaintance."

"And I yours, Mrs. Carfax." Zenobia smiled very slightly, as one would to a woman one had only just met. "May I offer my deepest sympathy on your recent bereavement. Everyone of sensibility must feel for you."

Helen looked almost taken aback; her mind had been on something else. "Thank you," she muttered. "Most kind of you . . ." Apparently she had already forgotten Zenobia's name.

The next thirty minutes passed in desultory conversation. James and his mother were obviously close, socially, if not emotionally. Zenobia watched them with intense interest, making occasional remarks to Helen sufficient to be civil, and now and again searching her face when she was watching her husband. From those trivial words, the exchanges of polite society, the pauses between, the flicker of resentments, suppressed pain, habits of manner so deeply ingrained as to be unconsciously adhered to, and the edge of fear unheard or ignored by others, Zenobia guessed at a whole history of hungers unmet.

She knew Mary Carfax and was not surprised that she

both spoiled and dominated her only son, flattering him, indulging his vanity and his appetites, and at the same time kept the purse strings tightly in her own jewel-encrusted fingers. His carefully well-mannered resentment was inevitable, his shifts between gratitude and rancor, his habit of dependence, his underlying knowledge that she thought him a fine man, the best, and his own whispering doubt that he had never justified such esteem and almost certainly never would. If it had been Mary Carfax who had been murdered, Zenobia would have known where to look immediately.

But it was Etheridge. The money leapt to mind, massive, lavish, all that even James Carfax could need to gain his precious freedom. But from whom? Only from Mary—it would tie him to Helen, now that the Married Women's Property Acts had been passed.

Or would it? One had only to glance at Helen's pale face, her eyes on James's or staring blindly through the window at the sky, to see she loved her husband far more than he did her. She praised him, she protected him, a faint flush of pleasure touched her cheeks when he spoke gently to her, her pain showed naked when he was patronizing or used her as the butt of his swift, light jokes, distasteful in their subtle cruelty. She would give him whatever he wanted in an attempt to purchase his love, and Zenobia's heart ached for her, knowing her pain would never cease. She was seeking something which he did not possess to give. Changes unimaginable would have to be wrought in James Carfax before he had the depth or the power within him from which to draw generous or untainted love. Zenobia had loved weak men herself, when she was alone in Africa, and old memories resurfaced, and old hungers. She had woken to the slow, scalding pain that her love would never be returned. You can draw little from a shallow vessel; the quality of feeling reflects the quality of the man—or woman. The soul with little courage, honor, or compassion may give what they have, but it will not satisfy a larger heart.

One day Helen Carfax would know that, would understand that she would never earn from James what he did not have to give her, or to anyone else.

Zenobia remembered some of her own romantic adventures, the rash giving, the clinging to hope, and wondered with a cold, sick fear if Helen had already paid the greatest price of all, having taken her father's life with her own hands, for the money to buy her husband's loyalty.

Then she looked again at the pale face with its white-rimmed eyes, now resting on James's elegant figure, and thought the fear was for him, not for herself. She was afraid that he had done the deed, or somehow contrived to have it done.

She stood up slowly, a trifle stiff from having sat so long.

"I am sure, Lady Mary, that you have family business to discuss and would care for a little privacy. It is such a delightful day I should like a short walk in the sun. Mrs. Carfax, perhaps you would be so kind as to accompany me?"

Helen looked startled, almost as if she had not understood.

"We might walk as far as the top of the road," Zenobia persisted. "I am sure the air would do us good, and I should appreciate your company, and perhaps your arm."

It was ridiculous—Zenobia was far stronger than Helen and assuredly had no need for support, but it was an invitation Helen could not civilly refuse, phrased in such terms. Obediently she excused herself to her husband and mother-in-law, and five minutes later she and Zenobia were outside in the sunny street.

It was a subject that could not possibly be approached directly, yet Zenobia felt impelled, even at the risk of causing serious offense, to speak to Helen as if she had been a daughter, a reflection of her own youth. She was prepared to mix truth of emotion with invention of setting in order to do it.

"My dear, I sympathize with you deeply," she began as soon as they were a few yards from the house. "I too lost my father in violent and distressing circumstances." She had not time to waste recounting that piece of fiction; it was merely an introduction. The story that mattered was of Zenobia's desperate attempt to win from a man a love of which he was not capable, and how instead she had lost her own integrity, paying a fortune for an article that did not exist, for her or for anyone.

She began slowly, extending her invented bereavement into her journeys to Africa, avoiding the numbing reality of Balaklava and Peter Holland's death. Instead she created first an imaginary father snatched in his late prime, then on to a suitor, a mixture of men she had known and cared for in one fashion or another—but never Peter.

"Oh my dear, I loved him so much," she sighed, looking not at Helen but at the briar hedge a little to their left. "He was handsome, and so considerate, such delightful and interesting company."

"What happened?" Helen asked out of politeness, not interest, because the silence seemed to require it.

Zenobia mixed disillusion with a modicum of poetic license.

"I gave him the finances for his trip, and unwisely many gifts towards it also."

Helen's whole attention was caught for the first time. "That is only natural—you loved him."

"And I wanted him to love me," Zenobia continued, aware that she was about to wound, perhaps intensely. "I even did things that on looking back I realize were dishonorable. I suppose I knew it at the time, had I been brave enough to admit it." She did not look at Helen, but kept her eyes on the white drifting clouds scudding across the sky ahead of them. "It took me a long time and much heartache before I understood that I had paid a high price for something which was not real, something I could never hope to gain."

"What?" Helen swallowed hard, and still Zenobia did not look at her. "What do you mean?"

"That it is an illusion many women have, my dear, that all men are capable of the kind of love we long for, and that if we are only faithful, generous, and patient enough they will give it to us in the end. Some people are not capable of that commitment. You cannot draw a deep draft from a shallow vessel, and to try to do so will only cost you your peace of mind, your good health, perhaps even your self-esteem, the integrity of your own ideals which are at the heart of all lasting happiness."

Helen said nothing for several minutes. There was no sound but the steady rhythm of their footsteps on the pavement, a bird singing in a high tree, green against the blue sky, and upon the main road the clop of horses' hooves and the hiss of carriage wheels.

At last Helen put her hand very gently on Zenobia's arm. "Thank you," she said with difficulty. "I think I have been doing the same thing. Perhaps you knew? But somehow I shall find the courage to cease now. I have already done enough damage. I have cast blame on the women fighting to be represented in Parliament, because I was desperate to direct the police away from my household, when in truth I have no idea that they have any guilt in my father's death. It was a shabby thing to do. I pray no one has been injured by it—except myself, for my poverty of spirit.

"It is a very hard truth to face, but—but I believe the time is past—" She stopped, unable to go on, and indeed words were unnecessary. Zenobia knew what she meant. She simply placed her hand over Helen's, and they continued to walk up the bright, sunlit street amid the hedges in silence.

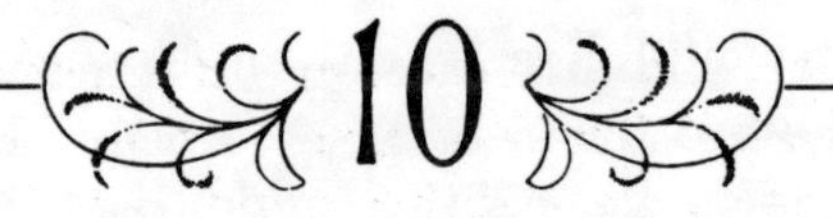

10

CHARLOTTE RETURNED HOME WITH a sense of failure. The visit to Parthenope Sheridan had produced nothing new. She was exactly what she seemed to be: a woman deep in the shock of bereavement and suffering the kind of guilt it is very common to feel when suddenly a member of the family is lost to one and there has been no time to speak of love, to repair old wounds, to apologize for misunderstandings and trivial angers and grudges over things now dwarfed by death.

There was no way for her even to guess if the emotion had been anything more, anything deeper. If there were jealousies, greeds, other lovers, Charlotte had caught no whisper of it, seen no clue she might follow, nor even had she formed questions to ask in her own mind.

The single step forward they had taken that day was that Zenobia was convinced that Helen Carfax was not a suspect, either directly or indirectly. James Carfax remained, although Zenobia did not believe he had the courage to have done it himself, nor the skill or power to have procured the service from someone else. Both Charlotte and Vespasia were inclined to agree with her.

Charlotte had told them of her own impressions of Florence Ivory, of the pity she had felt, the helplessness to counter Florence's anger, and of the terrible wound of injustice which remained inside the woman, poisoning everything that might otherwise have been love. Charlotte concluded reluctantly that she could not dismiss the idea that Florence might indeed be guilty, and they must prepare their minds for that possibility. She had found nothing to help their cause.

Different ideas came to her mind, ugly and terrible, of subtle plans, hatred cold and careful enough to design not only the death of someone known and close to them, but the corruption of another's soul, the leading to murder and all its long trail of nightmare and guilt. Was it conceivable that all the motives were separate and personal—and the link between them was deliberate conspiracy, each to fulfill the other's need? It was a monstrous thought, but they had been monstrous acts, and there seemed no other connection except their membership in Parliament, which they shared with six hundred other men, and that they walked home across Westminster Bridge.

Was Florence Ivory really deranged enough to kill, and to go on killing even after Etheridge was dead? Was her regard for life, even her own, so very little? Charlotte searched her heart, and did not know.

She organized Gracie in the kitchen, and Mrs. Phelps, the woman who came in twice a week to do the heavy work, and busied herself with linen and ironing. As she pushed the heavy flatiron back and forth over the linen, meanwhile heating a fresh iron on the stove, she recounted everything she and Aunt Vespasia and Zenobia Gunne had learned, and all that Pitt had told her—and she was left with a confusion of mind that grasped at hope and could not hold it. If not Florence, then who?

Did Barclay Hamilton's deep, unwavering aversion to his stepmother have anything to do with his father's death? Did he know or suspect something? That thought was no pleasanter; she had liked them both, and what cause could there be in their antipathy that would inspire murder now? Was the murderer a business or political enemy? Pitt had found neither.

James or Helen Carfax? Nobby Gunne had thought not, and her judgment seemed good. If their own investigations were worth anything—which was growing doubtful; never had Charlotte felt less confidence in herself—then it would be their judgment of character; their knowledge, as women, of other women; their intimacy with Society, which the police could not have; that would make a difference. They had engineered opportunities for observing their subjects in unguarded moments, obtaining confidences because their interest was unsuspected. If they discounted that advantage, then there was nothing left.

And Cuthbert Sheridan? As yet they knew nothing of him, except that his family seemed in no way unusual, nor did they seem to have any reason to desire his death. His widow was a woman newly discovering her own aspirations and for the first time in her life developing independent opinions. Perhaps they had quarreled, but one does not hire a cutthroat to murder one's husband because he disapproves of one's newfound political views, even if he forbids them outright. And there was nothing to suggest Cuthbert Sheridan had done that, was there?

Pitt was out now trying to learn something more of Sheridan's political, business, and private life. But what had he in common with the others that had marked him for death? She had not even a guess.

Her thoughts were interrupted by the postman, who brought the butcher's bill, the coal merchant's account, and a long letter from Emily. The bills were for a trifle less than expected, which was cheering: the price of mutton was three ha'pence a pound less than she had budgeted for. She put them on the kitchen mantel, then tore open Emily's latest letter.

Florence, Saturday

My dearest Charlotte,

What a perfectly marvelous city! Palaces with names that roll off the tongue, statues everywhere, and of such astounding beauty that I stand in the street and stare until passersby bump into me and I feel foolish, but I don't care. I think sometimes Jack pretends he is not with me! And the people! I used to think that those faces painted by da Vinci lived only in his imagination, or perhaps he had a fixation with one family and painted them over and over again. But Charlotte, there are people here who look exactly so! I saw a perfect "Madonna of the Rocks" standing in the piazza yesterday, feeding the birds while her carriage waited for her and her footman grew impatient. I think she may have been hoping to catch a glimpse of a lover, perhaps waiting for Dante to cross the bridge? I know I am in the wrong century—but who cares? It is all like a glorious poetic dream come true.

And I thought the golden light over the hills in Renaissance paintings was a mixture of the artist's license and the tint of old varnish. It isn't: the air really is different here, there is a warmth in its color, a shade of gold in the sky, the stones, even the trees. Utterly different from Venice, with all its shifting patterns, its blue sky and water, but every bit as lovely.

I think my favorite of all the statues is Donatello's Saint George. He is not very big, but oh so young! He has so much hope and courage in his face, as if he had newly seen God and was determined to overcome all the evil in the world to find his way back, to fight every dragon of selfishness and squalor, every dark idea of man, without having the least idea how long or how dreadful the fight would be. My heart aches for him, because I see Edward, and Daniel, too, in his innocence, and yet he lifts my spirits as well, because of his courage. I stand by the Bargello with the tears running down my face. Jack thinks I am becoming eccentric, or perhaps that the sun has affected me, but I think I have found my best self.

Truly I am having a marvelous time, and meeting so many interesting people. There is one woman here who has been twice betrothed, and jilted on both occasions. She must be close to thirty-five, and yet she approaches life with such an expectation of enjoyment that she is a pleasure to be with. They must be poor creatures indeed who abandoned her for some other. What shallow judgment some people have, to choose one for a pretty face or a docile air; they deserve to end up with someone of disagreeable temperament and with a whining tongue—and I hope they do! She has a kind of courage I find myself admiring more with each day. She is determined to be happy, to see what is good and to make the best of what is not. How different from some of our traveling companions!

And amid all the music and theater, carriage rides, dinners, even balls, there have been some disasters. We have been robbed, but fortunately not much of value was taken, and once the carriage wheel came off and we could not find anyone prepared to assist us. We were obliged to spend the night in a cold and noisy place between Pisa and Siena, where we were obviously unwelcome, and I vow there were rats!

But Jack is perfectly charming. I believe I shall be happy with him even when all the romance is settled, and we begin to live an ordinary life, seeing each other over the breakfast table and in the evenings. I must persuade him to find some occupation, simply because I cannot bear to have him around the house all day, or we should become tired of each other. Nor on the other hand should I wish to spend my time worrying whether he is in poor company. Have you noticed how tedious people are when they themselves are bored?

You know, I think happiness is to some extent

a matter of choice. And I have determined to be happy, and that Jack shall make me so—or at least I should say that I shall take every opportunity to be pleased.

I expect to be home in two weeks, and in many ways I am looking forward to it, especially to seeing you again. I really do miss you, and since I have not been able to receive letters from you, I am longing more than ever to know what you have been doing, and Thomas. You know, I think I miss Thomas as much as anybody I know! And of course I miss Edward.

I shall be there to visit you the day I return. Until then, take care of yourself and remember I love you,

Emily

Charlotte stood for a long time with the letter in her hand and a feeling of growing warmth. Without realizing it, she was smiling. She would love to have seen Florence, the colors and sights, the beautiful things, especially the Saint George, and the other splendors. But Emily was right: much of happiness was a choice, and she could choose to look at Emily's romance and glamor and envy her, or to look at the rare and precious friendship she had with Pitt, his gentleness, his tolerance of her adventures, his willingness to share with her his ideas and his emotions. She realized with a jolt of amazement and intense gratitude that since she had known Pitt she had never felt truly lonely. What was a lifetime of grand tours compared with that?

She spent the day working in the house, talking to herself as she went, tidying, rearranging, straightening, polishing. She sent Gracie out for flowers and fresh meat to make Pitt's favorite, steak and kidney pudding with a rich suet crust on top as light as a feather. She set the table in the parlor with linen and had the children washed and in their nightshirts when he came home.

She permitted them to run to the door to greet him and be hugged and kissed and sent to bed; then she threw her arms round his neck and held him tightly, saying nothing, just glad to have him there.

Pitt saw the linen and the flowers, saw that Emily had taken special care over every detail. He saw the golden pudding and the fresh vegetables and smelled the delicious steam rising from them, and he misunderstood it all. He thought of Micah Drummond's office and of the promotion, of Emily's letters, which he had not read, and all the new things a little more money would mean for Charlotte.

The more he thought of desk work, the more he hated the idea, but looking at Charlotte's smiling face across the table, at the feminine touches in his home—the flowers, the hand-painted lamp shades, the embroidered linen, the sewing box piled with fabric for the children's clothes—he felt it was a small price to pay for her happiness. He would do it, and he would try hard to see she never knew the cost. Smiling back, he began to share with her the events of the day, little as they had yielded about Cuthbert Sheridan or his family.

Charlotte went with Great-aunt Vespasia and Zenobia Gunne to attend the funeral of Cuthbert Sheridan, M.P. The weather had changed, and the mild winds and sun were replaced by sharp squalls which brought swords of soaking rain one moment, and a cold, glittering light gleaming on wet surfaces, running gutters, and dripping leaves the next.

The three of them traveled in Vespasia's carriage, for convenience and so they might compare observations, if any, although none of them held any strong hope of learning anything useful. The whole investigation seemed to have come to a standstill. According to Pitt, Charlotte informed them, even the police had progressed no further. If Florence Ivory had killed Sheridan, they had discovered no motive for it, nor any witness who even knew of a connection between them, let alone could place her at the scene with means or opportunity.

Vespasia sat upright in the carriage, dressed in lavender and black lace; Zenobia faced her, riding backwards. She wore a very fine, highly fashionable gown of dark slate blue overlaid with black in a fleur-de-lis design, stitched at the bosom with jet beads, the sleeves gathered at the shoulder. She wore with it a black hat which tilted alarmingly and threatened to take off altogether whenever a gust of wind veered to the east.

As had become her habit, Charlotte had borrowed an old dress of Vespasia's, of dark gray, and a black hat and cloak, and with her rich hair and honey warm skin the effect was remarkably becoming. Vespasia's lady's maid had done a few last-minute alterations, which removed from the gown the marks of five-year-old fashion, and now it was merely a very fine gown in which to attend a funeral and be distinguished but not ostentatious.

They arrived opportunely, after the mourners of duty, other members of Parliament and their wives, and immediately behind Charles Verdun, whom Vespasia knew and drew Charlotte's attention to in a whisper as they alighted and slowly walked the short distance from Prince's Road to the vestry of St. Mary's Church.

They were seated in their pew and able to observe Amethyst Hamilton when she arrived, walking straight and tall herself and a step in front of her brother, Sir Garnet Royce, refusing to accept the arm he offered her. Two paces behind them, holding a silk hat in his hand and looking suitably sad and more than a little harassed, came their younger brother Jasper, with a fair-haired woman who was presumably his wife. Charlotte identified them to Vespasia, and watched them discreetly as they were ushered to a pew in the far side three rows forward, which denied her the opportunity of seeing their faces. Sir Garnet was very striking with his high forehead and aquiline nose. The light from the south windows shone briefly on his silver head before the clouds blew across the sky again and the sunlight vanished. Charlotte noticed many eyes on him, and now and again he nodded in acknowledgment of some acquaintance, but his main attention seemed to be for his sister and her welfare, for which she appeared unaccountably ungrateful.

Jasper sat next to them in silence, fingering through his hymnal.

There was something of a stir as a well-known Cabinet figure arrived, representing the Prime Minister; after all this was a famous and shocking death. If Her Majesty's Government and their police force could not solve the crime and apprehend the criminal, they could at least be seen to pay all due respects.

Micah Drummond came in much more quietly and sat in the last pew, watching, although he had given up hope of learning anything of value. Neither Charlotte nor Vespasia saw Pitt standing at the very back, looking like one of the ushers, except for the pool of water collecting about his feet from his wet coat; but Charlotte knew he would be there.

At the far side among several other members of Parliament Charlotte saw the humorous, wing-browed face of Somerset Carlisle. She met his eyes for a moment before he saw Vespasia and inclined his head with the suggestion of a smile.

Then the Carfaxes arrived. James, in black, was remarkably elegant but paler than usual; his eyes downcast, he did not seek the glance of anyone else. His confidence in his charm seemed lacking, his old ease had fled. On his arm Helen walked calmly, and there was a peace in her face that added to her dignity. She drew her hand from James's arm before he had released it and sat with composure in the pew immediately to Charlotte's right.

Lady Mary came last. She looked magnificent, even regal. Her dress was highly fashionable; dark slate blue overlaid with black fleur-de-lis and stitched with jet beads across the throat and bosom, the sleeves gathered. A black hat adorned her head at a rakish angle, dashing and precarious. As she drew level with Charlotte, her eyes darted along the row, caught by Zenobia's gorgeous hat, her gown—and she froze, all the color draining from her already pallid face. Her black-gloved hand clenched on her black umbrella handle.

Behind her an usher murmured, "Excuse me, my lady," urging her to take her place. Shaking with fury, there was nothing she could do but obey.

Zenobia dived into her reticule for a handkerchief and failed to find one. Vespasia, who had seen Lady Mary arrive, handed her one with an unconcealed smile, and Zenobia proceeded to have a stifled fit of coughing—or laughter.

The organ was playing somber music in a minor key. Finally the widow came in, veiled and in unrelieved black, followed by her children, looking small and forlorn. A governess in black followed and knelt in the pew behind.

The sermon began. The familiar pattern of music and intoned prayer and responses, accompanied the monotonous, hollow voice of the vicar going through the ritual of acknowledging grief and giving it dignified and formal expression. Charlotte paid little attention to the words or the order, instead watching the Carfaxes as discreetly as she could from behind her prayer book.

Lady Mary stared in front of her with a fixed expression, studiously avoiding looking to her left at Zenobia. If she could have taken off her hat she would have, but that was impossible in church; even to alter its angle would be observed now and would only draw attention to the whole business.

Beside her James took part dutifully, rising when everyone else did, kneeling with his head bowed for prayer, sitting solemnly with his eyes on the vicar when he began the address. But the rather drawn look on his face, the strain and slow absorption of shock were not accounted for by grief. Nothing at all had suggested he knew Cuthbert Sheridan, and according to Zenobia a few days earlier he had certainly been in as good spirits as was decent after his father-in-law's death. In fact, he had seemed to her to exude a sort of confidence, a certainty of pleasures to come.

Charlotte mechanically sang the hymn, her mind far

from the words, and continued to watch James Carfax. The zest had gone out of him: in the last few days he had suffered a genuine loss.

The vicar was beginning his eulogy; Pitt would be listening to see if there was anything in it of the slightest use in the investigation, which was extremely unlikely. Charlotte turned her attention to Helen Carfax.

The vicar's voice rose and fell in a regular rhythm, sinking at the end of every sentence; curious how that made him sound so insincere, so devoid of all feeling. But it was the expected form and gave the proceedings a certain familiarity, which she supposed was uplifting to those who came for comfort.

Helen sat upright, her shoulders square, facing directly forward. During the entire service she had participated with something that looked like the very first germ of enthusiasm. There was a resolution in her quite unlike the distress and anxiety Zenobia and Pitt had described. And yet as Charlotte watched her gloved hands holding the hymn book in her lap, her pale cheeks, and the slight movement of her lips, she was quite certain that any relief Helen felt was only that of having reached some decision, not of having had her fear dissolve or turn out to be a shadow with no substance. Charlotte realized it was courage she was witnessing, not joy.

Had Helen somehow ascertained that her husband had had no part in her father's death? Or had the whole burden upon her been simply the pain of knowing that he did not love her with the depth and the commitment she longed for, which indeed he was incapable of doing. And now that she had faced the truth, tempered by the knowledge that it was a weakness in him, not in her, she had ceased to try to procure it by forfeiting her self-esteem, her dignity, and her own ideas of right. Perhaps it was a wholeness within herself she had recovered.

Three times during the service Charlotte saw James speak to her, and on each occasion she answered him civilly, in a whisper; but she turned to him not so much like a woman desperately in love, but rather with the patience of a mother towards a pestering child who is at the age when such things are to be expected. Now it was James who was surprised and confused. He was used to being the object of her suit, not the suitor, and the change was sharply unpleasant.

Charlotte smiled and thought with sweetness of Pitt standing at the back in his wet coat, watching and waiting, and in her mind she stood beside him, imagining her hand in his.

After the last hymn and the final amen, many rose to leave. Only the widow and the closest mourners followed the pallbearers and the coffin to the graveside.

It was a grim performance; nothing of the music and pageantry of the church, not a dealing with the spirit and the words of resurrection, but the tidying away of the mortal remains, the box with its unseen corpse, and the cold spring earth.

Here emotions might show raw, there might be in some face or some gesture a betrayal of the passions that moved the hearts beneath the black silk and bombazine, the barathea and broadcloth.

The sunlight was sharp outside, brilliant on the stone face of the church walls and the thick green grass sprouting around the gravestones. Old names were carved on them, and memories. Charlotte wondered if any of them had been murdered. It would hardly be written in the marble.

It was wet underfoot, and the clouds above were gray-bellied. The wind was chill, and any moment it might rain again. The pallbearers kept their even measured tread, balancing the load between them, the breeze tugging at the fluttering crepe on their black hats. They kept their faces downward, eyes to the earth, more probably from fear lest they slip than an abundance of piety.

Charlotte followed decently far behind the widow, managing to fall in step beside Amethyst Hamilton. Charlotte smiled briefly in recognition—this was not the place to renew an acquaintance with words—and kept close to her as she followed her brothers towards the great oblong hole in the earth with its fresh, dark sides falling away into an unseen bottom.

They gathered on three sides while the pallbearers lowered the coffin, and the grim ritual was played out, the wind whipping skirts and pulling at streamers of black crepe. Women held up black-gloved hands to secure their hats. Lady Mary and Zenobia put up their arms at exactly the same moment, and the two huge brims were pitched at even wilder angles. Someone tittered nervously and changed it into a theatrical cough. Lady Mary glared round for the culprit in vain. She skewered the ferrule of her umbrella into the ground with a vicious prod and stood with her chin high, looking straight ahead of her.

Charlotte watched Jasper Royce and his wife. She was well-dressed but unremarkably so and appeared to be there as a matter of duty. Jasper was a softer, less emphatic version of his brother. He had the same sweeping forehead but without the striking widow's peak. His brows were good, but straighter and less powerful; his mouth was more mobile, the lower lip a little fuller. He was not as individual, not nearly as striking, and yet, Charlotte thought, perhaps an easier man with whom to spend any degree of time.

Now he was bored; his glance wandered idly over the faces opposite him on the far side of the grave, and none seemed to catch his interest. He might have been thinking of dinner or the next day's patients, of anything but the purpose for which they were come.

Sir Garnet, on the other hand, was alert; in fact he seemed to be studying the others present quite as diligently as Charlotte herself, and she had to be careful he did not catch her eye and mark her observation of him. To stare at him as steadily as she was doing, if caught, would seem extraordinary and require an explanation.

He watched quietly as the coffin was lowered into the grave and the first drops of rain spattered on the hats and skirts of the ladies and the bare heads of the men, and umbrellas were twitched nervously, and left alone. Only one person broke his poise sufficiently to look up at the sky.

The vicar's voice grew a trifle more rapid.

Garnet Royce was tense; there were lines of strain in his face more deeply etched than there had been after Lockwood Hamilton's death. He shifted uneasily, watching, glancing about as if every movement might be of some importance, as though searching might yield him an answer he needed so badly that the pursuit of it dominated his mind.

Was there some factor he knew of that Charlotte did not? Or was it merely that his intelligence made him fully aware of the magnitude of these horrors, more so than the other mourners, who were come from personal grief, or a sympathy born of a similar loss? But what about the other members of Parliament? Did they not know that the newspapers were clamoring for an arrest, that people wrote letters demanding a solution, more police, a restoration of law in the streets and safety for the decent citizen going about his duty or his pleasures? There was talk of treason and sedition, criticism of the government, of the aristocracy, even of the Queen! There were very real fears of revolution and anarchy! The throne itself was in jeopardy, if the worst rumors were to be believed.

Perhaps Royce could see what others only imagined?

Or did he guess at a conspiracy of a private nature, a secret agreement to murder for profit, or whatever three quite separate motives might drive three people to ally with each other to make all the crimes look like the work of one fearful maniac.

Then was Amethyst after all at the heart of at least her husband's death, either as the perpetrator, or the cause?

It was over at last, and they were walking back towards the vestry. The rain came harder, the glittering shafts silver where the light caught them. It was unseemly to hurry. Lady Mary Carfax put up her umbrella, swinging it fiercely round and swiping at Zenobia's skirt with the sharp ferrule. It caught in a ruffle and tore a piece of silk away.

"I do beg your pardon," Lady Mary said with a tight smile of triumph.

"Not at all," Zenobia replied inclining her head. "I can recommend a good maker of spectacles, if you—"

"I can see perfectly well, thank you!" Lady Mary snapped.

"Then perhaps a cane?" Zenobia smiled. "To help your balance?"

Lady Mary trod sharply in a puddle, splashing them both, and swept on to speak to the Cabinet Minister's wife.

Everyone was hastening towards the shelter of the church, heads down, skirts held up off the wet grass. The men bent their backs and tried to move as fast as was consistent with any dignity at all.

Charlotte realized with irritation that she had dropped her handkerchief, which she had taken out and held to her eyes from time to time so that she might observe Garnet Royce undetected. It was one of the few lace-edged ones she had left and far too precious to lose simply for the sake of keeping dry. She excused herself from Aunt Vespasia and turned to retrace her steps back round the corner of the church and along the track towards the grave.

She had just rounded the corner and was coming up behind a large rococo gravestone when she saw two figures standing facing each other as if they had met unexpectedly the instant before. The man was Barclay Hamilton, his skin ashen and wet with rain, his hair plastered to his head. In the harsh daylight the pain in him was startlingly clear; he looked like a man suffering a long illness.

The woman was Amethyst. She blushed darkly, then the blood fled from her face and left her as white as he. She moved her hands almost as if to ward him off, a futile, fluttering gesture that died before it became anything. She did not look at him.

"I . . . I felt I ought to come," she said weakly.

"Of course," he agreed. "It is a respect one owes."

"Yes, I—" She bit her lip and stared at the middle button of his coat. "I don't suppose it helps, but I . . ."

"It might." He watched her face, absorbing every fleeting expression, staring as if he would mark it indelibly in his mind. "Perhaps in time she may feel . . . that it was good that people came."

"Yes." She made no move to leave. "I—I think I am glad people came to—to—" She was very close to weeping. The tears stood out in her eyes, and she swallowed hard. "To Lockwood's funeral." She took a deep breath and at last raised her face to meet his eyes. "I loved him, you know."

"Of course I know," he said so gently it was little more than a whisper. "Did you think I ever doubted it?

"No." She gulped helplessly as emotion and years of pent-up pain overtook her. "No!" And her body shook with sobs.

With a tenderness so profound it tugged at Charlotte's heart to watch them, he took her in his arms and held her while she wept, his cheek against her hair, then his lips, for a moment, brief and immeasurably private.

Charlotte shrank behind the gravestone and crept away in the rain. At last she understood the icy politeness, the tension between them, and the honor which kept them apart, their terrible loyalty to the man who had been her husband and his father. And his death had brought no freedom to them, the ban on such a love was not dissolved—it was forever.

Pitt attended the funeral without hope that he would learn anything of value. During the service he stood at the back and watched each person arrive. He saw Charlotte with Vespasia and a woman of striking appearance and much more fashionable than Charlotte had led him to expect, but he presumed she must be Zenobia Gunne. Perhaps he was more ignorant of the niceties of fichus and sleeves and bustles than he had thought.

Then he saw Lady Mary Carfax sweep in in a gown so nearly identical as to look like a copy, and he knew he had been right the first time.

He also saw the new, inner calmness in Helen Carfax, and the self-assurance that had deserted James, and recalled what Charlotte had told him about Zenobia's visit. One day, if it were possible without social awkwardness, he would like to meet Zenobia Gunne.

He had noticed Charles Verdun as one of the first to arrive, and remembered how much he had liked him. Yet a business rivalry between Verdun and Hamilton was not impossible. Heaven knew, nothing yet made any real pattern; there were only isolated elements, passions, injustices, terrible loss and hatred, possibilities of error in the dark, and always in the background the murmur of anarchy in the ugly, teeming back streets beyond Limehouse and Whitechapel and St. Giles. Or madness—which could be anywhere.

Hamilton and Etheridge were physically similar, of the same height and general build under an evening coat, both with longish, pale, clean-shaven faces and thick silver hair. Sheridan had been younger, and fair-haired, but within an inch of the height. And on the bridge, between the small spheres of light in the vast darkness of the sky and river, what difference was there to the eye between gray hair and blond?

Was it some grotesque, lunatic mistake? Or was the murderer totally sane in its purpose, and there a key to it which he had not even guessed at yet?

He watched the players as they sat in outward devotion through the tedious service. He noticed Somerset Carlisle, and remembered his strange, passionate morality which had held to such bizarre behavior when they had first met, years ago. He saw the widow and felt churlish to question her grief. He watched Jasper and Garnet Royce, and Amethyst Hamilton. He saw Barclay Hamilton deliberately sit as far from them as he could without drawing attention to himself by asking others to move.

When the service was over he did not follow them to the

graveside. He would be too conspicuous; no one would take him for family or associate. It would be a pointless intrusion.

Instead he hung back near the entrance to the vestry and watched. He saw Charlotte return and then look in her reticule and hurry back again out into the rain.

Micah Drummond stepped in a moment later, shaking the water off his hat and coat. He looked cold, and there was an increasing anxiety stamped in his face. Pitt could imagine the accusing stares his superior had endured from Members of Parliament, the asides from those in the Cabinet, the comments on police inefficiency.

Pitt caught his eye and smiled bleakly. They were no further forward, and they both knew it.

There was no time to talk, and to do so would compromise Pitt's "invisibility" as an apparent usher. A moment later Garnet Royce came in, heedless of the rain running down his face and dripping from the skirts of his coat onto the floor. He did not observe Pitt in the shadows but immediately approached Micah Drummond, his brow furrowed in earnestness.

"Poor Sheridan," he said briefly. "Tragedy—for everyone. Dreadful for his widow. Such a—a violent way to die. My sister is still suffering very much over poor Hamilton. Natural."

"Of course," Drummond agreed, his voice strained with the guilt he felt over his helplessness to do anything about it, to show that the investigation had taken a single step forward. He could offer nothing, and he would not lie.

It was not difficult for Royce to ask the next question. The silence invited it.

"Do you really think it is anarchists and revolutionaries? God knows, there are enough of them around! I have never heard so many rumors and whisperings of the collapse of the throne, and of new orders of violence. I know Her Majesty is not young and has undoubtedly taken her widowhood hard, but the people expect certain duties of a sovereign regardless of personal misfortune. And the Prince of Wales's behavior scarcely adds to the luster of the crown! And now the Duke of Clarence is causing gossip with his dissipation and irresponsibility. It seems everything we have taken half a millennium to build is in jeopardy, and we seem unable to stop wild murders in the heart of our capital city!" He looked frightened, not the panic of a hysterical or cowardly man, but the realization of one who sees clearly and is resolved to fight, knowing his anger immense and the prospect of victory uncertain.

Micah Drummond gave the only reply he could, but there was no pleasure in his thin face as he spoke. "We have investigated all the known sources of unrest, the insurrectionists and would-be revolutionaries of one sort and another, and we do have our agents and informers. But there is not a whisper that any of them ally themselves to the Westminster Cutthroat—in fact they seem little pleased by it! They want to win the common people, the little man whom society rejects or abuses, the man oppressed too far by overwork or underpayment. These lunatic murders improve no one's cause, not even the Fenians'."

Royce's face tightened as if some bleak fear had become reality.

"So you do not believe it is anarchists suddenly burst into open violence?"

"No, Sir Garnet, everything points away from it." Drummond looked down at his sodden boots, then up again. "But what it is, I don't know."

"Dear God, this is terrible." Royce closed his eyes in a moment of deep distress. "Here are we, you and I, the government and the law of the land, and we cannot protect ordinary people going about their lawful business at the heart of our city! Who will be next?" He looked up and stared at Drummond with brilliant eyes, almost silver in the light, now the rain had stopped outside. "You? Me? I tell you, nothing on earth would persuade me to walk home alone across Westminster Bridge after dark! And I feel a guilt, Mr. Drummond! All my life I have striven to make wise decisions, to develop strength of will and judgment, so that I might protect those weaker than myself, those it is given me both by God and by nature to care for. And here I am, incapable of exercising my own privileges and obligations because some lunatic is loose committing murder, apparently whenever he pleases!"

Drummond looked as if he had been struck, but he did not flinch. He opened his mouth to speak, but Royce cut in before he could find words.

"Good heavens, man, I'm not blaming you! How on earth does one find a random madman? It could be anybody! I daresay by daylight he looks the same as you or I. Or he may be any half clad beggar hunched in any doorway from here to Mile End or Woolwich or anywhere else. There are nearly four million people in the city. But we've got to find him! Do you know anything? Anything at all?"

Drummond let out his breath softly. "We know that he chooses his time with great care, because in spite of all the people around the Embankment and the entrance to the Houses of Parliament, the street vendors, prostitutes, and cabdrivers, no one has seen him."

"Or someone is lying!" Royce said quickly. "Perhaps he has an accomplice."

Drummond looked at him thoughtfully. "That supposes a kind of sanity—at least, on the part of one of them. Why should anyone aid in such a grotesque and profitless act unless they were paid?"

"I don't know," Royce admitted. "Perhaps the accomplice is really the instigator? He keeps a madman to commit his crimes for him?"

Drummond shivered. "It is grotesque, but I suppose it is possible. Someone driving a cab across the bridge, by night, with a madman inside, whom he lets loose just long enough to commit murder, then removes him from the scene before the body is discovered? At a good pace he could be along the Embankment, or going south up the Waterloo Road, and indistinguishable from a thousand others in a matter of moments—before the body is discovered or crime known. It's hideous."

"Indeed it is," Royce said huskily.

They stood in silence for a moment or two. Outside, the eaves dripped steadily and the shadows of mourners leaving passed across the doorway.

"If there is anything I can do," Royce said at last, "anything at all that will help, call on me. I mean it, Drummond—I will go to any lengths to catch this monster before he kills again."

"Thank you," Drummond accepted quietly. "If there is any way, I shall call on you."

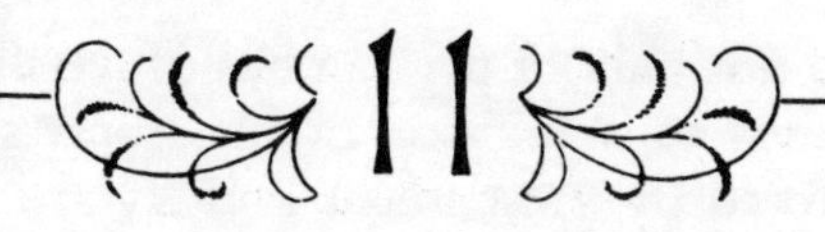

11

PITT LEFT THE FUNERAL and walked in the rain all the way down to the Albert Embankment. He was halfway across the Lambeth Bridge before he finally caught a cab back to the police station at Bow Street. It gave him time to think before he should see Micah Drummond again. What Garnet Royce had said was fearful—but it could not be discarded. It was possible some conspiracy existed, some person was using a madman to achieve his ends, taking him to the bridge, directing him to his victim, and then driving him away again afterwards. They had long ago questioned every cabby with a license to drive a carriage of any sort in London, and learned nothing of value. In the beginning it was conceivable one might have lied, for bribe or out of fear, but with three murders it was no longer a serious thought.

Every effort to discover a sane motive for all three crimes had failed. No battle for money or power, no motive of revenge, love, or hate tied all three victims, nothing that he or Drummond had been able even to imagine, still less to find. Even Charlotte, usually so perceptive, had nothing to offer, except that she feared Florence Ivory had a passion of hatred strong enough to have moved her to murder, and the courage to act once her mind was set.

Yet with Etheridge dead, what reason had she to kill Sheridan? Except precisely that reason—that there was none—and perhaps by that means to establish her innocence. Could she have killed Hamilton by mistake, believing him to be Etheridge, and then killed Sheridan simply because it was senseless, to remove herself from suspicion? She would have to be a woman not only of passion but of terrifying coldness. He did not want to think so. In his mind sharp and unfeigned, unmarked by pretense or guilt, was an understanding of the pain of a woman who had lost all she valued, her last child.

There was nothing to do but return to the most basic, prosaic police work, rechecking everything, looking for the inconsistency, for the person who had seen something, recalled something.

Micah Drummond was already in his office when Pitt came up the stairs and knocked.

"Come in," Drummond said quietly. He was standing by the fire waiting, warming himself and drying his wet clothes. His boots were dark with water and his trousers steamed gently. He moved sideways so Pitt might receive some of the fire's warmth. It was a small gesture, but Pitt was touched by the graciousness of it more than by any words of praise or sympathy Drummond might have offered.

"Well?" Drummond asked.

"Back to the beginning," Pitt replied. "Interview the witnesses again, the constables on the beat closest to the bridge, find the cabbies again, everyone who crossed the bridge or passed along either embankment within an hour of the crime, before or after. I'll speak to all the M.P.s in the House on any of the three nights. We'll question all the street vendors again."

Drummond looked at him with a flicker of hope in his eyes. "You think we might still find something?"

"I don't know." Pitt would not patronize him with groundless optimism. "But it's the best we have."

"You'll need at least six more constables—that's all the men I can spare. Where do you want them?"

"They can question the cabbies, beat constables, and witnesses, and help with the M.P.s. I'll start this afternoon, find the street vendors tonight."

"I'll see some of the M.P.s myself." Reluctantly Drummond moved away from the fire and took his wet overcoat off the hook where he had hung it. "Where shall we begin?"

The long, chill afternoon's work yielded nothing new. The following day Pitt began again, the only difference being that Charlotte had told him in a few sad words that the feeling between Barclay Hamilton and his father's wife was not the jealousy or the loathing they had supposed, but a profound and hopeless love. It brought him no satisfaction, only a respect for the honor which had kept them apart over so many years, and a sharp and painful pity.

He was so suddenly grateful for his own good fortune that it was like a bursting inside him, a flowering so riotous there was barely room for all the blooms.

He found the flower seller near the bridge, a woman with broad hips and a weathered face. It was impossible to guess her age, it might have been a healthy fifty or a weary thirty. She had a tray of fresh violets, blue, purple, and white, and she looked at him hopefully when she saw his purposeful approach. Then she recognized him as the policeman who had questioned her before, and the light faded from her face.

"I can't tell yer nuffin' more," she said before he spoke. "I sell flars ter them as wants 'em, an' 'as the odd word wiv gennelmen as is civil, n' more. I didn't see nuffin' w'en them men was murdered, poor souls, 'cept the same as I always sees, nor no cabbies stop, nor any workin' girls, 'ceptin' those I already told yer abaht. An' Freddie wot sells 'ot pies an' Bert as sells san'wiches."

Pitt fished in his pocket and pulled out a few pence and offered them to her. "Blue violets, please—or—just a moment, what about the white ones?"

"They's extra, cos they smells sweeter. White flars orften does. Ter make up fer the color p'raps?"

"Then give me some of each, if you will."

"There y'are, luv—but I still didn't see nuffin. I can't 'elp yer. Wish I could!"

"But you remember selling flowers to Sir Lockwood Hamilton?"

"Yeah, course I do! Sold 'im flars reg'lar. Nice gent 'e was, poor soul. Never 'aggled, like some as I could name. Some gents wot 'as fortunes'll 'aggle over a farvin'." She sighed heavily, and Pitt imagined her life; a quarter of a penny on a bunch of flowers meant a difference to her, and she was only mildly indignant that men who ate nine-course dinners as a way of life would argue with her over the cost of a slice of bread.

"Do you remember that night? It was an unusually late sitting."

"Bless yer, they 'as late sittin's an' late sittin's," she said with a wink rather more like a twitch. "Wot was they sittin' over, eh? An argy-bargy, new laws fer us all—or a good bottle o' port wine?"

"It was a fine night, nice enough to walk home with pleasure. Go over it all again in your mind for me. Please. Did you have supper? What did you eat? Did you buy it from someone here?"

"That's right!" she said with sudden cheer. "I got some pickled eels an' a slice of 'ot bread down Jacko's stand, 'long the Embankment."

"Then what? What time was that?"

"Dunno, luv."

"Yes you do. You would have heard Big Ben—think! You'd be waiting to catch the Members as they left the House."

She screwed up her face. "I 'eard ten—but that was afore I went down ter Jacko's."

"Did you hear eleven? Where were you when Big Ben struck eleven?"

Someone else came past and bought a bunch of purple violets before she replied. "I was talkin' ter Jacko. 'E said as it was a good night fer trade, and folk was still abaht, it bein' fine like. An' I said that was good, cos I'd gorn an' got an extra load o' flars, and they don't last."

"And then you came back up here sometime before the House rose," he prompted.

"No," she said, deep in thought, her brow furrowed. "That's wot I din' do! I got fed up wiv waitin' fer 'em, an I went up ter the Strand and the theaters. Sold all me flars there, I did."

"You can't have," Pitt argued. "That must have been another night. You sold flowers to Sir Lockwood Hamilton. Primroses. He was wearing fresh flowers when he was killed, and he didn't have them when he left the House a few minutes before he crossed the bridge."

"Primroses? I don't 'ave no primroses. Violets, me, this time o' year. All sorts later on, but violets now."

"Never primroses?" Pitt said carefully, a strange and dreadfully sensible idea opening up in his mind. "Would you swear to that?"

"Gor lumme! D'yer fink I sold flars all me life since I were six years old, and don' know the difference between a primrose nor a violet? Wot yer take me for?"

"Then who gave the primroses to Sir Lockwood Hamilton?"

"Someone wot poached my beat!" she said sourly. Then her face eased in innate fairness. "Not as I didn't go up the Strand, wot in't stric'ly my place, but . . ." She shrugged. "Sorry, ducky."

"I suppose you didn't sell primroses to Mr. Etheridge, or Mr. Sheridan either?"

"I told yer, I never sold primroses to no one!"

Pitt thrust his hands deep into his pockets and pulled out a sixpence. He gave it to her and took two more bunches of flowers.

"Well then, I wonder who did."

"Cor!" She let out her breath in a moan of incredulity, which turned to horror. "The Westminster Cutthroat! 'E sold 'em! Don' it fair make yer blood cold? It do mine!"

"Thank you!" Pitt turned on his heel and walked rapidly

away, then started to run, shouting and waving his arms for a cab.

"A flower seller?" Micah Drummond repeated, his brow puckered in surprise. He turned the thought over in his mind, examining it and finding it more and more acceptable.

"It gives me something to look for," Pitt said eagerly. "In a way, flower sellers are invisible, as long as you don't know that is what you are looking for. But once you do, they are a very definite body. They have their own territories, like birds. You won't get two of the same sort in one street."

"Birds?"

"The Parliament end of Westminster Bridge is usually Maisie Willis's patch; the night Hamilton was killed, as we know, she went up the Strand instead. But our cutthroat wouldn't know that in advance. He—or perhaps I should say *she*—seized the opportunity, and again when Etheridge and Sheridan were killed. She must have been waiting, watching for the opportunity. She might have been there several nights before the House rose when Maisie wasn't there, and she caught the man she wanted alone on the bridge. He probably stopped to buy flowers, not recognizing the seller in the half light, and naturally not expecting to see anyone he knew dressed in old clothes and with a tray of flowers!"

He leaned forward eagerly, the picture coming more sharply into his mind. "She, or he, took the money, gave him the flowers, and then reached up to pin them on for him"—he curved his right hand sharply sideways, fingers crooked as if to hold a razor—"and cut his throat. Then as he collapsed she propped him up against the lamppost and tied him to it with his own scarf, leaving the primroses in his buttonhole. She could hide the razor again on the tray of flowers and simply walk away. No one would notice her: she was a flower seller who had made a sale and pinned the flowers on her patron before leaving."

"She must be a damn strong woman!" Drummond said

with a shiver of distaste. "Or it might have been a man; it would be perfectly possible for a man to disguise himself as a flower seller, muffled up on a chilly spring night, hat drawn down, shawl round his neck and chin. How in hell do we find him, Pitt?"

"We have an actual person to ask about now! We'll start again with other M.P.s. She can't have sold only the one bunch of flowers—others will have bought as well. Someone may remember something about her. After all, it was unusual for it to be anyone other than Maisie, and it was unusual to have primroses rather than violets. We ought to learn at least her height, that's hard to disguise; a stoop is noticeable. And you can add weight easily enough with clothes, but you can't take it off. A man can look like an old woman, but it's very much harder to look like a young one: the bones and the skin are wrong. Did anyone notice hands? No doubt she wore mitts, but the size? A big man can't make his hands look like a woman's."

"Perhaps it *was* two people?" Drummond met Pitt's eyes and his own were bright with unhappiness, his features pinched and weary. "Perhaps the flowers were a decoy, to hold his attention while someone else attacked?"

Pitt knew what he was thinking. Africa Dowell with flowers while Florence Ivory crept up with a razor from behind, the victim turning at the last moment—the cuts had been made from the front with the left hand—and then both women together holding him and tying him to the lamppost. More dangerous; more likely they'd be noticed, two women leaving the scene. But not impossible.

"There must be clothes," he said levelly, forcing the picture from his mind's eye. "A flower seller in a lady's gown and cloak would be remarked instantly, and the M.P.s never mentioned that it was not the usual woman, therefore she must have looked something similar, of average height, broadly built, big shoulders and bosom, wide hips. Plain clothes, probably several layers; a hat and shawl, and probably a second shawl against the wind coming up off the river.

And most important of all, a tray of flowers. She had to buy some, not very many. She would want to look as if she were at the end of a long day's selling: four or five bunches would be enough. But she had to buy them somewhere."

"Didn't you say Florence Ivory had a garden?" Drummond asked, moving back to the fire again and staring up at Pitt as he bent to put more coal on it. The day was colder and there was a thin drizzle of rain running down the window. Both men felt the chill.

"Yes, but you can't pick primroses by the bunch day after day from a private garden."

"Can't you? How do you know so much about gardens, Pitt? Don't have a garden, do you? When do you find the time?" He looked round. "Mind, you'll have more when you're promoted after we tie up this case."

Pitt smiled thinly. "Yes—yes I will. Actually, we do have a small garden, but Charlotte does more in it than I do. I grew up in the country."

"Did you?" Drummond's eyebrows rose. "I didn't know that. Somehow I thought you were a Londoner. Amazing how little we know about people, even though we see them every day. So she bought primroses?"

"Yes, probably from the same source as other flower sellers. One of the markets. We can send men out to search."

"Good; arrange it. And questioning the M.P.s, I'll go out on that again too. Which of the people we know would be capable of passing as a street vendor? Surely not Lady Hamilton?"

"I doubt it, and I don't think Barclay Hamilton could pass himself off as a woman—he's far too tall, apart from anything else."

"Mrs. Sheridan?"

"Possibly."

"Helen Carfax?"

Pitt shrugged, the question was too hard. He could not visualize the pale, unhappy woman he had seen after her father's death, so torn with fears, so painfully in love with her husband, so wounded by his every small indifference, having the confidence and efficiency to acquire flowers and then stand on a street corner selling them to passing strangers so that she might commit murder. He remembered Maisie Willis's voice, casual, broad, idiosyncratic.

"I doubt she could master selling," he said frankly. "And James Carfax is the same as Barclay Hamilton, too tall not to be noticed."

"Florence Ivory?"

Florence had left her husband and found shelter for herself and her child, until Africa Dowell had taken her in. Perhaps she had also worked at something.

"Yes, I imagine she might. She certainly has the imagination and intelligence to do it, and the willpower."

Drummond leaned forward.

"Then, Pitt, we've got to catch her. We've got grounds to search her house now. We may find the clothes—if she means to do it again we almost certainly will. Dear God, she must be mad!"

"Yes," Pitt agreed with cold unhappiness. "Yes, I daresay she is, poor soul."

But the minutest search yielded only much-mended work clothes, gardening gloves, and kitchen aprons—nothing that would have dressed a flower seller—and only baskets and trugs for flowers, no trays such as street vendors use.

The third questioning of the members of Parliament produced a little more. Several men, when specifically pressed, recalled a different flower seller on the nights of the murders, but they could describe only the roughest details: she was rather larger than Maisie Willis, and taller they thought, but not much else. What they really recalled was that she had sold primroses instead of violets.

Was she very muffled with scarves or shawls?

Not particularly.

Was she young or old, dark or fair?

Definitely not young, nor, they thought, very old. Perhaps forty, perhaps fifty. For heaven's sake, who spends their time estimating the age of flower sellers?

A big woman, they all agreed, bigger than Maisie Willis. Then it was certainly not Florence Ivory. Africa Dowell padded out a little, her face grimed and made up to hide her fine fair skin, her hair bound in an old scarf or hat, a little dirt judiciously rubbed in?

He returned to Bow Street and met with Drummond to share his findings and consider the next step.

Drummond looked tired and beaten. The bottoms of his trousers were wet, his feet were cold, and he was exhausted with talking, with searching for a courteous way of asking over and over again questions that had already been answered with negatives, worn out with weighing, measuring and sifting every fragment of memory, every fact or suggestion, and knowing at the end of it no more than the beginning.

"Do you think she'll do it again?" he asked.

"Only God knows," Pitt replied, not blasphemously—he meant it. "But if she does, this time we know what to look for." Drummond pushed the blotter and the inkstand away and sat on the edge of his desk. "That could be weeks, months, or never."

Pitt looked at him. The same thought was mirrored in both their faces.

Drummond put it into words. "We must provoke her. We will have someone cross the bridge alone, after every late sitting. We will be close at hand; we can disguise ourselves as street vendors and cabbies."

"We haven't got a constable who can pass for an M.P."

Drummond pulled a very small face. "No, but I could. I'll go myself."

And for eight nights Micah Drummond slipped into the House of Commons strangers' gallery and sat there until the House rose, then mixed with the members as they left, talking for a few minutes with the one or two he knew. Then he turned and left, walking up past the great statue of Boadicea and onto Westminster Bridge. Twice he bought violets from

Maisie Willis, and once a hot pie from the vendor on the Embankment, but he saw no one with primroses, and no one approached him.

On the ninth evening, discouraged and tired, he was turning up his coat collar against a chilly wind and wraiths of fog coming off the river, when Garnet Royce came up to him.

"Good evening, Mr. Drummond."

"Oh, er, good evening, Sir Garnet."

Royce's face was tense. The lamplight gleamed on his high forehead and reflected the pale brilliance of his eyes.

"I know what you're doing, Mr. Drummond," he said very quietly. "And that it is not succeeding." He swallowed, his breath uneven, but he was a man used to being in command, of himself and of others. "And you won't succeed—not this way. I offered to help you before, and I meant it. Let me walk back across the bridge. If this lunatic means to strike again, I am a legitimate target: a real M.P. . . ." He faltered for a moment, then he cleared his throat and made a fierce effort to speak without a quaver. "A real M.P. who lives south of the river, and who could reasonably go home on foot on a fine night."

Drummond hesitated. All the risks swam before his eyes: his own guilt if anything were to happen to Royce, the charges that would be leveled against him. He winced as he thought how easily he could be accused of cowardice. And yet eight nights he had left the Palace of Westminster and walked alone across the bridge, and he'd achieved nothing. What Royce said was true: the cutthroat may well be insane, but she—or he—was not easily duped.

He knew Royce was afraid; he could see it in his eyes, in the fierce stare, in the nervous line of his mouth and the rigid way he held himself, seeming oblivious of the chill breeze and the clamor of other people busy less than twenty feet away, and yet for him they might have been geese on a lawn or pigeons in Trafalgar Square.

"You are a brave man, Sir Garnet," he said honestly. "I

accept your offer. I wish we could do it without you, but it seems we cannot." He saw Royce's chin rise a little higher, and the muscles in his throat tighten. The die was cast. "We shall be within a few yards of you all the time—cabbies, street vendors, drunks. I give you my word, we shall not allow you to be hurt." Please God he could keep it!

He told Pitt the following morning, sitting in his office by a roaring fire. The sight of its flames leaping up the chimney and the flicker and crackle of it seemed like an island of safety, a living companion as he thought of the night on the bridge. He had still had to cross it after speaking to Royce, still setting out at a measured pace into the gloom between the lamps, his footsteps falling dully on the wet pavement, veils of mist rising from the dark sheet of the water below, lights and voices from the bank distorted, far away.

Pitt was staring at him.

"Is there any other way?" Drummond asked helplessly. "We've got to stop her!"

"I know," Pitt agreed. "And if there's another way, I don't know what it is."

"I'll be there," Drummond added. "I can pretend to be a drunk coming home from the opera—"

"No!—sir!" Pitt was firm; at another time, with another man it would have been considered rudeness. "Sir, if we need Royce, then it is because the cutthroat knows you are not an M.P. For this to succeed Royce has to appear vulnerable, a victim alone, not a police decoy. You can't come any nearer than the Victoria Embankment. We'll have three constables at the far end, so he cannot escape that way, and we'll speak to the River Police so he doesn't get over the bridge and down to the water—though God knows how he'd do that. We'll have two constables dressed as street vendors at the House end, and I'll drive a cab across when Royce actually goes. If I stay a bit behind I can watch him; I'll get close enough without frightening anyone off. People always assume cabbies are watching the road."

"Can't we put a man actually on the bridge? As a drunk, or a beggar?" Drummond's face was pale, his nostrils pinched, and there was a transparent look to the skin across the top of his nose and under his eyes.

"No." Pitt felt no indecision. "If there is anyone else there, we'll frighten the cutthroat off."

Drummond tried one last time. "I gave Royce my word we'd protect him!"

There was nothing to say. They knew the dangers, and they understood that there was nothing else they could do.

For the next three nights the House rose early, and they kept watch, but with small hope of anything occurring. The fourth night the sky was heavy with unshed rain. The light was thin and darkness came early. The lamps along the Embankment looked like a string of fallen moons. The air smelled damp, and up and down the river the barges moved like wedges of darkness slicing the whispering, hissing water, with its broken reflections.

Under the statue of Boadicea with its magnificent horses, hooves flying, chariot careering forever in doomed heroic fight against the Roman invader dead two thousand years ago, a constable stood dressed as a sandwich vendor, his barrow in front of him, his neck muffled against the cold, his fingers blue in spite of his mittens, eyes watchful, waiting for Garnet Royce and ready to move out and follow him the moment anyone approached. His truncheon was hidden under his overcoat, but his hand knew exactly where it was.

At the entrance to the House of Commons another constable, dressed as a footman, stood to attention as though waiting for his master to approach with some message, but his eyes were searching for Garnet Royce—and a flower seller.

At the far end of the bridge on the south bank three

more constables waited; two on foot dressed as gentlemen with nothing better to do than idle away an evening looking for a little female company, and perhaps a trifle the worse for drink. The third constable drove a cab, which he kept standing twenty yards from the end of the bridge outside the first house on Bellevue Road, as though attending a fare who was visiting someone and might shortly return.

Micah Drummond stood in a doorway well out of the light on the Victoria Embankment and strained his eyes towards the New Palace Yard and the members of Parliament leaving. He could not make out any individuals, but he was as close as he dared be. He kept his face in shadow, his silk hat pulled forward and his scarf high round his chin. A passerby would have taken him for a gentleman who had celebrated rather too liberally and had stopped until his head cleared before going home. No one gave him a second glance.

Somewhere down the river towards the Pool of London the foghorns were sounding as the mist thickened and swept up with the incoming tide.

On the north bank, Pitt sat on the box of a second cab, on the Victoria Embankment just above the steps down to the water. He could see them all: the height of the cab seat gave him a vantage and also made his face less easy to recognize by a person on foot. He held the reins loosely in his hands while the horse shifted its weight restlessly.

Someone hailed him, and he called back, "Sorry guv, got a fare."

The man grumbled that he could see none but did not bother to argue.

Minutes ticked by. The members were beginning to disperse. The constable sold some of his sandwiches. Pitt hoped he did not sell them all, or he would have no excuse to remain there. A vendor out on a night like this, at this hour, with no wares to sell, would draw suspicion.

Where was Royce? What on earth was he doing? Pitt

could not blame him if his courage had failed; it would take a strong man to walk alone across Westminster Bridge tonight.

Big Ben struck quarter past eleven.

Pitt was longing to get down and go and look for Royce. If he had left by another way and gone west to Lambeth Bridge in a cab, they might wait here all night!

"Cabby! Twenty-five Great Peter Street. Come on, man! You're half asleep!"

"Sorry sir, I've already got a fare."

"Nonsense! There's no one here. Now pull yourself together and get a move on!" The man was middle-aged and brisk, his graying hair waved neatly and his expression was fast becoming irritated. He reached out a hand to open the cab door.

"I already have a fare, sir!" Pitt said sharply, his nerves betraying the fear he tried to force from his mind. "He's in there!" he poked a gloved finger in the general direction of the buildings along the Embankment. "I've got to wait for him."

The man swore under his breath and turned on his heel. He was an M.P. Pitt remembered seeing his photograph in *The Illustrated London News;* striking-looking man, well dressed, and—suddenly Pitt was as cold as if he had been drenched in ice water. He saw again in his mind's eye the pale blur of the flowers in the man's buttonhole—primroses!

His hand clenched so tight the horse started, throwing its head, and the harness clanked.

In his doorway Micah Drummond stiffened, but he could see nothing except Pitt, rigid on the cab box.

The wail of a foghorn drifted upriver and the lights reflected in the water danced along the shore.

Garnet Royce was coming down the street. He called out loudly to someone, his voice husky; he was frightened. His steps were uneven as he passed the sandwich vendor and started across the bridge. His back was straight, shoulders stiff, and never once did he look behind him.

Pitt moved his horse forward a few yards. A man with an umbrella passed between him and Royce. The sandwich vendor left his barrow, and the footman stopped looking in the direction of the New Palace Yard and walked towards the bridge as if he had changed his mind about waiting.

From the black shadow under Boadicea another figure appeared: heavyset, broad-backed, a thick shawl round her shoulders and carrying a vendor's tray of flowers. She ignored the footman—natural enough, footmen seldom bought flowers—and moved surprisingly swiftly after Royce across the bridge. He was walking steadily in the center of the footpath, looking neither right nor left, concentrating on the lights. He was precisely halfway across.

Micah Drummond came out of his doorway.

Pitt urged the horse forward into a brisk walk and turned it left over the bridge. He was only two or three yards behind the flower seller. He could see her figure silhouetted against the paler mist beyond. She was walking soft-footed, gaining on Royce. He did not seem to hear her.

He left the milky haze of one lamp with its triple globes and entered the void of darkness beyond. The mist was silver round the lights, and the droplets in the air gleamed like something beautiful and strange. His back was lit, showing the breadth of his shoulders, the precise angle of the rim of his hat, and his face was a mere lessening of the shadow, anonymous as he strode into the hollow of night between one lamp and the next.

Pitt held the reins so tightly his nails dug into his palms even through the wet wool of his mittens. He could feel the sweat cold on his body.

"Flowers, sir? You buy sweet primroses, sir?" The voice was hardly audible, high, like a little girl's.

Royce spun round. He was close enough to the light for his features to show clearly: his hair was hidden by the hat, but the sweeping brow was plain, the vivid eyes, the big bones. He saw the woman and the tray of primroses. He saw her take a bunch of flowers in one hand, the other drawing something from underneath them. His mouth opened in a soundless exclamation of terror—and glittering, superb victory.

Pitt let go of the reins and leapt from the cab box, landing hard on the slippery road. The woman swung her arm up with the razor in her hand, its blade open and shining in the light. "I got yer!" she screamed, flinging the tray off and sending the flowers spinning and scattering on the stones. "I got yer at last, Royce!"

Pitt was on top of her, bringing his truncheon down on her shoulder. The pain of it stopped her, brought her round sharply, face blank with surprise, the razor still high.

For a second they were all motionless: the madwoman with her black eyes and mouth open, the blade still in the air, Pitt with the truncheon clenched in his hand, and Royce ten feet beyond them.

Then Royce's hand went to his pocket, and before the woman could move, the shot rang out, and she took a stumbling step towards Pitt. There was another shot, and another, and she fell into the road and lay across the gutter, blood soaking her shawl, the razor tinkling thinly on the stones and the pale blossoms of the primroses lying around her.

Pitt bent over her for a moment. There was nothing to do. She was dead, shot cleanly through the heart from behind, as well as through the shoulder and the chest. He had no idea which bullet had killed her; it might have been any of the three.

He stood up slowly and looked at Royce, who was still standing with the gun in his hand, a revolver, black and polished, no longer hidden in the deep overcoat pocket. Royce's face was white, almost drained of expression; the fear had too recently left him.

"Good God, man—you nearly got yourself killed!" he said huskily. He passed his hand over his eyes and blinked, as though dizzy. He looked down at the woman. "Is she dead?"

"Yes."

"I'm sorry." Royce went towards her but stopped more

than a yard away. He passed the gun to Pitt, who took it reluctantly. Royce stared at the woman. "Although perhaps it is for the best. Poor creature may at last be at peace. This is cleaner than a rope."

Pitt could find no argument. Hanging was a grotesque and terrible thing, and why drag out a trial for a woman who was so patently insane? He faced Royce and tried to think of something appropriate to say.

"Thank you, Sir Garnet. We appreciate your courage—without it we might never have caught her." He held out his hand.

The constables were there from the south side of the bridge, and the pie vendor and the footman were approaching just beyond the circle of light. Micah Drummond stopped on the pavement and stared at the woman, then at Pitt and Royce.

Royce took Pitt's hand and wrung it so hard the flesh was bruised.

Micah Drummond knelt down and looked at the woman, moving the shawl away from her face, opening the front of it and searching for some mark of identity.

"Do you know her, sir?" he asked Royce.

"Know her? Good God, no!"

Drummond looked at her again, and when he turned back to them his voice was quiet, touched with compassion as well as horror.

"Some of her clothing comes from Bedlam. It looks as if she was in the asylum recently."

Pitt remembered what the woman's last words had been. He stared at Royce. "She knew you," he said quietly, very levelly. "She called you by name."

Royce was motionless, his eyes wide; then very slowly he went and looked down at the dead woman. No one spoke. Another foghorn sounded on the river.

"I—I'm not certain, but if she really has come from Bedlam, then it could be Elsie Draper, poor creature. She was lady's maid to my wife, seventeen years ago. She was a country woman, came with Naomi when we were married. Elsie was devoted to her, and when Naomi died she took it very badly. She became deranged, and we were obliged to have her committed. I—I admit, I had no idea she was homicidally insane. I wonder how in the name of heaven she came to be free."

"We haven't been notified of an escape," Drummond answered. "Presumably she was released. After seventeen years they may have thought her safe."

Royce gasped. "Safe!" The word hung in the damp air, with the slow-curling mist glowing in the lamplight.

"Come," Drummond stood up. "We'll get a mortuary van and take her away. Pitt, get your cab and take Sir Garnet home to. . . ?"

"Bethlehem Road," Royce replied. "Thank you. I confess, I feel suddenly very tired, and colder than I thought."

"Naturally we're very grateful." Drummond offered his hand. "All London is much in your debt."

"I'd rather you didn't mention my part," Royce said quickly. "It would seem . . ." He left the rest unsaid. "And I—I'd like to pay for a decent burial for her. She was a good servant before . . . before she lost her reason."

Pitt climbed back up onto the cab box. Drummond opened the door for Royce to climb in, and Pitt lifted the reins to urge the horse on.

Charlotte was asleep when Pitt got home, and he did not awaken her. He had no sense of the euphoria of having brought to a conclusion a long and dreadful case. The release of tension brought mostly weariness, and the next morning he slept in and had to rush out without breakfast.

He told Charlotte nothing. First he would make sure that what had seemed so apparent last night was really the truth. There would be time then to send her a message so she could tell Great-aunt Vespasia that Florence Ivory was no longer under suspicion. He simply told her the case was close to a conclusion, kissed her, and strode out of the house with her calling after him to explain.

Micah Drummond was already at the Bow Street Station. For the first time in weeks he looked as if he had slept without nightmares or frequent waking.

"Good morning, Pitt," he said, and held out his hand. "Congratulations, Chief Inspector. The case is closed. There is no doubt that wretched woman was responsible. There were other bloodstains on her clothes, old stains on her sleeves and apron, as there would be from the first murders. The razor had bloodstains on the blade and the handle. We checked with the chief medical officer at the Bethlehem lunatic asylum: she is Elsie Draper, committed for acute melancholia seventeen years ago and released from Bedlam two weeks before the murder of Lockwood Hamilton. She had never given them any trouble and seemed to have been a trifle simple, but never violent. A dreadful misjudgment, but there is nothing anyone can do now. The case is closed. The Home Secretary sent his congratulations this morning. The newspapers have printed extras." He smiled slowly. "Well done, Pitt. You can go home and take a few days off—you've earned it. You'll come back next week as Chief Inspector, with an office upstairs." He held out his hand.

Pitt took it and held it hard. "Thank you, sir," he said graciously—but it was not what he wanted.

12

PITT RETURNED HOME WITH a sense of relief only very slightly marred by a small question like a gnat bite at the back of his mind. The matter was closed. There could be no doubt whatsoever that Elsie Draper had been a criminal lunatic. She had murdered three men on Westminster Bridge and had tried to murder a fourth. Only Royce's courage in setting himself up as a decoy and the police who had warned and guarded him had prevented her almost certain success. And if it had not been Royce, it would have been someone else.

Now Pitt could take some time off and spend it with Charlotte and the children. Perhaps he could even get out into the garden. They could all work together, he with a spade, Jemima pulling weeds, Daniel carrying away rubbish, and Charlotte supervising. She was the only one who knew the overall design. He found himself smiling as he thought of it, as if his fingers were already in the earth, the warm sun on his back, and his family laughing and talking around him.

First Charlotte would go and tell Great-aunt Vespasia that Florence Ivory and Africa Dowell were no longer suspects. That would be one of the few real pleasures in this whole affair: to watch the fear and the anger disappear, to know the two women could pick up their lives again and begin to heal—that was, if they chose to, if Florence Ivory could let go of her rage.

He strode through the doorway and along the corridor to find Charlotte in the kitchen with her sleeves rolled up, kneading dough, and Gracie on the floor on her hands and knees. The whole room was filled with the smell of new bread. Daniel was outside in the garden running around with a hoop and Pitt could hear his crows of delight through the open window.

He put his arm round Charlotte and kissed her cheek and neck and throat, regardless of the flour and entirely ignoring Gracie.

"We've solved it!" he said after several minutes. "We caught the woman last night—in the act. Garnet Royce played decoy for us. She flew at him with a razor, and I jumped off the cab box to stop her, and Royce shot her, more or less to save me."

Charlotte stiffened and tried to draw back, fear rushing up inside her.

"No," he said quickly. "She wouldn't have gotten me; I had already struck her with a truncheon, and there were others coming. But it must have looked bad to Royce. Anyway, she was completely insane, poor creature, and this is better than a trial and a hanging. It's all over. And I'm a chief inspector."

This time she did pull away. She stared up at him, her cheeks flushed, her eyes wide, questioning.

"I'm proud of you, Thomas; you more than deserve it," she said, "But is it what you want?"

"Want?" Surely he had totally hidden his reluctance, his dislike of leaving the streets.

"You can have the honor of being asked, and still refuse," she said gently. "You don't have to take preferment if it means sitting in the station directing other men." Her eyes were perfectly steady and showed no shadow of wavering, nor any trace of regret for her words. "We don't need the money. You could stay as you are, doing what you are so good at. If you had been directing others instead of speaking to the people yourself, would this case be solved now?"

He thought of Maisie Willis and the violets, the long cold hours spent on the cab box, and the moment when he had realized the M.P. who had accosted him for a ride had fresh primroses in his buttonhole.

"I don't know," he said honestly. "It might be."

"And it might not! Thomas," she said, smiling now, "I want you to be doing what you enjoy and are best at. Anything else is too high a price to pay for a little more money, which we don't need. We can meet our expenses, and that is enough. What would we do with more? What is more precious than being able to do what you want?"

"I've accepted it," he said slowly.

"Then go back and tell him you have changed your mind. Please, Thomas."

He did not argue, he simply held her very closely for a long time, happiness singing inside him, beating like the wings of a great bird.

Gracie picked up her bucket and, humming a little song to herself, went out the back door to empty it down the drain.

"Tell me about it," Charlotte said presently. "How did you catch her—and who was she? Why did she do it? Why members of Parliament? Have you told Florence Ivory? Have you told Aunt Vespasia?"

"I haven't told anyone; I thought you'd like to."

"Oh yes—yes I would. I wish we had one of those telephones! Shall we go on the omnibus and tell her? Would you like a cup of tea first? Or are you hungry? What about luncheon?"

"Yes, yes, no, and it's too early," he replied.

"What?"

"Yes we'll go and see Aunt Vespasia, yes I'd like a cup of tea, no I'm not hungry, and it's too early for lunch. And your bread is rising."

"Oh. Then put on the kettle. I'll finish kneading the dough, and you can tell me who she was and how you caught her—and why she did it." And she went to the sink, washed her hands, and began again to pummel the bread dough, sprinkling more flour on the board.

Pitt filled the kettle and put it on the stove as he was bidden, then began to recount the story of Royce's offer and how they had carried it out. Of course she already knew about the abortive attempts with Micah Drummond.

"So it wasn't blind," she said when he finished. "I mean, she wasn't after members of Parliament in general. She knew Royce—you said she called out his name."

Pitt remembered the blaze of hatred on the woman's voice, the triumph in the moment she recognized him and knew beyond doubt it was he. "I've got you at last," she had said, and careless of the cab looming behind her, or Pitt leaping from it, she had lifted and swung the razor to kill. She was insane, a creature beyond the reach of reason, a destroyer—and yet there had been something very human in that hatred.

Charlotte's voice cut into his thoughts.

"Do you think she was after Royce all the time, and mistook the others for him? They all lived on the south side of the river, they all walked home, as it was not far, and they all had fair or gray hair."

"They were all Parliamentary Private Secretaries to the Home Secretary at some part in their careers. Except perhaps Royce himself—I don't know about him," he answered slowly. "I wonder what he was doing seventeen years ago."

She split the dough and put it into three tins and left them to rise. "You do think so! Why? Why did she hate Royce so much? Because he put her into Bedlam?"

"Perhaps." The faint dissatisfaction at the back of his mind was stronger, more like a prickle. It was Garnet Royce she had attacked, not Jasper, the doctor. Was that simply because he was the elder brother, the stronger, the one in whose house she had served? But what had turned melancholia over the death of her mistress into a homicidal mania such as he had seen on Westminster Bridge?

He finished his tea and stood up. "You go and tell Aunt Vespasia. I think I shall go back and talk to Drummond again."

"About Elsie Draper?"

"Yes; yes I think so."

* * *

All the way back to Bow Street he saw the newsboys carrying placards for extra editions. Headlines screamed WESTMINSTER CUTTHROAT CAUGHT! PARLIAMENT SAFE AGAIN! MANIAC SHOT DEAD ON WESTMINSTER BRIDGE! He bought a paper just before he went into the police station. Under the big black leader was an article on how the threat of anarchy had receded and law had prevailed once more, thanks to the skill and dedication of the Metropolitan Police and the daring of an unknown member of Parliament. The whole of the nation's capital rejoiced in the return of order and safety to the streets.

Micah Drummond was startled to see Pitt back so soon, and on a spring day when he might have found gardening such a pleasure.

"What is it, Pitt?" There was a shadow of alarm in his face.

Pitt closed the door behind him. "First of all, sir," he began, "I thank you for the promotion, but I would rather remain at my present rank, where I can go out on investigations myself, rather than supervise other men to do it. I think that is where my skill lies, and it is what I want to do."

Drummond smiled. There was a certain ruefulness in his eyes, and a relief. Either he had been expecting something less pleasant, or else in part at least he understood.

"I am not surprised," he said candidly. "And not entirely sorry. You would have made a good senior officer, but we should have lost a lot by taking you away from the streets. Secondhand judgment is never the same. I admire you for the choice; it is not easy to decline money, or status."

Pitt found himself blushing. The admiration of a man he both liked and respected was a precious thing. He hated now to have to pursue the matter of Elsie Draper, instead of merely thanking Drummond and going out. But the question pressed on his mind, clamoring for an answer. He felt an incompleteness like hunger.

"Thank you, sir." He let out his breath slowly. "Sir, I

would like to find out more about Elsie Draper—the madwoman. Just before she struck at Royce she called him by name. She wasn't killing at random; she hated him—personally. I'd like to know why."

Drummond stood still, looking down at the empty space on his desk, the quill and inkstand set in dark Welsh slate, unostentatious.

"I wanted to know too," he said. I wondered if she were after Royce all the time, and she mistook the first three for him. I couldn't find anything in common among them, except that they live on the south side of the river not far from Westminster Bridge, within walking distance, and they have a superficial physical resemblance. They have no special political opinions in common, but then a madwoman who has spent the last seventeen years in Bedlam would hardly care about such things. But I did inquire what Royce was doing seventeen years ago."

"Yes?"

Drummond's smile was tight, bleak. "He was Parliamentary Private Secretary to the Home Secretary." His eyes met Pitt's.

"So they all held that office!" Pitt exclaimed. "Perhaps that is why they died. She was looking for Royce, and she still thought of him in connection with the office he held when she worked in his house. She must have asked around, and she found three other men living south of the river who had held that position before she got the right one! But why did she hate him so long and so passionately?"

"Because he had her committed to Bedlam!"

"For melancholia? Perhaps. But may I go to Bedlam and ask about her, to see what they know?"

"Yes. Yes, Pitt—and tell me what you find."

The Bethlem Royal Hospital was in a huge old building on the Lambeth Road on the south side of the river, a block away from the Westminster Bridge Road where it curved up the hill away from the water and the Lambeth Palace Gardens, the official house of the Archbishop of Canterbury, Primate of all England. Bedlam, as it was commonly known, was another world, shut in, as far from sweetness and ease as the nightmare is from the sleeper's sane and healthful room, where flowers sit in a vase and the morning sunlight will presently stream through the curtains onto a solid floor.

Inside Bedlam was madness and despair. For centuries this hospital, whether within these walls or others, had been the last resort for those no human reason could reach. In earlier times they had been shackled night and day and tormented to exorcise them of devils. Those with a taste for such things had come by to watch them and taunt them for entertainment, as later generations might go to a carnival or a zoo, or a hanging.

Now treatment was more enlightened. Most of the restraining devices were gone, except for the most violent; but tortures of the mind still persisted, the terror and delusion, the misery, the endless imprisonment without hope.

Pitt had been in Newgate and Coldbath Fields, and for all the superintendent in his frock coat and the stewards and medical staff, the walls smelled the same and the air had a fetid taste. Pitt's credentials were examined before he was permitted the slightest courtesy.

"Elsie Draper?" the superintendent asked coldly. "I shall have to consult my records. What is it you wish to know? I assure you, when we released her she'd been calm and of good behavior for many years, nine or ten at least. She never gave the slightest indication of violence." He bristled, preparing for battle. "We cannot keep people indefinitely, you know, not if there is no need. We do not have endless facilities!"

"What was her original complaint?"

"Complaint?" The man asked sharply, sensitive to any criticism.

"Why was she admitted?"

"Acute melancholia. She was a simple woman, from some country area, who had followed her mistress when she married. As I understand it, her mistress died—of scarlet fever. Elsie Draper became deranged with grief, and her master was obliged to have her committed. Very charitable of him, I think, in the circumstances, instead of merely turning her out."

"Melancholia?"

"That is what I just said, Sergeant. . . ?"

"Inspector Pitt."

"Very well—Inspector! I don't know what else you think I can tell you. We cared for her for seventeen years, during which time she gave no indication that she was homicidal. She was perfectly able to care for herself when we released her, and no longer in need of medical attention, nor had we reason to fear she would be a burden upon the rest of the community."

Pitt did not argue; it was a moot point now, and this was not what he had come to find out.

"May I speak with those who attended her? And is there anyone among the other patients she spoke to? Someone who knew her?"

"I don't know what you imagine you can learn! We can all be wise with hindsight, you know!"

"I am not looking for signs that she was homicidal," Pitt said honestly. "I need to know other things: her reasons for acting as she did, or what she believed were her reasons."

"I cannot see how they can possibly matter now."

"I am not questioning your competence in your job, sir," Pitt replied a little testily. "Please do not question the way I do mine. If I did not believe this was necessary, I should be at home with my family, sitting in my garden."

The man's face grew still more pinched. "Very well, if that is what you wish. Be so good as to follow me," and he turned sharply on his heel and led the way down a chill stone corridor, up a flight of stairs, and along a further passageway to a door which opened into a large ward with ten beds in it. There were chairs beside the beds and set around at various places. It was Pitt's first sight of the inside of a lunatic asylum, and his immediate feeling was one of relief. There were enamel jugs with flowers, and here and there a cushion or a blanket which was obviously not institutional. A bright yellow cloth half covered one of the small tables.

Then he looked at the people, the matron standing near the window, with the spring sun coming in through the bars and falling on her gray dress and white cap and apron. Her face was worn with tension and the sight of misery, her eyes flat. Her large hands were red-knuckled, and she had a key chain hanging from her belt.

To the left of her a woman of an age impossible to judge sat on the floor, knees hunched up to her chin, rocking back and forth ceaselessly, whispering to herself. Her hair hung over her face, matted and unkempt. Another woman with a blotchy skin and hair scraped back in a tight knot sat staring vacantly, oblivious of them all. She saw some vision of despair that excluded everything else, and when two others spoke to her she took no notice whatsoever.

Three elderly women sat at a table playing cards with vicious intensity, even though they put down a different card each time and called it always by the same name, the three of clubs.

Another sat with an old news journal, which she held upside down, and kept repeating to herself. "I can't find it! I can't find it! I can't find it!"

"The Inspector wants to speak to someone who knew Elsie Draper," the Superintendent said tersely. "If you can find someone I should be obliged, Matron."

"In mercy's sake, what for?" the matron asked crossly. "What good can it do now, I'd like to know!"

"Is there anyone?" Pitt asked, trying to force himself to smile and failing. The hopelessness of the place was creeping into his skin—the confusion, the desperate faces that stared at him, the flickers of knowledge that they were betrayed from within. "I need to know!" He meant to keep his voice level, but a frantic note betrayed his feelings.

The matron had already heard every horror that there

was; little moved her, for she could no longer find the emotion to allow it to.

"Polly Tallboys," she said patiently. "I suppose she might. Here—Polly! Come here and speak to the gentleman. No need to be afraid. He won't hurt you. You just answer him properly."

"I dint do it!" Polly was a small woman with pale eyes that drooped downward at the corners, and as she came forward obediently her fingers twisted the gray cotton of her dress. "Honest I dint!"

Pitt moved away from the matron and sat down on one of the chairs, motioning Polly to do the same.

"I know that," he said agreeably. "Of course you didn't. I believe you."

"You do?" She was incredulous, uncertain what to do next.

"Sit down, Polly, please. I need your help."

"Mine?"

"Yes, please. You knew Elsie, didn't you? You were friends?"

"Elsie? Yeah, I knew Elsie. She's gorn 'ome."

"Yes, that's right." The elemental truth of the words wrenched his heart. "Elsie used to be in service, didn't she." He made it a statement, not a question; perhaps questions were more than she could handle. "Did she ever tell you anything about that?"

"Oh yeah!" Polly's vacant face lit up for a moment. "Lady's maid, she were—ever so grand. Said 'er mistress were the best lady in the world." Slowly the light faded from her eyes; tears filled them, spilling down her pallid cheeks, and she made no move to wipe them away.

Pitt took his handkerchief and leaned forward to dry her tears. It was a pointless gesture—she kept on crying—but he felt better for it. Somehow it made her seem more like a woman, less a thing broken and shut away.

"She died, Elsie's mistress, a long time ago," he prompted. "Elsie was very sad."

Polly nodded very slowly. "Starved, poor soul; starved to death, for Jesus' sake."

Pitt was startled. Perhaps this had been an idiotic idea, coming to Bedlam for an answer when he did not even know what the question was, and asking lunatics.

"Starved?" he repeated. "I thought she died of scarlet fever."

"Starved." She said the word carefully, but her voice sounded empty, as if she did not know what it meant.

"Is that what Elsie said?"

"That's what Elsie said. For Jesus."

"Did she say why?" It was a wildly optimistic question. What could this poor creature know, and what could it mean, having come from Elsie Draper's jumbled mind?

"For Jesus," Polly repeated, looking at him with clear, shallow eyes.

"How was it for Jesus?" Was it even worth asking?

Polly blinked. Pitt waited, trying to smile at her.

Her attention wandered.

"How was it for Jesus, this starving?" he prompted her.

"The church," she said with a sudden return of interest. "The church in an 'all on Bethlehem Road. She knew it were true, an' 'e wou'nt let 'er go. That's wot Elsie said. Foreign, they was. 'E seen God—an' Jesus."

"Who had, Polly?"

"I dunno."

"What were they called?"

"She never said. Least, I never 'eard."

"But they met in a hall in Bethlehem Road? Are you sure?"

She made a momentous effort at thought, brow furrowed, fingers clenched in her lap. "No," she said at last. "I dunno."

He reached out and touched her gently. "Never mind. You've helped very much. Thank you, Polly."

She smiled warily, then some part of her grasped that he was pleased, and the smile widened. "Oppression—that's wot Elsie said. Oppression . . . wickedness—terrible wickedness." She searched his face to see if he understood.

"Thank you, Polly. Now I must go and find out about what you have told me. I'm going to Bethlehem Road. Good-bye Polly."

She nodded. "Good-bye, Mr. . . ." She tried to think what to call him and failed.

"Thomas Pitt," he told her.

"Good-bye, Thomas Pitt," she echoed.

He thanked the matron, and a junior warder showed him out, unlocking the doors and locking them behind him. He left Bethlem Royal Hospital and went out into the sun with a feeling of pity so deep he wanted to run, to leave not only the great building but all memory of it behind. And yet his feet clung leadenly to the damp pavements; the individual faces were too sharp in his mind to be left behind like anonymous facts.

He walked to Bethlehem Road; it took him less than fifteen minutes. He did not want to find Royce but to see if he could find anyone who knew of the religious order that had met in a hall seventeen years ago. Someone there might remember Mrs. Royce and know something about her. He had no idea what he could find. He had nothing but a simple-minded woman's recollection of a lunatic's rambling obsessions.

There was still a small hall in the road, and according to the board outside it was open to hire by the public. He noted the name and address of the caretaker, and within another ten minutes he was sitting in a small cold front parlor opposite a stocky, elderly man with pince-nez on his nose and a large pocket handkerchief in his hand against the sneezing which frequently overtook him.

"How can I help you, Mr. Pitt?" he said, and sneezed hard.

"Were you caretaker of the Bethlehem Road Hall seventeen years ago, Mr. Plunkett?"

"I was, sir, I was. Is there some trouble about it?"

"None that I know of. Did you lease the hall to a religious organization on a regular basis?"

"I did, sir; most assuredly. Eccentric people. Very strange beliefs, they had. Didn't baptize children, because they said children came into the world pure from God, and weren't capable of sin until they were eight years old. Can't agree with that, certainly I can't. Man is born in sin. Had my own children baptized when they were two months old, like a Christian should. But they were always civil and sober people, modestly dressed, and worked hard and helped each other."

"Are they still meeting here?"

"Oh no sir. Don't know where they all went to, I'm sure I don't. They got less and less, about five years ago, then the last of 'em disappeared."

"Do you remember a Mrs. Royce, some seventeen years ago?"

"Mrs. Royce? No sir, no I don't. There were a few young ladies. Handsome and nicely mannered they were, but they've all gone now. I don't know where, I'm sure. Maybe got married and settled down to a decent life—forgot all that nonsense."

Pitt could not give up now.

"Do you remember anyone at all from seventeen years ago? It is important, Mr. Plunkett."

"Bless you, sir. If I can recall anything you are more than welcome to it. What was this Lady Royce like?"

"I am afraid I don't know. She died about that time, of scarlet fever, I think."

"Oh—oh my goodness! I wonder if that was the friend of Miss Forrester? Lizzie Forrester. Her friend died, poor soul."

Pitt kept the excitement out of his voice. It was only a thread, perhaps nothing—it might break in his hands.

"Where can I find Lizzie Forrester?"

"Bless you, I don't know, sir. But I think her parents

still live on Tower Street. Number twenty-three, as I recall. But someone'd tell you, if you were to go there and ask."

"Thank you! Thank you, Mr. Plunkett!" Pitt rose, shook the man's hand, and took his leave.

He did not even think of eating. He passed a public house, and the smell of fresh-baked pies did not even tempt him, so eager was he to find Lizzie Forrester and learn another side of the truth, something of the past of Elsie Draper which had sewn in her mind the seeds of such madness.

Tower Street was not hard to find: a couple questions of passersby and he was on the doorstep of number 23. It was a neat tradesman's-class front door, with a brass knocker in the shape of a horse's head. Pitt lifted it and let it fall. He stepped back and waited several minutes before a clean and dowdy maid answered it, not unlike the woman who did the heavy work in his own home.

"Yes sir?" she said in surprise.

"Good afternoon. Is this the home of Mr. or Mrs. Forrester?"

"Yes sir, it is."

"I am Inspector Pitt, from the Bow Street Police Station." He saw her face blanch and was instantly sorry for his clumsiness. "There's been no accident, ma'am, and no crime that concerns this household. It is just that someone here may once have been acquainted with a lady we would like to know more about—in order to understand events that have no connection with this family."

She was still highly dubious. Respectable people did not have the police in their houses—for any reason.

He tried again. "She was a very distinguished lady, the lady we wish to learn more about, but she died many years ago; therefore we cannot ask her."

"Well—well you'd better come in, an' I'll ask. You stay there!" She pointed to a spot on the hall floor on the worn red Turkey carpet next to the stand for sticks and umbrellas and the potted aspidistra. Pitt obeyed dutifully, waiting while she whisked away along the linoleum corridor past the stairs and the polished banisters, the samplers which read THE EYE OF GOD IS UPON YOU and THERE'S NO PLACE LIKE HOME, and a picture of Queen Victoria. He heard the servant rap on a door, then the latch open and close. Somewhere in the back parlor his person and his errand were being described.

It was fully five minutes before a middle-aged couple appeared, dressed in neat and well-worn clothes, he with a watch chain across his middle and she with a lace fichu at her neck pinned with a nice piece of Whitby jet.

"Mr. Forrester, sir?" Pitt inquired politely.

"Indeed. Jonas Forrester, at your service. This is Mrs. Forrester. What may we do for you? Martha says you are inquiring about a lady who died some time ago."

"I believe she was a friend of your daughter Elizabeth."

Forrester's face tightened, some of the fresh-scrubbed pinkness fading from it; his wife's hand gripped his arm.

"We have no daughter Elizabeth," he said levelly. "Catherine, Margaret, and Anabelle. I'm sorry; we cannot be of assistance."

Pitt looked at the very ordinary couple standing side by side in their hallway, faces set, hands clean, hair neat, the precise and God-fearing samplers on the wall, and wondered why on earth they should lie to him. What had Lizzie Forrester done that they should say she did not exist? Were they protecting her or disowning her?

He took a gamble. "The records say that you had a daughter Elizabeth born to you."

The color flooded back into Forrester's face, and his wife's hand flew from his arm to cover her mouth and suppress a gasp.

"It would be less painful for you to tell me the truth," Pitt said quietly. "Far better than my having to go and ask questions of other people until I uncover it for myself. Don't you agree?"

Forrester looked at him with intense dislike. "Very well—if you insist. Although we've done nothing to deserve this, nothing at all! Mary, my dear, there is no need for you to endure this. Wait for me in the back parlor. I shall return when it is done."

"But I think—" she began, taking a step forward.

"I have spoken, my dear," he said levelly, but there was insistence under his genteel tone. He did not intend to be argued with.

"But really, I think I should—"

"I don't care to repeat myself, my dear."

"Very well, if you say so." And obediently she withdrew, nodding miserably at Pitt in a sort of half recognition of his presence. She retreated back the way she had come, and again they heard the door latch open and close.

"No need for her to suffer," Mr. Forrester said tartly, his eyes on Pitt's face, hard and critical. "Poor woman has endured enough already. What is it you want to know? We have not seen Elizabeth in seventeen years, nor are we likely to ever again. She ceased to be our daughter then, and whatever the law says, she is none of ours. Although what concern it is of yours I fail to see!" He opened the front parlor door, twisting the handle hard, and showed Pitt into a cold room with too much furniture, all spotlessly clean. The tables were crammed with photographs, china figures, Japanese lacquer boxes, two stuffed birds and a stuffed and mounted weasel under glass, and numerous potted plants. He neither sat down himself nor offered Pitt a seat, although there were three perfectly good chairs, all with embroidered antimacassars on their backs. "I completely fail to see!" he repeated accusingly.

"Perhaps I could speak to Elizabeth myself?" Pitt asked.

"You cannot! Elizabeth went to America seventeen years ago. Best place for her. We don't know what happened to her there or where she is. In fact, she could be dead for all we know!" He said it with his chin high and his eyes bright, but Pitt caught a quaver in his voice, the first sign that there was pain as well as anger in him.

"I believe she belonged for a while to an unusual religious organization," Pitt began tentatively.

The pain vanished from Forrester's face, and only rage and bewilderment remained.

"Evildoers!" he said harshly. "Blasphemers, the lot of them." He shook with the depth of his outrage. "I don't know why they let them come into a God-fearing country and permit their wickedness to innocent people! That's what you should be doing—stopping wickedness like that! What's the use of your coming here seventeen years afterwards, I'd like to know? What good is that now, to us or to our Lizzie? Gone to join wicked men, she has, and never a word of her since. Mind, we're Christian people; we told her she'd be none of ours until she forsook her ways and came back to good Christian religion."

It was nothing to do with the case, but Pitt asked in spite of himself. "What was her religion, Mr. Forrester?"

"Blasphemy is what it was," he replied hotly. "Downright blasphemy against God, and all Christian people. Some charlatan who said he saw God, if you please! Said he saw God! And Jesus Christ! Separately! We believe in one God in this house, like all other decent people, and nobody is telling me some ignorant man with talk of magic and working miracles is going to have any part of me or mine. We told Elizabeth, forbade her to go to their meetings. We warned her of what would happen! Goodness knows how many hours her mother spent talking to her. But would she listen? No she wouldn't! Well in the end she went off to some place in America with the tricksters and wasters and fools who were taken in as she was, or saw a way to make a profit out of gullible women. You do everything you think is right, all you can do to keep your family God-fearing and Christian, and then they serve you like this! Well, Mrs. Forrester and I say we have no daughter Elizabeth, and that's how it is."

Pitt could see the man's grief, and his anger: he felt betrayed by his daughter and by circumstances, and it confused him, and the wound, for all his protestations, was not healed.

But Pitt had to pursue his own questioning.

"Was your daughter acquainted with a Mrs. Royce before she left England, Mr. Forrester?"

"Possibly. Yes, possibly she was. Another deluded young woman who would not take the counsel of her betters. But she died of typhoid or diphtheria as I recall."

"Scarlet fever, seventeen years ago."

"Was it! Poor soul. Dead without the time to repent, I daresay. What a tragedy. Still, the main damnation will be upon the heads of those who beguiled her away into idolatry and blasphemy against God."

"Did you know anything of Mrs. Royce, sir?"

"No. Never saw her. Wouldn't permit any of those people through my door. I lost one daughter, that's more than enough. But I heard Elizabeth speak of her often, as if she were quality." He sighed. "But I suppose being of gentle birth is no help to a woman, if she has a delicate constitution and a weak will. Women need looking after, sir, guarding from charlatans like that—that blasphemer!"

Pitt could not bear to give up. "Is there anyone who can tell me about Mrs. Royce? Did she ever write to your daughter? Would they have had mutual friends, anyone who still keeps that particular faith around here?"

"If there is, I don't know of them, sir, nor do I want to! Emissaries of the devil, performing his works!"

"It is important, Mr. Forrester." Was that the truth? To whom did it matter, after all these years? Pitt, because he wanted to know why Elsie Draper's sick mind had clung so passionately all the long years in Bedlam to her hatred for Garnet Royce? But what difference did it make now?

Forrester was looking uncomfortable, his eyes not quite steady on Pitt's face, his color mottled.

"Well, sir . . ."

"Yes?"

"Mrs. Royce did write some letters to Lizzie, after Lizzie'd gone. We didn't send them on. Didn't know where to send them, and we'd sworn we'd never speak of Lizzie again, like as though she were dead, which she was to us, but then since they weren't ours, we couldn't rightly destroy them either. We've still got them somewhere, up in the box room."

"May I?" Suddenly Pitt was shaking with excitement, a wild hope beating upwards like a bird inside him. "May I see them?"

"If you wish to. But I'll thank you not to mention it to my wife. You'll read them in the box room, sir, and that's my condition." He looked uncertain as to whether he might impose any condition upon the police, but his resolution to try was strong, his pale eyes defiant.

"Of course," Pitt conceded. He had no wish to cause distress. "Please show me the way."

Fifteen minutes later Pitt was crouched under the beams of the roof in a small, stuffy, ice cold box room where three large trunks lay open, a variety of cases for hats and mantles were piled high, and in front of him at last were the six precious letters addressed to Miss Lizzie Forrester and postmarked from April 28 to June 2, 1871. They were all sealed, exactly as they had arrived.

Carefully he slipped the edge of his penknife under the flap of the first envelope. The letter was in a young, feminine hand and seemed to have been written in some haste, as if interruption were feared.

19 Bethlehem Road
28th April 1871

My dearest Lizzie,

I have tried every art or plea I know, but it is no use, Garnet is adamant. He will not even listen to me. Every time I mention the Church he forbids me to speak. Three times in the last two days he has sent me to my room until I should come to my senses and leave the subject alone, forget it forever.

But how can I? I know no other such sweetness or truth on the face of the world! I have gone over everything I have heard the Brethren say, over and over it in my mind, and I find no fault in it. Surely some of it seemed strange at first, and far from what I had been raised to believe, but when I consider it in light of what my heart tells me, it all seems so very right and just.

I hope I may prevail upon him; he is a good and just man, and only desires what is right for me. I know from all my past both as his betrothed and as his wife that he desires to protect and care for me and guard me from all ill.

Pray for me, Lizzie, that I shall find the words to soften his heart so he will permit me to come again to the Church and share the sweet companionship of my Sisters and receive some instruction in the true teachings of the Saviour of All Mankind,

Your dearest friend,
Naomi Royce

The next letter was dated a week later.

Dearest Lizzie,

I hardly know how to begin! My husband and I have had the most dreadful disagreement. He has forbidden me ever to go to Church again, nor even to speak of the Gospel in the house. I must not mention the teachings or anything to do with the Brethren to him, nor try to explain to him why I know the Church is true, nor what makes me feel so.

I know it is hard for him! I do know it, believe me. I also was raised in the orthodox faith and believed it until I was eighteen years of age, when I began to find some of its doctrines did not answer the questions that cried out in my heart.

If God is such a holy and marvelous being as we are told—and I believe He is—and if He is our Father, as we are all taught, then how is it that we are such flawed creatures with no hope of growth, mere spiritual children, pygmies of such deformity of soul? I cannot believe it! I do not! There is endless hope for us, if only we will strive harder, learn who we are and stand upright, learn every good thing, seek after knowledge and wisdom, with the humility to let ourselves be taught. Then by the grace of Our Lord we shall become, in time, worthy to be called His children.

Garnet says I blaspheme, and he has ordered me to repent of it, and accompany him to a "proper" church every Sunday, as is my duty to God, to society, and to him.

I cannot! Lizzie, how can I deny the truth I know? Yet he will not listen to me. Pray for me that I may have courage, Lizzie!

May the Lord bless you and keep you,

Your dear friend,
Naomi Royce

The third letter had been written only three days after the second.

Dearest Lizzie,

It is Sunday, and Garnet has gone to his church. I am sitting in my room and the door is locked—from the outside. He has said that if I will not go to his "proper" church, as a Christian woman should, then I shall go nowhere else.

I must be content with that. If I cannot have my freedom to choose where and how I shall worship God, as we believe all human creatures should, then I shall remain here. I am resolved. I shall not go to his church, nor forswear my own conscience.

Elsie, my maid, is very good to me and brings my meals to my room. I don't know what I should do without her—she came with me when I was married, and seems to have no fear of Garnet. I know she will post this letter. I will have but three postage stamps left after I send this; after that Elsie has sworn she will evade the butler's eyes and deliver personally such letters as I write to you.

I hope next time I write I shall have better news.

In the meanwhile, keep your heart high and trust in God—no one ever trusted in Him in vain. He watches over all of us and will give us nothing more than we can bear.

Your devoted friend,
Naomi

The next letter bore no date, and the handwriting was more sprawling and unsteady.

Dearest Lizzie,

It seems I have come to the greatest decision of my life. Yesterday I prayed all day to question myself as rigorously in every particular as I might, examining my beliefs in the light of all that Garnet has said about our Faith being blasphemy, unnatural, and based upon the maunderings of a charlatan. He says that the Bible is sufficient for all the Christian world, and whoever adds to it in any way is wicked or deluded and should be denounced as such, that there is no further revelation, nor ever will be.

But the more I pray, the more firmly do I know that that is not so! God has not closed the heavens, the Truth has been restored, and I cannot deny it. On peril of losing my soul, I cannot!

What a terrible trial I am suffering! Oh Lizzie, I wish you were here so that just for a moment I might feel less alone. There is only Elsie, and bless her, she has no idea what I mean, but she does love me and will be loyal to me forever. And for that I am more grateful than I can say.

I had a dreadful quarrel with Garnet. He has told me that until I forswear this blasphemy I am to remain in my bedroom! I will, I told him I will, but I shall not eat until he permits me to choose for myself, by the light of my own conscience, what faith I will follow, and what I shall believe of God!

He was so angry. I think perhaps he truly believes he acts in my welfare, but Lizzie, I am a person—I have my own thoughts and my own heart! No one has the right to choose my path for me! They will not feel my pain, or my joy, nor be guilty of my sins. My soul is as precious as anyone else's. I have one life—this one—and I WILL choose!

And if Garnet will not permit me to leave my bedroom, then I shall not eat. In the end he will have to grant me my freedom to profess my own Faith. Then I shall be a dutiful and loving wife to him, fulfill all my callings both social and domestic, be modest and courteous and all else he would wish. But I will not forswear myself.

Your sister in the Gospel of Christ,
Naomi

The next letter was much shorter. Pitt opened it without even being aware of his frozen limbs or the cramp that was stealing through his legs.

Dearest Lizzie,

At first it was terribly difficult to keep my word. I grew so dreadfully hungry! Every book I picked up seemed to speak of food. I had such a headache, and I became cold so easily.

Now it is easier. It has been a whole week, and I feel tired and very faint, but the hunger has passed. I am still terribly cold, and Elsie piles the blankets and quilts on top of me as if I were a child. But I will not give in.

Pray for me!

Keep faith,
Naomi

The last letter was merely two lines, scribbled across the page, the writing faint and very hard to read.

Dearest Lizzie,

I fear if he relents it will be too late now. I am losing all my strength and cannot last much longer.

Naomi

Pitt sat in the cold box room oblivious of the rafters above him, the chill, the whole silent household below. Elsie was right; in her wild, mad brain she had held onto a core of truth all these years. Naomi Royce had died of starvation, rather than forswear the faith she believed. There had been no scarlet fever, only a religious order society would not have tolerated, a new belief that would have scandalized an M.P.'s constituency and caused him to be held up to ridicule.

So he had shut her in her room until she came to her senses.

Only he had misjudged the passion of her belief, and the strength of her heart. She had starved to death rather than deny her God. And what a scandal that would have been—an unconventional religious sect would be a small scandal compared with that! He would have lost his seat and his reputation. Locked in her room and starved to death: oppression, madness, suicide.

So he had called on his brother Jasper to pronounce that the death had been from scarlet fever. And then what had happened? The faithful Elsie had spoken the truth. They could not let that abroad—such whispers would mean ruin. Better bundle her off to Bedlam, where she would be silenced forever. Get Jasper to write up the forms, and the matter could be settled that night: melancholia over the death of her beloved mistress. Who would know any different? Who would miss her? Her stories would be taken as the ravings of a madwoman.

Pitt folded up the letters and put the envelopes in his inside pocket. When he stood up his legs were so cramped the pain made him gasp. He nearly fell down the steep ladder to the upstairs landing.

In the hallway the maid was waiting for him, face weary and a little frightened. The police always frightened her—and it was certainly not respectable to have them in the house.

"Did you get what you need, sir?"

"Yes, thank you. Will you tell Mr. Forrester I shall take the letters, and give him my thanks."

"Yes sir—thank you, sir." And she let him out into the late afternoon sun with a gasp of relief.

Micah Drummond stared at Pitt, his face white.

"There's nothing we can do! There was no crime—all right! God knows, this was sin—but who do we charge? And with what? Garnet Royce did what he thought best for his wife; he misjudged. She starved herself to death; she misjudged also. Then he did what he could to protect her reputation."

"His own reputation!"

"His own as well, but if we charged every man in London who did that we'd have half Society in jail."

"And half the middle classes aspiring to gentility as well," Pitt said chokingly. "But dear heaven, their wives weren't locked up to starve themselves to death so they shouldn't go to an inappropriate church! And how can any man take it upon himself to decide another person is insane and shut them in Bedlam for the rest of their lives? Just shut them away in a living tomb!"

"We've got to keep lunatics somewhere, Pitt."

Pitt slammed his fist on the desk, rattling the inkstand, unaware of the pain that shot through his hand; the outrage inside him was all he could feel.

"She wasn't a lunatic! Not before she was sent there! Dear God, what woman wouldn't lose her mind shut away in Bedlam for seventeen years? Have you ever been there? Can you even imagine it? Think what he has done to that woman. How can we let it happen? No wonder she tried to murder him—if she'd cut his throat it would have been an easy death compared with the slow torture he put her to."

"I know!" Drummond's voice cracked under the strain of his emotion. "I know that, Pitt! But Naomi Royce is dead, Elsie Draper is dead, and there is nothing we can charge anyone with. Garnet Royce only exercised the same rights and responsibilities any man does over his wife. A man and his wife are one in law: he votes for her, is financially and legally responsible for her, and he has always determined what her religion should be, and her social status as well. He didn't murder her."

Pitt sank down into his chair.

"And all we could charge Jasper with would be falsifying a death certificate for Naomi Royce. We couldn't prove it after seventeen years, but even if we could, no jury would convict."

"And committing Elsie Draper?"

Drummond looked at him with deep pain. "Pitt, you and I believe she was sane when she was committed, but it's only our belief against the word of a respected doctor. And God knows, she was certainly mad when she died!"

"And Naomi Royce's word!" He put his hand on the letters spread out on the desk between them. "We've got these!"

"The opinion of a woman who had embraced a strange religious sect and starved herself to death rather than obey her husband and come back to the orthodox faith? Who's going to convict a dog on the basis of that?"

"No one," Pitt said wearily. "No one."

"What are you going to do?"

"I don't know. May I keep these?"

"If you want—but you know you can't do anything with them. You can't accuse Royce."

"I know." Pitt picked up the letters, carefully folding them and putting them back in their envelopes and into the inside pocket of his coat. "I know, but I want to keep them. I don't want to forget."

Drummond smiled bitterly. "You won't. Neither shall I. Poor woman . . . poor woman!"

Charlotte looked up, eyes wide with horror. The tears ran down her cheeks unheeded and her hands holding the letters were shaking.

"Oh Thomas! It's too dreadful to have a name! How they must have suffered—first Naomi, and then poor Elsie. How that poor creature must have felt! To watch her mistress die slowly, growing weaker every day, and yet refusing to betray her truth, and Elsie helpless to do anything. Then when it had gone too far and she could not eat, even if she would, to watch her sink into unconsciousness and death. And when Elsie would not let them hush it all up and report it as scarlet fever, they told her she was mad, and bundled her away to spend the rest of her life behind the walls of a lunatic asylum." She seized his handkerchief from his pocket and blew her nose fiercely. "Thomas, what are we going to do?"

"Nothing. There is nothing we can do," he replied somberly.

"But that's preposterous!"

"There's been no crime committed." And he related what Drummond had said to him.

She stood stunned, too appalled to speak, knowing what he said was true, and that argument was pointless. And staring up at him, she was as aware of his pity and anger as she was of her own.

"Very well," she said at last. "I can see that. I am sure you would prosecute him if there were any grounds—of course you would. But there is no purpose in taking to law something which could never be acted upon. I think, if you don't mind, I shall show the letters to Great-aunt Vespasia tomorrow. I am sure she would like to know what the truth of the matter was. May I take them to her?" She half held them out to him, but it was only a gesture; she had not considered that he might refuse.

"If you wish." He was reluctant, and yet why should she not tell Vespasia? Perhaps they could comfort each other. She might want to talk about it further, and he was too exhausted by his own emotions to want to relive it. "Yes, of course."

"You must be tired." She put the letters in her apron pocket, regarding him gravely. "Why don't you sit down by the fire, and I shall make supper. Would you like a fresh kipper? I have two from the fishmonger today. And hot bread."

By late the following afternoon Charlotte knew precisely what she was going to do, and how she would accomplish it. No one would help her, at least not knowingly, but Great-aunt Vespasia would do all that was necessary, if she was asked the right way. Pitt had spent most of the day in the garden, but at five o'clock the weather had changed suddenly, a chill wind had sprung up from the east covering the sky with leaden clouds, and by nightfall there would be a freezing fog. He had come inside, then gone to sleep in front of the fire.

Charlotte did not disturb him. She left a leek and potato pie in the oven and a note on the kitchen table telling him she had gone to visit Aunt Vespasia. Since it was extremely cold and a fog was drifting in off the river, she took the rather expensive step of hiring a cab to take her all the way to Vespasia's house where she was received with pleasure and some surprise.

"Is anything wrong, my dear?" Vespasia asked, and looked at Charlotte more closely. "What is it? What has happened?"

Charlotte took the letters from her reticule and passed them over, explaining how Pitt had discovered them.

Vespasia opened them, adjusted her pince-nez on her nose, and read them slowly and without comment. Finally she put the last one down and sighed very quietly.

"How very terrible. Two lives wasted, and in such confusion and pain, over such terrible domination of one person by another. How unreasonably far we still have to go before we learn to treat each other with dignity. Thank you for showing them to me, Charlotte—although when I lie awake at night I shall wish you had not. I must speak to Somerset next time about the laws of lunacy; I am getting old to take up new causes about which I know nothing, but it will haunt me. What could be worse than madness, except to spend years as the only sane person in a fortress of the mad?"

"Don't! . . . I'm sorry. I should not have shown them to you."

"No, my dear. It was very natural." Vespasia put her hand over Charlotte's. "We wish to share our pain. And better you should have come to me than to poor Thomas. He has seen more than enough lately, and his helplessness must hurt him."

"Yes," Charlotte agreed; she knew it did. But it was nearly six o'clock and time to put the next part of her plan into progress. "I mean to visit Sir Garnet Royce, perhaps to deliver the letters to him." She saw Vespasia's body grow rigid. "After all, they are his, in a sense."

"Rubbish!" Vespasia snapped. "My dear Charlotte, you may be able to lie successfully to other people, although I doubt it, but please do not try it with me. You do not for a moment imagine they are Sir Garnet's property. They were written by his wife to a Miss Forrester, and if they cannot be delivered to her, then they are the property of Her Majesty's Postal Service. Nor would you give a fig if they were Sir Garnet's! What do you mean to do?"

There was no more purpose in lying; it had failed. "I mean to oblige him to know the truth, and to know that I know it," Charlotte replied. It was not all her plan, but it was part of it.

"Dangerous," Vespasia answered.

"Not if I take your carriage, with your coachman to drive me. Sir Garnet may be as angry as he likes, but he is not going to harm me. He would not dare. And I shall take only two letters, and leave the rest with you." She waited, watching Vespasia's face. Charlotte saw the doubt in it, as Vespasia argued back and forth with herself. "He deserves to know!" she said urgently. "The law cannot face him with it, but I can. And for Naomi's sake, and Elsie Draper's, I am going to. I shall arrive in a proper carriage, with a footman, and the servants will let me in. He cannot harm me! Please, Vespasia. All I want is the use of your carriage for an hour or two." She considered adding, "Otherwise I shall have to go by hansom," but it sounded too much like pressure, and Vespasia would not care for that.

"Very well. But I shall send Forbes as well, to ride on the box. That is my condition."

"Thank you, Aunt Vespasia. I shall leave at about seven, if that is acceptable to you. That way I shall be most likely to find him at home, since the House of Commons is not debating anything of importance today, so I have been told."

"Then you had better have supper." Vespasia's silver eyebrows rose. "I presume you have left something for poor Thomas to eat?"

"Yes of course I have. And a note to tell him I am visiting you and will be home at about half past eight or nine o'clock."

"Indeed," Vespasia said dryly. "Then I suppose we had better request the kitchen to send us something. Would you care for some jugged hare?"

An hour later Charlotte was sitting huddled up inside Vespasia's carriage while the horses drew it slowly through the fog-blinded streets from Belgravia, past the Palace of Westminster, across the bridge, and along the far side of the south bank towards Bethlehem Road. It was bitterly cold, and the dead air hung motionless, moisture freezing as it touched the icy stones. Half of her was dreading arrival, and yet she was so cold and the decision so firm in her mind that delay was of no value, there was nothing else to turn over or consider, nothing that would change her resolve. Garnet Royce was not going to be permitted to close his mind to Naomi, or Elsie Draper, and convince himself he had acted justly.

The carriage stopped, and she heard the footman's steps as he descended and a moment later the carriage door opened. She took his hand and alighted. The fog was so thick she could barely see the streetlamps on either side of her, and the houses on the far side of the street, no more than a slight darkening of the gray, curling vapors, a mark on the imagination.

"Thank you. I am sorry to ask you to wait here, but I hope I shall not be long."

"That's all right, ma'am," Forbes replied from the gloom just beyond. "Her ladyship said we were to wait for you right outside the door, and we shall."

Garnet Royce received her civilly enough, but his manner was distant and somewhat surprised. He had obviously forgotten her from her visit to Amethyst following Lockwood Hamilton's death, which was hardly surprising, and he now had no idea who she was. She did not waste time in niceties.

"I have come to see you, Sir Garnet, because I plan to

write a book—about a certain religious movement, to which your wife Naomi Royce belonged, before she died."

His face froze. "My wife was a member of the Church of England, ma'am. You have been misinformed."

"Not according to her letters," she replied, equally coldly. "She wrote several very personal, very tragic letters to a certain Lizzie Forrester, who was a member of the same movement. Miss Forrester emigrated to America, and the letters never reached her. They remained in this country, and have come into my hands."

He remained stony-faced, his hand near the bell rope.

She must hurry before she was thrown out. She opened her reticule and pulled out the pages she had brought. She began to read, starting with Naomi's account of her husband's forbidding her to attend the church of her conviction and sending her to her room until she should comply with his wishes, and her vow that she would refuse to eat until he allowed her the freedom of her own conscience. When Charlotte came to the end she looked up at Royce. The contempt in his eyes was blistering, and his hands clenched in front of him in rage.

"I can only assume that you are threatening to make this a scandal if I do not pay you. Blackmail is an ugly and dangerous profession, and I would advise you to give me the letters and leave before you damn yourself by making threats."

She saw the fear in him, and her own disgust hardened. She thought of Elsie Draper and a lifetime in Bedlam.

"I don't want anything from you, Sir Garnet," she said, her voice so grating it hurt her throat. "Except that you should know what you have done: you denied a woman the right to seek God in her own way and to follow her conscience in the manner of her belief. She would have obeyed you in all else! But you had to have everything, her mind and her soul. It would have been a scandal, wouldn't it? 'M.P.'s Wife Joins Extreme Religious Sect!' Your political party would have dropped you, all your Society friends! So you locked her in her room until she should obey you. Only you had not realized how passionately she believed, how strong she was—that she would die rather than renounce the truth she believed—and she did die!

"Oh how you must have panicked then. You sent for your brother to write a death certificate calling it scarlet fever"—she would not let him interrupt when he tried, raising her voice to drown him out—"and he agreed to do it, to avoid a scandal. 'M.P.'s Wife Commits Suicide in Locked Room! Did her husband drive her to it—or was she mad? Insanity in the family?'

"Only Elsie, loyal Elsie, wouldn't agree; she wanted to tell the truth—so you had her committed to Bedlam! Seventeen years in a madhouse, seventeen years of living death. No wonder when she got out she came hunting for you with a razor! God help her! If she wasn't mad when you put her in, she certainly was by the time she was allowed to leave!"

For many seconds of dreadful silence they stared at each other in mutual abhorrence. Then slowly his face changed. He caught a glimpse of what she meant, wild and heretical as it was to him, challenging all the rules he knew, overturning all order concerning the rights and obligations of the strong to protect the weak, to govern them for their own good—whatever their wishes. Then as he gazed at her those thoughts passed away; a conflict remained which Charlotte watched him wrestle with for several more minutes, while the clock on the mantelshelf ticked on, and far away someone dropped a tray in the kitchen.

"My wife was of fragile mind and disposition, madame. You did not know her. She was given to sudden fancies, and very easily prevailed upon by charlatans and people of feverish imagination. They sought money from her. That was not in her letters, perhaps, but it is so, and I was afraid of her being taken advantage of. I forbade them the house, as any man of responsibility would."

He swallowed hard, composing himself with difficulty,

banishing the horror he had caught such a dreadful sight of for an instant, forcing the words out.

"I misjudged her. She was more vulnerable to their blandishments than I realized, and in poor health, which affected her mind. I appreciate now that I should have called medical help for her long before I did. I imagined she was being willful, whereas she was in truth suffering delusions from fever, and the effects of designing people. I regret my actions; you do not know how I regretted them, how I have done over the years."

Charlotte felt her mastery was slipping away, somehow he was twisting what she had said. "But you had no right to decide what she should believe!" she cried out. "No one has the right to choose for someone else! How dare you? How dare you presume to judge another person as to what they should want? It is not protection, it is . . . it is . . ." She searched for the word. "It is dominion! And it is *wrong*!"

"It is the duty of the strong and the able to protect the weak, madame, and especially those born or given into their charge. And you will find that society will thank you little for seeking to make a profit out of my family's misfortune."

"And what about Elsie Draper? What about her life? You shut her away in a madhouse!"

A very slight smile touched the corners of his mouth.

"And do you contend, madame, that she was not mad?"

"Not when you put her away, no!" Charlotte was losing, and she saw it in his face, heard it in the stronger, calmer tone in his voice.

"You had better leave, madame. There is nothing for you here. If you write your book, and you mention the name of anyone in my family, I shall sue you for libel, and society will reject you for the cheap adventuress you are. Good day. My footman will show you out." And he rang the bell.

Five minutes later Charlotte was sitting in the carriage as the horses plodded slowly through the freezing fog down Bethlehem Road and back towards the Westminster Bridge and the darkness of the river. She had failed. She had not done more than shake his complacency for a few moments—just that brief space when he had glimpsed the idea that he had been guilty of a monstrous oppression. Then self-justification had swept back and everything was as before; he was powerful, complacent, secure. To think that she had even been frightened! How needless—he had dismissed her without any emotion but disgust. He had not even asked for the letters!

They were coming down onto the bridge now; she heard the difference in the echo of the horses' hooves. The fog was very dense and the ice slippery on the stones. She felt the occasional jolt as an animal lost and regained its footing.

"What were they stopping for?

There was a rap on the carriage door and Forbes opened it.

"Ma'am, there is a gentleman wishes to speak to you."

"A gentleman?"

"Yes. He said it was confidential, if you would not mind stepping out for a moment; it would be more decorous than his climbing in."

"Who is it?"

"I don't know, ma'am. I don't recognize him, and to tell the truth, I wouldn't recognize my own brother on a night like this. But I shall be right here, ma'am, only a few yards from you. He said to tell you it was about passing a new law guaranteeing freedom of conscience."

Freedom of conscience? Could something she had said have touched Garnet Royce after all?

She stepped out, taking Forbes's hand and steadying herself on the ice-glazed pavement. She saw the figure dimly, only a few feet away. It was Garnet Royce, muffled up against the bitter night. He must have relented as soon as she had left, and followed her carriage; they had traveled at no more than walking pace.

"I'm sorry," he said immediately. "I realize I misjudged you. Your motives were not selfish, as I presumed. If I might have a moment of your time. . . ?" He took a step away from the carriage to be out of earshot of Forbes and the coachman.

She followed, understanding his desire for privacy. It was a highly delicate matter.

"I was too zealous, I confess. I treated Naomi as if she were a child. You are right. An adult woman, whether married or single, should have the freedom to follow her conscience and to embrace whatever religious teaching she will."

"You mentioned a law?" Could it be that after all something good would come of this? "Could such a law be framed?"

"I don't know," he said so softly she was obliged to move closer to hear him. "But I am certainly in a position to discover what can be done, and to introduce such a bill. If you would tell me what you think would be of benefit to all woman, and yet still keep order and protect the weak and the ignorant from exploitation. It is not easy."

She thought about it, trying frantically to come up with some sensible answer. A law? She had never thought of legal means. And yet he was very serious, his eyes with their clear silver-blue irises were bright in the triple lamplight and the halo of the fog. She could barely see even the outline of the carriage.

She looked back at him, and it was then she saw the sudden change in his expression, the gleam of passion as his lips twisted back from his teeth and his arm darted forward, his black-gloved hand clamping over her lips before she could cry out. She was being pushed backwards towards the balustrade and the long drop to the river!

She kicked as hard as she could, but it was useless. She tried to bite and only bruised her mouth. The balustrade was digging into her back. In a moment she would be lifted over and thrown into the void, then the freezing water would close over her, and darkness, and her lungs would fill to bursting. No one would survive the river tonight.

She swung her other hand round and jabbed for his eyes with outstretched fingers. There was a stifled yell of pain, muffled by the fog. He lunged forward to strike her but his feet gave way on the ice, and for a desperate second he hung on the balustrade, arms and legs flailing. Then, like a wounded bird, he went over and dropped into the long chasm of the night and the river. She did not even hear the splash as the water received him; the fog drowned it in choking silence.

She stood leaning on the rail, sick and shaking. The sweat of a few moments ago was now freezing on her skin. She felt too weak with fear and guilt even to stand without support.

"Ma'am!"

She stood rigid, not even breathing.

"Ma'am? Are you all right?"

It was Forbes, looming up, invisible until he was almost on top of her.

"Yes." Her voice sounded thin, unrecognizable.

"Are you sure, ma'am. You look . . . unwell. Did the gentleman—trouble you? If he did—"

"No!" She swallowed hard. There seemed to be an obstruction in her throat, and her knees were wobbling so, she feared to walk. How could she explain what happened? Would they think she had pushed him over, murdered him? Who would believe her? And what was she guilty of anyway? Would they believe she had not tried after all to blackmail him, and pushed him over the bridge when he had threatened to expose her to the police?

"Ma'am, I think, if you will forgive me, that you should get back into the carriage and permit me to drive you back to Lady Cumming-Gould."

"No—no thank you, Forbes. Will you take me to the Bow Street Police Station? I have an—an incident to report."

"Yes ma'am, if that is what you wish."

Gratefully she took his arm, and awkwardly, tripping over the step, she half fell inside the carriage and sat there shivering while they covered the short distance across the rest of the bridge and up the north side to Bow Street.

Forbes helped her out again, now severely anxious for her welfare, going with her past the duty sergeant and up the stairs to Micah Drummond's office.

Drummond looked at her in alarm, then at Forbes. "Go and get Inspector Pitt!" he commanded. "Immediately, man!"

Forbes turned on his heel and ran down the stairs two at a time.

"Sit down, Mrs. Pitt." Drummond half carried her to his own chair. "Now tell me what on earth has happened. Are you ill?"

She wanted above anything else to fall into Pitt's arms and be held, to weep herself into exhaustion and to sleep, but first she must explain, now, before Pitt came. It was her fault, not his, and the very least she owed him was not to involve him in the blame, and to spare him the anguish of her explanation.

Slowly and carefully, between sips of brandy, which she loathed, and staring at Micah Drummond's strained and gentle face, she recounted precisely what she had done, and how Garnet Royce had responded. She saw the reflection of fear and anger in his eyes, his perception of what would happen before she reached that part of the account herself, and the briefest flicker of admiration for what she had said.

She faltered when she told him how Royce had slipped on the ice and plunged over the balustrade into the river, but slowly, with her eyes shut, she found the words, though they were inadequate to express her terror and her guilt.

She opened her eyes and looked at him. What would he do to her? To Pitt? Had she jeopardized not only herself but Thomas also? She was bitterly ashamed and afraid.

Drummond held both her hands.

"There can be no doubt that he is dead," he said slowly. "No one could live in the river in this weather, even if he survived the fall. The River Police will find him presently; maybe tomorrow, maybe later, depending on the tide. There are three conclusions they can come to: suicide, accident, or murder. You were the last person known to have seen him alive, so they will come to question you."

She wanted to speak but her voice would not come. It was even worse than she had thought!

His hands tightened over hers. "It was an accident, which occurred in the course of his attempting to commit murder. It seems his dread of scandal was so great he would kill to keep his position. But we cannot prove that, and it would be wiser not to try. It would distress his family and achieve nothing. I think the best thing would be for me to go to the River Police and tell them that he received letters written by his late wife which distressed him profoundly, and we fear that they may have disturbed the balance of his mind—which is perfectly true. Then they may draw whatever conclusions they wish, but I imagine they will find it to have been suicide. That would be the best thing, in the circumstances. There is no need to tar his name with accusations that cannot be proved."

She searched his face, finding only gentleness there. The relief was so intense it was like the easing of a cramp, painful and exquisite. The tears would no longer be stayed, and she buried her head in her hands and sobbed with pity, exhaustion, and overwhelming, devastating gratitude.

She did not even see Pitt come in the door, ashen-faced, Forbes at his elbow, but she felt his arms go round her as she breathed in the familiar smell of his coat, feeling the texture of it under her cheek.